Gothic Romance

Also by Emmanuel Carrère

The Mustache

Gothic Romance

Emmanuel Carrère

Translated by Lanie Goodman

CHARLES SCRIBNER'S SONS

NEW YORK

© P.O.L. éditeur, 1984

English-language translation copyright © 1990 by Macmillan Publishing
Company, a division of Macmillan, Inc.

Charles Scribner's Sons
Macmillan Publishing Company
866 Third Avenue, New York, NY 10022
Collier Macmillan Canada, Inc.

Library of Congress Cataloging-in-Publication Data
Carrère, Emmanuel, 1957–
[Bravoure. English]
Gothic romance / Emmanuel Carrère; translated by Lanie Goodman.
p.   cm.
Translation of: Bravoure.
ISBN 0-684-19199-7
I. Title.
PQ2663.A7678B713   1990   89-24215   CIP
843'.914—dc20

10 9 8 7 6 5 4 3 2 1

Printed in the United States of America

A NOTE ON THE TEXT

The author has taken advantage of this translation
to revise and edit his novel.

ACKNOWLEDGMENTS

The author wishes to acknowledge his reliance for certain details of this novel upon James Rieger's erudite introduction to *Frankenstein* (University of Chicago Press, 1974).

Gothic Romance

CHAPTER I

Moving no farther, he peers into the damp shadows of the hall. Then, before the door swings closed, he glances back at the street, now blocked from sight. The house has no furniture, and he, no remaining possessions. All he has left is his own body to carry, but that's enough to exhaust him. Everything seems to weigh more between these thick walls, beginning with the massive oak door, whose threshold he crosses less and less frequently. Every move is an effort, as if the laws of gravity had suddenly multiplied and the earth's magnetic force had become more oppressive in this particular place in London.

Sometimes, no sooner inside, instead of sucking in his shallow breath and climbing the flight of stairs that leads from the narrow hallway to his closet, he kneels down in front of the door. Then, with his eye glued to a crack, he peeks outside. Despite his limited field of vision, he enjoys these lookout sessions, at least he did at first. It's still the best way for him to view the world: without being seen, without having to get involved or play any part in it.

When he's out in public, he envisions those situations that might threaten his retreat. He has to make certain, for example, that no one sees him push open his front door or remove the board, which looks as if it's nailed shut but in fact is not. Though the alley is fairly deserted, occasionally he has to walk past the entranceway two or three times all because he has crossed paths with someone, and must therefore put him on a false trail by simply continuing on his way. There have been times when upon his return the passerby

1

would still be there sniffing around, in the midst of a conversation with an acquaintance, or even examining the façade, evaluating the damage that the deserted mansion had weathered over time. If such were the case, he'd walk past him once again, avoiding the man's gaze for fear that the latter might find something suspicious about all these comings and goings or in his own general appearance. Alerted, Polidori would slip away from the scene as one might remove a piece of evidence to forestall an investigation. He quickens his step, imagining the effect this little coincidence has on the honest citizen out for some air: this man with the guilty look on his face, he thinks, who for no apparent reason has just walked by me once more, is taking a stroll, just as I am. But no, he is not just out for a walk. Strangely enough, he seems too disengaged to have time for a stroll. This man has nothing to do, but he is definitely not taking a leisurely walk. In all likelihood he's in hiding. He dreads any interaction with his fellowman; his only connection with any of them is his fear of seeing them stationed in front of his lair, barring his entry. It's even possible that once inside, he might drill little holes in the wall, shielding himself from the rest of the world, but still able to observe it.

One day, on his way home, Polidori turned down the street and unexpectedly came upon a middle-aged man with the air of a ruffian, his knee bent in front of the doorstep in exactly the same position as the one he himself adopts whenever engaged in spying from behind the door. The crack must have been exactly at eye level. Cold sweat poured down his frail spine, though he was truly in no danger. The man, who had just removed a pebble from his shoe, immediately stood up and walked off in the opposite direction. He wonders what might have happened had he been on the other side of the door, his eye glued to the thin crack. If the troublemaker had suddenly knelt down, his glance would have caught Polidori unawares, on the lookout. The following night he dreamed of this horrible moment in which the gaze of a man outside his door betrayed his own, the instant when their eyes met. He awoke as was his custom: by raising the lid of one eye, and then the other, he could generally keep his eyes from dancing a jig in their sockets, which would occur more and more frequently under the shock of an emotion. Opening one eye, he saw another eye, the black eye of a stranger that was nearly glued to his. He didn't even cry out; it was as if he were dead. He was awake, yet the nightmare continued. Very well then, he was dead. Without blinking, he stared calmly at the eye, open wide, so close to his that he could barely focus on the white surrounding the dilated pupil. He had never seen an eye at such close range. Then, confident that rigor mortis would prevent the dreaded jig from starting, he opened the other eye, certain of what he was about to see: a symmetrical eye, just as close, almost touching his. But in fact, all that he saw was the curve of a cheek, Teresa's cheek; she had been watching him sleep for the past hour.

CHAPTER II

Teresa lends a kind of childish grace to her occasional prostitution, which is what allows her to survive. A trifle idiotic, Polidori thinks. Although she must cater to the whims of her customers, who demand more than innocent caresses, she often affects the manner of a little girl, a provocation better suited to charm an aging sugar daddy than a troubled, sexually frustrated man. In the three weeks they've been living together in the empty house, she has only made love with Polidori once. Neither she, who does this for her livelihood, nor the young man, rendered impotent by self-hatred and opium

3

abuse, seems to care very much, and they haven't repeated the experience. But she reserves for him the light caresses that her customers often refuse. When they're together, she often winds the curls of her hair around Polidori's toes, biting his nails, or granting her favorite treat, which she calls a butterfly kiss. She places her eyelids close to a sensitive spot on his body and flutters her eyelashes several times, brushing against the proffered skin.

On that particular night, Teresa, weary of watching him sleep, or perhaps in an attempt to pull him gently out of the bad dreams contorting his face, gave him a butterfly kiss directly on his eyelids. And so when he opened his eye, he could only see hers, just an eyelash length away. Grasping the situation, he pretended that he'd merely opened his eyes out of reflex and hadn't been awakened, to discourage Teresa from pursuing her little indulgences. If she suspected as much, she would understand that she should stop what she was doing. Several minutes later he cautiously opened one eye and discovered that Teresa's, at a slight distance from his, were presently closed. She wheezed with every breath. At another time in his life, given his penchant for symmetry, Polidori would have offered a butterfly kiss in return, but symmetry no longer has any meaning between his eyes and those of a stranger. His eyes only serve to avoid others. Against his own will, they behave like elusive, frightened animals. His ears serve to record what others say, not out of sympathy or curiosity, but to detect any hidden threats; his lips, to lock in anything that might escape and make its way to foreign ears. His hands are used to fill his torn pockets or stay folded behind his back, or else to write pages that no one will ever read. His genitals remain shriveled in his undergarments. All in all, his entire person shuts itself off in the somber recesses where neither strange eyes, lips, nor hands can reach him. It is the only thing he desires: to be out of reach.

This is why Teresa's presence is so oppressive to him, although he knows that she's as furtive and frightened as he is. He can't bear to have her touch him—something she does not out of sensuality so much as to establish an intimate bond or at least some sort of closeness, however precarious. He brushes her aside because of her moist palms; he forbids her to speak to him. He'd drive her out of the house if he could. Yet it was she who had offered to share her auspicious shelter after they'd met on the bank of the Serpentine, where she'd found him lying, exhausted. But this indebtedness wouldn't stop him. He's merely afraid that if he tells her to leave, she might inform other vagabonds of his existence. Furthermore, she's the one who provides their sustenance, who brings home their daily crust of bread, a jug of cold water, and sometimes a bit of cheese or lard. And now that he rarely goes out, she procures the laudanum that he so desperately needs, from the one-armed pharmacist whom he had saved from prison, perhaps from hanging, when he was still a doctor and had testified for him in a case of poisoning. Ever since, the pharmacist has supplied him free of charge, and for this reason alone, he's the only person with whom Polidori has remained in contact.

He pays back these favors by tolerating Teresa's timorous presence and sharing the straw mattress—which is, of course, hers. He must seem mysterious if not seductive to this poor girl of seventeen with red, blotchy skin, slender on top and wide around the hips. He sometimes wonders what she could possibly think of him, yet quickly tires of these hypotheses, he who all his life had taken such pleasure in that sort of thing. She might take him for a young man from a wealthy family, wounded in an unhappy love affair, or for an escaped convict, or simply a vagabond. But it hardly matters now, this image she has of him, reflected in those perpetually tearful, imploring eyes. She's just one more burden, acceptable because of certain practical advantages.

From inside and out, everything weighs on Polidori. He's worn out from twenty-four years of a deathly life, twenty-odd years of promises. Happiness is something he's never known, but ambitions, yes, and even confidence. He'd been a kind of child prodigy. His sisters had admired him; his sketches had been charming. At the age of nineteen, his thesis on somnambulism had made him the youngest doctor to graduate from the University of Edinburgh. It's only in the last four years that everything has started to go wrong. Ever since he'd left England, to accompany Lord Byron, his life has been nothing more than a slow and precise deterioration, a series of failures; in short, a catastrophe, and a catastrophe that has already run its course. These twenty-four years have progressed like a malevolent conspiracy, slyly at first, then openly, to bring him here, to this clandestine refuge in Soho, to this soggy straw mattress that he, in his weakened state, must share with an ugly and well-meaning whore. If only he could consider himself a pariah, a different type of being, an undiscovered genius! But no, he is just an ordinary failure, driven by his mediocre talents and lofty ambitions to an anonymous fall from grace. Just one of the hundreds of poor lads who roam the streets of London every night in search of a shelter, a temporary salvation. But it's already too late for them. Polidori, who mistrusts men in general, disdains above all those who resemble him. What's left of his self-image, formed at eighteen, prohibits him from dealing with others who have also lost their social position—from frequenting the taverns where they conjure up from the past, like ghosts or stillborn children: how this one's musical talents had been wasted, how another's poetic promise hadn't survived, and how a third had nurtured vague dreams of glory. At least Polidori will stand alone until the very end. Or at worst, he'll remain burdened with someone like Teresa, with whom he had nothing in common.

He can no longer resuscitate the illusion that he's hit bottom, and therefore need only give himself a good kick to rise back up to the surface. He's well aware that it's an illusion, because he's used it far too often; there have already been several occasions where he's tried and his enthusiasm has failed him. And now, even more than in the past, the bottom to which he has descended has changed from a solid, reliable surface to something like quicksand, where the feet slide and sink instead of springing back.

This is why Polidori doesn't even dream anymore. He knows that this house is his last asylum, that after this it will all be over. He also realizes that one of the most pernicious aspects of his personal tragedy is his pathetic inclination toward desperate acts. Ever since the age of twenty there had been many times when, all bitterness aside, he'd rationally taken stock of what was keeping him alive. He'd always come to the conclusions now imposing on him with an even stronger, if useless, lucidity. He had been a failure as a doctor, banished from the profession, an unlucky gambler, and a playwright without a play, ridiculed in the literary world where he'd dreamed of a career. Penniless, friendless, and too ashamed to ask help from his family, who presume him dead, he has nothing, absolutely nothing left to lose. Nor anything to gain—whatever he does now, it's too late.

He'd wanted to commit suicide for the first time upon his return to England three years ago, having learned of the fate assigned to his *Vampire* manuscript by the publisher Colburn, and of his own literary pretensions according to Mary Shelley, in the preface of *Frankenstein*. After much hesitation he'd narrowed down his choices to a pistol. From behind the counter the gunsmith, one eye closed, had watched him enter. His other eye remained wide open, despite the tensed muscles that held a watchmaker's magnifying glass, used as a monocle, apparently to see at a distance. He was very old, extremely frail, and even a young man as weak as Polidori could have knocked him down with a mere brush of the hand. Polidori thought that since he was determined to die, there was nothing to stop him from stealing the pistol instead of buying it. He didn't need to do it—he still had quite enough money for this last purchase—but he suddenly realized that all his life, he who had dreamed of adventure, risks, and intense emotions frowned on by society, had never stolen, never so much as taken a penny from anyone (which he'd later been obliged to do, but out of poverty and without any flair). Before he died, since he was going to die, he could at least grant himself that one luxury. Less than two feet were between him and the old man, who, as Polidori approached, had replaced his magnifying glass with another that he'd dug out of a box. Polidori couldn't understand, for that matter, how this man who was nearly blind was able to select the lens suited to each situation in so short a time.

The idea of stealing only occurred to him as he'd set foot in the shop. Polidori hadn't had time to prepare a speech, to rehearse it in his head, or to say it aloud, knowing only he could appreciate its effect. Placing both hands on the counter, careful not to let them shake, he wanted to say, "Give me a pistol" with enough polite resolve that the gunsmith would understand that it was a matter of giving it to him and not selling it, and that he'd be better off not discussing the issue any further with such a determined man. However, as if he'd already exhausted this line, another sprang from his lips. "I want a pistol," he said, and felt like weeping upon hearing his own words. His life at that moment seemed to be hanging by a thread, not on the basis of his decision to kill himself, but on whether he would buy or steal the pistol. In a certain respect, if he succeeded in stealing it, he needn't bother to commit suicide. In doing so, he would have performed a positive action and might benefit from it as from a favorable omen. At least he hadn't said, "I want to buy a pistol."

"Of course, sir," said the gunsmith. "We've got plenty of pistols. Is there a particular type that you prefer?"

Polidori's entire being had concentrated on the fact that he must not answer, that if he did, a conversation would ensue, and he'd wind up buying the pistol. But as soon as he'd become aware of this, another thought began to gnaw at him. He asked himself—and the moment he asked himself, he realized that the whole matter had taken a turn for the worse—if he actually had a preferred brand or not. No, of course not, he knew nothing about pistols, and he owed everything he'd learned about the way they were handled to Lord Byron. Now, Byron was a connoisseur; he had preferred brands, and adored giving long lectures on the subject. He was a great poet and a great lover of pistols—of course, he pretended to take pride in that aspect of his personality. In a sudden flash Polidori recalled a conversation at the Villa Diodati: Byron, apropos, had been comparing several brands, unconcerned that no one present was interested in the subject. Neither Shelley, who was listening to his speech and smiling affectionately, indifferent to pistols but charmed by his friend's enthusiasm, nor Mary, who was bored, nor he, Polidori, who had nevertheless thought it wise, out of fear and the pleasure of hearing his own voice, to contradict Byron by bitterly defending a make that of course he knew nothing about. "Ah," Byron had exclaimed, "if Polly is a Brewer devotee, I have nothing more to say!" And now, he answered the gunsmith timidly.

"A Brewer, perhaps. . . ."

"I see that the gentleman is a connoisseur," said the old

9

man, changing his lens once again. So instead of taking him by the shoulders and shaking him, smashing the window and grabbing any pistol at random, Polidori could not prevent himself from contemplating the following question: Were Brewers good or bad pistols? Was it Byron, in fact, who didn't know what he was talking about? Or was it the gunsmith, who as a polite salesman would regularly admire the expertise of his customers, even if they asked him for a pellet gun with which to hunt deer? He finally left the shop with the Brewer in a neat package under his arm. It had cost him two thirds of what had been in his pocket. It was a superior weapon, beautifully finished, and although he would never use it, he felt sad when one month later it was stolen, along with his baggage, in a Sussex inn. The proprietor had exasperated him, remarking that one had to be incredibly unlucky to be robbed in an establishment where nothing like that had ever happened before. He'd repeated it at least three times.

Of course, he hadn't committed suicide after all, and he wouldn't have done it even if he'd had the courage to steal the pistol. He wanted to give himself another chance, and consequently, before it had been stolen, the pistol had come to represent this last chance, rather than his pride. Armed with a weapon such as this, he could, if he wanted to, return to the gunsmith's shop and threaten to rob the cash register. But after thinking about it, he imagined the police's reaction to the garbled deposition of the old man. "He attacked me with a pistol that he'd purchased the night before; he was very polite and paid in cash. . . ." And the mere idea of passing for an uncertain beginner, small fry not even worth pursuing in the eyes of these gendarmes, was enough to make him decide against it. He could also rob someone in the street, anyone at all, or follow Lord Byron, or that traitor, the perfidious Mary. He could rejoin them in Europe and kill them, take out his vengeance for all the humiliations he had endured, or else seek revenge for everything he had suffered, kill a few innocent bystanders before killing himself. But he did nothing of the sort. Desperate he was, but unable to benefit from the few advantages that this state might confer: indifference, courage, a contempt for death, and most of all, for life.

CHAPTER III

In the past, whenever his suffering had become too much to bear, he was able to delude himself, occupy his mind—so prone to delirious thoughts—by creating an image of the future Polidori: rich, famous, and calm, who would sometimes think back to his various former selves with affectionate irony. At the age of twenty, when his hosts at Diodati had mocked him, and when even he himself could not think of the tragedy he was in the process of writing without flying into a scornful rage, he tried to imagine the Polidori of age twenty-five. Even Byron would pale next to this shining star, this Polidori whose tragedies had been applauded and whose poems had been published and zealously read. And this Polidori, smiled upon by the gods, would remember the efforts that his first tragedy had cost him, the discouragement he had felt because of its slow progress. How stupid I was then, he would say to himself, sniffing a glass of sherry. And the bouquet of this future sherry, the conviction and self-assurance of the prosperous drinker he'd envisioned would momentarily sweep the young man, who at this time was indeed quite stupid, off his feet. His confidence would be renewed, his despair under control. After all, it is unlikely that a chrysalis ever hopes to turn into a butterfly, but it turns into one nonetheless.

However, little by little, the destiny of this budding genius

11

had taken an unfortunate turn and had come to an abrupt halt. As the years that separated them gradually diminished, the future Polidori, who would have everything he'd ever dreamed of by the age of twenty-five, became less and less of a reality. He'd had to keep putting off the day of reckoning, like a coquettish woman who at the age of forty resigns herself to growing old, adding, let's say, five years in one fell swoop, so that she admits to being thirty and no longer twenty-five, until she discovers that she's really forty-five and is sick with grief. The mythical contented Polidori had aged in this way, in periodic bursts, and one day, assuming that the other confused Polidori lived a long life, he would be obliged to imagine his elder double as a benevolent fossil. He would even find serenity in the loss rather than the realization of his illusions. No, that was impossible. Instead of looking his age, the double should die, no matter what, to put an end to this sordid agony. His guiding star—which in spite of his pain along the way had made him hope that the narrow path he'd taken would somehow lead to glory and happiness—this star had gone out after a few pathetic flickers and had banished his comforting illusions into a zone of darkness.

Now all he had left was the opium. His habit began during the time of his return to England and his failed suicide, coinciding with the very real death of the ideal Polidori. At this point, his health was already in an extreme state of decline, and the drug would ward off his shaking spells, his awful stomachaches, and the violent spasms that agitated his eyes after a strong emotion. The opium took the edge off. In numbing his senses, it made him indifferent to a fate that seemed like someone else's, someone living in China whose soul and passions could be explored with purely scientific curiosity. For it also encouraged intellectual activity that could be accomplished calmly, without qualms or prejudices, as in a laboratory. He marveled at discovering within himself a certain manner of thinking, a certain personality trait that, had he been lucid, would have put him to shame. He developed brilliant theories, plots for novels or plays, and their futility only troubled him during the increasingly rare moments when he wasn't under the influence. He almost took pleasure in the nightmarish intervals when he'd be tortured by the recognition of his failures, knowing that he'd need twenty—soon thirty, soon fifty drops of laudanum diluted in a glass of warm water to return to a complex, colorful reality. Yet it was within his grasp, dictated by his own will; he could march right into it with the nonchalance of a conqueror.

His idyll with the drug did not last. After a few months the charted course leading to this magic kingdom had changed. The stream of reveries on which, until then, Polidori had drifted down as if on a river, stretched out in a boat watching the treetops above sail by, had become more turbulent. Bubbling foam had surfaced; reefs jutted out of the water. Nearby, the thundering roar of waterfalls warned of an imminent catastrophe.

The opium had at first lent a rigorous fluidity to his inner musings: words flowed smoothly, one attracting another as thought took shape; nothing remained, but nothing was omitted. Now, on the contrary, a sentence that began in a graceful manner became a distortion. Rather than coming to an end to let another phrase take over, it would persist, reaching out when there was nothing more to grasp, stumbling on words that were suddenly devoid of their meaning or had been passed on to the enemy, lying in ambush like a cannibal in the jungle. When the explorer had first landed, the cannibal had cautiously refrained from showing any sign of life to avoid frightening him away. Now, without actually revealing himself, he leaves traces of his presence everywhere; scraps of a meal, a poorly extinguished fire, footprints where the number of toes purposely varies from one day to the next. He plays with his prey, creeps into his words, and uses idiomatic expressions from his own country to work against him. He employs others to be on the lookout, with whom he undoubtedly communicates through some secret channel, since he's enlisted into his service such figures as Byron and the Shelleys. Each day a monstrous, incomprehensible desire drives Polidori back to the torture chamber, into the labyrinth of his brain, where from now on he's no longer alone. After trying so long to avoid it, he would almost be willing to consider ordinary lucidity a state of bliss. He wishes to be able to maintain it, not by a sudden burst of determination or for health reasons, but to escape the nightmarish drama in which he's constantly plunged.

Between dying of thirst or drinking water that you know to be poisoned, there isn't much of a choice: you will always drink, because extreme suffering forces one to take some kind of action, no matter what it is. Your bowels racked with pain, the thirst increases and you take another drink. Polidori fails miserably in his attempts to break his habit, in plans designed to reduce the daily number of drops of laudanum: at the moment, he's taking three hundred. He had, for example, begged the pharmacist to cut off his supply of opium, and disregard all his pleas. But later he had begged him so much for the opposite that the pharmacist had finally given in. And besides, now it was Teresa who went to see him. These resolutions that were never kept would bring back memories, breaking down the plans Polidori had once made in order to facilitate the pursuit of his work.

Before leaving London, Byron had received from his editor, John Murray, a rather large sum that, according to Murray's phrase, was supposed to serve to "facilitate the pursuit of his work." The poet had immediately squandered this sum, then ordered a magnificent carriage, an exact replica of Napoleon's, and sent the bill to Murray, pointing out that with this vehicle he could pursue his work in the required fashion. While traveling, this became one of his favorite jokes. Whenever another coach went faster than theirs, he'd lean out the door and call to the driver, "My work! My work! It's got to be pursued!" And once the coach had been passed, he would burst into laughter and improvise a few lines of verse. Polidori, who acted as both doctor and secretary, took note of this, thinking to himself that one couldn't really accuse him of stealing from the honest Murray.

In spite of, or perhaps because of this emulation of the poet, Polidori pursued his work just as he pursued this contented image of himself, a reflection in the water constantly disturbed by the pebbles he threw in. Each one of these projectiles had broken, had shattered into millions of elusive bits certain mental structures that at first had taken the form of his famous tragedies. These always ended in the baroque-style vestibule—where the action was supposed to begin—and ended in a prosaic manner almost as if the hero had been denied his entrance by a valet, and was doomed by this rebuff never to bring his torments to the stage. Shattered, too, was the story of a vampire he had sketched at the Villa Diodati and finished the following year at the home of the countess of Breuss, whose well-known fortune struck him as a mocking emblem of his own destiny.

Nevertheless, he had written out this entire story. For once in his life, aside from his medical thesis, he'd been able to mark the words "The End" at the bottom of a page covered with his own handwriting. Preceding that were approximately thirty other pages—or hundreds if one counted the rough drafts. The story was his own; his name should have been printed above the title, *The Vampire;* strangers should have read it and retained this name in the back of their minds. Out of a lifetime of failure, at least this evidence would have remained, a rectangular slim volume that could be held in one's hand, a testimony to the passage of John William Polidori through this world.

He had never found out exactly what had happened. During the entire year that followed, he had mulled over certain events, so important to him that he could not understand how the people who had played a part in them had forgotten so quickly. Upon his return to London, after two years of travel with Byron, then without Byron, he had seen his story published under the name of Lord B. Then there had been a review, an unfavorable one, for that matter, in which the anonymous critic insinuated in a pointlessly mysterious and roundabout way that everyone knew quite well that *The Vampire* had been written by Byron.

Polidori trembled as he read the article; his legs gave way beneath him. He'd rushed to his publisher's office as soon as he'd had the strength, and Colburn had had him shown to the door. He had turned to the countess of Breuss, who had been his patron during his stay in Germany. He had entrusted his manuscript to her, not so much in the hope that she would encourage its publication as in an attempt to win her esteem by making it appear that he had other works hidden away. In doing so, he both feared and hoped that she would ask for other samples of this imaginary opus, but she expressed no curiosity, and the interest she had had in the easily offended young doctor quickly faded.

But she was in London and had agreed to see him. As soon as he'd been ushered into her boudoir, she informed him that she was about to leave for the country, and although it was a great pleasure to see him again, she barely had any time to devote to him. She had no memory of the manuscript, and in his efforts to make her remember, Polidori, fists clenched and livid with rage, had great difficulty in controlling his

16

trembling. Fatigued by the rantings of a madman, and to deter this madman from fainting on her carpet, she finally conceded that he had indeed given her a fantastic story the year before and that she in turn had entrusted it to the publisher Colburn, without, in fact, even having read it. Yes, of course it had been under his name, John William Polidori. If he had said Milton, she would have also said Milton. She dismissed him.

He returned to Colburn's office, met with another barricade, which was all the more insulting since everyone else was passing through quite easily. In the waiting room an old man had begun to put out the candles. They were closing up. In desperation Polidori stood up, forcing himself to ignore the floor reeling at his feet, and declared that he was Lord Byron's secretary and had come on his behalf. At that moment a corpulent man walked out of the office that must have been Colburn's and took a key from his waistcoat pocket to lock the door. With his back turned to Polidori, he grumbled, "And you've come on behalf of His Grace to protest, is that it? His Grace isn't satisfied? His Grace doesn't like it when we have him sign any piece of nonsense to make it sell?" He put the key back into his pocket and turned around. Then, undoubtedly noticing the agitated state of his visitor, he continued somewhat more graciously, "Listen here, my friend. I received a letter from your master. I wrote back to him no later than yesterday and I don't see what more I can tell you. Some person wrote a preposterous story, not very good, I grant you that, but we all have to survive somehow. He signed it with a pseudonym. On top of that, some imbeciles thought they recognized the name of a famous poet behind this pseudonym. That's their business, not mine. Neither is it any business of the famous poet, believe me. One should only heed the rich. His true readers, if there are any, will surely know that the story isn't his. He should forget the whole affair, give up the idea of making amends, and everyone will be happy."

Polidori had lost control over the movements of his eyes, which rolled from right to left, faster and faster, sweeping back and forth over his field of vision, in the middle of which stood the publisher, who appeared to be troubled. Polidori's gaze passed over him so quickly that he couldn't be entirely certain. Perhaps he was amused.

"But what about the real author?" sputtered the young man.

"God rest his soul," said Colburn. "He died, apparently. According to His Grace, it was a young Italian doctor, his former secretary. Come on, my friend, we're closing up. Kindly pay my respects to your master, and with no ill feelings. . . ."

He was pushed out the door.

CHAPTER IV

He idled about London, drinking. One time he came to at the police station. They told him that he had created quite a scandal, and had fainted in front of the bookstall displaying copies of a novel currently in vogue, *Frankenstein*, by Mary Shelley. In his delirium he'd repeated these two names over and over, that of the author and of the eponymous hero. As they set him free the police jokingly referred to him by this nickname, and several days later he met up with a crowd of drunks who greeted him like an old friend, yelling, "Frankenstein, Frankenstein, here comes Frankenstein!" He fled, failed in his attempted suicide, and left London.

He was unable to remember the days that followed his visit to Colburn, and fearful that in his drunken stupor he had run to every newspaper, bookstore, and antechamber of literary renown to claim the authorship of his *Vampire*, or maybe even of *Frankenstein*. And that he had maligned Byron, Mary Shelley, and the entire world. In any case he was certain that he'd made a terrible fool of himself, so that whenever he eventually summoned enough courage to write a story or a poem, he wouldn't be able to present it anywhere without an exchange of knowing smiles between the secretaries, lackeys, and couriers. He convinced himself that he had traded in the reputation of a clown for an oppressive yet protective anonymity; that his name, which had already been changed by the drunks into Frankenstein, had now become a professional password in literary society (where, several weeks earlier, he had still dreamed of making his triumphant debut). For them it represented all the unfortunate authors who would be shown the door, those enlightened souls lacking brilliance, the eternal beggars.

But worse was still to come. Despite his aversion to it, he could not escape *Frankenstein*. The success of this novel was odious to him, but it was everywhere he turned; it had been brought to the stage, plates were being decorated with its characters, people were talking about it all the way out in the provinces, at the tables of country inns. He read it while in Sussex. Already, in the first few pages, he recognized some of the ideas he had breathed to Mary four years ago, in order to please her—for she had been the only one who sometimes treated him with kindness. Now she owed him the theme of her novel and by the same token, her sudden glory. She had stolen the idea and the glory *from him*, and this is how she was thanking him! In a short preface she referred to the summer spent on Lake Geneva, the evenings at the Villa Diodati, the little clique that she belonged to, composed of Shelley, Lord Byron, and he—he, Polidori, cited as a minor character, a humble bit player, even though Claire, for example, had been mercifully forgotten. She told how Byron had proposed a game—that each of them write a ghost story, based on the model of the ones that Polidori, yes, him again, had bought from a peddler passing through Sécheron—how "the two poets" had abandoned their preliminary drafts, and how she had continued with hers. Then came the horrid paragraph that she'd devoted to him, and that he knew by heart:

Poor Polidori had some terrible idea about a skull-headed lady who was so punished for peeping through a keyhole— what to see I forget: something very shocking and wrong, of course; but when she was reduced to a worse condition than the renowned Tom of Coventry, he did not know what to do with her and was obliged to dispatch her to the tomb of the Capulets, the only place for which she was fitted.

It was false from beginning to end. Never had he had such an absurd idea. He could fully remember having sketched out the plot of his ill-fated *Vampire*—for unlike her, he had ideas—and having told Mary about a galvanic experiment that had taken place in Glasgow: the resurrection of a dying man, which she had drawn upon for the plot of *Frankenstein*. And as for skull-headed ladies, it was Shelley who, on those drunken evenings, had seen her with cruel eyes on the tips of her breasts, something she'd obviously kept to herself.

Why had she written this? What pleasure could she, with her fortune and fame, have possibly derived from ridiculing an obscure young man who had never done her harm? With whom, moreover, she had been gentle and friendly? He thought back to the graceful and serious adolescent he had known, whom he had loved without telling her or even admitting it to himself, and who, four years later, had become this harpy now determined to humiliate him. How could anyone change to such an extent? Perhaps it wasn't really her; perhaps she'd been replaced. Yes, that was it. Without anyone knowing, the exquisite soul of Mary Shelley had been sucked out by some kind of vampire, who now possessed her, dictated her thoughts, her writing, and had driven her toward the sole objective of ruining John William Polidori. The resentment he felt this time was no longer dispersed by the evidence of a widespread conspiracy against him (at first he had hated Byron, then realized that the responsibility was shared by Madame de Breuss, Colburn, the critics, and the myriad of unknown enemies that made up his audience). From then on all his hatred was concentrated on the one and only Mary Shelley, this vampire, this creature suddenly possessed by a demon whom he swore he would kill. Unfortunately, his pistol had been stolen. Then he found out that Mary was living in Italy and he didn't have a penny to get there. Even so, he could very well picture himself following her all over the world, just as Victor Frankenstein follows the monster he's created all the way to the ice of the North Pole.

But he lacked the courage; his trembling body was of little use to him. He decided against it. For an entire year he went from one shelter to another, ruminating over his humiliation, as well as the symmetry he saw at play in the two events that, in the space of a week, had sealed his fate. He had written a story, just one, that had been attributed to someone else, and this other person had immediately disclaimed it as being unworthy of him. And in return, the only trace of his work as a writer that would remain on this earth was an ironic summary of a completely fabricated story whose sole purpose was to ridicule him. All of the mirrors were warped; never again could they reflect the image of the ideal Polidori, the one who at age twenty-five would be admired and famous. And if that Polidori, projected into an increasingly distant future, had still, at that point, lost every hope of eventual self-fulfillment, it wouldn't be the sole fault of the impotent Polidori, who had proved incapable of writing a work that would have made him famous. It would also be the fault of the world for having dressed him in a clown's costume, so that if ever he'd been able to write the work he'd always dreamed of, even if it had surpassed the brilliance of Shakespeare, this brilliance would never be recognized. Even before reading it, the publishers would see the author's signature and howl with laughter.

"What's so funny?"

"You won't believe it, it's that poor Polidori again! I thought he was dead, but apparently he's still writing his skull-headed-lady stories. Into the wastebasket it goes!"

"Beware now. Before you know it, he'll be back in your antechamber, rolling his eyes and fainting on your carpet. . . ."

CHAPTER V

From then on, no matter what happened (if anything else were to happen) and no matter what he wrote (if he were to write anything more) he would have to go about it in disguise. His name and identity were useless to him. But there was really nothing new about his situation. Although it hadn't assumed the proportions of a tragic destiny, he had already toyed with this idea when he'd parted from Byron, on his way to Italy. He had traveled in Germany, rushing full speed ahead in the opposite direction of the majestic carriage of imperial pretentiousness.

During the first few weeks, strangely enough, he had felt lighthearted. The colors of the ideal Polidori were revived in the mirror and the distance that separated them seemed to diminish with every turn of the coach wheels. They had dismissed him like a valet, but in fact he suddenly wasn't a valet any longer. He clutched the first draft of his story in his bag, the story that would soon open the doors to the literary salons of London. And besides, he could lie, he could take advantage of the anonymity of his encounters while traveling to converse. For a brief moment, time enough for a discreet rehearsal before a wealthy audience, he could try on the glittering costume of the true Polidori: a young English poet, soon to be famous, who was wandering about Europe for his own amusement.

He had always enjoyed passing himself off as someone else, and this inclination had been both encouraged and kept in check during the past spring, when he'd been traveling with Lord Byron, in the famous carriage, on their way to Switzerland. Byron had never missed an opportunity to play a practical joke. Had he been alone, Polidori would have been tempted to pass himself off as no other than Lord Byron, or at least someone else of comparable literary stature, whereas Lord Byron, on the contrary, delighted in exploiting his incognito in the most outlandish ways. The roles he chose to play were not prestigious (they would have become so, had the poet announced himself) but almost buffoonish in nature. The purpose of these creations was less to flatter his vanity, already well satisfied, than to disconcert his spectators—and if that failed, his accomplice, for Polidori was obliged to participate.

Byron adored exotic disguises, and the coach, full of intendants, trailing the carriage from a good distance away, carried in it an entire supply of them worthy of any theatrical costumer specializing in Turkish accessories. One night, at the very beginning of the trip, they stopped at an inn near the battlefield of Waterloo, where the imperial army had been defeated the year before. Although the costume-filled coach was also equipped with a pantry and everything needed for a refined midnight feast, Byron wanted to parade around the inn's dining room in a little corporal's costume. But then he saw that the gray frock coat didn't suit him. Changing his mind, he dressed himself in a pair of harem pants, Turkish slippers, and a vest embroidered with fake jewels, and put Polidori in charge of knotting a complicated turban around his head. Then Byron sent him off as a dispatcher with a cumbersome hookah and a little vial in his hands, to announce his arrival and order a bowl of boiling water. After this, he made his entrance in his Grand Panjandrum costume, as incognito as possible, since the veil pinned to the tassel of his turban concealed his face.

The moment he was seated, he leaned over the steaming bowl and poured in the contents of the vial, composed of several drops of an oily and foul-smelling liquid. The folds of his silk veil were draped around his bent torso, forming a desert tent over the soup bowls, planted at the edge of the guest table. From this tent emerged two well-kept hands, the wrists floating in a wave of embroidery, the fingers laden with rings. At regular intervals one of these hands would wave a distress signal, until Polidori, standing over him like a servant, would produce the hookah pipe, which was gropingly seized and guided under the tent.

The combined effect of the inhalation and the smoke, which gave off a sickening odor of wilted geraniums, gradually turned the other guests green. Yet they didn't dare protest, simply proving that incredible cheek will grant one a certain authority. And besides, perhaps this powerful figure had the material means to impose it. The traveling salesmen who looked with astonishment upon their strange table companion hidden under his veil clearly wondered whether the inn wasn't in fact surrounded by a troop of cruel eunuchs. Ready and waiting, their plump fingers fondling their scimitars, they would make sure that anyone who didn't show proper respect for their master would lose more than his appetite. This fearful respect had quickly spread throughout the entire inn, and no one uttered a word. The caliph (or the vizier, or the bey, or the pasha—they weren't really certain) and his attendant set an example by keeping silent. Not a soul dared to move from his seat, or even allow his chair to creak. And for nearly an hour the only sound in the room was the monotonous gurgle of the hookah, and the Turk's deep breathing, followed by loud exhaling noises that made his veil flutter. During the next few days Byron and Polidori had a splendid time imagining what the spectators must have thought of their show, the stories they had told their families and friends, and the increasingly distorted versions that had spread ever since.

Of all of Byron's practical jokes, this was the only one in which Polidori had spontaneously collaborated and with enjoyment. It had taken place at the beginning of their trip, before he had become bitter. A young man fresh from the university, haloed with the prestige earned by his thesis, he had simply wormed his way into the inner circle—on an equal footing, he thought—of England's most famous poet. He had smiled somewhat condescendingly, but without losing his temper, when his father, who had once served as secretary to the poet Alfieri in Italy, had noisily congratulated him for renewing a family tradition that he had once obviously scorned. But in his eyes, the position of secretary to a poet was only a stepping-stone to becoming a well-known poet himself.

On the eve of their departure, in the large mansion on Piccadilly Terrace, he had recited the first act of one of the tragedies that he'd been working on. Hobson and Scrope Davies, two friends of Byron's, had poked fun at him, but the poet had reread the best passages aloud and made encouraging comments. Once their travels began, he had shown him a certain friendship. Polidori was ecstatic from this intimacy with such a great man—Byron had separated him from the common herd (hardly worth the effort of a practical joke). Yet he had never suspected how unbearable his position as a servant would soon become. Sometimes, while amusing themselves at the expense of mortal men, the gods will elect a human ancillary who is suddenly led to believe that he's established himself on Olympus. And once his masters tire of his services, he finds himself a stranger among his peers, in the same way that an informer, once freed by the police, has nothing more to do with the good-for-nothings whom he has betrayed.

Polidori realized this three weeks after the euphoric Turkish episode (in which he had proudly played his part), when Byron was obliged to pay a visit to Madame de Staël. Undoubtedly inspired by a farce performed for them by some Italian actors in Grenoble, the poet had decided on a whim that they would exchange roles. He had proposed the plan to him with all the mischief of a child, so infectious at that particular moment that Polidori had failed to see how such a masquerade could prove humiliating to him. Besides, Byron surely hadn't realized it himself, for he was still favorably disposed toward his doctor. Hardly wishing to play a nasty trick on him, he had simply been more interested in playing an amusing one on Madame de Staël.

One man followed the other with an affected humility that was already unpleasant; Polidori had never acted so obsequiously—he was a doctor, not a subordinate. It was only after they arrived in Coppet and were announced in the drawing room (where Madame de Staël and several friends were expecting them, impatient to see the famous and scandalous Lord Byron) that the young man was able to evaluate the true extent of the disaster, realizing the offense that would be taken not only at the final explanation, but even prior to this ordeal, at his obvious incapacity to carry out the role as planned. Never could he, under their observant stares, be as witty, loquacious, and seductive as Lord Byron. For a moment he hoped he could get out of this fix by affecting an attitude that certain provincial readers associated with Byron's person, based on the strength of the poems of his youth: an obstinate silence, an austere and melancholic stance.

Polidori greeted them coldly, making a general survey of the room, where everything, the decor and the friendly smiles of the guests, prompted him to bow and scrape. And in doing so, he could distinctly sense their surprise. What? This was Lord Byron? This almost beardless young man who was so awkward, so self-conscious? To make matters worse, his disguise, already unconvincing, was further compromised by his bright-colored clothing. If only he'd been able to remain in his somber black dress, in which he was often mistaken for a clergyman. At least it would have been appropriate for a morose poet, unconcerned with his attire and lost in poetic contemplation! But Byron had insisted that he put on a pair of Chinese periwinkle-blue pants, a short red velvet jacket, and that he unbutton the neck of his shirt. Waves of lacy ruffles spilled over the braided loops of the jacket, fastened with a single button. As it was, Byron preferred ample clothing, and Polidori, who had neither his broad build nor his corpulence, was floating in it. It was the dress of a man who intends to attract attention, not disillusion, and absolutely incompatible with a reserved and aloof manner. Decked out in this fashion, Polidori resembled a clown who has just been kicked out of the ring, but remains silent, barely repressing his desire to weep.

He looked at Byron, who stood in the doorway of the room,

daring neither to step forward, nor backward into the vestibule. So this was how his master saw him: staring at the tips
of his black shoes, twisting his hat in his hands. The audience's attention was so riveted on the disappointing Lord
Byron that no one had the gallantry to invite his companion
in to join the company.

As a last resort, and because he hoped that Byron would
put an end to his torture (even if this kind intention had been
carried out, it would have only led to the next form of pun-
ishment), Polidori strode across the drawing room, took Byron
by the arm, and brought him into the center of the circle.
Panic-stricken, he wondered whether he should introduce him
as Polidori (which was what they had agreed upon, but he
now realized that the more he emphasized the symmetry of
their exchanged roles, the more stinging his humiliation would
become) or under an imaginary name. That was assuming,
at least, that this grotesque character portrayed by Byron was
one of pure invention, like the Beloved of the Prophet, and
not a caricature of Polidori. Undoubtedly the best solution
would have been for him to take the initiative and reveal the
hoax straightaway, but it simply hadn't occurred to him at
the time. Anxious to find a fictional name (though any name
would have done the trick: Mr. Smith, Mr. Jones, Captain
Walton . . .), he frantically came up with, "I present to you
Doctor Polidori," pronouncing each syllable with an hysterical obstinacy. Byron bowed, as if intimidated by the guests,
looking gratefully at his master. "My friend," he added all
in one breath, immediately aware of the catastrophe that
would result from this pledge of friendship granted to an
inferior in public.

Assuming an air of sly humility, Byron began rubbing his
hands with delight but then stopped, and clasping them together, he said in a falsetto, "Milord is too kind. . . ." Then,
hobbling along in such a way that everyone would notice the

celebrated limp that Polidori had forgotten to imitate, he gaped with feigned astonishment (so intense that Polidori momentarily forgot about the guests) and exclaimed, "But Milord has lost his limp!"

Polidori should have appreciated this act of mercy. Realizing that he'd gone too far, that the joke had turned sour, Byron had decided to put an end to it. He'd let himself be recognized at his own expense, by drawing attention, with his usual dramatic flair, to a personal detail that was nevertheless a painful subject to him. He even pointed his thumb toward the sky, like a Roman emperor bestowing his grace on a defeated but courageous gladiator. However, in his bewilderment, the young man didn't grasp the meaning of this sudden about-face. All he could see in front of him was a sort of sneering demon, twisting and turning on his clubfoot, bulging out of the black suit that was his, Polidori's. Standing there, distraught, in the middle of the drawing room, he lost all self-control and murmured in the dead silence, "I am not that man," while the stunned audience looked on, unable to comprehend the startling turn that this drama was taking right before their eyes, nor the true significance of the imposter's words.

Proclaiming them as if they were his last, he was not certain which man he was referring to: the pitiful character he was playing, or himself, the one who had consented to play this character, or perhaps the one whom Byron was playing. Before collapsing in a faint, he repeated under his breath, "I am not that man," and indeed from that day on, he was on his way to becoming nobody.

CHAPTER VI

From that day on, he lost favor with Byron as well. While Byron reproached himself for having offended Polidori, he also believed that he'd done everything possible to help him save face. By fainting, Polidori had put him in the absurd position of a practical joker, the kind who pulls a chair out from under a guest just about to be seated, only to declare afterward that he nearly died with laughter when the guest fell down and broke his spine. Besides, whatever harm had been inflicted on Polidori had seemed innocent enough. Later on, at the Villa Diodati, he'd never really treated him like a scapegoat, but the young man had already adopted this role so willingly that everything took an unpleasant turn.

Polidori was more easily offended now, having been ridiculed in public, and he always dreaded meeting someone who had witnessed his nervous fit. He was pained to see Byron returning often to Coppet, where he was certain they spent their time making fun of him (he wouldn't have accompanied him there for anything in the world). He was jealous of Shelley and detected conspiracies everywhere he turned, intended to discredit him or steal the great ideas in his tragedies. Byron's presence, his visible annoyance, and his scoffing banter became so unbearable to him that, while he regretted not having proudly taken the initiative, he felt a sense of relief when the poet, who was leaving to spend the autumn in Italy, advised him to visit Germany.

Traveling alone, he rediscovered the freedom that had been denied him, and along with it a fondness for masks, which he could now pick and choose at will. He made use of the opportunity to imagine all sorts of flattering fabrications that no ironic look could contradict. Unfortunately, his financial means prevented him from playing the part of the wealthy traveler. But by the same token, it was possible that certain political circumstances or an unhappy love affair had forced him to move about with discretion, using a disguise, which is what he insinuated to the more gullible minds he encountered.

In this way he'd persuaded a French governess on her way to Cologne, diligently reading a translation of *Werther*, that she'd made the acquaintance of Louis XVII. A dewy-eyed myopic pastor with a quivering chin had been tempted to give up his faith for a secret emissary of the General of the Jesuits, a pale young man dressed in black whose pleasing, regular features were almost always contorted with sarcasm. From his obviously depraved lips flowed a stream of whispered mumblings about a new race who would conquer the world (and whose good graces had to be won), diabolical experiments, vampires—and above all, no matter what happened, this must remain a secret.

In his empty house in London, Polidori had seen this pastor one more time, in a dream. On his deathbed, which had been prepared in the sunniest room of a Swiss chalet scented with edelweiss, the old man turns to his son-in-law, a pastor like himself, and in one breath, murmurs something about an encounter with the Evil One. The son-in-law doesn't understand a word of it, but he nods earnestly, watching the doctor out of the corner of his eye. The doctor, standing at the foot of the bed, lowers his gaze in a sign of sympathetic complicity. The patient is delirious; his hour is near. This pale reflection of a former mask sinks into the depths of the mirror. Polidori is shaking all over. He has died little by little in the minds of those he has encountered, the same way that he is dead, and undoubtedly has been for quite a while, in the mind of a man he recalls as having been the most satisfying of his German interlocutors. A mixed satisfaction, as always, for at the time Polidori's intention (which worked out well in his dreams and very badly in reality) was that his interlocutor demonstrate both the capability of listening attentively to everything that he, Polidori, had to say, as well as an undeniable superiority in terms of age and prestige. In fact, all those whom he considered superior to himself (and whom he already resented for that very reason) became rapidly impatient with his combination of flattery and arrogance. As a result he was constantly snubbed. However, when he met the German poet named Clemens in a literary café in Berlin, the latter had been drunk, lonely, and eager to pour out his heart. For this he'd needed a means of detaining his listener, and had therefore allowed the other a reasonable amount of time to pour out his heart as well.

A long and chaotic conversation had ensued. Clemens complained a great deal, and like an old man, continually deplored the contrast between his present life and his idyllic youth, which couldn't have been that long ago. Judging from his troubled, childlike face, this rather fat gentleman hardly looked more than thirty. Polidori took advantage of every sorrowful pause (a sign of the poet's consternation before the swift passage of time, as well as his drunken inability to keep the conversation on track) to slip in a mysterious allusion to the top-secret mission that had brought him to Germany. But each time the other would start in again, telling him about his years at school, about his sister, who as a young girl had won the heart of Goethe (here, Polidori pricked up his ears; he was always interested in intimate friends of famous people) and went on to malign Goethe (Polidori trusted his judgment) then to describe his sister's husband, a certain Joachim, who was presently a lord in a château somewhere in eastern Prussia.

He was also a poet (Polidori found it irritating that everyone was a poet) and a rare storyteller. He chattered on until dawn in a haze of alcohol, recounting his adventures and a story that Joachim had written about a mandrake (Polidori tried in vain to get a word in about his *Vampire*), all of this mixed in with personal memories, recollections of poems or stories he'd read, thoughts about the moral benefits of Roman Catholicism, and comments on the café's regular customers, who were thinning out little by little.

Polidori was so drunk that he listened attentively. But it was only after they'd been thrown out, trudging down the narrow streets, holding on to the arm of the poet (who staggered along, threatening halfheartedly to throw himself into the river) that he finally managed to squeeze in a kind of monologue. Passing over his top-secret mission (the likelihood of which, at this point, could be no better judged by his companion than he) Polidori introduced himself as a famous English poet. "A poet?" repeated Clemens with disgust, when all along he had given the impression that nobody worthwhile could be anything else. Without waiting for a reply, he launched into drunken praise of Shakespeare and above all, Ossian, who had just been translated into German. From these two examples he concluded that over the last few centuries the art of literature had become increasingly banal, which he attributed once again to the Reformation. Overwrought from the alcohol, no doubt, a perverse and imaginative demon drove Polidori into claiming otherwise—that Ossian's ballads, far from having been rediscovered by a scholar, were in fact contemporary fakes, and that his father even knew the author.

Seeing that Clemens didn't believe him, he took it even further and calmly assured him that this type of abuse was quite common in English literature, that authors were even permitted to publish using another's name, a fact of which foreigners were often unaware. Now carried away by his own idea, he evoked a civilization that would indulge in a kind of graphomania, where all literary creation would be mixed

33

together, where pseudonyms, pastiches, plagiarism, falsely attributed and antedated works would ultimately reign. He himself, for example, in his spare time, outside of his own work, which he doubted would be published before another century or two, had written poems that were quite well known, under the name of Lord Byron. (Upon his return to England he thought of this tale, which had turned out to be partially true in the worst possible way, and persuaded himself that he'd been right all along about Ossian, although he had never been able to verify it.) As a matter of fact, he continued, he had just spent several months traveling with an actor from the Old Vic who, in view of the popularity of these poems, had been instructed by the editor to impersonate the imaginary and aristocratic man of letters right under the noses of the gullible readers of the Continent. This second-rate actor was somewhat of a brute, but a docile brute with an imposing presence. Every morning Polidori would help him rehearse lines of verse and choose the right words to embellish his conversation for any number of social situations that could arise during their tour. These witty expressions had been specially adapted by Polidori, according to their prospective audience. For the minister who was also a renowned hunter they had decided to tell anecdotes about hunting; for the playwright it was the paradoxes of the theater. Moreover, many of these repartees could only begin with a specific phrase. Obviously, while at supper or in the loge at the opera, it would have been impossible for Polidori to prompt him, and therefore his artistic pleasure was derived from forcing one of the guests, whose complicity would never be suspected, into unwittingly doing it himself.

Although the German poet was much too drunk to appreciate such finesse (which probably would have escaped him even when sober), Polidori fervently described the giddiness of the accomplice off in the shadows, who imposes his power on an innocent victim, then entwines him so skillfully into the web of his own words that ultimately those very syllables, arbitrarily decided upon by the demigod, now spring from his lips one by one. Up until the last moment, the other listens attentively to the conversation in which he is to intervene. Once the signal is given, the *primo uomo*, the false Byron, remains doubtful as to whether this plan will actually succeed. And the moment the predetermined syllables are finally pronounced, he adds his retort to the phrase at once, trying to avoid winking at his mentor, who has triumphed once again. The latter begins to feel like a kind of universal ventriloquist, giving his cues to one man and imposing them on another without his knowing. Seized with an exhilaration that his humble pose conceals (officially, he's nothing more than the secretary to this great man), he dreams, like the juggler, of increasing the number of pins; adding one, two, three marionettes to the theater under his control; making all of the guests in the drawing room or in the opera loge utter the words he's imagined.

He had often experienced the effect of this omnipotence, he confessed to Clemens. Amid the general conversation, the false Byron spouted phrases, his audience broke into laughter, and he, Polidori, remained slightly off to the side, nodding his head with half-closed eyes, like a playwright listening to superb actors reciting his play. The lines flowed one after the other, in the right order; the delivery of the dialogue was respected. At times the author in the wings would intervene to encourage the action, pulling a few strings with a mere look. And he could delight in the knowledge that all these people who thought that they were in control of the situation were in fact portraying characters and enunciating words that had sprung entirely from his own imagination. What were poetic raptures compared with these?

Clemens, his face sagging with fatigue, said in a listless

voice that all of this reminded him of the ecstatic virgins of Tyrol, and Polidori (more for his own personal pleasure than to impress his companion, who having established this inept resemblance, fell asleep at last in the gutter) smiled proudly, as if he had planned all along to make him utter these words. It was almost as though this statement were proof neither of Clemens' intoxication nor of his own free will. On the contrary, it was evidence of his submission to the hypnotist, who had gotten him to say things that perhaps made no sense to him at all.

CHAPTER VII

It's the opium that induces these imaginary dramas. In some of these fantasies Polidori envisions a large audience, who regularly assemble in a grand drawing room with luxurious and antiquated furnishings in the style of the king of France, Louis XV. This drawing room is a combination of the one at Coppet and Madame de Breuss's, where day after day, for almost two months, he had read aloud to the thoughtless aristocrat. Among the guests in the drawing room, the faces within the range of his peripheral vision seem somehow familiar to him. Yet as soon as he actually focuses on one in particular, it turns out to be the face of a stranger. Consequently he finds himself in a room swarming with characters who, if he were to look at them closely, might be Madame de Breuss, Byron, Bonstetten, Madame de Staël, Shelley, Mary, Colburn, the Chevalier Pictet, the Marquis Saporati and even Teresa, who is terribly out of place in this setting. Whereas those standing in front of him are not so much strangers as people who, in short, have the negative distinc-

tion of being neither Madame de Breuss, nor Byron, nor
Bonstetten. . . . When he enters the room, these characters,
who have so far been silent, suddenly begin to speak among
themselves. He perceives this indistinct murmur much in the
same way as he did the faces: he vaguely understands what
is being said on either side of him, but nothing at all of what
follows from the pencil-lined lips of the German princess,
who might as well be speaking in Javanese. He is even more
frightened by this problem of perception, since by some monstrous increase of talent, the glib chatter that surrounds
him—of this he is certain—springs from his inner thoughts.
Everything they say comes from his own mind; he speaks
through their lips but doesn't understand a word of the cacophony. For instead of his brain calmly organizing the arguments, dividing the dialogues among the speakers—who
would animate it, not letting the subjects overlap any more
than they would in normal conversation—instead of taking
the initiative and savoring the pleasure of universal control,
as he'd boasted, it is the guests in the drawing room who
ransack his brain, snatching bits of barely formulated
phrases, chewing on them and spitting them out, then helping
themselves to more, exchanging them among themselves like
drunken dogs in a mad scramble for the spoils. He had
previously thought of himself as a hypnotist, prevailing upon
a coterie of somnambulists, but instead he has been assaulted
by a horde of vampires who make themselves even more
horrible by sucking out the minds of others.

A continual stream of thoughts and phrases gushes from a
thousand points in his brain, but he is unable to stop it, not
a single word. He's now immersed in the verbal chaos as if
it were his own blood. This nightmare demands his undivided
attention, which is constantly thwarted and carries with it a
sense of danger. It is as though the assembled group, ap-

parently indifferent to his presence (ordinarily, he remains in the doorway), were simply waiting for a signal to surround him and tear him to pieces, laughing contemptuously. Yet he is the one who gives this signal, since they only exist because of him, and he's afraid to give it, or afraid that someone inside him will give it for him.

More and more frequently upon entering the drawing room in his dream, he finds the guests seated at a small table, a secretary, or at the corner of a desk, completely absorbed in the task of writing, never once bothering to look up from their paper. Whenever this takes place, Polidori is relieved at first, for all in all, he prefers the scratching sound of the pens to the cacophony of the conversations. But no sooner is he relieved than a thought occurs to him, and he realizes that this thought is being scrupulously noted by one of the clerks, disguised as a member of high society. Suddenly another idea begins to gnaw at him: that this group of ten or twenty people (he can no longer count nor identify them) is working without a moment's respite in order to transcribe every thought that runs through his head.

He envisions himself walking across the drawing room, standing behind one of the zealous scribes, and looking over his shoulder. The man's hand diligently scratches away and the pen grates, without a second of hesitation or remorse to slacken the pace. Perhaps this hand is Byron's; maybe it's Mary's; maybe it's Teresa's, she who doesn't even know how to write!

And if he does manage to read it, what will he actually find? The thoughts he knows he has just had, namely his own hesitation in discovering what he is about to read? Or something even more surprising? Perhaps the scribe whom he's been observing is not supposed to record Polidori's central train of thought, which he can barely follow himself. Perhaps instead it's a peripheral thought, adventitious, unformulated and gratuitously linked to a word from the principal associative chain; a thought that will, in turn, list all the subtleties of this word, or in the case of a proper name, draw up an historical account of his relationship with that person.

Polidori often dreams of rushing into the drawing room and collecting the papers, like a professor. After all, he has never really dreamed of anything else but transcribing his thoughts from day to day, hoping that this copy would finally be accurate. And what has he amassed up until now? Only despicable rubbish. He takes perverse pleasure in contemplating the inventory as he stands in the doorway of the drawing room: a thesis in medicine, *Disputatio Medica Inauguralis de Oneirodynia* (congratulations from the jury, please!), then the unfinished tragedies (let us cite among many others *Cajetan*, a Spanish drama, and *Boadicea*, an imitation of a classical subject), half-empty notebooks, a story he can no longer even claim as his own, and finally some lines of verse that hammer in his brain with malevolent irony, evoking his most undesirable acquaintances. This flattering address (in French, no less) had been dedicated to Charles, Madame de Breuss's son, who had served in the imperial army:

> *Jeune guerrier dans l'armée du premier des héros,*
> *Dans la cause de la France dédaignant le repos,*
> *Que la chute de vos ans soit tranquille et heureuse*
> *Comme fut l'aube de vos jours éclatante et glorieuse.*

This is his only accomplishment. But the rest, which has built up in his mind and whose unknown charms have never been captured on paper—the rest he is certain exists in black and white in the archives of the drawing room. Throughout his entire life they have been writing it all down. He has to get his hands on these archives, find the way to the repository.

* * *

Another dreadful thought: What goes on in the drawing room when he isn't there? His visitations take place more frequently, thanks to the opium, but they have begun fairly recently and last only as long as his sluggish stupor. Obviously his plan to collect the papers and appropriate the archives calls for a certain academic suspicion; the skepticism of a professor well acquainted with the laziness and lack of discipline of his students. Undoubtedly these students would never create an uproar in his presence, as had Madame de Breuss's other son, the younger one, for whom he had served as a tutor (he recalled with horror this pudgy, devious child whose ears stuck out, and who, just to provoke him, knowing that he would never dare to inform his mother, would undo his breeches during the lessons and masturbate with a vengeance, chortling with laughter). But what if they only pretend to be busy at work, after his arrival has been announced by someone on the lookout? Once he turns his back and goes home to London, to Teresa, to his wretched quarters, the hooting and whistling will start up again. Mocking him, they'll rip up all the papers. Then as a kind of penalty they will appoint the loser of some game (which is surely obscene) to remain on duty to prevent Polidori's mind from plunging entirely into the darkness.

He would have to stay there, camp out in the drawing room and keep up a relentlessly close watch; otherwise the scribes would cut off all supplies to the machinery. The corridors of his brain would be deserted, except for a kind of senile night watchman, dragging his felt-slippered feet, half asleep, a trembling and sickly dwarf who has been reduced into mumbling the same sentence over and over ("I am not that man, I am not that man, I am not that man. . . .") or perhaps the same word, the same name, that might even be his own ("Frankenstein, Frankenstein, Frankenstein . . .") so that he would never forget it, so that he wouldn't have to stop talking. It was just like Polidori in his empty house, afraid to fall asleep and surrender to the opium, knowing that he'll have nightmares, and that once he's inside the nightmare, he'll be struggling to remain asleep so that he won't have to leave his lookout post in the drawing room, or ring the recess bell for the dunces and the destruction of his own mind.

CHAPTER VIII

One day Polidori tries an experiment. He stands in the doorway of the drawing room where the clerks work with excessive zeal, as if hoping to trick him. Not daring to venture inside, he decides to withdraw and let a few moments pass before discreetly returning, so he can catch the guests unawares once they think he has gone. Walking away, he deliberately squeaks his shoes on the wooden floor of the antechamber, an oval-shaped room punctuated by half-columns. Between the columns the walls are decorated with frescoes, mythological scenes that he observes lingeringly, one after the other, as if he were visiting a museum. He then realizes that the only rooms of the château he has ever seen are the drawing room, and just a few moments ago, the antechamber. Perhaps a more thorough visit would prove to be instructive.

Besides the double glass doors that lead to the drawing room, there are two other massive wooden doors in the antechamber, smaller and perfectly symmetrical. Pressing down vainly on the handle of the door on the right, he realizes that it opens from the opposite direction, and pulls the door toward him, enters, and walks down a narrow, dimly lit hallway. Next he reaches a large room with French windows, but once he draws nearer, intending to open the shutters and take a

41

look at the park outside, he discovers that they are firmly nailed shut, like all the windows of his hideout in London. He passes through other rooms, follows other corridors, and walks down a stairway, trying all the doors, pulling at them.

The last one leads to the first-floor landing, within a couple of paces of his miserable dwelling.

He recognizes it once the door is closed behind him. He has never crossed its threshold before, never even tried to push it open. During the weeks that he's been hiding out in this abandoned residence, he's had neither the curiosity nor perhaps the courage to make the proprietor's rounds—nor, most likely, has Teresa. When viewing it from the street (when was the last time?), he could safely say that it was a two-story mansion, topped by a pretentious turret. But the only thing he knows about its interior layout is, in sequence, the heavy door at the entrance, the crack, the narrow alleyway leading to the stairs, the stairway, the landing, and the room on the right, more like a closet, where he and Teresa had set up their quarters in the hope that the tinier their dwelling, the more protected they would be.

The effects of the opium subsiding, Polidori is now lucid enough to realize that the drawing room where his life and his work are being transcribed is purely his own fantasy, and therefore could not possibly be concealed within the London mansion. He finds himself in familiar surroundings, sitting on the straw mattress with his knees drawn up to his chin. Teresa isn't there. However, her basket is lying on the floor, the water supply has been replenished, and a bottle of laudanum has been conspicuously set next to the pitcher. Everything is conspicuous in this bare room, and Polidori reflects that the tragedy of his life has never been so obvious to him before, like a tangible object placed directly in front of him.

It had been decided that Teresa would make a trip that

day to the pharmacist, who grows poisonous mushrooms. Polidori is surprised by the unusual size of the flask. The pharmacist ordinarily gives Teresa a small stoppered bottle each time she comes, but this one, at first glance, looks as though it contains five times more than usual. This extravagant amount could perhaps explain her absence, or maybe her supplier merely wanted to give the young man certain ideas by providing him with a highly lethal dose. He bursts into laughter. What if it were a birthday present? He's not sure of the date, but he recently remembered that he would be turning twenty-five in three days' time. In any case, the event deserves to be celebrated. He allows himself a glass with twenty-five drops in it.

He decides to resume his inspection of the mansion, counting on the drug to help him find the drawing room. One thing worries him: as long as he hasn't yet located it inside the house, and as long as it has come to him in a dream (he has never been conscious of any movement prior to his standing in the doorway), nearly all of his opiated visions have carried him there. And ever since he imposed the idea of a path that leads from his refuge to the drawing room, he senses that it will be more difficult to find, that never again, perhaps, will he be able to watch over the scribes in charge of registering or dictating his thoughts. Nevertheless he manages to pull himself into an upright position. From the renewed lassitude of his muscles he can feel the drug beginning to spread throughout his body. He leaves his closet.

He is going to have to retrace his steps, but also resign himself to the fact that the memory of his last expedition is not a reliable one. Still, there is one detail about which he is absolutely certain: between the drawing room and his shelter he had constantly pulled the doors toward him. Therefore, between his shelter and the drawing room, any door that could be pushed open would be an encouraging sign. So he tries pushing the doors. His candle, held at an arm's length, conjures the predictably spooky shadows on the damp-stained walls. He doesn't recognize a thing. Did he have a candle on his way back? He can't remember.

He feels surprisingly lucid, almost alert. Knowing the effects of the opium, he is constantly waiting for an obtuse angle to get sharper and sharper, then grip him like a pair of pliers, or for the floor to cave in, or the walls to close in on him. He is watching for these outward signs, confident that the changes in his physical surroundings will serve as the indication of how drugged he is. But nothing moves. To make sure that the house isn't creating some kind of illusion, some semblance of order before his very eyes (when it is actually undermining him, burning all the bridges, modifying its own layout as soon as he has gone past), he returns to the landing without any difficulty, then starts out again, somewhat troubled by this strange lull. He pushes the doors and none offers any resistance. It's even odd: if he had tried to pull them instead, none would have yielded.

At one point he arrives in a room without windows, the size of which suggests that it was reserved for banquets. As a reference mark, he notes the total absence of a wooden floor, which has been replaced instead by a long stretch of limestone eroded by large puddles of stagnant water. In the rooms he presently occupies, wooden planks are loose and falling apart. Some are missing, but there's still something left of the floor. The same is true for all the rooms that he has been through, if he remembers correctly. But here, perhaps, it was a question of a particularly precious floor. Had it been a work of art that someone had carried off or stolen, taking it up piece by piece only to be reassembled somewhere else? Unless one were to explain this removal not by the value of the floor itself, but by the documents that it concealed, which had been seized after a hasty unnailing of the floorboards. He's frightened enough by this possibility to reconsider the object of his search. In waking from his dream, he had recklessly thrown himself into this venture, if only to put an end to his prostration: clenched teeth, throbbing temples, trembling hands, and most of all, eyes that dart back and forth like startled animals. Remembering this horribly familiar state, he wonders how he was able to elude it, how he had ever summoned the energy to stand up, walk through empty rooms, push open doors, and arrive in this strange parlor where he suspects they have removed certain compromising documents.

Which documents? He no longer knows. He falls to his knees on the hard floor, then rolls onto his side, into the middle of a large puddle. He feels as if he's fallen from a dizzying height and has landed at the bottom of a well, not daring to move for fear that his bones are broken. His right cheek is lying in the puddle, which reaches the corner of his mouth. He wants to take a drink but cannot. He feels no pain, only irritation at not being able to move his eyes, frozen in place like a broken mechanical doll whose half-closed lids have been jammed into position. And now they're stuck in the lower corner of his sockets, thinks Polidori, being pulled by the earth's gravity like all his other organs. He has reached the bottom, his eyes will no longer focus—except upon the surface of the puddle gleaming softly in the shadows, reflecting the curve of his cheek and the bridge of his nose.

CHAPTER IX

Night has fallen. Not a glimmer of light filters through the nailed shutters. A few sounds drift up from the street: horse's hooves, the echo of a voice. Polidori crawls for what seems like a very long time, sleeps for a very long time as well, certain that he'll never wake up, then crawls some more and finally reaches the drawing room. He recognizes it by its voluminous size, but the furniture has disappeared, the French windows have been boarded up, and the parquet has also been taken up. The congregation of scribes has abandoned its duties, leaving only a minor employee to perform the task, and even she has fallen asleep. With her back to the wall, legs spread, and coarse cotton skirt raised all the way to her stomach, Teresa is snoring softly, her chin propped upon her chest. Her right hand is lying in a puddle, where a drop of water has just plummeted from the ceiling. Polidori wonders where this drop has come from, and as another one falls he also hears the raging storm outside, which he hadn't noticed before.

Teresa gives a slight groan, wrinkling her nose, as if she'd heard it as well, and leans her drooping head on her left shoulder. Without a sound Polidori approaches and crouches down next to her. He is overcome with rage. So this is what happens to his mind during his absence! The responsibility is passed on to this miserable creature, to this sleepyhead, to this illiterate! So far he had only depended on her for minor material needs. And now it has become his duty to furnish her with thoughts, because thanks to her his mind is as empty as the drawing room where she has fallen asleep.

Polidori gazes at the puddle of water next to the sleeping girl, which is steadily increasing in size, drop by drop. Then he looks at the cracked ceiling, the porous walls, decorated with light-colored stains where pictures must have once hung. He lingers there a moment, kneeling down beside Teresa. If he were to kill her, wouldn't that make him the master of the drawing room? Wouldn't he then regain the power that, like everything else, had been taken from him? Polidori wonders how to execute this sensible plan. It is important both that she realize that he's going to kill her, and that she not put up too much of a struggle, for he lacks the necessary physical strength. The ideal solution would be a weapon that would unequivocally guarantee his superiority and therefore qualify as a threat. A razor, for instance, which he could negligently wield, idly describing the manner in which he's prepared to use it to his victim, who is astonished at first, then increasingly distressed by the bad turn this joke is taking until the moment she realizes that it isn't a joke after all. The sharp blade is pressing on her throat; it presses, makes an incision, then slices. Unfortunately, he has left the razor in his toilet kit back in his makeshift quarters, and it is out of the question for him to try to find either one. There were no blunt objects he could use either, such as a chandelier, or a lead pipe— nothing. Nothing but his bare hands and the alternative of strangulation, which would mean taking her by surprise, given their nearly equal strength.

He pours some of the melted wax around the wick of his candle onto the floor and thrusts the candle into it. Then, checking to make sure that his hands aren't trembling, he makes sweeping gestures that form two gigantic shadows on the wall behind Teresa. He brings his hands up to his own throat to animate the shadows, and momentarily enjoys watching his startled silhouette on the wall. He can change their scale simply by distancing himself or drawing nearer to the candle. To prevent his shadow from stretching across the ceiling and towering over him, he falls to his knees so that it only projects onto the wall, then exaggerates the hold around his neck, his thumbs tightly gripping his Adam's apple. His ears are throbbing with blood; his vision blurs. He lets go.

Teresa, now awake, is groggily observing his little trick with interest. He smiles sweetly and proposes a game. In a voice still thick with sleep she tells him that she's been looking for him everywhere; she's been worried about him. She wanted to—

He interrupts her. First the game.

To keep the flame from going out he explains the rules to her in a whisper. She must imitate every move he makes.

She nods her head in agreement.

Frowning, Polidori tells her that he hasn't yet nodded his head; he has merely moved his lips in a way that she must then immediately copy.

"I understand," Teresa says humbly, which only provokes a torrent of mumbled insults. No, she doesn't understand; if she had understood, she wouldn't have said so, she would have repeated his explanation by mouthing the words.

He has to go through the rules three times before she finally starts to imitate him clumsily, but this slowness is also a guarantee that she'll have as much trouble getting out of the game later as she had getting into it. If he were to announce abruptly that it was over, she would undoubtedly do the same, for fear that he was testing her. Certain of her obedience, Polidori starts the game with a few exercises for beginners —hand gestures, an entire repertoire of facial movements that are easily imitated, such as wrinkling one's forehead, scowling, or blinking in an exaggerated way—anything that Teresa could diligently reproduce an instant later. At least he's the one who is imposing the rules.

Now for something more difficult. Without a sound he slowly and precisely mouths the words *I am going to kill you*. Teresa, her eyes riveted on his lips, silently copies each movement. Polidori wonders what this submissive mimicry would sound like if she were speaking aloud. She doesn't seem very worried about grasping the meaning; she already has enough to do, merely trying to keep up with the shapes forming on Polidori's lips. Once again he voicelessly mouths,

Say it out loud! fully realizing that she will not understand. And in fact she repeats the phrase without doing what she is told—probably mouthing it incorrectly as well.

I am going to kill you, he repeats, accentuating each syllable even more distinctly.

I (mouth open wide, like a silent scream) *am* (lips pressed firmly together) *go-ing* (lips puckered, then pulled back into a forced smile) *to* (lips pouted, tongue striking his front teeth) *kill* (lips stretched into a half-smile, teeth clenched) *you* (lips curled, menacingly thrust forward).

She imitates him perfectly, without a single mistake.

Oh, so you're going to kill me? he continues, sneering as if he'd just exposed her true thoughts, which she'd hoped to conceal. Teresa hesitates for a moment before trying to copy his grimace, whose meaning she has possibly guessed. Her tormentor reacts to what he has insidiously made her say.

Polidori swiftly brings his hands back around his own throat and starts to squeeze. She does the same. Now, how can he get her to strangle herself without actually having to strangle himself as well? She's had sufficient practice in the game and is stupid enough to die after him, if he decides to die. But he doesn't want to die now, and certainly not like this; he's still got some details to take care of. So the main thing is to mislead her so that she presses harder and longer than he does. Imperceptibly loosening his grip, he notes that the infinitesimal relaxation of his fingers hasn't escaped Teresa who, like him, is greedily sucking in air. He realizes that she will do exactly the same as he does, that she'll use the same amount of force—proving that she's a good student—and that it will become a no-win situation. Every move the aggressor makes will be reproduced by his opponent a fraction of a second later.

But—no, that's just it. This fraction of a second can be used in his favor. To pull off a similar sort of circumstance in a chess game, the board is arranged in such a way that only the white pieces, the symmetry suddenly destroyed, can benefit. For the first time in his life, he's the one with the winning pieces.

He is going to have to play hard. He removes his hands from his own neck and places them on Teresa's, pressing slightly, ever so slightly, near her earlobes. The girl's hands immediately adopt an identical position around his neck; the appalling expression on her face reflects her fear both of being strangled and of playing the game poorly. Polidori wonders what his own expression reveals—perhaps the same fear. Seizing both her ears, he bangs Teresa's head against the wall as hard as he can. He's laughing the entire time: there is no wall behind him, that's the whole point. Even if she had reacted, he would have only come up against a void! And Byron, the imbecile, who always said that one is never safe unless one's back is to the wall!

He bangs away blindly, laughing. He smashes her skull against the wall—first it's Mary's, then Byron's, then Colburn's. . . . Her hands are waving in the air around him. She lets go, her bones snap, the panicked arms drop. Only her fingers continue to quiver, and subside once he lets her collapse onto the floor like a rag doll. The wall is stained with dark spots. He laughs.

He pulls himself back up. He is now hiccupping with laughter. To try to control it, he concentrates on finding a convincing comparison to his present state of affairs. Doesn't he resemble a passenger of a ship who discovers, in the middle of the night, that the hull has been demolished by an iceberg and that the crew has already fled in the lifeboats? Distraught and alone, he paces the gangways, which slant more and more, until he's almost walking on the walls. He can hear the creaking—the pressure is rising, shattering the wood. The dull roar of the water invades the shipwrecked vessel, and there is a mindless and furious hammering from the engine room, into which he rushes, frantically descending the rungs of the metal ladder. He is already ankle-deep in water, the icy whirlpool imperceptibly rising, when he discovers that he isn't, in fact, alone. He has been abandoned, together with the simpleminded cabin boy, who, mad with fear, is chopping the boiler to pieces with a hatchet. He's the one who's making this hammering noise, hacking away with drunken terror. Soon it will all explode. No—the passenger takes control of the situation and drives the hatchet into the boy's skull, splitting his stupid smile in two, from top to bottom, bathing his drooling mouth with blood, and now he is alone once again, this time for good. The hammering hasn't ceased, but he realizes that it's coming from his throbbing temples. He has just warded off a great danger, the explosion of the boiler (not to mention all the other risks he would have taken in the company of the mad cabin boy), but the water is crashing, rising up to his waist. If he has escaped the explosion and the hatchet, it is only to better appreciate what it is like to drown. No need to try and fight it: he would have to seal the punctured hull, bail out the water that the ship was soaking up like a sponge, subdue the panicked boiler, which was spewing great jets of incoherent steam, as if the idiotic soul of the cabin boy had taken refuge in its belly—all at the same time. The entire crew, had they remained, wouldn't have been enough. Any move he made would only spread the effects of the catastrophe: he could pick up a pail, fill it with foaming water, now up to his chest, and empty it over his shoulder. That was all he could do.

How absurd. He would have to die. But beforehand, he would leave a testament inside a bottle, throw it to the sea. Quick, up to the captain's quarters! He must take advantage of this brief lull to compose his message. That way, when the wreckage is found, they'll know what became of the sacrificed passenger. If the lifeboat survives the storm, once ashore, the cowards who abandoned him will perhaps go on to lead happy and respectable lives. Their crime must be known—perhaps they will even be hanged because of this posthumous message. Polidori smiles. His hiccups have vanished. This wouldn't be the first time that he's calmed his fears and found comfort in the construction of a metaphor. This one stands on its own; its solid terms create the impression of a refuge, the very last before the end. For he has reached the end. He has only to seal his fate by describing his torture and exposing his tormentors: the ship's crew, the scribes in the drawing room, Byron, Shelley, Colburn, Madame de Breuss, and Mary. Especially Mary. First and foremost Mary, the most cunning and vicious of the vampires who throughout his life have sucked out his thoughts, ravaged his brain. The truth must be told about *Frankenstein*, this inflicted, deceitful, frozen image of his soul. Before he disappears, he must put things in order, disclose every detail about the imposture, attack them on their own terms, beneath their masks, since they have managed to discredit his own true face; since he has no face left.

Quick, up to the captain's quarters.

There he'll find paper, ink, and something to end it once and for all, after he's put the final word on his indictment.

Leaving behind Teresa's corpse, which will soon be carried off by the water, he takes a few steps and breaks into a run. He must pull the doors open. He has spent his entire life pushing them, which only drove him lower and lower, down into the hold. Now it's this urgency that controls him, guides him. He runs, impulsively pulling at the doors; his elbows tucked at his side, he climbs stairways, passes from one threshold to another, never worrying whether or not they look familiar. The gangways parade past him—quick, he pulls open more doors, strides through the rooms without turning his head, paying attention to nothing else, walking straight ahead—quick, up to the captain's quarters. He knows that he's headed toward the closet. He opens the last door.

He enters. It's hardly surprising. The captain's quarters look nothing like the cabin of a ship, though the shape—a sharp triangle—might have been part of the bow cutting through the ice. . . . But he needn't give any thought to that. Nor to the strange furnishings, the worn carpet on the floor, the sink in the corner, the telephone on the nightstand, nor the mirror above the dresser, in which the reflection of the captain looms into view as he approaches it. It's the face of an old man—well, not too old—who looks a bit like him. But he's not at all surprised to be here, though he knows nothing whatsoever about how to use the telephone or why the diesel engine is rumbling below, from the street. Above all, he has no idea what he will write on these blank pages sitting on the dressing table, in front of the mirror, and in front of him as well.

He will offer no resistance, he will simply obey the captain's orders, write down whatever is dictated. He knows he can trust the captain; feels, in a way, as if he has finally met his creator. He will sit in front of the dresser, on the black vinyl stool, just like the captain's reflection, pulling his trousers at the knees to hold the crease. They sit down; the captain smiles at him, then smiles at his own reflection as if it were familiar to him, as if he had just met up with an old friend. Because the mirror reaches the top of the dresser, Polidori can see the captain's hands: one hand is resting on the sheet of paper; the other, firmly gripping a ballpoint pen, sets down the first words:

I am . . .

The captain glances up to make sure that the other one is following him, that he's not going too fast. It is easy to imitate the captain, to write along with him, and copy the movements of his hand. Easy to trust him. The captain knows what to say.

I am a man who is tired, ill, and frightened. On this night I have decided to put my memories in writing. I wish to be as brief as possible, for I haven't much time. . . .

The captain looks at his wristwatch: almost midnight.

. . . The clock will soon strike midnight. I expect that I can endure until the morning, locked in my laboratory, the oak door barricaded with heavy furniture, but I fear that this situation cannot go on much longer. I don't even dream of escaping anymore. What would I say and to whom? They would lock me up in an asylum—or worse, they would put me in the custody of one of my relatives. And should they believe my adventures, they would certainly hang me.

I stopped writing for a moment to look at my face in the mirror and scrutinize my prematurely aging features. "I am that man," I said to myself aloud. I recognized the timbre of my voice, my intonations, I saw my lips forming the syllables that had been dictated by my brain. I looked down at the scribbled page and also recognized this delicate, sloping hand-writing, which I can still consider my own. Now I shall pick up my pen once more, for I am eager to tell the world about the unfortunate soul by the name of Victor Frankenstein, and correct the lies that a successful novelist has been guilty of inventing.

One more word before I finally embark upon my last night on earth. I am quite conscious of the futility of this memoir.

Inevitably it will fall into the hands of my tormentors, who will be amused by it: I can already hear Elizabeth's peals of laughter. Undoubtedly she'll lose no time sending a copy to the novelist, to whom I will shortly return. As odious as I might find this prospect, I can no longer delude myself. On this night I would like to imagine that I am writing to someone, to a young, adoring woman, to a just and honest man. But what do I know of young, adoring women or just and honest men? What do I know of men anymore?

A final word of introduction—the very last. I should like to refute a detail of which I shall speak no more. My name is not Frankenstein and I shall not reveal my true name. This pseudonym (so transparent that it did not fool those who know me well) owes its existence to a literary adaptation of my life, in which, as I've said, I must rectify the countless errors. I am not that man, and I do not bear that abhorred name. However, should I go down in posterity, it shall be under this name, for I have no illusions that I am addressing these stillborn lines to posterity, as one throws a bottle into the sea. And so, without further ceremony, I shall retain it. Only let it be known: it is a cruel fate to recount one's life in the form of a rebuttal that will never be published.

CHAPTER X

It is true that I am by birth a Genevese and that I turned toward the sciences at an early age. My father was my first teacher, as my grandfather has been his, and it had gone on like that for centuries. Our family annals make mention of a certain Frankenstein, student of Paracelsus, the latter even envisioning this man as his successor in the circuitous pursuit of alchemy. At the time, the master and his disciple were supposedly on the verge of breathing life into a homunculus. However, the documents pertaining to this matter are so discreet that it is difficult to sort out whether or not their hopes were ever fulfilled.

I believe in family destiny. I believe that for those who have had a particular solicitude or spitefulness bestowed upon them by the Creator, there shall come a time when a descendant will complete what his ancestor has begun. He who comes first is almost always ignored. Everyone hopes to be the last, to behold the fruit of the labor that has been germinating over a long period of time. I, too, fancied myself as the last link who would justify the chain, and perhaps I was not entirely mistaken. Undoubtedly, the end of our family line, which I know is drawing near, will also serve to forewarn of the end of the world, or at least, of the race of men who now prevail upon this earth. There are more mediocre accomplishments than this.

As is widely known, I studied in Ingolstadt, and I steadily progressed toward the goal dictated by my origins. The medical school, where I had been sent by my father, offered a cautious and empirical education. However, after searching through the libraries, consulting with equal enthusiasm the moldy archives and the most recent publications; after confronting, doubting, and endlessly experimenting, I fathomed the mysteries of anatomy, chemistry, and above all, of galvanism. At first my professors, impressed with my ardor, placed all their hopes in me, so that at age nineteen I was the youngest ever to graduate from the university. But they soon lost interest in my research, seeing that I was leaning toward the most obscure aspects of their disciplines, which were taught on the basis of clear and well-proven theories. But this was only true for the best of them. The others were content to repeat their errors and conserve their prejudices. In tissue pathology they proceeded according to the Brownian school, distinguishing between sthenic and asthenic maladies, and consequently prescribing

*remedies that were either fortifying or soothing, such as pep-
percorns or hopel-dopel. Or they would simply bleed patients
whenever they weren't entirely certain, giving little thought to
the causes that produced these elusive symptoms. I believe that
most of them associated names like Galvani, Volta, or Priestley
with images of picturesque inventions: an operating table
equipped with lightning conductors or an apparatus designed
to jolt dead frogs.*

*Despite the eccentricity of my research, I inspired neither
hatred nor fear. They recognized my superiority; they took me
for an original, easy to get on with, attributing my inclination
for the bizarre, the forbidden, the inexplicable to my frequent
travel and my literary friends. For it is true that in order to
enter the depths of science, I had to delve into the mysteries
of poetry. I would move from one to the other, from the dissection tables to the bohemian literary life. And this incessant
movement back and forth, this constant confrontation between
channels within my mind was by no means a sign of indecision
or dilettantism, as my father had often feared. The dear man
was born in a century where poetry and science had nothing
to do with one another, and this cultured chemist and friend
of Lavater thought that he was paying sufficient tribute to the
muses by reading his Kotzebue every night by the fireplace, as
a diversion from the laboratory.*

*As for myself, whenever the torpor of my intellectual faculties
weighed too heavily upon me, I would join Clerval, my childhood friend, who was studying theology and Romance lan-
guages. He would take me on long walks along the banks of
the Danube, and during our lofty conversations my entire being
soared above the poplars, which appeared to grow faster there
than anywhere else—or so it seemed—toward the birth of a
new spirit. In the literary circles frequented by Clerval young
philosophers were weaving subtle connections between diurnal
thought and nocturnal dreams, analyzing the natural elements*

in terms of poetic intuition. I often scoffed at their paltry scientific knowledge, but I enjoyed hearing them describe the universe as an immense cosmic circuit and the inanimate world as its mirror image that we carry in our hearts and minds, affirming that one cannot claim to be a philosopher without knowing the laws of nature, nor shall they be known unless one is some sort of poet.

Like many others I had started to keep a journal of my dreams, convinced that there were secrets to be unlocked and that fantasies were the key. This effort even spurred me to draft several short stories and scribble down poems that brought me many compliments. Today I regret not having pursued this path; yet any path would have been preferable to the one that I ultimately chose. But if I felt the inspiration seething within me, I also failed to channel it. It is easy enough to sit at one's desk facing a ream of white paper. Unfortunately, thoughts are free, numerous, and swift, and soon disperse into a thousand directions, none of which are indicated on the page. One needs as many hunters to track them down as poachers to set the traps, and when I happened to find one, only a dead carcass remained. Everything that was alive in my mind inevitably expired under my awkward pen.

The more I studied anatomy, on the contrary, the more it seemed that, under my scalpel, lifeless matter might be animated, that blood might be made to flow in the veins of cadavers. It is hardly an exaggeration to say that this dream dates back to a distant period of my life. Though it hadn't any precise form, I was already obsessed by it. Of course, I never confided it to anyone at the medical school, where my fellow students shrugged their shoulders whenever anyone spoke of Mesmer. My poet friends, on the other hand, were astonished when, to humor them and win their esteem, I boasted of having performed experiments that were still only in their imaginary stages. However, since they were equally amazed by stories about mandrakes, golems, and noblemen deprived of their own shadows, their infatuation was but a passing moment of flattery.

Once spring arrived, Clerval would organize outings where he was often joined by his colleague Clemens, a robust, stocky lad who wrote poetry, and at times, his sister, Bettina, a ravishing and fiery young woman. My fascination with her highly audacious ideas caught more than just her attention. The countryside around Ingolstadt is beautiful, and the French troops there were a discreet presence. The four of us would take the hills by storm, armed with walking sticks and our rucksacks. Clemens, who had taken to collecting popular folksongs, lingered in every village inn to extract these tunes from the local drunkards, and he would later reproduce them for us to admire. Most were inept, and I recall with a smile the day that our young, naïve friend, extremely proud of his provincial find, gravely sang us something that sounded much like an aria by Piccinni—a composer he scorned, though he knew nothing about him, but who, by some miracle of rural diffusion, had charmed the ears of some dirt-rumped music lover.

I also remember one evening, a storm deterring us from sleeping outdoors, we were obliged to seek shelter in a Benedictine abbey. When it came time to retire, after dinner and abundant drink, the good friar accompanied us to our quarters, reserved for passing travelers. It turned out to be a vast room, clean and well aired, that had been divided in half by a thick wooden partition. But compared with the stone walls of the abbey, at least three feet in width, it looked as if it were made of paper. This partition allowed the Benedictine hosts to provide lodgings for the occasional woman—since it was out of the question for the two sexes to mingle in the dormitory. The friar, who had had a good deal to drink, jokingly advised us that on our next visit we ought to come equipped with a man's disguise for Bettina. He gave us a wink, laughing heartily.

Then, once the two sexes had been separated, he closed the door with a double turn of the key and wished us all a good night.

I believe that none of us slept for a single minute. Our mouths and ears glued to the dividing wall, the three of us sat there in constant conversation with Bettina, who, alone in her cell, claimed she was dying of fright, and deigning to prove it, she burst into joyous laughter after every other sentence. We had already spent countless evenings together discussing poetry and philosophy, so when the hour had advanced and the familiar specters glided into our midst like hovering vapors around the punch, we told ghost stories. But the solemnity of the place, the giddy combination of physical fatigue and alcohol, and the strangeness of the circumstance turned that particular night into a unique occasion for us all.

Today I can no longer recall the content of this conversation, neither what was said nor, above all, the unforeseen chain of associations that carried us from a single stroke of the imagination to an entire story, from a confidence to a verbal obsession. I was soon to lose sight of my comrades, with the exception of Clerval; I do not know if they are still alive today or if they have retained my image in their memory. However, I think of them often, as they are the only three beings capable of proving that this night of enchantment had actually occurred, in all its reckless abandon, capricious mastery, and astonishing clarity. "Nocturnal dreams are private," Clerval later wrote to me, "and waking dreams are shared, and only through this sharing is the idea of reality founded." Did the four of us share a nocturnal dream? In any case, we were united by this intoxicated feeling, or at least by the collective memory of this feeling, as well as the common gaps in this recollection. For whatever I am presently unable to recall, we could not even remember the next morning. Each sentence had erased the preceding one, and when the bells tolled the morning hour, the last sentence spilled over into a void, dragged down by the weight of the others. No sooner was it uttered than it had already been forgotten. In the midst of my elation I felt twinges of bitterness as well, for whenever I got carried away with the beginning of a brilliant reflection or a dramatic effect, I tried not only to speak and immediately share my emotion, but also to hold it back. I wanted to detain my words and those of my companions. The wave would break before I had had the chance to appreciate the landscape of which I had only caught a glimpse while sitting atop its crest; I already found myself on the crest of the following wave, spotting another landscape that was equally magnificent but just as ephemeral. To memorize these landscapes I would have liked to make some sort of imprint on my mind, utilizing a thought or a word to which I attributed mnemonic significance, then hoping that they would reemerge from my memory the following day, still attached by a thread to the living tissue of our phrases. And the next day, I thought, I would be convinced that it had been a dream, that I had uttered this stranded word, sole vestige of the night, while asleep. To ward off this deception and reap the spoils of this insane pursuit, we promised one another not to forget a single word as they glittered before us with their multiple meanings. Perhaps by repeating a word over and over, the four of us could polish it inside our mouths until it recovered its true brilliance. If it survived within us, this would at least prove that something had truly occurred, that it had indeed been pronounced as well as heard.

And by the next day, of course, these open-sesame words had been stripped of their magic. We blushed with shame while reciting them, as if their baldness of style, shriveled by the sun, had offended the brilliance of the night. We were like drunkards, embarrassed to find ourselves sober. Later, if these words were uttered back and forth among us, they became like contraband jewels within innocuous phrases. They did not conjure up that spring night, only our common conviction of having lived through it, and we often felt the need to test one another's certitude to reaffirm our own.

I realize that this anecdote is disappointing, like the glib talk of a juggler who announces an extraordinary show—until one comprehends, after having waited there impatiently for a half hour, that the extraordinary show was the announcement itself. So let us simply say that reality is also disappointing, and speak of it no more. It is getting late.

CHAPTER XI

The captain stops writing. It's not as if he were hesitating; quite the contrary—he knows where he's headed. For several weeks (at times he would even gladly say for all his life) he's been mulling over the sentences of the manuscript. He is merely taking down his own dictation. But now he needs a break. He briefly glances at himself in the mirror above the dressing table, where, wedged into one of the corners, is a framed portrait of Polidori's pale face, the night of his suicide. Then he stands up, goes to the window, and cranks up the metal shutters. From his room on the third floor he has a view of the small square and the pub, which has just opened. A couple is walking out of it, elegant in contrast to the prole-tarian look of the neighborhood customers, who are, for the most part, Chinese shopkeepers. The captain wonders what motive could have prompted these young people to meet in an establishment that was so far from the type of place that they usually frequented, and from their own neighborhood. Perhaps it was a game, another one. He could join in by tossing them false leads, creating short-circuits. . . . He smiles. The girl walking near the curb, constantly tucking her hair behind her ear in a graceful manner, is wearing a pair of harem pants and a short white jacket. In this Chinese suburb where women are rarely seen, she stands out even more. Most of the time there are only men rushing about the square, slamming their car doors, going in and out of the pub. It's a Saturday. By her casually chic dress, the girl reminds the captain a bit of Brigitte. Lowering the shutters once more so that the room is lit only by the pale colors of the wallpaper, he walks toward the bed, grabs the telephone on the night table, and dials a number—not Brigitte's, but Ann's.

Even though the ringing awakens her, Ann is not surprised or particularly annoyed, as it quite naturally interrupts her dream about a telephone wake-up service. For the last several weeks she's been woken up every day by this public service. She doesn't have an alarm clock anymore; someone stole it and she hasn't yet replaced it. At least she considers it stolen. As unpleasant and, above all, as unlikely as this hypothesis might seem concerning an inexpensive object bought in a supermarket, it's the only one that seems possible. Despite her careful search, the alarm clock—an item not easily left behind at a friend's home, like a lighter or a pair of red wool gloves—was not anywhere to be found, and she's sure that she has never taken it out of her apartment. Nothing else is missing, so it seems that a thief must have broken into her place with the sole intention of stealing an alarm clock. Ever since this incident she has been calling the wake-up service nearly every night and even has brief conversations with the employee. It's always the same one, a very young man, judging from his voice. If Ann should ask to be awakened at seven o'clock in the morning, he will want to know why she is getting up so early. At noontime he'll wish her a pleasant evening. They'll chat a bit. It's for this reason that in her dream she has come to consider the employee as a kind of supreme arbitrator, the sovereign magistrate of sleep in all of London. She must be ready for his calls at all times and not unplug the phone, not put on her answering machine as she had one day, which had only brought her a reproachful message from the young man: in the two months he'd been at this job so he could earn a little money during the summer vacation, this was the first time that a customer had requested his services, and then had switched on an answering machine, preventing him from performing the task that she herself had asked him to do.

Ann gropes for the telephone lying at the foot of the bed, but it's not the wake-up service. There is no sound on the line, not even breathing in her ear. Ever since she has been living alone, she has grown accustomed to anonymous calls in the middle of the night—but it's not the middle of the night; the sun is filtering through the venetian blinds. Luckily she has never been subjected to the persecution of sex maniacs who whisper terrible things, but on the other hand, she has often received these silent phone calls. No doubt they were from some young boys who were in love with her, probably calling from a phone booth; one of them had covered the receiver in vain with his hand, for fear of being betrayed by his breathing. They would remain in the phone booth for quite some time, a block of dim light at some deserted intersection. They would keep trying every now and then, hoping that she'd finally say one of their names in a questioning tone of voice. But there was no chance of that ever happening and besides, she wouldn't even know which name to declare.

She murmurs, "Jim," anyway, in a sleepy voice that should give her caller something to cry about, then hears the click of the receiver and listens to three or four busy signals. The guy must not have hung up the phone, only pushed down on the hook to cut off the call. He lingers in the booth for a moment, dumbfounded, wondering perhaps who Jim is, then lets go of the receiver and leaves it dangling, slamming the door. But then again, perhaps it was nothing like that at all.

She looks at her watch. Past noon. She leaps out of bed, opens the shutters, and goes to take a shower.

Before he hangs up the phone, the captain does in fact push down the hook with his forefinger. It had been far too early to telephone, he thought. (He is indifferent to Jim.) He fixes a time to call her back: seven-thirty, and returns to the dressing table, the mirror, and the manuscript.

CHAPTER XII

I completed my studies in 1809 and returned to my father's home in Geneva to fulfill my destiny. I had been a brilliant, if not unusual, medical student. I had been a poet and a friend of poets. Now I would become a Frankenstein. As it had been planned since our childhood, I married my dear cousin Elizabeth, and immediately after our honeymoon I began my work, alone. I had a laboratory installed in a villa that we owned several miles from the city, and there, for seven years, I verified experiments that dated back to the intuitions of my youth. I dreamed of disrupting the cosmos, stripping this bottomless well of the necessary ebb and flow, to rival the god whom man had invented for lack of an explanation of nature. In devoting myself to dissection, and the galvanic resurrection of small animals, I was working slightly outside his domain; a minor contraband god who was advancing a few seconds faster than the hands on the dial, set by the great clockmaker himself.

By the beginning of the summer of 1816, my experiments

with field mice, frogs, and even a dog had satisfied me so fully that I felt ready to take the final step toward the process of creation: that of man.

Would I restore life to cadavers or attempt an even more insane enterprise: to create limb from limb—borrowed from the morgues and artistically assembled—the human body that would serve as a receptacle for the life-flow emanating from the spheres? I hesitated. The turn of events would decide for me.

My dearest Elizabeth, whose warm, resplendent body lay beside mine every night, and who gave me the courage each morning to labor over decomposed cadavers, my Elizabeth fell ill—a harmless chill, caught during a walk through the woods cut short by a sudden storm, so that I was not overly alarmed when she took to her bed for several days. Then her symptoms became slightly more pronounced, and a relapse made me fully conscious of several menacing signs that I had observed in recent years. I was a doctor—no use in deluding myself. Elizabeth's condition was growing worse each day. The consumption was spreading implacably, torturing her emaciated body. She would never see the autumn.

Any man who has loved will understand my despair. While in my laboratory, by then in total disarray, or in the room where Elizabeth vainly sought rest, imploring me to put an end to her suffering, I was forced to hide my tears and only barely succeeded.

One night I sat up with my beloved, settled into the large armchair by her bedside, watching over her once splendid bosom, now heaving. All of a sudden I was struck by the clarity of the situation. I had been banging my head against a wall, confronted by my own powerlessness to cure her and to arrest the flow of a biological process, when the very goal of my lifework, so close to triumph, was to leap over this wall. I broke out in a cold sweat; I nearly rejoiced, surprised that I hadn't thought of it before. I was about to open a door in the wall of life, and I would no longer be crossing its threshold alone; like the threshold to the chalet we had already crossed in Chamonix where our honeymoon had been spent, I would be carrying my wife in my arms. And if I failed, I would also die. But I wouldn't fail. Never before had I had such a powerful incentive to practice my art.

There was no use waiting. I would have to hasten Elizabeth's death so that the disease would not irreversibly alter her organism. To restore her life I would have to kill her first.

This will sound monstrous, perhaps, but once I had clearly made up my mind, this imperative hardly daunted me. One must not forget that I had not slept for three days, that my studies had brought me to the point where nothing more could surprise me, and most of all, that this monstrous act was my only chance, rather than lying there prostrate with grief. And so all my former ideas were erased by this powerful suggestion, which had imposed itself as a last resort.

I violently shook my head several times, as if trying to rid myself of a bad dream, and went downstairs. I ordered my horse to be saddled, and galloped all the way to the laboratory, where I concocted a lethal potion, an opium derivative, that I put into a small stoppered bottle, and returned home at full speed. The night was beautiful and clear. I had scarcely been gone two hours.

I remember this nocturnal trip home: the gates closing behind me, my footsteps on the marble tiles of the vestibule, and outside the windows, the groom, grumbling as he led my horse to the stable, and the sound of wooden clogs on the gravel. The entire household was asleep, the sort of restless sleep that grips a family when someone is dying. Holding my vial of poison, I returned to the room and resumed my position in the chair. The velvet upholstery was damp, as if I had spilled something or had unwittingly relieved my bladder. The room had a foul odor. I reached over for the silver tray on the night table, which held a glass and a carafe of water. I poured several drops from the vial into the glass, then added some water. Elizabeth tossed and turned, sighing hoarsely in her sleep.

Later she awoke. When she saw me in the dimness of the night lamp, she gave me a sad smile. I seem to remember her murmuring something that I cannot recall. Nevertheless, they were her last words.

Her hand groped along the night table, and for a moment I fancied that her veins were casting shadows on the wall. She seized the glass and brought it to her lips. Hypnotized, I watched her drink, her head thrown back, until not a drop was left. I could see every bead of sweat on her straining neck. Then she fell back to sleep. I remained in my chair in a stupor until the rays of dawn filtered through the shutters. Yet I could not truly say at what time she ceased to live. With the palm of my hand I smothered the night lamp. The pale flame flickered and went out. Then, with my fingers spread, I closed the eyes of my beloved.

I left the room and headed for the stable, where I somehow harnessed the horses to the carriage, then drove to the doorstep of our residence. I was terrified of being seen, but the household was still asleep. Upstairs in the room, I made certain that the passage was clear and wrapped Elizabeth in the sheet as if it were a shroud, bloodstained from her coughing the night before. She was as light as a child, but as I tensed my muscles I could feel her tortured body getting heavier every minute with the cold weight of death.

I carried her like a parcel down the deserted corridors, then hoisted her up onto the seat of the hoodless carriage waiting in front of the door. I met with some difficulty trying to prop her up against me, into a position that was natural enough to fool any possible encounters. I finally succeeded in doing so by pulling her head and chest onto my lap. A fold of the sheet came undone to reveal her bare shoulder, on which I placed my trembling lips. She must have bitten herself to withstand the pain; her skin, in any case, was full of teeth marks.

Dazed, I lingered there for a moment, kissing her shoulder, heedless of any danger. Then I caught hold of myself, whipped the two horses, and for the second time in those last few hours, set out again in the direction of the cottage where my laboratory was located. As Elizabeth was constantly thrown against me during the bumpy voyage, she resumed her loving gestures, even in death. With her head thrown back on my knees and an arm dangling on the edge of the seat, one might have thought that she was still alive; she looked much like a child in a fitful sleep, wrapped in blankets so as not to catch cold. I must have wept as I drove the carriage. The sun was shooting upward between the foothills, and the tears on my face, rolling onto the one close beside me, looked as though they were flowing from her own lifeless, astonished eyes.

Upon arrival at the laboratory, I carried Elizabeth inside, laid her on the operating table that had previously served for the dog, and set to work. Less fortunate than Orpheus, I was forced to look into her cold, still eyes, and furrow through her inanimate body to bring it back to life. I was acting not only as a surgeon, a chemist, and a galvanist, but above all— which gave me the strength to carry on—as a lover. It was my love that intercepted the lightning and tamed the ether spirits that would enter into this cherished tabernacle.

At last, Elizabeth's hand stirred slightly, as if to protest against the violence being inflicted upon her. I clenched my teeth, sharing her pain and recalling the identical reaction of the tortured dog. But my exaltation was at its peak, more intense than the heights of a loving embrace. As the corners of her mouth began to twitch, and her strained neck began to twist from side to side as if trying to drive off a nightmarish spirit, I caught a glance of myself in the metal gleam of the slender knife I had used to make the incisions. In the distorted reflection my face was lit with a triumph that no man before me had ever worn. If somewhere there exists a paradise and a hell, I could already envision them. My paradise would be the preservation of this moment for all eternity, and my hell, the moment that followed it and every moment thereafter. My carefree youth, spent pursuing an ideal that I had still thought impossible until the instant I had achieved it, had brought me in a single bound to the pinnacle of my endeavors. But no sooner had the zenith been reached than the incline gaped below, which I would be forced to descend in the midst of bitterness, tears, and blood. I should have died the moment that Elizabeth, her eyes still closed, sprang back to life—after my supreme science had served to revive my supreme love, but before I could discover where this science and love would lead me. For I have seen too much of life.

CHAPTER XIII

Elizabeth's lashes fluttered two or three times very rapidly. Instantly my triumph gave way to apprehension. I had been expelled from paradise. What would she say, if she were to speak? And what would I tell her myself? How could I explain to her what had happened? What would she remember from the kingdom of the dead? I recall hoping that she would simply call out my name. Drunk with love, she would pull me toward her, at the risk of snapping the hundreds of tangled cords around her naked body which, like Ariadne's ball of string, had rescued her from the labyrinth where specters awaited. An inner voice from the depths of my being conjured the inflection, the timbre, and the sound of this "Victor . . ." that I will never hear again, and that sometimes comes back to haunt me in my nightmares. I bent over her face so closely that our noses rubbed together, just like an Eskimo kiss. It had amused us so much growing up together that we had kept it up as a childlike and affectionate ritual.

Finally she opened her eyes. Cold sweat poured down my spine. The black of her dilated pupils had completely invaded her irises, so that only tiny circles of periwinkle blue remained. Then, once her lids were entirely open, the circles disappeared. Her eyes were now so black as to be unearthly. The sole image that comes to mind is that of a well with nothing surrounding it. No curbstone, no bucket, nothing to contain its blackness, so that nothing exists but this well; it is both the world itself and all that it engulfs. I stepped back, recoiling from Elizabeth's face. More dumbfounded by her expression than by my extreme fatigue and nervous tension, I felt my taut muscles giving way, my body sapped of its energy, and very slowly, I let myself slide to the foot of the operating table. I have learned, since that day, the undeniable happiness of withdrawing from the world by losing consciousness.

The captain closes his eyes for a few moments, then rubs them. When he stands up to use the phone, his legs are numb. Stretching, he dials Julian's number. Julian answers immediately.

"It's me," says the captain. "I'm calling to let you know about a slight change. I've decided that Elizabeth will have to be satisfied with black eyes. It's more dignified."

"Oh. You think so?"

Julian sounds disappointed.

"It's a shame," he appeals. "Instead of breasts—I found that rather picturesque. And it's even authentic. It also means that I memorized 'Christabel' for no reason."

"It might come in handy at social gatherings. And then

71

you can even make use of it in Brighton, if you like. Once you're there, you can do whatever you want, ad-lib. It's only in the preliminary stages that I'm afraid things might go badly."

"All right," Julian concedes.

"So go out and buy yourself some dark glasses for Monday. We're going for realism."

He hangs up the phone and returns to the dressing table.

When I abruptly came to my senses, it was night and I was lying in my bed. I heard an earsplitting scream and then realized that it was my own. I fell silent and suddenly it all came back to me. With surprising serenity, I concluded that I had just had a nightmare. I had dreamed that I had res-urrected Elizabeth, and that she had looked at me with trans-formed eyes. A complete fantasy: why would I have resurrected her? I had dreamed that she was dead. But then, why would she be dead? I had dreamed that she was ill, that I had married a woman named Elizabeth, that my name was Victor Fran-kenstein, that I lived in Switzerland, that I was doing forbidden research. . . . I smiled. I was in fact only in my bed, safe and sound. I was about to curl up, the blanket snugly tucked around my body, when the sound of hurried footsteps caused me to prick up my ears. I now recognized my room, and saw that the person who had opened the door and entered was Louise, the elderly governess who had been with our family her entire life—the Frankenstein family, which meant that I would have to resign myself to being a part of it, with all the terrible consequences that this premise implied.

"Oh, Master Victor," she hiccuped, clasping her pudgy hands and shrugging dramatically, "so you are awake. You were having a nightmare."

I realized that she was alluding to my scream. I remembered who I was, that this woman had taken care of me during my childhood, that my father lived in this house, but I didn't dare push my recollections any further.

"You're going to be terribly pleased, Master Victor," Louise continued in a whining voice that contradicted the promised happiness. "Madame Elizabeth is out of danger. The doctors have said so!"

Elizabeth, my wife, was out of danger. So it was true that she had been dying. . . . I could no longer hide behind my protective amnesia.

"And what about her eyes, Louise, her eyes?" I asked in a whisper, not daring to look at the old woman.

"Oh, Master Victor, how did you know? They turned black, as black as coal."

And she went on to compare this phenomenon, which she attributed to the illness, to other equally spectacular occurrences. Her sister's hair had turned white in one hour on the day their father died. For that matter, her father's hair had fallen out suddenly when, in the middle of dinner, the old Jacobin had learned of Robespierre's execution. He was too choked with emotion to swallow his soup, because entire handfuls of hair were floating in his plate. A lad from her village had woken up one day with an additional toe on his left foot. The evening before, he had gone for a walk and passed under some gallows, and had no doubt trodden on a mandrake, born of the tears of the hanged fellow. . . .

I listened for a moment in stunned silence to this insane litany, then pushed aside the covers and leaped out of bed, ignoring Louise's protests that I was ill, that the doctors had ordered me to rest. Indeed, the brusqueness of my gesture produced a shooting pain in my jaw, which once aroused, would not disappear.

"Where is Madame Elizabeth?" I asked.

"But . . . in her room. She's asleep . . . It's late. . . . Tomorrow. . . ."

73

I went into the corridor, tiptoeing into the chambers where the night before—unless it had been quite some time before that—I had murdered my beloved. I hesitated in front of the door. My jaw was throbbing. I finally entered the room, bathed in moonlight streaming through the open window. The odor of agony and dried blood had been replaced with the scent of an armful of freshly cut roses, arranged in a vase on top of the small table. A thorn scratched my cheek as I walked past. I approached the large canopy bed where Elizabeth was quietly resting, resumed my seat in the chair, and listened to her steady breathing as she slept. Apparently she was out of danger. I let a moment pass, unable to determine whether my thoughts were veering toward joy or terror. I closed my eyes. Then I heard Elizabeth's voice calling my name, as I had once dreamed she would when she came back to life.

I took Elizabeth's outstretched hand in mine, delighting in her cool touch: her fever had even disappeared. Then I sat down on the edge of the bed as she propped herself up, threw her arms around me, and drew me near. The suddenness of her gesture caused the sheet to slide from her body, as when she had been dead, and I noticed that contrary to custom, she was naked. Even in summer she always slept in a nightgown. Her breasts were pressed tightly against my chest. In the tussle that followed, Elizabeth showed a fire and an audacity that I had never known in her before. She abandoned all sense of modesty, and I was suddenly aware of my own contradictory feelings.

In my youth there had been ardent, experienced mistresses whose raptures had only heightened the intensity of my own. Yet once I had married Elizabeth, my puritan upbringing made me thankful for her prudery. What one expects from a chance encounter does not befit one's own wife. Nevertheless, after several months of marriage, I would have liked her to let herself go a bit more, not only to give variety to our lovemaking, but above all because I hoped that a bit of licentiousness might create a greater intimacy between us, like a sweetly shared secret. And now that Elizabeth manifested the very freedom I had prayed for during carnal exchange, she seemed infinitely more distant than in previous times. No sooner would I enter her room than she would present herself to me without preliminaries, asking me to possess her, crying out and arching her back as though electric shocks were going through her; she clawed at my neck, thrust me inside her, soaked the sheets with our heated embraces. At the height of ecstasy, she would call out my name over and over, and this frenzy, contrary to all expectations, stole her away from me. At the moment of orgasm, suddenly exasperated, I scratched her cheek, roughly pushing aside the veil of hair that had come undone and was hiding her face. Instantly frozen, she leaned over me and fixed her gaze onto mine. It was then that I saw her black eyes. Devastated, I tore myself away from her and rolled to the side. As we had carried out our desires near the edge of the bed, I fell onto the floor, and rather than confronting her eyes again, I remained stretched out on the carpet. A trickle of water running down my legs explained the noise that had accompanied my fall: I had kicked over the vase of roses.

My face to the floor, I could hear the parquet creaking under the weight of Elizabeth, who was climbing down to join me. I felt her hands on my body, colder than ice. She brushed her lips on my shoulder and gently forced me to turn over. She was crouching down beside me, naked, and the moon, perfectly framed in the open window behind her, silhouetted the shadowy contours of her body with a sinuous halo of milky light. I knew that nothing more remained around the black of her pupils, not even a thin blue circle. And this time I felt treachery in the way she murmured my name, though it was the closest that I would ever be to hearing it again from her. Every night thereafter, she would creep into my inner ear with a dull pounding, quickening my pulse. She lay there beside me, stretched out on the carpet in the puddle of rose water. I stayed awake all night, staring longingly into her closed eyes, still unaware that I held in my arms what can only be called the monster of Frankenstein.

CHAPTER XIV

Elizabeth was a charming monster indeed. In the beginning only her eyes differentiated her from the way she looked before. She recovered her curves and the color in her cheeks, as well as the radiant smile that had made me fall in love with her. The doctors at the medical school marveled at her miraculous recovery, attributing it to divine intervention, for lack of a better explanation as to how this dying woman had managed to get to the country cottage several miles away, and further-more, how she had safely returned, even diligently maneu-vering the transport of her sick husband. They soon stopped treating her like a convalescent, and must have consoled them-selves by pampering me instead, to help me recover from the shock and the repeated attacks of neuralgia from a dental accident. The day I had resuscitated Elizabeth, I had ground my teeth for so long and so violently that I had broken all my molars without even realizing it.

On the night I have just described, the death and resurrection of Elizabeth had converged in my mind and were now merely a fragment of blurred memory; I was even under the illusion that I could obliterate it, like the bad dream it so closely resembled. How can I express, without foreshadowing what was to come, the strange and contradictory feelings that as-sailed me whenever I was near my wife? This adorable creature, my passionate mistress, had seen the Styx. I had rescued her from that place only to re-create her. As much as I tried to tell myself that I had "cured" Elizabeth, this euphemism was like the one used to refer to a deceased person as someone who has "departed on a long journey." Despite the blindness into which I had been lured, I knew in my heart that she was no longer a creature of God, but of man. "Is what we create ever our own?" We used to ask ourselves this question in Ingolstadt when, provoked by the discussion of autonomous existence, mandrakes and other creatures would glide from our feverish minds, and would even turn against us. When Elizabeth had been a woman like any other, molded and given life by the Creator, I was never troubled by her independence. Her self-possession had struck me as the most natural thing in the world. Now that she was mine because she had sprung from my own hands, I feared that she would escape me. Perhaps God, if He exists, understands what I felt so strongly on that first night while making love to the revived Elizabeth: we are able to love and possess what is not ours without too much trouble. But as soon as someone owes you their entire existence, he (or she) becomes dreadfully distant. No one is more disarming than a Demiurge. It is for this reason that Elizabeth, though apparently unchanged, terrified me. How would I be treated by my own creation?

My foreboding about the night of our second honeymoon was well founded. Elizabeth was indeed different and she wasted no time proving it. We now kept separate rooms, and at first, without admitting it, I avoided being alone with her, but she often came to join me during the night. I did not lock my door, fearing that it might grieve her. I still wanted to convince myself that her transformation existed only in my own mind, that my uneasiness might upset Elizabeth, who was so sensitive, and I felt guilty that she might guess the truth. However, as time went on, this hypothesis became increasingly improbable. My malaise did not escape Elizabeth for a single moment. On the contrary, it amused her. In public she took pains not to act differently from before. My father even confessed one day that it was difficult to remember her with blue eyes. On the other hand, she took advantage of our private conversations to slip into an entirely different temperament. The modest and shy young woman, with a somewhat limited critical mind, was replaced by a cruel and calculating person. She made fun of the slurping noises that my father made while eating his soup, and ridiculed the guests at our dinner table for harmless trifles. She would evoke our shared and precious memories only to mock them. I didn't dare ask her the reasons for this change. I understood them all too well. One night she informed me that she knew everything about her incredible resurrection, and did not bat an eyelash when recalling her death during those several hours. It was the first time we had ever spoken of it.

"Don't think that I hold it against you," she teased. "On the contrary. Only I would have loved to see the look on your face when you gave me the poison."

"How do you know about that?"

"I know a lot of things; more than you do, anyway. I know what happened before and afterward, and also during."

"What do you mean?"

"Ah, you're much too curious. But don't worry, you'll find out one day, just like everyone else."

From that day on, she often spoke of her rebirth, assuring me that the moment of triumph after my successful experiment was nothing compared with the joy of reemerging from the shadows of limbo. To hear her speak, it was as though she were now made of invincible steel, stronger and wiser. It was merely a pity, she laughingly added, that I couldn't perform the experiment on myself and breathe life into a perfect Frankenstein who would easily replace the distracted scientist and exhausted lover that I had become. (This sarcastic remark, alluding to the extravagant demands of her sensuality, which I could not completely satisfy, was quite typical of the new Elizabeth.)

Elizabeth's proselytizing rapidly turned into an obsession. One often observes this behavior in those who are afflicted in some way, who rhapsodize to anyone who will listen on the incomparable joy it brings them. An acquaintance in Ingolstadt, covered with tattoos from head to toe, tried to rally all his friends into copying him. The magnificent Beethoven— according to my friend Clerval, who had known his assistant, Schindler—had advised young musicians to pierce their eardrums to better appreciate his musical scores. Some of them actually claimed that they had done so to flatter him, and they would stroll about with an ear trumpet.

In any case, according to Elizabeth, the treatment that she had undergone had brought out a budding personality that was infinitely superior to her former self; like a chrysalis turning into a butterfly, she was glad to cast off the worn clothing that had constricted her—it was all I could do to keep myself from telling her just how much I missed that old clothing. I must let the world benefit from this miraculous method, she pleaded, as if it were a sort of rejuvenating potion, or a fountain of youth, or some other old wives' remedy. I protested that under no circumstances would I risk killing for such uncertain ends. But Elizabeth merely burst into laughter and declared me a fool.

CHAPTER XV

Barely a month after Elizabeth's resurrection, a terrible incident threw us into despair. My brothers Ernest and William, along with several friends, had decided to take a walk in the forest. Elizabeth, now in perfect health, joined the group as well. I would have gladly done the same if I hadn't been called to the city for a business matter. The group came home later than expected; night had already fallen. They asked me if young William had already returned. I hadn't seen him. He had disappeared during the excursion. He had lingered in the woods, no doubt, looking for plants for his herbarium. The others had assumed that he had continued on home. Alarmed, we returned to the forest with torches to look for our precious little boy. At last, about five o'clock in the morning, Ernest found the poor child—who, only that afternoon, had been active and blooming with health—in the undergrowth. He was lying in the grass, pale and motionless; on his neck were the bluish fingerprints of the murderer.

We carried him back to the house. From our anguished expressions Elizabeth was able to guess the horrifying news. Tears streaming from her eyes, she leaned over the tiny cadaver, examined his neck, and clasping her hands, exclaimed, "Oh, God! I have murdered my darling child!" Then she fainted, and was restored with extreme difficulty. Once revived, she could only weep and sigh. When I asked the meaning of her strange outburst, she told us how, that same evening, William had begged her to let him wear a very valuable miniature of his mother that she owned. The locket was gone, and was clearly the temptation that led the murderer to kill the poor child.

Overcome with sorrow, I forced myself to console the weeping Elizabeth, who blamed herself for this horrible turn of events. I accompanied her to her chambers, fearing that if she fainted, she would only add to the turmoil. Despite my own grief, I was sincerely moved by her reaction, worthy of the generous, tender soul that had once been Elizabeth. However, as soon as I had shut the bedroom door behind us, she turned to me with a gay smile and withdrew from the bodice of her dress

the notorious locket, which she held out defiantly. Flabbergasted, I did not dare try to understand, and began to stam-
mer. Elizabeth willingly explained it to me.

"Of course," she said, "I'm the one who strangled him. And
you're the one who is going to revive him. My little brother-
in-law will be just like I am! I already love him, do you know
that?"

At that moment it was I who thought about murdering
Elizabeth.

"Come now," she continued in a mischievous tone of voice,
"don't do anything foolish. Otherwise I'll scream and tell them
that I found the locket in your clothing. I'll show them your
laboratory and convince everyone that you wanted to test one
of your latest discoveries on William. Which is precisely what
you are going to do, for that matter. And meanwhile, you are
going to plant this locket in someone else's belongings. Whomever you like. The little Moritz girl, who's so fond of jewelry.
I'm sure she'll be delighted."

Elizabeth smiled again, with appalling perversity. But the
power of her ink-black stare was so intense, and I so distraught,
that I seized the object and left the room. As if in a dream—
like the time I poisoned Elizabeth—I walked through the corridors leading to the room of the young German governess,
Justine Moritz. As I'd suspected, she wasn't there. She must
have been downstairs at William's side, with the others. I was
so caught up in the machinery of my own creation that I
observed my own gestures and thoughts with the detachment
of a stranger. It merely seemed curious that I had reached this
point.

Later a chain of events occurred before I had a moment to
reflect on what had transpired. My poor little brother was
buried the following day, and afterward the locket was found
in Justine Moritz's drawer, among some enticing lingerie that
one never would have suspected of this innocent girl. Everything

favored my plan. The entire city was fascinated by the inquiry; crowds assembled in front of the municipal buildings where the investigation was taking place. Justine's interrogation went on into the night for so long that I was able to hurry to the cemetery, and enter with impunity into our family vault, which was still open. I stole William's remains from the tiny coffin and replaced them with those of a dog, which had already begun to reek. I put everything back into place and carried the body to the laboratory, where I spent the night reviving it with the spark of life that I had snatched from the cosmos.

William opened his eyes into the world from which he had so suddenly departed. They had turned from hazel to black. Nothing seemed to surprise him, not my laboratory, nor my uneasiness, nor the fact that he was being kept there in secret. When his murderer arrived, he welcomed her with open arms. Under the pretense that she needed rest and solitude, Elizabeth moved into the cottage to take care of William while I returned to Geneva, so that my absence would not arouse suspicion. During each of my brief visits, I found the two of them increasingly more intimate, getting along better than when they had been alive. I was worried, like a mother who is jealous of the nurse, afraid that her child might prefer the other—but then, what else could I do?

Justine Moritz's trial took place a week after the discovery of the incriminating evidence. Despite her touching protestations of innocence, there was little doubt that she would be convicted, and no one was surprised. The poor girl was hanged the day after the verdict.

Immediately afterward Elizabeth and William—who seemed perfectly conscious of what had befallen him—pressed me to retrieve the body in order to resuscitate Justine. Their insistence, like their complicity, frightened me, but I could not refrain from restoring life, however dubious the simulation, to an innocent girl whom I had deliberately driven to the gallows. I waited until the cadaver was transferred to the morgue, and bribed the night watchman.

By the third experiment, something strange took hold: it had become a habit. I resuscitated the dead the same way one sets a fracture. No longer was I grinding my teeth. Justine, who had been plunged into the Styx without any explanation for such an excruciating injustice, now came back to life with no questions asked. Her eyes had nevertheless turned black. She quite naturally joined the little colony already made up of William and Elizabeth. William allowed himself to be rocked in the same arms that had cruelly strangled him. The two women watched him play, engaged in lively conversation, as if one hadn't sent the other to the scaffold. Yet all three re-membered everything about their former lives as well as the circumstances of their deaths, which, ironically, provided them with reasons for mutual gratitude. It was as if Elizabeth had been right after all; as if murder ensured entrance into a very exclusive club. So, in this secluded spot in the Swiss country-side, a society of specters with ink-black eyes was secretly forming, from which, after each of my visits, I felt bitterly excluded.

Unexpectedly we were obliged to leave this forested haven, where the sun seemed to shine on the dead with a peculiar tenderness, while I was made to feel out of place, having remained among the living.

A little river flowed near the cottage. William would sometimes go boating there, under the watchful eye of Justine. One day, without taking notice of the downstream current, they drifted beyond the limits of our property. Vigorously paddling against the current, before they could correct their mistake, a peasant drinking nut wine on the bank recognized the girl (news of her hanging had recently monopolized the local gazette) and the child she had strangled. The rumor spread quickly, though it remained vague. Three days later we were surrounded by silent hostility. The village mayor, a pious and well-to-do farmer, paid us a visit for no apparent reason. Then the local policeman, who knew of a terrible story at such and such a place, where a common wall had prompted a litigation over grazing rights, came over to tell me about it as his eyes darted around the room.

These visits were of no avail, for the three living dead no longer left the cellar, where the laboratory was located, and could only be reached by a carefully hidden trapdoor. But the situation had become unbearable. As swiftly and discreetly as possible, I prepared for our departure. At Elizabeth's urging, I packed some of my equipment into cases, selecting what would be essential to me in exile. Justine and William departed first, in a closed carriage that William drove himself. Elizabeth and I were to join them later on. It would have been unthinkable, several weeks earlier, to allow this timid girl and this twelve-year-old child to make the trip alone, but like Elizabeth, their rebirth had given them an alarming confidence. William seemed much older than his years and spoke with the self-assurance of a mature man.

We spent several trying days back in Geneva. Many of our friends owned neighboring villas, and the vague and contradictory hearsay that had gone around the village had spread to the city. Though they had nothing specific for which to reproach us, we were looked upon as a source of embarrassment. My father was affected by it, and I realized from his troubled and awkward attitude that he wondered if some essential part of my life had somehow escaped him.

Elizabeth soon received a letter from Justine, who arranged a rendezvous on the other side of the lake, in a town called Sécheron. We were still able to leave without being hindered

84

by the authorities. Several days later it would have been impossible, since the investigation had led to the exhumation of William and Justine and thus the discovery that their bodies had disappeared. My father gave Elizabeth and me his blessing, but I sensed that he did so a bit reluctantly. What did he imagine, without daring to ask? And I, what could I possibly have told him? I never saw him again, and he died, unable to grant me more than a dutiful embrace. He must have forgiven me, though he had remained ignorant of what there was to forgive.

Having worked out the Genevese chapter successfully, the captain pauses once again. He weighs the bundle of paper with satisfaction, now covered with his neat, delicate handwriting, and with not a single word crossed out. He numbers them: thirty-four pages already—nothing to sneer at. And still he's only, let's say, halfway through. He looks at his watch: almost five-thirty. He had better hurry if he wants Ann to find the manuscript tonight. So the captain picks up the phone again, dials the girl's number, and is annoyed to hear the recorded voice on the answering machine. The message is banal and impersonal: "I'm not here right now but I will call you back if you leave a message after the beep." He refrains from doing so. Even if she is there, perhaps she doesn't want to answer. Besides, this system of screening calls is intolerable. He hangs up, rings the reception desk, and asks them to bring up some tea and Chinese pastries. He is hungry. Meanwhile, since there is no time to be wasted, he returns to his writing.

CHAPTER XVI

We met up with Justine and William at the Hotel d'Angleterre in Sécheron. They were waiting in the parlor, chatting comfortably with some English tourists about the weather. When we arrived, a furious storm was brewing. From the windows of the hotel overlooking the lake, we watched the shivering surface, the gray, powerful waves roused by the storm rising up in different directions. A small sailboat was struggling to return to the port, fighting the current, and we anxiously followed the passenger's efforts with a pair of binoculars belonging to one of the English tourists, who was passing it back and forth.

The owner of the binoculars wore many rings. He was clearly well informed on the subject of navigation but was rather boastful in his knowledge. He was approximately my age, well proportioned though on the corpulent side, and there was something Middle Eastern about his face. He spoke in a loud voice, making authoritative remarks on the navigator's efforts, addressing himself both to the company at large and to one of his friends in particular, a tall, lanky, true-blue Englishman with a cherrywood pipe in his mouth, whose demeanor would suddenly switch from an almost apathetic equanimity to a state of agitation. He was listening to the foppish Turk in silence, staring vaguely off into the distance, when all of a sudden, without any apparent reason, he let go of his pipe and began waving his arms about like the blades of a windmill, his nostrils flaring, his eyes like daggers. There was also a younger fellow with a pale, anxious countenance and somber eyes, and—I've saved the best for last—flanked by these three men, a ravishing young woman, almost a child. She couldn't have been more than eighteen. I was immediately taken with her ash-blond hair, her gray eyes, and the delicate shape of her face. Despite the difference in their features, she emanated a purity that reminded me of the former Elizabeth.

Though the boat was out of danger, the storm was far from over. I had wanted to order horses, but was told that an accident had occurred on the route to Plainpalais. Many trees had fallen onto the road, and a coach had been badly damaged . . .

All these details, were they really necessary, especially when there was so little time? the captain wondered. At that moment there was a knock at the door.

"One minute," he said, then went on to finish his sentence:

. . . and we would have to assume that the relay of horses would be disrupted until the following afternoon. Therefore, we would have to spend the night at the Hotel d'Angleterre.

He stands up to open the locked door, and lets in the receptionist, who is carrying the tray of tea and pastries.

He is Chinese, about twenty years old, pale, stocky, his hair impeccably blown dry, wearing a pair of black trousers fitted at the waist and wide at the bottom, and an open white shirt with a large pointed collar. Just as he is about to leave, the captain detains him. He asks him to convey an important message, giving him a good tip: he is to take the note that the captain is about to write and deliver it to Ann by hand. He will give him her address in Battersea. If she's not there, he must wait for her and then phone him back, once his mission has been accomplished. The young man accepts; he'll be going off duty at six o'clock.

Once he is alone again, the captain takes small sips of his tea, and fighting the desire to stretch out for a few minutes on the bed, he begins the dramatic final scene of his story.

* * *

Dinner was served at the guests' table, where we found ourselves seated together, all eight of us. It turned out that the English tourists were on their way back to the villas that they had rented for the summer, near Plainpalais, after a two-week excursion in Chamonix. At first the conversation revolved around the country's beautiful landscapes; the majestic Mont Blanc and the sea of ice that had highly impressed them. However innocent, this subject put me ill at ease, for as I might have already mentioned, Elizabeth and I had spent our honeymoon in Chamonix, seven years earlier. And so it was painful to listen to the new Elizabeth conjure up these memories, which I would have preferred to have shared solely with the former one. She recounted them with diabolical malice, changing certain anecdotes, tossing out phrases with double meanings that wounded me even more cruelly when William and Justine smiled with an air of complicity, as if they had been present in our nuptial chambers. I sensed that the three of them had united themselves against me. At the risk of saying more than was necessary, I waited for a chance to disconcert them in return, a sort of one-upmanship where I would even threaten to betray the secret that bound the four of us together as inextricably as if we had committed a common crime. I had also had a good deal to drink.

In the middle of one of his agitated fits, the tall, lanky fellow with the long teeth and flowing hair, whom they called Percy, told how during their stay at Montanvert an avalanche had claimed several lives but at the same time had uncovered a cadaver, perfectly preserved in the ice, an enormous man dressed in crude animal skins. For a week tourists and villagers had paraded past the block of ice jutting out of the debris, and had contemplated the hideous creature as if it were on display in a shopwindow. Nobody spoke of anything else. At the Montanvert inn, each guest offered his own explanation. One claimed that the creature had been taken by surprise in an avalanche several centuries ago, perhaps during the Middle Ages; yet there was nothing about its clothing that evoked a particular era. According to another, who had read Far Eastern travel stories, it was the cousin of the Abominable Snowman, known as the yeti in Nepal, and often recognized by the terrified mountain dwellers by its huge footprints. Then the young woman, who hardly spoke, made a strange remark. Everyone, she said, agreed that they had found the creature in ice repulsive, and she did not deny having experienced a profound malaise when she had seen it herself. But this incontestable hideousness did not stem from the irregularity of its features or some sort of deformity. This body of colossal stature was well built, and each feature, when contemplated on its own, might even have served as a sculptor's model. However, the general effect was flawed because of the unfortunate juxtaposition of these perfect parts. And laughing at her own audacity, the young woman declared that she imagined it as exactly like a rough cast of Adam that had been abandoned by its dissatisfied Creator.

At first I had listened to this anecdote somewhat distractedly, for I could have quoted at least two or three others like it. These types of discoveries occur frequently here in our mountains, and few but the tourists are impressed. I had even noticed, while reading the stories in the local gazettes, that glacier victims always seem to have some bizarre trait, doubtless exaggerated by the reporter with space to fill. They had recently recovered the remains of a bearded woman, and the year before that, the body of a Malayan whose hiking outfit concealed an exotic costume of magnificent silk. The description given by the fellow named Percy was far less disturbing than the bold interpretation of the young woman. But before I was able to obtain any further information, I was startled to hear Elizabeth exclaim, "Ah! We are saved!"

Justine and William stared at her in astonishment. They

had undoubtedly guessed, before I had, the practical joke that Elizabeth had just thought up. Their discomfort and the strangeness of the remark did not escape our table companions, who inquired as to the meaning of these words. Elizabeth remained silent for a moment, making certain that everyone present was hanging on her words. And then, like a hero of a novel who decides to spend the whole night recounting the story of his life to passing strangers, she solemnly declared that the final act of the tragedy had now been consummated. She wanted to tell the entire story to her audience, but she demanded that it be kept a secret. In the look exchanged between Justine and William, I sensed their common apprehension, and experienced a bitter joy, knowing that they, too, had been caught unawares at that moment. However, we could not unobtrusively silence Elizabeth, who was savoring our anxiety nearly as much as the curiosity of the English people. At last she began to speak.

I thought that I would faint when she announced that the hero of her story was none other than her own cousin, a Genevese doctor named Victor Frankenstein—I've already said that this is not my name, but it does bear a strong resemblance. She briefly described the childhood of this Frankenstein, more or less as I have in the beginning of this account—which is, in fact, an approximation of what I now recall of her story. On this occasion I realized that she hadn't overlooked a single detail of my student life, though I had never said a word to her about it.

Justine, William, and I were dumbfounded. But oddly enough, after a few minutes, the combined effect of the wine (four more bottles of which had been ordered by the exotic Turkish-looking Englishman, who drank only sparkling water) and above all, Elizabeth's gift for storytelling, made us take a childlike pleasure in this apocryphal confession, and forget all about the risks it entailed. Soon I caught myself interrupting the storyteller, but not to silence her as would have been wise, but to add a detail or start in again on the same episode. William and Justine contributed their share as well. I might have thought I was back in Ingolstadt, during the happy times. Moreover, I felt a disturbing complicity with Elizabeth after having participated in her improvised story. Disturbing because this sentiment would never have been possible with the former Elizabeth, whose candor would have made her unaware of any sort of hoax, and because it was also impossible with the new Elizabeth, who felt only hostility toward me. In recalling this night, I sometimes wonder whether a true closeness might have sprung up between us, had I played my part more skillfully. But even if it had continued, what difference would it have made? Would I ever have crossed over to their side?

And so Elizabeth told the story of my life, taking care to cast a doubt as to the identity of the hero and the present company. She spoke as if it concerned a third party, or even fictional characters, yet allowing the English people to think that each of her sentences contained a secret message to her companions, though perhaps an ironic one. Which was exactly the case.

At the crucial moment she became delirious. Instead of recounting her illness and her resurrection, she imagined that (the idea that had in fact occurred to me) my experiments had led me to breathe life into a hideous monster, made of bits and pieces of cadavers, meticulously assembled in a vain concern for beauty, which among other reasons, had driven me to endow this creature with a colossal stature.

No sooner had he been brought to life under my care than the monster took advantage of my having fainted (her cousin Frankenstein fainted easily, she stated) only to escape and disappear into the mountains. Rejected by mankind, he obstinately begrudged his creator and turned against him by strangling his younger brother.

"Oh, the scoundrel!" cried William, who was madly enjoying himself. I would have liked to break his neck.

Next it was his schoolmate's turn to die—Henry Clerval. Clenching my fists, I began to wonder if she hadn't actually murdered him and could only admit to it in this roundabout way. Threatening to continue his crimes, the monster ordered his maker to provide him with a female companion in his own image. Under this condition, he promised to go off into exile far from mankind, to some desert in South America. Mad with torment and rage, and conscious of the risk he would be taking by either accepting or refusing to grant this wish, Frankenstein tried to dodge the issue. He ceaselessly bemoaned his fate, and I admit that I felt a morbid pleasure in completing my own portrait as a spineless simpleton who could do no more than lament his sorrows after each massacre, surprised that the elevated purity of the Swiss mountains had not inspired nobler sentiments in this creature.

Then the English girl began to talk about Rousseau and how much she pitied poor Victor, but Elizabeth cut short her effusive outburst and continued, weaving herself into the story, but remaining anonymous. Frankenstein, she said, had just married his cousin Elizabeth, and fearing that the monster might attack her next, he wound up accepting his condition. Unable to create a new Eve from Adam's rib, he went back to sewing together cadavers' parts, stitching in arteries, and transplanting tissues.

Irritated by the brusqueness with which Elizabeth had interrupted the sympathetic girl who admired Rousseau and took pity on Victor, I interrupted the story myself and took over with an authoritative tone. In order to survey Frankenstein's progress in the fabrication of his female companion, the monster, according to my account, prowled around the villa where the laboratory was situated. One night he imprudently pressed his face against the window and the hideous desire reflected in his expression upset Victor so greatly that, preferring to die rather than re-create this nightmarish being, he seized an ax and went on a rampage, furiously destroying the work in progress. The meticulously sutured body parts flew to the far corners of the laboratory, blood was spurting, bottles were breaking, even a goosefleshed breast was hurled right into the face of the monster, who began to howl with sorrow and rage. Standing in the midst of this carnage, trembling, covered with blood and guts, Frankenstein waited for his creature to advance toward him so that he could tear him to pieces as well. He closed his eyes, but when he reopened them, the monster had disappeared. Then he heard heavy footsteps hastening upstairs, and realized in a flash that he had just sealed Elizabeth's fate. Still holding the ax, he bounded up the stairs, tripped on one of the steps, swore aloud, then heard the awful scream as it echoed. He kept running until he reached the nuptial suite, where the door had been ripped off its hinges and the furniture had been overturned. Dressed in her nightgown, Elizabeth was thrown across the disheveled bed. The open window banged in the wind. The lifeless body was all that remained in the room.

I had improvised this gruesome episode in the most realistic way possible, becoming more and more feverish as I neared the ending. I sat back down, breathless. Nevertheless, I felt calmer for having unburdened such violence in the story I had told. I, in turn, closed my eyes and was struck with the absurd idea that this gesture had exposed me as the hero of the story that I had just told in the third person. Elizabeth doubtless had the same thought.

"Please forgive my cousin," she said. "This is such a painful memory for him."

I opened my eyes again. They were all staring at me.

"Your cousin?" the girl asked. "So then . . . ?"

"My cousin, that's right. Why hide it any longer? You have before you the wretched Victor Frankenstein."

*This revelation was met with another silence. On the sly,
Elizabeth gaily winked at me, exactly as she had done before
while confessing to William's murder. Now that the effect of
the alcohol had subsided, I once again began to wonder where
this dangerous joke would lead us. Not knowing what countenance to adopt, and incapable of fainting on the spot, I fell
back on the easiest role I could play—the grief-stricken man
unable to react to what is being said by those around him.*

*"What happened next?" the young man with the somber air
asked eagerly.*

*"After that," my cousin replied solemnly, "the man you see
before you lived only for revenge. He tracked down the monster
and followed him all over the world, to kill him or be killed
by him. He wanted no other destiny."*

*"I see," the young man murmured. (And though I don't
know why, I was struck by the idea that he did indeed understand, but that he was the only one who did.)*

*"He almost had him, somewhere near the North Pole. The
creator and his creature found themselves face to face, on the
ice floe, but one of nature's tricks prevented this final combat
from being fought. Pardon me, dear Victor," she said glancing
in my direction, "but I think it would be better if we got this
over with."*

*"You're probably right," I agreed all in one breath, won-
dering how she intended to end it. I tried to regain control of
the story, but she was faster than I.*

*"An extraordinary sight, I assure you! Victor was holding
the monster with the tip of his sword, when suddenly the ice
cracked open. Their little islands drifted for several hours without either of them being able to overtake the other. Victor
waved his fist and brandished his sword in the direction of the
monster, who only sneered and stuck out his tongue—he was
out of reach. He even made obscene gestures," Elizabeth added,
giving me a compassionate glance as if this detail had been*

more painful than the rest. The Englishmen, moreover, were equally shocked, and the pretty girl let out a whimper of prudish delight that struck me as ridiculous.

"Finally they were separated by a current," Elizabeth continued with dramatic effect. "Three days passed before a whaling vessel rescued Victor, who was unconscious and half dead from cold and hunger. As soon as he had recovered enough strength to stand on the deck, he didn't budge until Copenhagen, scanning the vast expanse of ice night and day in the hope of spotting the monster. All in vain, alas."

Elizabeth fell silent for a moment, then went on in a touching, tragic tone. "Not long ago Victor returned to the house of his ancestors, more desperate than ever. His wife, his brother, and his friends had perished at the hands of the hideous creature, and fate had cheated him out of his sole reason for living: vengeance. He thought that his enemy had died in the snows of the North Pole, and here he finds him imprisoned in the ice of Montanvert, only miles away from his point of departure.

"How terribly ironic!" William pompously remarked.

"Indeed. Everything has come full circle; death has done its deed. From now on, what other purpose shall give him the strength to live?"

"Oh, Victor," she cried, dramatically taking my hand and cruelly digging her nails into my palm, "if only the love of your family could make you take heart! If you wanted to, knowing that we live for you, couldn't you try to live for us? Having sacrificed my youth, I ask for no other reward!"

As you can imagine, this speech made me extremely uncomfortable. Hiding my face in my hands, the living epitome of sorrow, I knew that I had become a topic of general interest and could not hope to divert their attention right away. I also sensed that our listeners were dying to ask me questions but did not dare, out of respect for my suffering. Furthermore, I

95

believe they didn't really know what questions to ask after this crazy story. They were probably wondering whether it was true, and if that were the case, what could have prompted us to tell it to strangers? And if it wasn't, which was more likely, what truthful episodes could have inspired us? What were the ties that bound us together, what private conflicts had they inadvertently become involved in, as silent accomplices to a discussion that appeared in every way to be a settlement of some sort of dispute? These questions hovered over the dinner table in a cloud of embarrassed confusion, and, to maintain decorum, would not be dispersed.

I was worried. Why had Elizabeth transformed our story in such extravagant terms? And why had I made the foolish mistake of intervening? To give the illusion of an ephemeral complicity with Elizabeth? Or was it to accomplish through words, and by procuration, a murder that I had dreamed of committing but would not admit to myself? I had caught an ironic smile on my wife's face while I had been speaking. She was clearly amused by my account of her death and the relentless passion with which this massacre had been described. And she amused herself even further with her own retorts, to show that I had been defeated and reduced to a state of submission that I already sensed would become my true fate. But for the moment, within the strict limits of the tale we had fabricated, I still had time to react. I nervously dropped my hands from my face and looked up. They were still staring at me, all of them.

"Don't worry, dear cousin," I said, turning toward Elizabeth, who had kept her hand on top of mine. "Rest assured —I shall live! I shall live and mourn those who were dear to me, but it shall not be for vengeance's sake. The gods did not rob me of that! You are all, perhaps, unaware that, this monster whose remains are exhibited in Montanvert—I'm the one who killed him!"

"Oh, I'm so happy!" Elizabeth cried, stifling the oohs and ahs that arose from the table. The stupidity of her remark was, moreover, simply in response to my own. I cannot understand why the fact that I had killed the murderer of my family should have consoled me in my loss, nor why this entire affair should have enchanted Elizabeth. But the very nature of these kinds of improvisations is that chance will impose its absurd stakes, and this additional declaration was an indication of the riposte that Elizabeth was preparing. She reiterated how happy she was and cast a silent look toward the others, inviting them to manifest their joy as well.

"Ah, excellent, excellent!" shouted little William, whose pubescent voice had already begun to break. "Congratulations, Victor! What admirable swordsmanship! Victor killed the monster, did you hear that?"

He turned to the English people to be his witnesses. And as this brusque transition from the depths of abandon to an exaggerated joviality appeared to disconcert them, he whispered something into the ear of his neighbor, the tall, lanky character with the shaggy hair, who looked surprised at first, then nodded his head with an air of understanding. He, in turn, leaned toward his companion, the pretty young woman. There was a moment of silence, whispers around the table, and then embarrassment.

"Now, Victor," Elizabeth said to me in the coaxing tone of a governess addressing a stubborn child, "you must be very tired. . . ."

"Yes," added William, who was now standing. Slipping behind my chair, he took me firmly by the arm—the little monster!—and said, "It's time for you to go to bed."

I immediately broke free of his grasp. "Stop this farce at once," I grumbled. "No one is amused by it."

"Come now, dear Victor, you must be reasonable. You need your rest."

I knocked over my chair as I stood up and eyed William contemptuously. This enemy of mine, ready to abuse me physically and pass me off as insane, this was my little brother, the gentle and affectionate child who, three weeks before, had still been playing with his ball. I heard Justine whisper something, and at the other end of the table, the foppish Turk declared that his friend Polly was a doctor (but the somber young man whom he designated did not make a move to intervene—in the midst of this excitement, he was the only one who seemed lost in his thoughts, and for this I was grateful).

"No, don't worry," Elizabeth immediately responded, "everything will be all right. It's not your fault. You couldn't have known that the story of the wild man in the ice . . ."

William took advantage of my confusion to take hold of my arm once again; this snot-nosed twelve-year-old had the grip of a German soldier. The Turkish-looking fop drew nearer to come to his aid. I realized that it was useless to resist. No matter what I said, and especially if I told the truth, they would attribute it to my madness, which proved that Elizabeth's explanation of our digressions had been a stroke of genius. After all, it was perhaps the best way to avoid any unfortunate consequences.

Complying with their wishes, I was irritated when, after I had left the dinner table with a perfectly idiotic grin on my face, Elizabeth, who led me back to my room, continued the charade that she had just initiated.

Being a good sport, I congratulated her on having won the match, but she answered me with the mild tone of a patient nurse who, in private, had no further motive to speak this way than the pleasure of humiliation.

I got into bed furious. I kept imagining the conversation downstairs, my wife, my brother, and the smooth-tongued

Justine explaining how, during my fits of madness, they were forced to acquiesce and humor me in the face of my delirium, by entering into my game, even playing the parts of the fictional characters who inhabited my demented mind. I angrily envisioned the woeful compassion of the English foursome, William, making pretentious speeches, and above all, Elizabeth, with the pained and dignified expression of someone who has greatly suffered. Yet at the same time I wondered if they were right—if I hadn't actually gone stark, raving mad. I imagined myself as a terrible burden in their lives, now devoted to watching over a brother, a husband, a friend, who would not give up his horrid, ludicrous ideas, who as long as he lived would consider them his enemies, as a clan of living dead who were conspiring against him. . . .

Later on, I heard Elizabeth come upstairs and open the door to the adjoining room occupied by Justine and William. There were murmurs and stifled laughter. They were making fun of me, no doubt. Elizabeth soon joined me in bed, lay down beside me, and immediately fell asleep. My anger kept me awake. I got up, went to the window, and opened the shutters slightly. The rain had stopped and a strong earthy scent rose from the drenched garden. On the terrace, someone was speaking softly in English. Bending over cautiously to avoid being seen, I recognized the girl called Mary by her companions. She stood there, staring straight ahead, leaning against the railing that separated the terrace from the garden. Directly beneath my observation post, I could make out the dark figure of a man sitting on a stone bench. Every so often, puffs of smoke would drift into the air above this figure, and the aroma of strongly scented tobacco helped me identify him as the tall, shaggy-looking fellow. At that particular moment neither of them spoke. Then I heard a voice, almost certain that they were talking about me. But even if this had been the case, it was too late to overhear their conversation. The girl spun around, giving me a chance to admire her oval face bathed in moonlight, and addressed her companion.

"I'm going up to bed now. Will you be long?"

"No," the other replied. "I'll be up shortly. The night is so beautiful."

"And what about me?"

Instead of answering, the young man merely chuckled politely, as if his desire to be original prohibited him from simply saying, "So are you." However, he found no other reply, and so by chuckling, he was also admitting to Mary's verbal triumph. She must have interpreted it this way as well, for I saw her smile as she headed toward the French doors that linked the terrace to the room where we had dined. She paused a moment before going inside, and although the shutters prevented me from seeing her, I imagined her on the threshold, her hands clasped around the doorframe.

"Come quickly," she said. "Come, Percy."

"I'm coming," said Percy, who hadn't budged.

Once he was alone, he tapped his pipe against the wall and struck a flint to relight it. From my viewpoint directly overhead, I only had to lean forward slightly to see the red glow of his pipe, which he covered with the palm of his hand until it glowed even redder, at which point Percy was apparently satisfied, and calmly began to puff on it at long, steady intervals. The care with which he had performed this operation gave me reason to believe that he would remain there a while longer. Taking heed not to wake Elizabeth, I crossed the room, noiselessly opened the door, and took up my post on the landing. From there, I dominated the stairway. A floorboard creaked; the bars of the railing suddenly danced in the candlelight, announcing Mary's arrival. My heart was pounding. At that moment I was even prepared to die, if I could speak to her first. Ever since Elizabeth's death, my life had become a night-

mare into which I had sunk deeper and deeper with every passing day. I had been unable to confide in anyone. The only ones who knew—and probably knew more than I did—were my enemies with the black eyes who assumed the appearance of my family. For once, at least, a human being had to be told the whole story—as I am doing tonight in writing this memoir—but I am afraid that no human being will ever read it. Did I already have an inkling? In any case, this girl who had spoken so ardently of Rousseau now appeared to be my last chance. If anyone in the world should know who Victor Frankenstein had been, it was surely her (or else the pale young man, but I preferred to confide in a woman).

The lifeless eyes of the stuffed deer mounted on the wall flashed in the dim, flickering candlelight. Tiptoeing, I followed Mary, and no sooner had she closed the door of her room than I locked it behind me.

When she saw me, she opened her mouth, upon which I firmly placed my hand. I had to. When it is past midnight and a girl finds a wild-looking man in her room who was presented as a madman during dinner, she is obliged to scream.

"I won't hurt you," I breathed into her ear. "Please don't scream."

Then I remained silent, holding her close to me. I had acted on an irrational impulse, having surprised her like this, wishing to tell her everything without planning what I would say next. And now that she was in a position to listen, though against her will and for a very short time—Percy would be coming upstairs soon—I didn't know what to say. No matter what I said, she wouldn't believe me; my story would only be looked upon as new proof of my insanity, sufficiently certified by my behavior.

My hand still pressed on her mouth, I stepped back a bit so that I could look into her eyes. They were light gray, which gave me the ludicrous hope that she would venture to listen to me and perhaps believe me. I said to her in what was no doubt an exaggeratedly calm voice, "You have nothing to fear. I am going to take my hand away now, and it will be up to you. If you don't cry out, I shall tell you my story and then leave, giving you my blessing. If you do cry out, I won't do you any harm. I am at your mercy—it's for you to decide."

I was pleased with the beginning of my speech, full of nobility, and let my hand drop with grandiose simplicity. Or rather, I started to do so, but as soon as I withdrew my palm from her mouth, I realized that she was about to scream at the top of her lungs. Then everything happened very quickly. By the time this scream was rising in her throat and her intention was transforming into sound, I had panicked, and forgetting my promise, I stifled this sound by squeezing the girl's neck. Her body went limp and heavy in my arms. My strength failed me and I laid her down on the bed, allowing myself a moment's respite, just time enough for my rapidly pounding heart to recover a tolerable rhythm. During this ridiculously brief moment, I felt as if I were waiting for salvation. It was one of those absurd spells that occur when there is no way out of a situation, and so one begins to dream: the hotel would be struck by lightning and annihilate us all, there would be no trace of my heinous crime, nor of my victim, Elizabeth, myself, anyone—it would all be over.

The sound of footsteps in the corridor roused me from my exhausted, helpless state. Someone was coming, probably the shaggy-haired Percy, and I couldn't do anything about it. Outside of the providential cataclysm that I had prayed for, nothing could prevent him from opening the door, seeing his wife's cadaver on the bed, and the murderer standing beside her with trembling hands. . . .

The footsteps came to a halt in front of the door. Then in walked Elizabeth, who took one look at the situation and said with a mocking smile, "Well done."

We carried the body into our room, fortunately without encountering anyone in the corridor.

The telephone rings.

"The note has been delivered," says the young Chinese.

"Good," replies the captain, who hangs up immediately. It is getting dark. Ann will be arriving soon, if everything works as planned. He barely has an hour left to finish.

He hears the sound of footsteps in the hallway. Someone on their way to the toilet, no doubt.

CHAPTER XVII

I hear footsteps outside my door and the sound of furniture being moved about. It is dawn, the end is near; I must quickly finish my story without further ado.

The following morning, Mary rejoined her idiotic Englishman, the lanky poet. Had he been worried about her disappearance during the night? How had he reacted to her black eyes when she walked through the door of their room? I shall never know, for we left the Hotel d'Angleterre before dawn, then, like fugitives, crossed hurriedly through France and boarded the ship in Calais. I had contacted a former schoolmate of mine in Geneva, a surgeon named Robert Knox, who after his studies in Germany, had come back to settle in Edinburgh, where he apparently had a great many patients. He had agreed to welcome us and help us get established.

But I have neither the time nor the desire to recount what my life was like in Edinburgh. Until now, I had never left the foggy city. I lived in a beautiful home there. I soon entered into partnership with Knox, and up until last week, we ran the surgery unit of the city hospital. I was a respected doctor, a prestigious professor. My wife's beauty made us popular in high society; William grew up to be a brilliant cavalryman. What more can I say?

Only this: that the hybrid beings who made up my family (I shudder to use that sacred word to designate strangers who conspired in my downfall) had only strengthened their hold on me during these past years. I was forced to obey Elizabeth, Justine, and William like a slave, and others as well. I truly believe that they would have gotten rid of me if they hadn't still needed my talent and skill to carry out their monstrous plan.

Though thoroughly integrated into the world of mankind, they found themselves more excluded than the worst of criminals. A thief is shunned by his society, whereas they were like travelers with a perfect knowledge of the country, in a world that smiled upon them. The warm welcome of the natives did not keep them from remaining foreigners. And rather than attempting to be like the others, forgetting what it was that made them different, they decided that the others would become like them, and therefore to abolish any difference. Rather than conforming to an ideal, they themselves wanted to be the ideal and they put me in charge of transforming the world, as I had already transformed them. Knox's accidental death (that is, they assured me that it was accidental, but I don't really believe it) enabled him to join their ranks, resuscitated under my care. During his lifetime I had rather counted on the support of this honest practitioner, even though I had never dared to confide in him. His second life turned him into one more enemy.

Under Elizabeth's influence, our activities began to spread beyond our own sphere. One morning I found two sinister-

looking men at my home, who deposited a large cloth sack in the vestibule of my laboratory and advised me not to worry about where it had come from. Doctor Knox, they told me, had assured them that I would pay upon delivery of the package. Partially opening the sack, I found the body of a poor woman named Tess Nicholson, who only the night before, had been peddling her meager charms and had recently consulted me at the charity hospital. As I threatened the two murderers (there was no doubt that they had killed her during the night), declaring that I would call the police, Knox arrived and with an intolerable self-assurance ordered me to pay his "friends."

"Mr. Burke and Mr. Hare work for us, my dear Victor. Since the morgue cannot provide us with enough suitable material, we have to find it somewhere else. If you raise a fuss, it shall only be used against you."

Trembling with horror and rage, conscious that I had now become a veritable criminal, I was forced to make up my mind and pay my "employees."

I bestowed poor Tess with life, then continued with others. For several years the purveyors continued to supply my laboratory. I experienced certain failures, some due to my fatigue, and others through my lack of will. Whenever this was the case, the two partners would dispose of the mutilated bodies in some alley. This also explains the abominable wave of crime that bathed Edinburgh in blood at the time. But these failures only represented a tiny proportion of my activity, and the body snatchers, paid increasingly fatter sums, were in fact strangling and stabbing far more unfortunate people than the police were ever aware of. Most of them were, as Knox called it, "reinstated into the circuit"; that is to say, they returned to their former existence after a brief disappearance, for which they were generally able to provide a plausible explanation. All the same, Burke and Hare chose their victims in the slums of the city, where missing persons, runaways, and abnormal occurrences were quite common. Only their eyes would, at times, pose a problem.

As time went on, obliged by the excess of material, I populated Edinburgh with the products of my reprehensible enterprise. The thieves, prostitutes, beggars, and even several prominent citizens, surprised by my assassins during their nocturnal escapades, had all become my creatures, only to escape immediately thereafter. Many would frequently visit our home, where Elizabeth welcomed and conversed with them. There was an abrupt silence whenever I set foot in the room. I had no power over the work of my bloodstained hands. From bodies that had been emptied of their autochthonous souls, I tirelessly replaced them with souls more perverse, derived from ether; I became an impotent god, ridiculed by a society of ghosts, who, recruited by my family, began to disseminate, crossbreed, and multiply. All my attempts to rise against them were in vain. They made me understand that I was nothing but an enslaved artisan in the workshop, ultimately as insignificant as the two miserable thugs who supplied me with human flesh.

I remember these years as a sort of hell to which I had almost become accustomed. There were several moments of despair, various plans to escape or commit suicide, but above all, I was plunged into a deep and heavy stupor from my toil and its familiar horror. It was almost as if living in this cold, damp city where I had been condemned to spend the rest of my days, I barely missed the meadows, valleys, and blue skies of the Continent and of my youth.

I no longer even tried to confide in anyone; the episode with Mary had scorched any further desire. Several years earlier Elizabeth had me read the famous novel Frankenstein, *entirely based on the tale we had fabricated at the inn for the benefit of the English tourists. I was angered by it, but how would I have felt if she had told the truth, as I have attempted to summarize it here tonight, as I would have liked to tell it to her, that other night in Sécheron? In the end she did indeed find out, but too late, and through Elizabeth, with whom she still corresponds. I even suspect that Elizabeth and William advised her to write her novel. She was, and still is on their side, and it is only natural that she would use her talent to throw everyone off the trail with a literary fantasy that chronicles a conquest in which she had been in the front lines. When Elizabeth finds this manuscript after my death, I am convinced that she will give it to her to read, and since it is probably in her hands at this very moment, it is to her that I am addressing myself. Or rather to the young, innocent girl with the gentle gray eyes who might have listened to me. You must find all of this highly amusing, don't you, Mrs. Shelley?*

Ann giggles with excitement in the taxi. The driver is Chinese, probably from Malaysia or Singapore. As she observes his slender neck occasionally swiveling from right to left—as if he were trying to keep his features immobile, even his eyes, and figured it less compromising to move his entire head, as mechanically as the gun turret of a tank—Ann calculates what the chances are that he, too, works for Captain Walton. She had found him cruising right in front of her flat, ready to pick her up as soon as she had left the building. She wishes she hadn't hailed the taxi. If she hadn't waved, she would have been certain. Would he have driven slowly along the sidewalk and proposed his services? Yes, without a doubt. It can't just be a coincidence. As it is, the young man who had brought her the note and had waited outside her door had been Chinese. Come to think of it, it hadn't even occurred to her to ask him how he had gotten into the building despite the entry code. But he had vanished so quickly. . . .

Though not exactly his custom (at least to Ann's knowledge, but she hardly knows him, she would have to ask Brigitte), all these enigmatic gestures were typical of Captain Walton's style. She had not only recognized his neat handwriting, in contrast to the illegible signature, but also his taste for cheap intrigue. Yes, cheap. Still, that doesn't stop her from being intrigued all the same. Not once had it occurred to her to refuse to obey the instructions in the note: she must wait for a telephone call at precisely ten o'clock in a phone booth at the corner of St. Dunstan Road and East Appold Street, both of which she has never heard of before.

In spite of everything, Ann is surprised by her own submissiveness. She has even respected the order not to say anything about it to anyone. Coming from anyone else but Walton, one might suspect it was a trap. With him, one can only expect something childish, a practical joke that is no doubt amusing, or some kind of staged production, perhaps, to wish her a happy birthday. She had celebrated her twenty-fourth birthday the night before; he could have found that out through Brigitte. She thought about giving her a call, if for no other reason than to find out whether he had ever pulled anything like this on her. But she realized that Brigitte wouldn't tell her if it was to be a surprise; therefore, she might as well be conscientious and do as she was told, and not spoil it.

Judging from the way things are going, she can easily imagine a Chinese dinner in her honor, with all the young women of Mecklemburgh Gardens and the captain beaming at the head of the table (in uniform—why not? He must have one somewhere), proud to have skillfully arranged these little touches of Oriental atmosphere, something along the lines of a clandestine opium den of which he was so fond. It was the first thing that she had noticed when she had walked into his office: that profusion of ivory and jade Buddhas, all that colonial paraphernalia; besides, he almost seemed Chinese himself, with his extreme politeness, his high cheekbones, his slightly slanted eyes, and his indefinable age. He had lived in Asia for a long time, but to listen to him speak, one would think he'd lived everywhere for a long time. Which was—if one were to add up all his supposedly long stays in Hong Kong, Manila, Brasília, Vienna, Cape Town, Novosibirsk, Santiago de Chile, or the Kerguelen Islands—what made his age so indefinable. One was obliged to take some of his remarks with a grain of salt. Ann suspects him of deliberately isolating himself, exaggerating to such an extent that his listeners would only be more confused: this overactive imagination is, in his case, merely a courtesy. She remembers the first time she visited him and heard the secretary requesting a connection with Melbourne on behalf of Captain Walton (afterward she had heard him refer to himself with this title, but had no idea of which army, or most likely, which navy he had served in; without knowing why, she could picture him as a sailor). He had greeted her with a smile, and had gestured for her to come in and sit down, holding the receiver propped between his shoulder and his beardless cheek, in the midst of a conversation with some Australian businessman. Right before he hung up, he had inquired if his T-shirts were dry. While chatting with the captain later on, Ann was dying to ask him the meaning of this question, what his motivation was for trying to make her believe that his laundry was being washed and dried in Melbourne. And why T-shirts? It was impossible to imagine him in anything but a pin-striped gray flannel suit and a conservative tie. And how had the caller on the other end of the line reacted to this preposterous incident? Captain Robert Walton is exactly the kind of man to interrupt and perhaps compromise himself in a serious discussion for the sole pleasure of disconcerting a young lady who has just entered his colonial office. He can flaunt both his sophistication and absurdly casual style of dress, never thinking for a single moment that she will believe him. By the same token, it is because of these personality traits, both twisted and indifferent to their own confabulations, that Ann has begun to develop a liking for this place, to the point where she is allowing herself to be led by a Chinese taxi driver to an overtly mysterious rendezvous.

As I became more and more skilled in my operations, and my losses became increasingly rare, Knox made progress as well; from assistant and evil spirit, he turned into master and executioner. A month ago, when he succeeded at one of these resurrections alone (which I thought only I was capable of doing), I was cowardly enough to fear for my life. Since I was no longer useful and one of my creatures could now give birth to others—assuming my accursed task without a nagging conscience—there was no further reason to let me live. I sensed that all those around me were scheming, including Knox and Elizabeth—who, in fact, were openly having an affair. And to this day, if I am still alive, it is undoubtedly due to the scandal that has just broken out and has distracted my tormentors from my existence.

It had been several years since I had recorded any more than a few rare failures in my operations, but Knox, who was a novice, did not succeed with the majority of them. As a result, the series of crimes that took place several years ago, which were considered a closed affair, or else had been solved, began all over again. Burke and Hare were grudgingly obliged to resume the part of their job that they liked the least: the disposal of the bodies. Eight days ago, Burke stupidly got himself arrested, and there is anger in the streets. They are demanding the name of his employer, and Knox suspects that the scoundrel may have confessed. Yesterday a panic-stricken Elizabeth made it clear that if Knox were in danger, it would become vitally important to find a successor; someone who would know how to perform these frightening operations, which were indispensable to their plan, and who would also be on the side of the creatures. I am well aware of what these words imply. Burke, who has just been sentenced, will soon be hanged, and perhaps Knox as well. His final operation, if there is enough time, will be reserved for me. Someone will have to carry on his work. Not only must I die, but I shall also be reborn in their camp, in order to serve them.

Yesterday, December 8, 1828, I locked myself in my laboratory, sealed off all the exits, and spent the night writing this, for no one in particular. Or for you, Mrs. Shelley, which is the same thing. I hear sounds in the corridor. Knox will undoubtedly be arrested this morning, but they will somehow find a way of forcing me out of my refuge, murdering me, and operating on me before he gets taken in. I am waiting.

The captain puts down his pen. His hand is numb, but the work is finished. He is waiting. He smiles at himself in the mirror with satisfaction. Now Frankenstein can die, the shipwreck where Polidori still lives can sink, he can finally leave this corner room, and the game will continue. He is waiting.

CHAPTER XVIII

The rain comes down in such thick sheets that she can't even read the names of the streets on the signposts, gazing out the cab window. She notices that many of them are in Chinese, pagodalike neon signs that break up the gray monotony of the cottages, one after another. Yet the driver had avoided the center of town, leaving the Asian neighborhoods far behind. Not having paid close attention to the itinerary, Ann realizes that they have driven along the banks of the river and are now in the suburbs. The heat inside the car is beginning to make her feel drowsy. She rolls down the window, but is pelted with rain and promptly rolls it back up again. She went to bed too late last night, and she's tired.

A quarter to ten. She hopes they are far from the meeting place so she can doze a little in the taxi, sheltered from the rain, and guided by the silent Chinese, whose head pivots back and forth from time to time. While she thinks about his posture again, she suddenly notices that the taxi has stopped and is idling. The diesel motor purrs. The driver has turned around and now faces her. At first she thinks that he hasn't moved his shoulders, which would mean that he is able to rotate his neck a hundred and eighty degrees. No, that couldn't be, but from what she can make out from behind the window, he's holding himself at a three-quarters profile. Seeing his face for the first time, she discovers with surprise that he's not Chinese at all. She must be crazy.

The captain finishes writing the preface, places it on top of the manuscript, which he carefully stacks, lining up the pages on the edge of the dressing table. Then he puts it away in a manila folder. He turns out the light, cranks up the metal shutters, and looks out the window.

"Here we are," the driver repeats.

Ann didn't hear him the first time, but she's sure that he's said it twice and is grateful that he knows enough not to raise his voice. She digs into her purse and pays the fare. The price confirms her hunch that she had fallen asleep. She's in no mood for party favors, even if they are Chinese, let alone a room filled with laughing people. She thinks vaguely of Jim.

Either by coincidence or because someone else has informed him of her destination, the driver has pulled up right in front of the telephone booth, its yellow glare illuminating the intersection. Ann could almost open the door of the booth without moving from the car. She gets out anyway, hears the motor gunning, and suddenly realizes that there's someone in the booth. It's a sinister-looking guy in his twenties with a shaved head, sitting on the floor, talking into the receiver in a high-pitched voice. He looks up at her, fuming. She closes the door and goes back to sit in the taxi. The driver turns off the motor but makes no comment. He resumes his driving position, without turning back toward his passenger. Once again, he looks Chinese. Ann doesn't dare say a word, not even to thank him for waiting. They both remain silent in the car. After a while the young man, presumably Chinese, turns the key of the engine, but only to put on the windshield wipers. The worn rubber makes a steady two-note squeak that is actually somewhat soothing: it drowns out fragments of the skinhead's conversation that occasionally drift from the phone booth.

The door finally opens, the guy walks out, turns up the collar of his leather jacket, and runs off. Ann is relieved to see that he's not going to stay in the vicinity. She mumbles her thanks to the driver, who doesn't seem to hear her, and enters the phone booth.

Two minutes to ten. The skinhead had neglected to hang up, and has left the receiver dangling. Ann can barely hear the dial tone; she's afraid that he has broken the phone. She places the receiver back on the hook, delighted to hear the click, then the dial tone, and prepares to wait. The taxi still hasn't moved. At the moment she can see the driver's profile and his presence troubles her. The fact that he's not Chinese makes it less obvious that he's playing a part in the surprise organized by Walton. And therefore, his silent stratagem is becoming inexplicable, almost worrisome. And what could he be thinking, watching her stand in a phone booth out in the suburbs, without making a call? True, he's still looking straight ahead and can't see her unless he discreetly rolls his eyes in her direction. It would be impossible to put him on a false trail by picking up the receiver and pretending to talk; then she wouldn't get her call. In desperation she plucks up the courage to tap her index finger against the glass of the booth to attract his attention. He turns his head toward her, and she signals in a way that is intended to mean that he can leave, that she won't be needing him any longer. But, for fear of insulting him, dryly dismissing him when he has actually turned out to be cooperative, she finally gives an indecisive wave that could just as easily be an invitation to join her in the phone booth. Nevertheless, the driver grasps her meaning and pulls away. He comes to a stop, on the other side of the intersection, partially hidden by the corner building. The taillights of the taxi are visible from the glass booth, one of the few bright spots piercing through the darkness along with the blinking sign and an occasional lit window of a hotel—probably the Cheng Hotel, which protrudes into the intersection. Like the bow of a ship, the angle is so sharp that it makes one wonder who would want to stay in such slanted rooms.

Two minutes past ten. Ann decides to wait five more minutes, and then she'll leave. She hopes that no one else wants to use the phone booth, but the neighborhood seems deserted. Strange for a Saturday night. The prospect of a practical joke seems more and more improbable, although she can't think of any alternatives, and her uneasiness heightens. Perhaps someone is spying on her from a dark window above.

The captain is, indeed.

It is still raining. Ann feels uncomfortably warm. How stupid of her to wear a leather suit in the middle of summer! And stockings too! She had gotten dressed expecting a party, and it was the only decent thing she could find in her closet. And furthermore, the elastic is too tight around her waist. She reaches under her skirt, making sure that no one can see her, and quickly peels off her stockings, rolling them into a ball and letting them drop to the floor of the booth, right in the middle of the puddle under her feet. No use holding on to them; they already have a run. A fine mist has formed under the dial of her watch. She's afraid that the water might have ruined the mechanism, but the big hand is moving along normally, and at exactly the moment that the five-minute grace period has run out, the telephone rings.

She picks up the receiver. "I've been waiting here for ten minutes," she says acidly.

"Only seven," answers a strange voice, undoubtedly muffled by a handkerchief or a stocking.

Ann glances down to see if her stockings are still there.

"But you haven't been waiting in vain," the voice continues. "Do you see the hotel on your right, where the lights are?"

She is certain that her caller can see her. If one were to stand directly in front of the telephone in the booth, one would be facing the neon sign of the Cheng Hotel. In order for it to be on the right, one had to be leaning against the phone at an angle, as she is now. She spins around on her heels a quarter of a turn.

"It's right in front of me," she lies, but the unknown caller does not pick up on it.

"Very well. When I hang up, you will walk out of the phone booth and go into that hotel. Go to the reception desk and tell them that you're a friend of Mr. Polidori. I'll spell it: P-O-L-I-D-O-R-I; it's an Italian name. You'll say that he's asked you to pick up some papers of his. They'll give you the key to the room; they've already been informed. You will take these papers and return home. That will be all for tonight. So long."

* * *

The captain hangs up the phone and leaves the room. Now it's his turn to play dead.

Ann hears the click, leaves the phone booth, and heads toward the hotel with rapid strides. At the reception desk, half-concealed behind a drooping plant on the counter, a stout woman carefully pours water from an electric kettle into a cup with a tea bag in it. She is unquestionably Chinese. With the kettle poised in midair, she is startled by the sound of the bell as the door closes. Ann faithfully carries out the orders of her anonymous caller, and as promised, the Chinese woman is not surprised. However, instead of giving her the key from the board behind her chair, she takes one out of a straw basket filled with sewing accessories, where something is moving under a piece of cloth, some kind of bird, perhaps.

Confident that the mystery is about to be solved, Ann climbs the dimly lit staircase, decorated with faded wallpaper, and has no trouble finding the hallway on the third floor. She opens the door of room 306 and gropes for the light switch. When the overhead light flickers feebly several times, she notices that she is in one of those corner rooms whose shape she had tried to imagine from outside. Approximately four meters wide at its base, where the door is located, the room tapers off in such a way that at least one half of its surface is unusable. Near the base of the triangle, arranged along the length of the two sharply angled walls, are a few essential pieces of furniture: a single bed flanked by a night table on one side, and on the other, near the rust-stained sink, a dressing table with a tarnished mirror above it. Both the walls in the narrow part of the room have windows, and pushing aside the curtains, Ann notices that one of them has been walled up with cement. The other faces the intersection, with a view of the phone booth through the G of the neon sign, the last letter of the word Cheng. A manila folder has been conspicuously placed on the dressing table. Ann opens it. It contains a thick pile of manuscript pages, covered with Captain Walton's easily recognizable handwriting. At first she thinks that he has secretly written a romance novel like the kind she and Brigitte produce for his collection, and that he's letting her be the first to read it, which is certainly very nice of him. But if that's the surprise, it is hard to account for the elaborate production around her.

Intrigued, but also prepared to be disappointed, she flops down on the black vinyl stool and starts to read the first lines of the manuscript.

On Tuesday, September 8, 1821, in an abandoned house in London, the bodies of two young people were discovered, later identified as Teresa Hobster, a poor streetwalker in Soho, and John William Polidori . . .

Ann winces. This affair is taking a morbid turn that she finds unpleasant. Obviously it concerns neither a birthday dinner nor a romance novel, in which any form of violence is forbidden.

. . . doctor in medicine from the University of Edinburgh barred from the medical profession two years ago, prosecuted by the court of justice for gambling debts. Both had disappeared a month before. It was established by the coroner that Teresa Hobster died of strangulation and Polidori, of massive doses of laudanum. It was also surmised, though never proved, that one had murdered the other before committing suicide. The matter was closed. Among the few possessions of the deceased found in the house, a manuscript in Polidori's handwriting was held for a while in the police archives. In 1827 his family tried to reclaim this manuscript, after having seen the inven-

117

tory, but it was discovered that it had vanished. You have before you the complete version of this document. Take it with you, familiarize yourself with it, and above all, keep it in a safe place. Do not mention it to anyone whomsoever, until you are given the signal.

This preliminary warning leaves Ann perplexed. The nature of the joke escapes her, not to mention its humor. She closes the folder, deciding to postpone her reading until later, puts it under her arm, and leaves the room without turning off the light. What a strange evening.

"Did you find what you were looking for?" asks the Chinese woman at the reception desk.

"Yes, thank you. Tell me, has Mr. Polidori lived here for a long time?"

"Oh, he doesn't live here. He only comes around every now and then. But he pays for the whole year. He left just a little while ago. Stayed the whole day without going out. I even thought he might be ill. You know, it happens a lot in the hotel business—people will take a room and then don't budge for hours. It must be depressing. It scares me a little; you never know what they're up to. I once had a very proper-looking gentleman who stayed in his room like that, all alone, for a week. He didn't want us to make up the room, and when he left, well, he had relieved himself all over the place. It was disgusting, took an entire day to clean it up. We're also afraid that people might commit suicide, or that they're in hiding. Thieves, murderers, you never know; we always ask to see their identification, but they have fake ones. But Mr. Polidori, he's not a problem."

"Do you think you could describe him to me?" Ann asks and immediately regrets her question, noting that the fat woman, suddenly attentive, is eyeing her with suspicion.

"But you do know him, don't you?"

"Yes, of course. It's just that . . . It's just that, you understand, the last time I saw him, he talked about shaving off his beard, and I wanted to know . . ."

"His beard?"

Ann realizes she's made another blunder. Obviously Captain Walton doesn't have a beard, and if he's been frequenting the hotel for a long time . . .

"Oh," she replies, "I guess whenever he sees me, he wears a fake one. He loves to play practical jokes."

She leaves without waiting for a reply.

CHAPTER XIX

The taxi is parked in front of the hotel. The rain hasn't let up. Ann considers walking away, but almost mechanically she opens the door, sinks into the backseat, and the driver starts up the engine without even asking her destination. During the ride she vainly attempts to read a few pages of the manuscript, taking advantage of a street lamp or while stopping for a red light; she succeeds only in tiring her eyes. She starts to light a cigarette. Without turning around, the driver taps his finger on the dividing window that separates them, then points to the NO SMOKING sign next to the meter. Ann nervously crumbles the cigarette between her fingers.

By the time she gets out of the taxi in front of her building, the rain has stopped. The air is now pleasantly cool.

On her way up to the fourth floor, where her flat is located, she looks at herself in the elevator mirror. In this light she looks deathly pale, even when she's looking well, which is presently not the case. Her features are drawn and her hair is a mess. She's afraid that Jim might surprise her by waiting in front of her door; not that it's ever happened before, but nearly every time she takes the elevator she imagines that it could happen. And if she knows Jim, the day it does happen, it'll be exactly at a time like this, when all she wants is to be left alone. True, the code outside the front door of the building had been changed three weeks ago and Jim doesn't know the new one. But then, the young Chinese in Ray-Bans managed to get inside.

As she undresses she makes some coffee and brings it into her room. She slips on a terry-cloth robe that used to be white, but turned a pinkish purple after an unfortunate passage in the washing machine. She lies down on the bed and automatically stirs the coffee with her spoon even though it has not been sweetened. Then she opens the manila folder.

She begins by rereading the first page, without really understanding why Captain Walton (if, in fact, it is him, but it must be him—it's in his handwriting) has recopied the manuscript of a doctor who died in 1821. Why, with this absurd lead, is he letting her in on this enormous secret, and does he rent a room in some fleabag hotel in the suburbs using this doctor's name?

Turning the page, she frowns. She must continue. She becomes even more baffled as she reads on. The author of the manuscript, whether he is the so-called Polidori or Walton, presents himself as a man who's at the end of his rope, which at first is easily explained by his impending suicide. But he claims to be forty years old, which doesn't apply to Walton, who is older, nor to Polidori, who is apparently younger. And all this about a laboratory, invisible enemies, and suddenly, on the second page, it's neither Polidori nor Walton, but Victor Frankenstein who is writing. Ann doesn't understand at all. Naturally, this name conjures up a cloud of images: the face of the actor Boris Karloff, with those screw bolts in his neck—electrodes, no doubt—his greasy bangs, his heavy eyelids, his woundlike mouth, all in black and white, like a prewar American film. Jim adored that type of thing; he had even taken her to see a retrospective at the National Film Theatre, but she's not sure if she saw the real Boris Karloff. So many actors who came after him had copied his makeup, his heavy step, and wore the same animal-skin costume. However, unlike many of the people in the audience, she knew that Frankenstein was not this familiar monster's name—immortalized by a famous performance, hundreds of films and comic books—but the name of his creator, a mad scientist whose face, on the other hand, she cannot recall in the film. She also knows that before becoming a popular myth, *Frankenstein* was a novel, written in the nineteenth century by Mary Shelley, the wife of the poet.

She soon realizes that she'll have to read this book to judge how the text by the so-called Polidori, fictitiously attributed to Frankenstein himself, varies from the official version. Resolving to fill this literary gap right away, and somewhat irritated by the string of private jokes, most of which escape her, she reads on nonetheless. The entire beginning strikes her as tedious; she leafs through it without enthusiasm, only lingering over the episode of the night spent by the narrator and his schoolmates in the abbey. It reminds her of similar experiences: those sessions of verbal improvisation—like the Surrealists' *cadavre exquis*—in the country, with Jim and his friends. Yet, by the next day, after that shared excitement and uncontrollable laughter, they could not remember anything more precise than Frankenstein had on the night spent in the abbey: fragments of anecdotes, rendered absurd by the flow of words, which had been carried by the ebbing tide, and left stranded on the shore of the evening; the sublime memory of a wondrous experience that they had lived through together, out of which nothing remained but the empty pass-

121

words. Ann fully understands this nostalgia, of never wanting to completely dissociate oneself, lose track of the people with whom one has shared such moments. But now, there are no more passwords possible with Jim, nor with any of his friends.

The telephone rings. It's Brigitte, who as usual doesn't wait for a hello, doesn't apologize for calling so late, only tells her to come over to her place. They're having a great time —they're all racking their brains, trying to improve the flimsy plot of *The Starry Nights of Vanessa*. Ann hesitates, but she wants to finish reading the manuscript. Also, if she does go there, she might reveal the secret by asking Brigitte if she knows about the latest obsession of their employer, and if she has anything to do with it. Ann prefers to say that she's tired and promises, before hanging up, to drop by the following day.

The next part of the manuscript isn't any more entertaining. Once again, she lacks the essential references. Beyond the passage about the English tourists, which she likes but which is all too brief, there are the same old repetitive deaths and resurrections, cadavers being lugged around, cavalcades in the corridors, doors being pushed open, and private jokes that she doesn't understand. Monotonous. It's the typical cliché of the story written in one night, in a dire situation. What a disappointment. Ann vainly waits for the emergence of a monster that corresponds to the traditional cinematic image and is more puzzled by the time she reaches the end than when she'd begun. Exhausted as well. She drops the folder at the foot of her bed, switches on the answering machine, which she hasn't even played back since she returned—too bad—and drifts off to sleep.

CHAPTER XX

She wakes up late. Since the bookstores and the libraries are closed on Sundays, she telephones a few of her friends who might own a copy of *Frankenstein*. But they either don't answer or reply politely that they don't have the book, surprised by her sudden curiosity about such an out-of-date novel. She vows that in the future she will associate with people who are more cultured.

She leaves her apartment. Outside, the sun is shining. A fairly good-looking young man approaches her, but she brushes him off sweetly. "Maybe another time," she tells him. Crossing the Albert Bridge, she walks at a leisurely pace toward Brigitte's apartment in Chelsea. On the way, she stops in a French pastry shop to buy some croissants. The croissants make her think about a vacation. Why not go to France for a few days? To the Riviera? She could sit in an outdoor café every morning—she remembers one in particular, on a little square, like the one in Catania where she used to meet Jim. There would be swinging garden chairs covered with flowered fabric; she would have café au lait with croissants. Then later she'd change to a straighter chair and work for several hours in the sun, sitting at a fake-marble table. In a week or ten days she'd be able to finish *The Fickle Beauty*, which is due next month. The only problem would be typing it. She can't picture herself typing in a French outdoor café. The noise would disturb the tranquillity of siesta time; the Don Juans in their open shirts would be leaning over her shoulder and asking her what she was writing. And to write it out by hand—when she'd just have to type it up later—would be a waste of time and violate the principles she had set for herself when she'd begun to work for Captain Walton. She only has to produce one romance novel every three months, and she earns enough to live the way she pleases. But if she finishes one off in a month, she can have the next two months free. To carry out this plan, once the outline has been established, the text has to be composed directly on the typewriter. She'd be better off finishing the book in London, sticking to a strict schedule (which means spending hours with Brigitte elaborating on complicated work schedules, considerably cutting into the time that should be used for planning) and taking a vacation afterward.

The rules of the series, spelled out in a little brochure for the in-house writers that hardly ever leaves her desk, provide a formula for books of the same genre, subject to slight modifications, such as the name of the hero, certain mishaps, the time period, and the geographical location. Although the names and the details of the plot are left up to the authors, Captain Walton is the one to choose the period and the place, with the help of synoptic charts outlining the history of the world during the last two centuries, as well as a world map that hangs in his office, studded with little flags that mark the allotment of territories used in the series.

As a result, Ann's third novel has been set at the beginning of the nineteenth century, in France and Italy. Thus, the fickle beauty, whose name is Bernadette, is one of those rare flowers from the highest ranks of Parisian society during the Restoration. There are carriages, crinolines, and outings in the Bois de Boulogne. In the first chapter her parents fix her engagement to Amédée des Ormes, a young man of equally aristocratic lineage, but who is terribly boring. Bernadette's virginity is beyond reproach, for all the novels published by Captain Walton are exemplary in their chasteness. This is actually the hardest and, at the same time, the most amusing part of the job: being forced to imagine passionate intrigues in which sex is strictly forbidden. According to custom—and the brochure—the novels must end in marriage, and one is free to imagine, if need be, that it is also consummated. However, this depravity only occurs in the half page following the last sentence of the twelfth and final chapter—and undoubtedly in the frustrated and feverish imaginations of the famous readers whose tastes and demands Walton claims to understand, and which he obliges his writers to respect to the letter. It is, however, expected—or rather tolerated—that in chapter six, an unforeseen and romantic circumstance will force the hero and heroine into an intimate situation so that they may, as a result, "unknowingly exchange kisses." Upon reading this paragraph in her brochure, Ann smiled and asked her employer how, in his opinion, two people could unknowingly exchange kisses.

"Ah, but that's for you to figure out!" he had replied. "No one is obliged to include sex in my novels; that clause was practically imposed upon me by our friend Brigitte, and I have to admit that our readers seem satisfied. But it's optional. In fact, it's the only one that is, and you can easily omit it. It's the one final kiss that is sacred. The one at the altar, or at least somewhere nearby, and on the lips! However, if you do leave out the kiss in chapter six, I imagine that our readers will be disappointed, since they're accustomed to it. But once, every now and then, won't hurt them—they'll just eagerly await our next publication."

Ann had said that she had nothing against kissing on the lips, even in chapter six, but to her knowledge, this was a conscious act, at least from the point of view of the protagonists.

"No rapes, please!" the captain had protested. "That's disgusting. And besides, deliberate acts, you know . . . There are a lot less of them than you'd think. After all, nothing proves that we're not in the process of unknowingly exchanging kisses, you and I."

Following this conversation, Ann carefully studied the sixth chapter of several of the books in the series Walton had given her as a present on her way out the door. Most of the time, the authors worked their way around the problem by interpreting "unknowingly" as "dutifully," shamelessly resorting to a situation where, like fugitives who don't want to be recognized by their pursuers, they are forced to hide their faces by pretending to kiss. In the most daring of these books this compulsory kiss would degenerate into a "French kiss": lips would part, tongues would intertwine, and a delicious warmth would flood the girl's breast. The story was inevitably told from her point of view.

With the fickle beauty, Bernadette, Ann intends to use a method in chapter six that has never been attempted in the history of the series: hypnosis. At the beginning of the story Bernadette has sneaked away from a ball where Amédée was languidly stepping on her toes. She meets a very handsome young man named Gérard, a poet, who falls madly in love with her, and they flee to Italy together, living a bohemian life in carefree, simple poverty. Chapter three is a transposition of Ann's trip to Catania with Jim a year ago, into the conventional and anachronistic jargon of the series. However, since the end of this holiday is still a painful memory for her, the story takes a very different turn with the emergence of a third character, a friend of Gérard's. This Tim Bishop, an international champion boxer and an ostentatious dandy as well, pays a visit to the lovers, showers them with gifts, and both disturbs and attracts the innocent heroine. In chapter six, which Ann has put off, the couple will be drawn into a hypnosis session, where Tim and Bernadette will exchange kisses.

When she had shown this synopsis to Captain Walton two weeks ago, Ann was afraid he'd ask her to make some changes. In effect, the more or less marital cohabitation between Bernadette and the poet Gérard violates the rules of the series, even if she provides them with separate rooms and nightgowns buttoned up to the neck. But, contrary to all expectations, the captain kept making little nods of approval as he read, saying, "Ah, that's very good, very good," when he reached the brief description of Tim Bishop, the dandified boxer. Bishop had been inspired by Ann's admiration (inherited from Jim) for Miles Davis: a feline, elegant hero, a capricious and predatory prima donna. Since it was going so well, she suggested that Tim Bishop could possibly be black, but the captain, who obviously wasn't thinking of Miles Davis and probably didn't know who he was anyway, said no, it wasn't necessary, it was fine the way it was. "Very good. Really, very good," he repeated several times with a pensive air. He also thought that the hypnosis was an excellent idea and then suddenly launched into a pedantic speech about how mesmerism had come into vogue at the end of the eighteenth century.

CHAPTER XXI

When Ann finds Brigitte, she's just getting out of bed, nursing a migraine. Her basement apartment looks like the morning after a high-society orgy: cigarette butts stained with lipstick strewn about the cream-colored carpet, lamps still lit that hadn't been turned off during the night. The living room, smartly stripped of its furniture, smells of stale tobacco, a mixture of perfumes, and a musty odor. It also reeks of a staged event—the pictures have been taken off the wall and turned around, so that only the frames are visible to the guests.

Reemerging from the bathroom, where she had turned on the faucets for her bath, triggering bizarre noises from the decrepit plumbing, Brigitte steps over the typed pages stained with various liquids. "Oh, what pigs!" She sighs, and starts to gather up the scattered manuscript of *The Starry Nights of Vanessa*. Kneeling down, barefoot, she reads a few sentences aloud and laughs, running her hands through her hair. In the morning light her scar is more noticeable. Embarrassed, Ann averts her gaze. She goes over to open the basement window, and raises the awning, happy to air out the room.

A former model, Brigitte was left with a very visible scar on her right cheek from a car accident. At first she wore her hair draped over one eye like Veronica Lake, then renounced her profession and recycled her talents by churning out romance novels for Captain Walton. Ann is very fond of her, and admires the fact that her accident has not made her bitter. She also likes the quaint way Brigitte always knows what is fashionable. Jim used to jokingly refer to her as the "swinging London" type.

Having collected her manuscript, Brigitte goes back into the bathroom and turns off the faucets. It doesn't stop the racket, which sounds like someone scraping the pipes with a set of metal hooks, but Brigitte gives a long sigh of relief once she is in the tub. Ann checks to make sure that no one has used the electric coffeepot as an ashtray, since it's sitting on the carpet in the living room, and starts to prepare some coffee. Brigitte shouts that there are no more filters, but Ann makes do with some cotton she finds in the bathroom closet. Then, after a cursory glance at the kitchen, discouraged by the mountain of dirty dishes piled in the sink, she finds a glass used to hold toothbrushes, pours the coffee into it, and brings it to Brigitte.

Her friend takes a sip and makes a face. Throwing her head back, she completely immerses herself in the bathtub. Her hair is swirling in the water; she massages her head, then resurfaces, letting out a deep breath.

"Brigitte . . ." Ann begins.

"Yes?"

"You haven't, by any chance, read *Frankenstein*?"

"*Frankenstein*, the novel?"

"Yes, by Mary Shelley."

"It's funny that you should ask me that. Look over there on the floor, near the laundry basket. It's got to be there."

Ann bends down, pushes aside a wet towel, and picks up the book. On the green cover is a picture of a hideous character with a scarred face, very different from the Boris Karloff monster. Under the title, in large gothic letters is:

OR The MODERN PROMETheus
The 1818 Text

All the way at the bottom is the name of the author, Mary Wollstonecraft Shelley, above the notice, in small roman type, "complete edition, edited and annotated by James Rieger."

"I noticed it earlier, when I came into the bathroom. Somebody must have left it here last night—there were so many people. Anyway, it's the first time I've ever seen it. Why are you so interested in this book?"

"Someone told me about it," Ann replies cautiously. "Can I take it?"

"Go ahead. If anyone asks for it, I'll tell them you have it."

Sitting on the toilet seat, Ann leafs through the book, a university press paperback edition, full of notes on the bottom of each page. She notices some annotations written in pencil and passages that have been underlined. Closing her eyes to keep the shampoo from stinging, Brigitte massages her scalp, her arms held up in a self-consciously graceful pose.

When Ann first arrived, she'd considered informing her friend of the whole story. But now it is clear that Brigitte won't tell her a thing. She knows the captain much better than Ann does; it's hardly a coincidence that a copy of *Frankenstein* is lying around her bathroom. Better to play the game, and try to get her friend to talk without actually giving herself away.

"You know," she finally blurts out—like someone who has been twisting around in a seat for ten minutes before deciding what to say—"you know, it's the captain who suggested I read it."

"Read what?" Brigitte says, engrossed in her shampoo.

"Frankenstein."

"Oh, really? Now he's recommending books to you? Be careful."

She plunges her head underwater and shakes out her hair to rinse it. Coming back up to the surface, she continues, giggling, "If he offers you candy, refuse. He's an old lecher."

Being a few years older and supposedly more experienced, Brigitte enjoys treating Ann like an innocent little sister, describing a world of satyrs ready to jump on her.

"It's disgusting," replies Ann dryly, "to rinse your hair in the bathwater. Hasn't anyone ever told you that?"

"Yes, but the shower sprays all over the place, so I use it as little as possible."

"Have you seen him recently?"

"Frankenstein?"

"Walton."

"No, he must be away. He wasn't there on Friday, and neither were you. Which is strange. Admit it, you were together."

Every Friday, in Mecklemburgh Gardens, in his office filled with Chinese curios, Captain Walton holds a meeting for the authors of his series. The purpose of this weekly ritual is strictly social: during tea and scones with raisins, they exchange news about their heroines as if they were real people who were unfortunately unable to attend the meeting. On her first visit, shepherded by Brigitte, Ann (who had paged through one of Brigitte's romance novels at her home) was extremely surprised to see the authors. Brigitte had never spoken of them, and from the look of the books, she had imagined a group of idealistic young women, and perhaps some older incestuous couples. She had attributed her friend's inventive snobbery to having chosen a livelihood and a milieu far removed from the sort of people with whom, as a rule, she would usually socialize. And here she had found herself in the company of a half dozen young women, of whom at least four were pretty and the other two, elegant, dressed in the latest styles, the kind worn in the world of fashion, the movies, or public relations. Ann had been intimidated by their casual manner, and even by their pseudonyms, which they used as often as possible and which sounded like the assumed names of courtesans of *La Belle Époque*.

She had yet to make the acquaintance of Captain Walton, this impeccably dressed little man, with the old-fashioned elegance of a government minister. He was engrossed in a conversation concerning the fate of Priscilla Darryl-Kenna (the Darryl-Kenna crystal heiress) in the fairy-tale kingdom where her fiancé, Enguerrand de Lastours, had suddenly become addicted to gambling. Since Laura Fitzlowins, the author responsible for the destiny of this young aristocrat, lacked the necessary knowledge of casino games, the captain had launched into a lecture, full of personal anecdotes about incredible card stunts, memorable scams, and dear friends of his who had blown their brains out one sweet summer night dressed in their tuxedos.

As early as this first meeting, Ann had discovered the resourceful imagination of her future employer. She paid him another visit with Brigitte, submitting a synopsis, which her friend, like an attentive mother, had closely supervised. Before long she had written her first romance novel.

That was six months ago. Ever since, she's regularly attended the Friday teas, having made friends with the other young women who make up Captain Walton's little circle. She also pays him a personal visit from time to time. Whenever she's in the neighborhood, she goes up to the first floor of 18 Mecklemburgh Gardens, and chats with the secretary, who immediately shows her into the comfortable office of a country gentleman nostalgic for the British colonies of the Far East. The captain is usually busy making telephone calls concerning the ironing of his T-shirts in Melbourne (T-shirts!), Stock Exchange transactions in Reykjavik, or the weather in East Java, subjects that he discusses with her afterward in great detail. He gets her to talk about herself as well, without asking questions or playing the role (that he nevertheless would be inclined to play) of the doting uncle to whom the clever niece confides her little stories. No, he always remains discreet, affable, and attentive, inspiring her trust while at the same time making her uneasy. Ann thinks that he could have been a father confessor or a psychoanalyst, or some kind of court priest with all his affected benevolence, curiosity, and eloquent charm. Not a military man, at any rate, despite the fact that he seems attached to this title. Or then again, perhaps he is. Captain Walton is quite possibly one of those officers, the power behind the general staff, who actually pulls the strings, protected by a civilian activity as innocent as publishing romance novels, betraying government secrets to the Far East, based on his fondness for duplicity rather than any ideological conviction.

At times she reproaches herself for confiding in him, but she always ends up going back. And Brigitte, who teases her about it, also pays him similar visits. Ann was somewhat disturbed the day she found herself actually lying. Chatting about her day on the phone with Brigitte, she'd said nothing about having tea with Captain Walton in Mecklemburgh Gardens. No reason to hide this; yet she'd hidden it anyway, inventing an errand to fill the gap in her day. And what proof does she have that Brigitte isn't lying to her as well? She pictures herself running into Brigitte in the doorway or in the waiting room, where the secretary sits, each one using the same excuse: "Oh, I happened to be in the neighborhood, so I just dropped by to say hello," which would be the absolute truth. But then why this embarrassed and apologetic tone in their voices?

Besides, disregarding the insidious charm that he exerts on them, there is still something suspicious about Captain Walton's business. Ann doesn't know much about the publishing circle that specializes in genre novels, producing two new titles per series a month. While she lacks a means of comparison, the surprise of her first visit must be due to something more than naïveté. Where did these obviously wealthy young women come from? Why do they gravitate every Friday to an affable, smiling officer who serves them tea? And what about the generous sums given in exchange for a manuscript, when in fact, there is no proof that the captain's authors are qualified to write books in the first place? For they are extremely well paid. Ann knows an acquaintance of Jim's who earns his living cranking out spy novels. The poor guy is not without talent, but he works like a dog, and after ten years of this debasing literary slavery he earns four or five times less money per book than they do.

"What do you expect?" Brigitte says when she tells her the result of her comparative survey. "We're high-class whores. The work is the same, but we're more beautiful, and established in a better neighborhood by a wealthier pimp. That's the only difference."

Ann thinks that this reasoning is economically unsound—
if one high-class whore is worth more than another, it's because the client pays more, and Walton's books are sold at
the same price as those written by Jim's friend. But of course,
they are published regularly and can be found on the stands
of any drugstore or train station. Once, while traveling on the
Hovercraft, she had sat across from a woman reading her
Love Is a Bird in Flight, and had been slightly touched. She
had already received two substantial checks, and would be
getting a third when she turned in *The Fickle Beauty*. It was
all legitimate. What more did she want? It was just odd, that's
all.

CHAPTER XXII

"Would you pass me my robe, please?" Brigitte asks, sitting
up in the tub. She had just rinsed her hair, using the shower
attachment this time. Ann gets up and closes the bathroom
door halfway to reach for the hook where the bathrobe is
hanging. At that moment the phone rings, and she freezes.

"Do you want me to get it? The phone, I mean."

Before Brigitte can reply, the ringing has stopped. In the
next room Ann hears a male voice saying "Hello" as he stifles
a yawn.

"Is there someone in there?" Ann stammers stupidly.

"Hey! Why don't you make yourself right at home?" Brigitte
calls out, still standing in the bathtub. "Yes," she answers
Ann in her normal voice. "A guy. I don't think you know
him."

"No, I don't think so," says the thin guy with curly hair,
advancing toward the doorway, stark naked, with the phone
in one hand and the receiver in the other. "It's for you."

His feet get tangled in the telephone cord that he's dragged in from the other room, and he leans against the doorframe to avoid losing his balance. Ann reaches for the robe, but instead grabs the receiver that he's holding out to her.

"Don't tell anyone about the manuscript," a voice says.

This is absurd, she thinks. It sounds like the young man from the wake-up service. He has that same abrupt manner of hanging up right after the last syllable. Speaking to the dial tone, she mumbles, "I'm not an idiot."

Then, in spite of the obvious contradiction, she says to her companions, "Wrong number."

She's absolutely certain that it was the wake-up service.

"But your name is Ann, right?" the guy says, stroking his beard. And without waiting for an answer, he adds, "Mine's Allan."

They both look at Brigitte, who opens her mouth to say something and then stops herself. Ann suddenly feels ridiculous, fully clothed between these two nudists. She hands the robe to Brigitte, who slips it on, using the collar as a towel to dry her hair.

"I brought some croissants," Ann says. "And I'm going to make some more coffee."

Carrying the phone, she leaves the bathroom and brushes against the young man, who announces, as if it were earth-shattering news, that in the meantime he's going to put on his glasses.

"I can hardly see a thing without them," he explains.

Ann crouches down, dials the number of the wake-up service, and gets a woman's voice that she's never heard before. Naturally, the service operates even during the day, but the employees are on shifts. Besides, it's Sunday. The boy must have called her from his own home, and the idea that this voice has a home somewhere disturbs her. She'll call back tonight.

The three of them squat down on the living-room carpet, Brigitte still draped in her robe, and Allan in baggy corduroy pants and a T-shirt with some cartoon character on it. His glasses rest at the end of his long nose. After getting dressed in the bedroom, he'd stopped in the bathroom to shave with the disposable razor ordinarily used for Brigitte's underarms—she has her legs waxed. He returns holding the volume of *Frankenstein* that Ann had dropped when she had almost rushed to answer the phone.

"Who's reading this?" he asks, biting into his croissant.

"Ann," says Brigitte.

"Well, hope you enjoy it. And I don't mean to sound pedantic, but this one is, by far the best possible edition. There are a lot of different ones, some with better notes, which can be important for a book like this."

"I haven't started it yet," Ann admits.

"So you're interested in Frankenstein too?" Brigitte asks Allan. "It's unbelievable. Ever since last night everyone has been talking to me about that book. Is it the latest trend, or what?"

"That's right," Allan answers. "This summer, it's the Frankenstein look. Animal skins, electrodes, and everything."

He stands up and walks around the room, imitating the plodding gait of movie monsters. The corner of his mouth sags and his eyelids droop, giving him a blank yet bloodthirsty expression.

"And what about the Frankenstein look in the feminine version?" Ann asks, thinking herself very clever. (Will he mention Elizabeth?)

Allan doesn't react. Either he was expecting it, or he's a good actor, or as a last hypothesis, he doesn't know anything about it. He continues to gesticulate, clumsily flapping his arms around in the air, as if rage had deprived him of all muscular coordination, then collapses heavily onto the floor. He springs back up, and resumes his seat in front of the breakfast tray, nearly knocking over the coffeepot.

"You should see his videos," Brigitte tells Ann. "He's made a couple of videos of himself making faces; it's his forte. Some of them go on for almost an hour. His features barely move and still, his expression is constantly changing. It's very scary."

"I love to scare people," Allan confesses good-naturedly.

"Is that why you're interested in Frankenstein?" Ann asks.

"Not in Frankenstein directly, but in Shelley. I was going to do my thesis on him."

"A thesis in what?" Brigitte inquires. "You never told me anything about that."

"In literature. But that was a long time ago. I dropped it."

He throws his arms up in the air, then, miming the descent of falling paper, lets them fall.

"And what do you do now, besides shoot videos of yourself making faces?"

Ann wishes she hadn't asked this question. She envies the ease with which Brigitte is able to strike up conversations with people without getting into the inevitable interrogation about professions, where they live, and all the conventions that she pretends not to care about.

"What do I do now?" Allan repeats, as if he were thinking about the question. "Not much. I play dead."

"Play dead?"

"Yeah. Next weekend, I get to play dead. Last month I was the murderer; it'll be a nice change."

Given Brigitte's surprise, Ann deduces that even if she's just spent the night with Allan, she doesn't know him much better than Ann does, unless she's pretending. Or unless Allan said that for the mere pleasure of disconcerting them;

he seems like the kind of guy who would, the slightly irritating mad-dog type. He probably has no trouble approaching girls on the street, telling them all sorts of farfetched stories.

"Yes," he explains, after enjoying the dramatic impact of his statement. "I go to a hotel in Brighton with a whole group of friends and other people I don't know, but they pay for it. And they pay quite a lot, as a matter of fact. During the weekend there's a crime, generally followed by one or two others; the people who pay are in charge of the investigation. We give them clues, and on Sunday the detective explains everything. Who killed whom, why, and how. It's called a murder party; it's been a great success. The hotel has to turn away people several months in advance."

"How exciting!" Brigitte exclaims mockingly.

"I think I once read an article about it in a magazine," Ann says.

"I wouldn't be surprised. Each time, there's at least one reporter who comes to do a story on it. The people at the hotel are thrilled. It's great exposure."

"And what about you?" Brigitte asks. "Do you know who the murderer is?"

"Yes, especially when it's me. But this time I'll be the first one to die. Nothing to it. I fall off my chair during dinner on Friday night, an ambulance comes, they take me away on a stretcher, and I'm free until Sunday noon. Then I reappear to say hello to everyone and modestly sign a few autographs." He mimes this, somewhat unconvincingly. "The idea is to remain out of sight."

"So where do you go?"

"I still don't know what I'll do this time—it's the first time I get to die. Maybe go back to London, maybe take a trip to the coast if the weather's nice. Or else I'll stay in my room, sit in front of the mirror, and rehearse some new faces. Or reread *Frankenstein*. We'll see. You want to come along?"

"Not this weekend," Brigitte says. "I've got to finish *Vanessa*. But another time, yes, I'd love to. Preferably in autumn. Brighton is a living hell in the summer."

Allan turns to Ann. "What about you?"

"Why not?"

"And *The Fickle Beauty*?" Brigitte reminds her.

"*The Fickle Beauty* can wait," Allan says firmly. "Really, you should come."

They exchange phone numbers as Brigitte looks on with a sarcastic smile. She doesn't seem to be particularly attached to Allan, and Ann figures that the prospect of an affair between her two friends rather amuses her. Brigitte is generous with her romantic conquests; this also is part of her personality. Ann thinks this sexual liberation is outmoded (in fact, she tells herself smugly that her friend, usually in the know, is actually a little behind the times). Then they discuss *The Starry Nights of Vanessa*, which Brigitte hopes to finish over the weekend and hand in to Walton at the beginning of the week, provided he's back from his trip. They go on to *The Fickle Beauty*. Ann and Brigitte freely combine the two plots, and summarize them to Allan, who laughs heartily. They arrange meetings between their respective characters, which ultimately turn into an orgy.

Allan is somewhat familiar with the story of Vanessa, which, as Brigitte had said on the phone, had already been discussed by her guests the night before. He finds Bernadette's story, which is new to him, quite interesting. One day, he says jokingly to Ann, if she manages to sell the rights to her novel for a movie, he knows the perfect actor to play Tim Bishop, the flashy boxer—one of his friends who's a jazz trumpet player and occasional actor. He's already appeared in two avant-garde films and a TV series, but is above all an exceptionally good trumpet player.

"That's funny," Ann says. "I was actually thinking of someone like Miles Davis."

Brigitte says that she prefers David Bowie, but Allan protests, No, Miles Davis is a much better idea.

"You know who your story reminds me of a little? Lord Byron and the Shelleys."

"Them again!" Brigitte moans. (Ann is thinking the same thing.)

"Hey, I know what I'm talking about. In his time Byron was like Miles Davis: a big star. Opulence, sports cars, cool brilliance, the sudden whims of a superstar, scandals, all of that. . . ."

"I'll have you know," Brigitte remarks, "that those characters are a dime a dozen. The mysterious, dark, and handsome type. A necessary figure perhaps, but not particularly original."

"But still. . . . And besides, there's the boxing, which Byron was supposedly more interested in than poetry. And then that whole love triangle between the fickle beauty, the sweet, simpleminded poet, and the great predator who threatens their relationship. Listen, I'm going to tell you the story of the summer of 1816, on the shore of Lake Geneva."

"Good idea." Ann chuckles.

"You already know it?"

"I've heard a little about it. Someone at school told me."

Either this was an incredible coincidence, or Allan must have read the manuscript. And what did Brigitte have to do with all this?

"Well, I don't know it," she protests. "Tell us!"

"All right. So, it happened in 1816. Percy Bysshe Shelley, the poet by the very same name, had just kidnapped the tender-aged Mary Godwin from her family. He knew her father

quite well—a grumpy philosopher type. They traveled together all over Europe, living on love, just like Gérard and
Bernadette: always on the road, two angelic vagabonds. After
crossing through France, they arrived in Switzerland, were
enraptured by the mountains, quoted Rousseau with tears in
their eyes, gave the finger to Voltaire's statue in Ferney, and
settled in for the summer on the shore of Lake Geneva in a
little cottage called Montalègre. Simple but convenient."

"You certainly are well informed," Brigitte says.

"Why shouldn't I be? Remember, I started a thesis on it.
One morning Lord Byron arrives with great ceremony. Enter
the rock star, disrupting the daily routine of their holiday,
and in violent contrast to the Shelleys' love and peace and
brown-rice tendencies. Oh, I forgot to mention that Percy and
Mary were traveling with their newborn baby, and with Mary's
half sister, Claire."

"She always gets left out," Brigitte observes rather mys-
teriously.

Allan scowls momentarily, then sets his glasses firmly on
the tip of his nose and continues. "It's important to know that
Shelley had a thing about carrying off women in twos. The
first time he got married, the sister of his wife, Harriet, came
along with them, and Claire did the same. The neighbors
imagined all sorts of wicked debauchery, which probably
never occurred; Shelley believed in communal living. Any-
how, Claire, undoubtedly jealous of Mary's handsome poet,
found no better way to prove herself than to try to seduce
England's most famous poet, namely Lord Byron. It happened
in London before the departure—she made up an elaborate
farce with a masked rendezvous, to offer herself to him. But
after two days Byron got tired of Claire and dropped her.
Later on, since he had left for Geneva, she managed to get
closer to the Byron clique through the Shelleys, much to
Byron's horror, although he soon became friendly with Shel-

ley. He moved into a sumptuous villa right nearby, and they all spent the summer together, going boating and writing poetry."

"And so?" Brigitte asks. "Did Mary sleep with Byron?"

"No. I don't think there ever was a chapter six, with the protagonists unknowingly exchanging kisses. But it was a bizarre situation. Mary adored and admired Shelley, who was totally unknown. On the other hand, she found herself constantly in the presence of a poet who was one of the most famous men on earth, and naturally, it affected her. At the same time, despite the differences of personality and fame, Shelley and Byron admired one another. Byron, because he had good taste and no illusions about his celebrity; Shelley, because it came naturally to him and he was not inclined to be jealous. Between the two of them, Mary must not have felt terribly comfortable."

"You're right, it's just like *The Fickle Beauty*," Brigitte teases.

"Every evening," Allan continues, "they would all get together at Byron's, on the terrace of the Villa Diodati. I should also mention that the summer of 1816 was the worst of the century; it never stopped raining. To entertain themselves, they played backgammon, which was called trictrac back then, and read ghost stories translated from German, which was sort of a trend at the time. One night Byron suggested that each of them write a ghost story as a diversion. So they set out to work on it, the four of them. . . ."

"You mean," Ann asks, "Byron, the Shelleys, and Claire?"

"No, not Claire. She was already out of it. Since Byron couldn't stand her, she stayed in Montalègre, pining away and wondering whether she should tell him that she was pregnant. The fourth was Byron's doctor, who also served as his secretary, a certain Polidori."

Startled, Ann suddenly drops one of the empty coffee cups she had been stacking on the tray.

"What's the matter?" Brigitte asks.

Ann apologizes, runs into the kitchen to get a sponge, asking Allan to wait for her to finish the story. She leans against the edge of the sink, trying to think for a minute, then returns to the living room and attempts to make the heavily sweetened coffee stains disappear from the carpet. Allan continues his lesson in literary history.

"Mary was the only one who really kept the bet. Shelley began a story, but quickly realized that he was not comfortable with prose. First he'd write it in verse, and then change it. Anyway, he eventually gave up. There was also some complicated story between Byron and Polidori—I can't remember the details anymore, but if you're interested, I think it's explained very thoroughly in the critical commentary by this American professor. As I recall, Byron began a story about a vampire, which he abandoned and which Polidori retrieved and published, claiming that it was Byron's, who then denied having written it; in short, it's all very confusing and only of interest to historians. As for Mary, she waited the longest to get started, but one night she had a nightmare that was a combination of their conversations on galvanism, the living dead, and those sorts of things, which ultimately yielded the novel *Frankenstein*. She was nineteen. And that's the story."

Allan picks up the book at his feet and pages through it.

"And what about Polidori?" Ann asks. "What happened to him?"

"Not much. He committed suicide several years later. In fact, almost all of them died young. Shelley drowned in 1822, Byron caught typhoid fever in Missolonghi in 1824 or '25. Only Mary survived until the 1850s, and devoted herself to perpetuating Percy's legend. She went on to write a number of novels and essays, but nothing nearly as good as *Frankenstein*. It's a magnificent book, you know."

He begins leafing through it again, and stops at an underlined sentence, which he reads aloud:

"Do not laugh like that, I beg of you!"

"Apparently, Shelley had a very unpleasant laugh and a high-pitched voice," he comments. "He often amused himself by trying to scare people."

On that note, Allan looks at his watch and declares that he's got to get going.

As he slips on his tweed jacket, too heavy for the season, he reminds Ann of her promise to accompany him to Brighton the next weekend. Ann laughs and points out that she's made no promises. Fifteen minutes later, when she's about to leave, Brigitte assures her with a wink that she's scored and that she'll have nothing to complain about if she goes along: Allan is great in bed.

CHAPTER XXIII

She arrives home around four o'clock, slightly depressed by the lazy Sunday mood in the streets. Like every afternoon since the beginning of August.

There are thick clouds hiding the sun, it won't be long before the storm breaks.

As she is about to enter the elevator, the concierge steps out of her glass booth, where she spends the day surveying a control panel that looks like the type one would find in an airplane. Several months ago Ann had refused to participate in the installment costs for a closed-circuit TV, insisted upon by the security-minded tenants. The TV had been installed anyway, her maintenance bill had gone up automatically, and for a long time the concierge had resented her because of her opposition.

"A man was here to see you," she says. "He tapped on the window, but he didn't have the code, so I didn't let him in. I suppose I did the right thing."

"Well, I wasn't home anyway."

"That's what I told him, but he said that he had your key. I also found that a little surprising."

Ann feels her upper lip trembling and bites it. It could only be Jim. But as if she were reading her mind, the concierge, who knows Jim by sight, then adds, "It wasn't your friend. You know, the one who always came around."

"No, of course not," Ann says blankly. "What did he look like?"

The concierge describes a small, dark-haired man, well dressed but unshaven, who had seemed very agitated. He might have been Italian. Ann makes her promise not to let in any strangers who claim to have her key. The concierge tells her that she knows how to do her job, and assumes an offended and vindictive air that stays with Ann all the way to the elevator. She turns her back to the corner where the camera is hidden, then briskly walks down the corridor and closes the door of her flat as if someone were following her.

She spends the rest of the afternoon and evening stretched out on her bed, a box of cookies within arm's reach, reading *Frankenstein*. She had put on a record, but realizes that it doesn't fit in with her reading, and vainly searches for a more appropriate one. Most of the time, however incongruous they might seem, the fortuitous associations between books and musical works are extremely obvious to her. For example, *And Then There Were None* by Agatha Christie and the dances of *Prince Igor*: one of the melodies even assumes the rhythm

145

of the counting rhyme that punctuates the murders perpetrated by the mad magistrate on his island off Devon. But in this case, no. She closes the cover of the stereo.

From the very first page the book surprises her. The narrator is named Robert Walton, the captain of a ship that is approaching the North Pole. If this is the key to the mystery, she has to admit that it falls short of her expectations. As far as Ann is concerned, there is no need to get madly excited just because someone happens to have the same name (a common one, at that) and the same title as a character in a book. No need, for that matter, to try to extract another version of this novel (in which, to top it off, the character in question isn't even mentioned). Besides, even in *Frankenstein*, Captain Walton disappears fairly early. In the beginning he is near the North Pole, feeling somewhat bored on his ship, and so he writes to his sister, telling her about his sailors, complaining about his loneliness—nothing too terribly interesting. One has to wait until the fourth letter, when, off the shores of Arkhangelsk, he rescues a shipwrecked man drifting on an ice floe that is shrinking dangerously in size. After several days the survivor of the shipwreck is feeling better, and although violently melancholic (he's apparently had many misfortunes), strikes up a friendship with the good Captain Walton, to whom he tells his life story (and Walton, in turn, tells it to his sister). The real story begins here: it consists of Victor Frankenstein's memories, religiously recorded by Captain Robert Walton, whose role stops there. Obviously, Ann muses, if Captain Walton (the real one from Mecklemburgh Gardens) had called himself Raskolnikov or Philip Marlowe, perhaps she would have embarked on an even greater adventure. Well, never mind. She continues her reading.

After this preamble, Frankenstein's youth closely resembles the one described in the manuscript, which Ann frequently consults as a means of comparison. Though equally verbose, it does not, however, include any details on his student life, nor the magical night in the abbey. His cousin Elizabeth is present, as well as his little brother, William. On the other hand, Mary Shelley's novel strays from the manuscript (of course it's the manuscript that strays from the novel, but the order of Ann's reading has confused her) at the crucial moment of the monster's creation. Instead of resuscitating a changed Elizabeth, Frankenstein breathes life into a creature fabricated *ex nihilo*, and basically conforms to the vulgar image made popular by the cinema. Ridiculed by mankind, frightened by his ugliness, the monster turns cruel, kills little William, then Elizabeth, and then the friend, Clerval, to avenge his creator, who refuses to give him a companion. And Frankenstein, mad with rage, ends up following him all the way to the North Pole, where after having almost caught up with him, he is rescued by Captain Walton, who reappears in the last chapter to inform his sister of the moral he has derived from this entire somber affair. As a matter of fact, it's almost the same story as the one Frankenstein and Elizabeth tell Mary Shelley in the manuscript.

If she has to compare them, Ann thinks she prefers the real *Frankenstein* to the Polidori-Walton version. Allan was right: the book by this nineteen-year-old girl is magnificent. Slightly dated, of course, with all its emotion, moralizing sermons, pantheistic effusion. But moving, nevertheless, even if it is ridiculous to see the poor monster shedding bitter tears while reading Rousseau and Gibbon, pained by his existence, rejected by all. The poignant sorrow of the last few pages lends a compassionate depth to the story, which was absent from the pedantic text—full of private jokes— that she had read the night before. But still, a comparative study of their literary merits wouldn't get her very far; this business called for questions that a detective might ask. Ann takes a piece of paper and writes in big letters, on the left side of the page:

WHO?

and on the right side:

WHY?

Then she meticulously retraces the capital letters and the question marks, which have become enormous. Finally, under the column WHY? she jots down three names:

> Victor Frankenstein
> John William Polidori
> Captain Robert Walton

Okay, now: a character in a novel (doubled by a narrator in the two versions of this novel); a real person, but one who has been dead for the past century and a half; and finally, a living person whom she knows, but who has inexplicably disappeared several days ago, and who is also a character in the novel, the confidant of the first character.

In all likelihood the manuscript is the work of the third person who wrote or (if she believes him) recopied it in the hotel room where Ann found it. It is already peculiar that Captain Walton (the real one), so fussy about his material needs, should lock himself up in a fleabag hotel to write a second version of the story of Frankenstein. But it is odder still that he attributes it to neither Frankenstein, nor his namesake (whose insignificant role could easily have been developed), but instead to an obscure figure, peripheral to literary history, namely John William Polidori. A biographical note, included in the invaluable introduction by Professor

James Rieger (of the University of Rochester, also author of *The Mutiny Within: The Heresies of P . B . Shelley*) summarizes Polidori's brief existence in these terms:

> He came from a literary family, and had grown up in the Italian expatriate milieu of Soho. His father, Gaetano Polidori, had been the secretary of the poet Alfieri, and his sister would later become the mother of Christina, Dante Gabriel, and William Michael Rossetti—the latter would, in 1876, publish his uncle's diaries.
>
> His literary pretensions, his jealousy of Byron and Shelley, his habit of biting his nails, his "eternal nonsense and *tracasseries*," as Byron put it, were a constant source of friction during the summer of 1816. A swaggering yet timid soul, he once challenged Shelley to a duel, also and most likely because he knew that the poet was a pacifist. At which point Byron proposed to fill in for Shelley, and the incident ended there. Two years later, after a trip to Germany, the young doctor returned to London, where he committed suicide in 1821, leaving behind him two volumes of wretched verse, some unfinished plays, and *The Vampire*, a tale. Published in 1819, born of the famous bet made at the Villa Diodati, this story was attributed to Byron by for quite some time, despite the poet's assertion, in which he stated, "I have a personal grudge against vampires, and the little knowledge I have of their habits would certainly never have inspired me to devote a tale to them, particularly one as bad as this."

The available evidence (James Rieger adds further on) indicates that "poor Polidori," not Byron, was Shelley's interlocutor in the scientific conversation that precipitated Mary's germinal nightmare image of the monster.

At the bottom of the page Ann notes the name of William Michael Rossetti, editor of Polidori's diary, a reference that might be useful if she decides to pursue her research. No sooner has she written the words down than she sits up in bed and smiles. She would have to be crazy to even consider doing research on the basis of a hoax like this. She's got better things to do: for instance, finish *The Fickle Beauty*, which most certainly will not be a masterpiece of narrative prose, but will make enough money for her to live comfortably until the winter; that is, she thinks bitterly, enough to pay her concierge for the closed-circuit TV that gives her the creeps.

She sits down at the bridge table where she keeps her typewriter and, in a folder, the first five chapters. She rereads a couple of pages. Immediately sick of it, she decides that it's too late to get back to work anyway. Since the evening is shot, she might as well devote it to an absurd enigma, but at least an entertaining one. Tomorrow she will see the real Captain Walton and ask him the meaning of all this. She'll show him that had she persevered, she easily would have found the key to the mystery on her own. She'll spell out her clues, her conclusions, and display her talent as a detective, which might even be helpful to her next weekend. She'll definitely go to Brighton with Allan—she likes him. She thinks about calling him right away to accept his invitation and to ask *him* for an explanation. No doubt he knows what's going on. Though perhaps Brigitte doesn't. Ann clearly sensed it this afternoon when it had become a game between Allan and herself, going right over the head of Brigitte, who couldn't understand why everyone was getting so excited about *Frankenstein*. Or else she, too, was acting, but without giving herself away or putting her cards on the table. No, that wasn't like her. In the end Ann doesn't telephone either one.

However, she does call the wake-up service, and after hearing the voice of the young man she knows, she is absolutely certain that it was him this morning. No need to try and trick her. He sounds surprised. Obviously he would never have taken it upon himself to call her like that; and what's more, he doesn't work during the day. He clearly thinks she's crazy, or else he's also playing a role. Of course, it isn't very likely that in a farce, a treasure hunt, or God knows what, the wake-up service would be solicited. But then again, why not? She is so sure that she recognized his voice, and his denials seem so sincere and bewildered that they must be feigned. Perhaps the night before Brigitte had asked him to ring her place on Sunday morning and ask for Ann; he would have accepted, he's an amiable young man. Then it hits her like a boomerang.

"Listen," she says to the young man, "do me a favor. Call 702-9876"—it's Brigitte's number—"now, and just say one thing."

"It's not really allowed, but . . . well, for you . . . What is it?"

She pauses a moment. Ann must show Brigitte that she is manipulating the game and is capable of throwing her off track, if she so desires.

"Just this: 'The girl with the manuscript is going to catch up with you and pass you by. Be careful.' Then hang up immediately."

The young man on the line laughs.

"Hey, is this some sort of espionage?"

"Yeah, that's it."

Then Ann returns to her notes, crosses out the list under the question WHY? and firmly writes, "Robert Walton = J. W. Polidori = Victor Frankenstein." Then she circles the name Polidori and puts another question mark above the whole thing. This is getting her nowhere.

So, what about the motives? WHY?

As for Frankenstein, he's got to be taken at his word, since he *is* the narrator. He simply wants to recount his life, and as he specifically states, to correct the errors of the official version—which he also specifically states that he has inspired.

Suddenly it is easy to guess Polidori's motives. Embittered by the failure of his own works and by the success of Mary, to whom he had virtually given the idea for her bestseller (since he had told a story of this kind in her presence), he in turn wrote his own version of the story, solely to identify himself with Frankenstein and to denigrate Mary, transforming her into a zombie and insinuating that she wasn't the true author of her novel. It's terribly complicated, but it does make sense.

Only Captain Walton remains, and the only possible motive she can ascribe to him is the pleasure of disconcerting her with this fortuitous coincidence of names. Unless he were a descendant of the Walton in the novel. No, of course not. She laughs at herself for having seriously believed it even for one moment; fictional heroes do not have descendants. Or else, a Captain Walton, whom Mary Shelley had personally known, had actually existed in the beginning of the century and she had put him into her novel—it was, after all, a possibility. But even so, why doesn't *that* Walton play any part in the manuscript? And why, when he is obviously the initiator of this whole story, does he disappear without a trace and turn it over to that sinister Polidori? And Brigitte, what does she have to do with all this? And Allan? And herself? Why her? Just what did they expect of her?

CHAPTER XXIV

The telephone wakes her early the next morning. It's Brigitte, asking if she wants to play squash. Still half asleep, Ann declines the invitation, saying that she was planning to go to the British Museum to do some research.

"Research?" Brigitte shrieks. "Why are you doing research? Who put that into your head? Was it Allan, with all that talk about his thesis?" Ann swears that he has nothing to do with it: she simply wants to gather some material for her novel.

"A novel? You're writing a novel? Are you crazy?"

"Yes, I am. Aren't you?"

"Ah," Brigitte says, reassured. "You scared me. I thought you were talking about a real novel with subtle psychological motives and interior monologues. But you're still crazy to try to document *The Fickle Beauty.*"

"Do you know how they lived in Italy at the beginning of the nineteenth century?"

"No more than how they did in St. Petersburg in 1880—no, not really. But why don't you just ask the captain? He knows all that."

"If he's not away on another trip."

"That's possible," Brigitte admits. "He must be in Italy, in 1820, gathering material for you."

She tries again, insisting that Ann should forgo her research for the squash game. Then, to make amends, she offers to come pick her up, since she has the car, and drop her off at the British Museum. Ann falls back to sleep, wondering whether it wouldn't be more fun to go play squash after all. Everything that happened that weekend—the Chinese hotel, the manuscript—now seems far away, unreal. But she'd still like to know how Brigitte had reacted to the call from the wake-up service—if he had actually called her.

Brigitte wakes her up again when she rings the bell. She knows the entry code to the building. It is almost the same scene as the previous night, except it takes less time, since Ann settles for a shower. Brigitte keeps going in and out of the bathroom to the living room, shrieking every time Ann splashes her, looking at herself in the clouded mirror over the sink, then leafing through *The Fickle Beauty* manuscript, reciting aloud the passage that Ann had found so irritating when she reread it the night before.

"That's enough," she cries, slightly annoyed. "That's enough, that's enough," Brigitte echoes, but she stops reading. Not a word about the wake-up service. Perhaps she hadn't been home last night. Or else she had reasons for keeping it to herself. Ann suddenly thinks of the *Frankenstein* manuscript and is afraid that her friend might notice it. She remembers having left it at the foot of her bed. She quickly finishes her shower, but the cardboard folder is still there; Brigitte hasn't touched it. Ann is disturbed by her own sense of relief.

In the car, Brigitte launches into a lively conversation, casually saying that she'd spent the evening at home working, but makes no mention of a suspicious phone call. She drops Ann off in front of the British Museum and pulls away with an exaggerated, friendly wave.

Once in the library, Ann begins by digging through the catalogues. There are two and a half drawers crammed with reference cards of books devoted to Shelley. Mary, his wife, only gets half a drawerful, but it's still discouraging. She tries Walton, and finds four entries with the first name of Robert (two of whom are jurists, judging from the titles of their many publications), but not a single captain. Too bad. Polidori remains (John William), whose tale *The Vampire* has been published in several editions. She notes the reference number, as well as that of the *Journal*, published thanks to William Michael Rossetti. Once her request slips have been sent to the basement, she sits down in her assigned seat to wait for the books.

An elderly man wearing spats takes notes from a huge book, his tongue sticking out. Judging from the thickness of the pages that have already been turned and the stack of paper used, Ann begins to think that he's carefully recopying the entire book. Which is surprising, since there's a sign at the beginning of each row stating that a photocopying service is available for all library users. She's surrounded by other scholars busily at work: those perpetual student types, badly dressed. One is quivering with tics, and the other two are albinos. Two out of eight people, that's statistically abnormal, she calculates. However, far from being depressed, Ann realizes that she looks out of place—in a flattering way—among this unattractive group. Not only because she's young and pretty, but because instead of pursuing a methodical and sterile task, she now finds herself in an unusual, even romantic situation (perhaps dangerous as well) in which she will carry out some important research without anyone's knowledge.

The books she has requested finally arrive at the table.

The Vampire is part of an anthology of Gothic short stories, augmented by a lengthy introduction from which she gleans little more than what she already knew from Professor Rieger. The actual story is only about twenty pages, and not much to get enthusiastic about. It tells of an evil nobleman, Lord Ruthven, who behaves the way vampires traditionally do. Moreover, the author of the preface acknowledges that the writer lacks imagination and concedes a merely historical interest in his tale, emphasizing, while on that subject, that the Lord Ruthven character was directly inspired by Lord

Byron (to whom *The Vampire* was in fact attributed, although Byron denied it). That was all. Ann now unties the slim volume of the *Journal*, whose shredded binding has been kept together with string rather than glue. First, she reads the introduction by William Michael Rossetti, the nephew, who presents the document as a lesson in literary history and tries to revive the memory of his uncle. Chiefly known through Byron's acid remarks in his own journal, Polidori was unfairly portrayed as a peevish, dull person—while at age nineteen, he had been the youngest to graduate from the medical school of the University of Edinburgh. The preserved fragments of his personal dramas were worthy of attention, not to mention his immortal *Vampire*. . . . Enough of this.

However, on page 32 the Rossetti nephew reaches the tragic death of his hero, and solemnly announces that he shall simply reproduce the report made by the coro . . .

. . . ner, Ann says to herself, looking up at the next page in the hopes of finding some mention of the name Captain Walton.

But pages 33–34 and 35–36 are missing, half an inch from the binding, as if someone had torn them out with a ruler.

Ann doesn't know whether to be angry or to rejoice. Putting aside the hypothesis of a coincidence, if someone is set on destroying the works in the British Museum to prevent access to a document, that means the document in question contains a serious lead, and that her intuition was right: one way or another, Captain Walton is involved in Polidori's suspicious death. It hardly matters that he only exists in a novel, or that a hundred and sixty-three years later, she rapidly calculates—he most definitely has something to do with it.

To clear her conscience, she leafs through the book, page after page, to make sure that no others have been removed; that is, no others of any interest. Unless, of course, the mysterious vandal had been counting on this type of reaction and had maliciously left some decisive evidence at her disposal. She forces herself to at least skim through the diary, which in spite of Rossetti's assertions, strikes her as deadly boring: played trictrac, visited the home of Rousseau, dined at Madame de T——s. Captain Walton is never mentioned.

Ann returns the book to the counter and leaves the library. Stopping at three rare-book stores near the museum, she asks for Polidori's diaries and journals, not really hoping to find them, but rather to hear some bookseller grumble, "What is it with this Polidori chap anyway? You're the second person this morning to ask about him." Her efforts are in vain—everyone tells her that they've been out of print for a long time but that she'd have no trouble finding them at the British Museum.

It is getting cloudy. She takes the bus home in the early afternoon. Feeling tired, she allows herself a short nap. She doesn't bother to unplug the answering machine, or listen to the messages that might have been left during her absence.

CHAPTER XXV

She wakes up in a sweat, probably because of the heat and an approaching storm. The open window knocks loudly; the papers from the bridge table are strewn all over the carpet. And she'd had a nightmare, inspired by her visit to the British Museum. She was accused of having torn out the pages of a book. The elderly scholar with the spats who had sat next to her that morning was doggedly following her, waving an illegible reference card, with Brigitte alongside him. Her mind still foggy, Ann thinks that she should have notified someone about the two missing pages; otherwise the next reader—if there ever was another reader—might notice it. They'd look back in the archives for the reference card of the last borrower, find her name, trace it back to her . . .

She makes a face, gets up, takes off her soaked T-shirt, and wearing only her panties, picks up the pages scattered by the wind. Then she closes the window, presses her naked breasts against the pane, and takes a deep breath. How lucky she is not to have any houses facing hers, only a construction site across the street. The sky is mauve, with traces of black. Uneasy on her feet, she returns to the middle of the room and slides down onto the floor, near the bed, where the cardboard folder containing the manuscript still lies. She halfheartedly picks it up and opens it.

Instead of the manuscript pages, there is nothing but a ream of white paper.

For a moment Ann is completely stupefied. The first idea that occurs to her is that she's been dreaming—that this whole business about the manuscript, Frankenstein, Polidori, the visit to the Chinese hotel, the corner room, are all part of her fitful sleep—like the conspiracy between Brigitte and the old scholar in spats, who tried to make her return the pages that she hadn't torn out. The London summer must be getting to her.

As her eyes wander around the room she notices the paperback edition of *Frankenstein*. And some papers on Mary Shelley that, as far as she can recall, have no reason to be there. Someone has clearly stolen the manuscript.

The cleaning woman. She comes in once a week, and not on Mondays. But supposing she had come this past Monday—sometimes she changes her day without notice, and she has the key—why would she have stolen the manuscript? Or thrown it in the trash bin, perhaps? No, she always puts everything back in place with meticulous care. And besides, there's the ream of typing paper with exactly the same thickness.

Brigitte.

Of course, it's Brigitte, who had had plenty of time to make the switch while she'd been taking a shower. It could only be her. But why? Assuming it was an impromptu practical joke, it doesn't make sense. It was definitely a calculated plan: Brigitte had come with the white paper in her big gym bag, under the clothes and the rackets. Unless . . . Ann examines the stack of typing paper sitting on her table. But she no longer remembers how thick it had been the night before, or if the pile had diminished. Therefore, it's impossible to decide whether the theft was premeditated or spontaneous.

She unplugs the answering machine and dials her friend's number. "We're sorry, all the circuits are busy at this time," a computerized voice answers. "Please try your call again." She calls back right away and gets the same response.

The sky darkens. Outside, the pigeons fly rapidly in circles, crossing paths and swerving away from one another at the last minute, flapping their wings to avoid a collision. There is something panicky about the figures they trace. The coming storm, no doubt. Recently there had been one almost every night; nothing gets washed away, nor does the humidity drop. She flings the window wide open and leans out to observe the deserted street. It's a quiet neighborhood, too quiet, surrounded by recently constructed buildings full of offices. But, at a quarter to nine, they are long since empty. A jogger passes, taking small strides toward the park. Just in front of her apartment, almost directly below her window, a blue Triumph pulls up and parks at an angle. The driver turns off the motor. Not another sound in the street, except for the piercing cries of the birds. She waits for someone to get out of the car and slam the door, the sound of footsteps echoing on the sidewalk. But no one gets out. From where she stands she can see only the roof of the car. After waiting a while longer, she concludes that she's acting like an imbecile, goes back to the phone by the bed, and redials Brigitte's number. The computerized voice again. She hangs up and returns to the window. She should really listen to her answering machine.

The car hasn't budged. Perhaps the driver got out while Ann was on the phone. He would have had to close the door very softly; otherwise she would have heard it. You can hear sounds very clearly from the street, and she had been listening; she had even considered moving near the window with the telephone, but it seemed too ridiculous, so she hadn't. Now she regrets it. She thinks about going downstairs to the lobby: the car is parked right in front of the entrance of the building; she would be able to look through the glass door without being seen, to find out whether there was anyone inside. But by the time she left and took the elevator, if there was no one there, it wouldn't mean a thing. If she were on better terms with the concierge, she could call to ask if there was someone inside the blue Triumph parked just outside the building, and visible from her booth. But this solution is out of the question: the woman would think she was crazy and would never let her forget it.

Ann realizes she's trembling. Instead of moving away from the window to get a clean blouse from the closet, she pulls the damp T-shirt on the carpet toward her and slips it on. Her nipples are erect with excitement.

She looks back and forth, from the street—where no one is in sight—to the telephone, both hoping and fearing that it will ring. The answering machine is too far away for her to listen to it right now. So she keeps trying to call Brigitte, without moving from the window this time, and upon hearing the computerized voice, she realizes how relieved she is. She's afraid to hear her friend's voice, and wouldn't dare ask her why she stole the manuscript or the reason for all this nonsense. However absurd it is, she has to admit that she considers Brigitte an enemy.

An elderly couple pass by in the street, very slowly. She could call out to them and ask if there was anyone in the car, using a plausible explanation, but which one? By the time she found one, the couple would already have turned the corner.

She has to talk to someone. Who? She realizes she doesn't really know that many people. Brigitte isn't answering and she doesn't feel like speaking to her anyway. Jim is out of the question, or anyone she's met through him. Which left her so-called close friends, guys she'd gone to bed with, usually for a brief period of time, or old acquaintances from college.

She decides to call Tom, a friend with whom she'd had an affair last winter, just after her father had died. They've hardly seen each other since, but occasionally they call one another; he's very fond of her. And he doesn't know Brigitte, or Walton, or anyone in that circle—he has nothing to do with any of that.

Ann is glad to hear his voice, calm and resonant, like a late-night talk-show host on the BBC. He seems pleased that she's phoned him, and apparently doesn't expect a specific reason for her calling. It's just to chat, to make a simple date for dinner one night, that's enough. So they talk for a while. Ann feels reassured, but worried at the same time: talking to Tom is so comforting that it becomes impossible to explain to him that she's been going around in circles in her flat, watching a car without being able to determine whether the driver has gotten out or not. Not to mention the manuscript, Frankenstein, and Brigitte's betrayal, but she has no intention of bringing that up. Still observing the car out the corner of her eye, she finally ends up admitting that she's feeling down, and was hoping that Tom would offer to come and see her, or take her to dinner tonight. He gets the message and seems sincerely sorry: he has a business engagement that he can't possibly break; in fact, he was just getting ready to leave, but if she likes, he can stop by later.

Ann knows that Tom is very attracted to her, and that their breakup, which she had initiated, had saddened him. If she offers to spend the night with him, he'll accept. Foolishly, she still doesn't want to give the impression that she's counting on his visit, and replies that she's not really sure, she'll probably go out as well, but he can always try to call her later on in the evening. With a little laugh, he promises that he will, and hangs up.

She's alone again.

The car is still outside.

There is the sound of a horn, but from very far away on Albert Road. All of a sudden Ann senses real fear, which she had kept at bay during the phone call, but it's now back, more forceful and intense than ever. She gets up and paces the room in the semidarkness without turning on the lights. She pours herself a glass of gin and downs it in one gulp. She makes a face, wincing from the burn of the alcohol, which she doesn't tolerate well. Then she rushes toward the phone, and dials Tom's number again. Her finger is shaking. She's going to ask him to cancel his dinner, no matter how important, so that he can come over right away. She'll insist, even cry if need be, until he accepts. And he will.

The voice of an elderly woman. Wrong number.

She apologizes and starts over.

"You have reached the home of Thomas Ellison," Tom's voice replies, even deeper and calmer than usual, with Gato Barbieri playing sax in the background. "I'm sorry I'm out at the moment, but I'll call you back if you leave a message after the beep."

Ann hangs up after the beep, cutting off Gato Barbieri at the height of orgasm, then recalls that people with answering machines, including herself, will often keep them on even when they're at home, then take the call, interrupting the message, if they feel like talking to the person whose voice they've recognized. She redials the number, listens to the tape again, then says that he absolutely has to pick up if he's still there, even if he's in a hurry, that it's urgent. But apparently he has already left. Ann loathes Gato Barbieri.

Near panic, she downs a second glass of gin, closing her eyes as though the liquid might sting them. She has to get out and take a walk. But she knows very well that she's afraid to leave the building, afraid of the car that is waiting outside. She thinks about who else she can call, refers back to the mental list she'd made fifteen minutes ago, and now eliminates Brigitte, Jim, Allan, and the Walton circle. "I've got to calm down," she says aloud, clenching her fists. The sound of her voice in the silence of the room frightens her. She repeats the same sentence, more softly this time, as she enters the bathroom, where she turns on the bathtub faucets. While the water runs she waits in the tiny front hall, not knowing what else to do. She glues her ear to the door, then strikes up the courage to open it halfway to see if anyone is in the hallway. She used to do this often when she and Jim first split up. She would open the door just to make sure that he wasn't there, waiting for her to let him in.

No, there is no one there, no other noise but the almost imperceptible, incessant hum that seems to come from the evenly spaced ceiling lights.

She returns to the bathroom, which is now like a sauna. The faucets don't work very well, so she always turns them on one after the other: first the hot water, then the cold.

The tub is filled with scalding water, and an opaque mist covers the mirror above the sink. She yanks her clothes off, then goes back into the living room to get the phone and the answering machine, which she carries into the bathroom. She sets them on the tile floor, within arm's reach. Easing into the tub, she turns the cold water on in the shower attachment, immersing it so that it makes no noise, only a whirlpool. Blood throbs in her ears; how stupid of her to drink.

She lets her arm dry off on the rim of the tub, then pushes the REWIND button of the answering machine and plays it back.

First message: "Mission accomplished. I called the number that you told me to. Hey, you aren't by any chance playing one of those role games, like *Dungeons and Dragons*?"

It's the guy from the wake-up service. He must have left the message in the morning, or during the night. Ann wonders exactly what a role game is. She had vaguely heard of *Dungeons and Dragons*, the game inspired by Tolkien that suburban executive types played over and over again for months, assigning various roles, attributes, and powers.

Second message. Brigitte: "How did your research go? I'll call you tomorrow. Bye." The call must have come in the afternoon.

Third message. The guy from the wake-up service again, who simply says, "You'd better watch out too," and hangs up.

Ann clenches her teeth. She rewinds the tape and listens to the messages, to compare the voice of the good-humored young man who had so kindly gone along with her jokes and this menacing one, telling her to watch out. There's no doubt; it is indeed the same person.

Now she's really scared, but doesn't dare call the wake-up service to demand an explanation. Besides, she's well aware that the guy will not admit to having made the first phone call. But then again, perhaps he will. So should she call the police? What would she tell them? To listen to her answering machine?

She shivers, and glances around her. The sink and the mirror are on her right—she can see them out of the corner of her eye, but it seems to her that someone has traced some letters on the fogged mirror. And the steam has only formed minutes ago; it's even evaporating as the cold water runs in the bath. Yet she can plainly see the letters from the side. They are still clear, though not for long.

If she doesn't get out of the bathtub right away, the message will disappear.

And if she gets out, if she discovers that there is in fact a message, a word, a threat, then it means that she's not alone in the flat.

Ann no longer dares to move. Her fingers grip the rim of the bathtub, ready to support and help her stand up, so that she can get out of the water, take one step sideways, and check the mirror.

The phone is lying on the tile floor, within arm's reach. And so is the innocent black box of the answering machine.

The bathroom door is ajar, opening onto the dark hallway. She can make out the pale moldings in the background. A dry towel is draped over the door, which is why she can't close it. But she wouldn't have closed it anyway, because of the heat.

She can no longer distinguish the letters on the mirror from an angle. The steam is evaporating. She's going to miss her chance again and will never be sure.

She splashes the tile floor as she gets up.

No more steam, the surface of the mirror is clear.

Standing there naked, she listens to the clinking pipes of the plumbing, coming from somewhere around the water heater, a huge white tank suspended from the ceiling. Someone could probably store dead bodies in it, or anything, for that matter. And since she hasn't drained the tub yet, there's no reason to be hearing these noises.

She looks at her reflection, her anxious face, the beads of sweat on her forehead and her breasts, as if she were in a sauna. She can also see the bathroom door behind her, and the green towel slung over it.

So, the green towel is drying over the door, and of course, if she looks at it carefully, it is easy for her to imagine that the folds of this towel are, in fact, moving; no doubt, a hand on the other side of the door is going to grab it, let it slide down; then the door will suddenly open onto the empty hallway. And someone will be out there.

She reaches to adjust the mirror, so the door is perfectly framed by it, then presses her hands on the glass. The knocking noises start up again, even louder. She turns around and pulls the towel herself. No one is holding on to it. She wraps it around her body, pushes the door open, inspects the hall, and trembling, goes back into the dark living room.

Now she's curled up on the bed, wondering how she got there, how the telephone and the answering machine have been put back in their place with the night lamp on, as if this moment of her life—ever since she'd reached toward the towel—had been wiped from her memory.

She drinks another glass of gin and listens. The muffled sounds of reggae drift up from the street below, probably from an enormous cassette player that some Jamaican guy in a warm-up suit is lugging around. She tries to make out the words, as if they could be sending her a message, but the music, instead of gradually dying out, suddenly stops.

Silence.

She is waiting.

She pours herself another gin.

Will she be able to hold out like this until morning?

She is waiting.

The doorbell rings.

She hates this doorbell, two perfectly even tones, shrill and solemn at the same time.

"Tom?" she says in a faint voice.

But she knows that it can't be Tom. Even if he had come without bothering to telephone, he didn't know the entry code. Unless someone else from the building had gone in or out at the same time.

"Tom?" she repeats nonetheless.

The doorbell rings again.

Suddenly realizing that she's been speaking so softly that no one in the corridor could possibly hear her, she stands up. Now someone is knocking on the door, with one finger.

"Open up!" says a voice she's never heard before.

"Who are you?" she stammers.

"You don't know me but it's very important. I've got to talk to you. Open the door."

"I'm going to call the police."

"No, you won't, because I'll break down the door first."

Ann takes two steps backward, toward the living room. The carpet absorbs the noise; he might think she was still in the hallway.

"Come back!" he says with authority.

She freezes.

"Listen," the voice says, "I'm coming in, no matter what. So you might as well avoid any damage and just be so kind as to open the door. I'm not going to hurt you. I swear, it's very important."

Ann realizes that he really is going to knock down the door and that she won't have time to call the police. She's so frightened that she obeys—walks over to the door and turns the latch. Anything to get it over with.

"You've got to get out of here," the man tells her as he steps inside.

"You're crazy."

He takes her by the arm, drags her into the living room, and leaves her standing there as he collapses on the bed. In the midst of this activity, Ann's towel drops to the floor and she makes no attempt to pick it up. The man doesn't either. He seems terribly tired.

"Listen," he says. "You're in danger. I guess you might have noticed it these past few days. All I want to do is get you to a safe place. So get dressed. We've got to go."

"Where?" Ann murmurs.

"I told you, to a safe place. Hurry up."

He reaches over for the gin and takes a long swig straight from the bottle.

"You want some?"

Ann shakes her head. Tears are clouding her vision. He stands up again. He's barely taller than she is, about thirty, on the heavy side, with a handsome Roman profile beginning to get fleshy. He takes Ann by the shoulders, looks her straight in the eyes so that she is forced to open them again. Then he says, more gently, "You've got to trust me. You have every reason to be afraid, but not of me. I'm on your side in this whole business."

Ann bows her head, weeping silently. Her entire body is trembling. He lifts her chin with his finger, once again very gently. He has beautiful green eyes.

"Now get dressed and then we'll leave. Okay?"

Ann nods in agreement, mainly so that she can look down again. The man lets go of her arms. She shuffles toward the bathroom and on her way takes a swig of gin straight from the bottle as he had done. Mechanically she slips on a pair of jeans and the same damp T-shirt. She turns away from the mirror, which reflects her distorted features. As she puts on

168

her pumps the phone rings and she loses her balance trying
to rush into the living room to answer it. But he has already
picked it up.

"No," he says, "she's not here right now."

Resigned, Ann stands there facing him. She doesn't even
attempt to grab the phone away from him.

"Probably later tonight," he replies in an even voice, then
adds, "a friend," and hangs up.

He picks up a pair of dark glasses on the bridge table and
holds them out to her.

"And don't forget to wear these."

CHAPTER XXVI

In the sinister ceiling light of the elevator, he gives Ann a
weary, almost forced smile. He's also wearing jeans, but the
horrible kind made by certain sportswear companies with a
neatly pressed crease. His shirt is half unbuttoned, revealing
a hairy chest and a shiny chain in the worst taste; a gold
razor blade for fake, high-class junkies. He takes out a pair
of Ray-Bans from his breast pocket and puts them on.

"You don't wear contact lenses either," he says to Ann.
"That's not very smart."

Ann doesn't answer.

They walk through the lobby without turning on the light,
passing in front of the concierge's empty glass booth. The
man guides Ann, lightly steering her elbow, and she thinks
that if he were threatening her with a gun hidden under a
raincoat or a newspaper, no one would be able to tell the
difference. He puts her into the blue Triumph, starts up the
engine, and heads toward the docks. Ann remains silent and
so does he. He drives fast, precisely. After a while he asks,

"You didn't tell anyone about the disappearance of the manuscript?"

Ann shakes her head. And although he couldn't have seen this mute denial, since his eyes are on the road, he comments, "Well, thank God for that." A few minutes later he adds, "My name is Julian."

Once again they lapse into silence. They drive on like this for a good fifteen minutes, crossing through several neighborhoods, from deserted warehouses near the river to crowded streets. Ann, huddled up in the bucket seat, looks out the window, vainly trying to identify the route. She doesn't know London very well, and in fact only frequents a few neighborhoods. Whenever they slow down, she peers at the people in the cars they pass. If only they would notice her, remember her features, her panicked expression! But she doesn't dare attract their attention by signaling or waving. Their faces are swallowed up by the darkness; they won't remember a thing about her. She reaches up to take off her dark glasses, but he firmly stops her.

"Are you crazy or what?"

Later, at a red light where a police car is parked nearby, she is tempted to dash out and call for help. But the light turns green and the car starts moving before she can decide.

They enter the suburbs, and it isn't until the last minute that Ann recognizes the route leading to the Cheng Hotel. They pull up in front of it. The telephone booth at the intersection is still bathed in yellow light, but tonight, perhaps because it's not raining, there are people strolling down the street, mostly Chinese men in short-sleeved shirts. The warm air smells of pastry, thrown into the trash bins.

Ann allows herself to be led, as if on her way to the gallows. There is little more she can do. She's caught in a trap about which she knows nothing. Kidnapped in the heart of London, she blew her last chance to escape. They walk up the steps leading to the lobby, and her abductor takes the key from behind the deserted front desk. Climbing up the narrow stairway, she reflects that she wouldn't be surprised if he kills her once they reach the landing. She hesitates for a moment, only to be reprimanded by the hand that is guiding her elbow. He opens the door to the corner room where she had found the manuscript two days earlier. Then he asks her if she is hungry. She shakes her head once more. He says that he'll be back in a minute. Standing there alone, with her arms dangling at her sides, she doesn't even consider walking out of the room, although the door is open.

Then he is back, holding two glasses and a small ceramic flask, which he sets on the dressing table.

"Wu-Chiao-Pi," he says, "a Chinese liqueur. It's very good."

He fills the two glasses with an amber liquid, and holds one out to her. When he takes a sip, she automatically imitates him, without tasting the flavor of the alcohol. It doesn't even occur to her that she shouldn't be drinking, to conserve whatever is left of her lucidity. If he told her to jump out of the window, she would probably do it.

He refills the glasses, sits down on the black vinyl stool, and gestures for her to do the same on the bed. Then, while warming the drink with his hands, he says, "Now you've got to listen to me."

Ann nods weakly.

"What I'm about to tell you may sound absurd. You're going to think that I'm crazy. But you only have one choice, and that is to believe me. It's a question of life or death. I won't be able to protect you much longer, no matter what you do."

Ann brings the glass to her lips, but he reaches out and takes it away from her.

"That's enough for now. You'll be drunk. Have you read the manuscript?"

"Yes."

Hunched over, her arms gripping her knees, she is gradually inching toward the other end of the bed, wedged into the sharp corner.

"All right," says the young man. "Now you have to believe me. Everything in that manuscript is true."

Ann notices that he pauses to judge the impact of his words, the implications of which she clearly does not grasp.

"So what does that mean?" she asks feebly, not out of curiosity, but because she senses that he expects a question.

"That means, since one can read between the lines, that in 1816 there was an invasion in Switzerland. I could tell you it was Martians, extraterrestrials, anything—I have no idea. In any case, they were intelligent beings from the outside. These—I don't know what to call them—beings took advantage of the experiments performed by Frankenstein, who attempted to revive his wife, in order to infiltrate the earth. Elizabeth was the first human being who was . . . replaced, and if you read the manuscript, you know how, in the course of several years, all those like her began to multiply among themselves, not only in Switzerland, but in England, then all over Europe and throughout the world. It has been exactly one hundred and sixty-eight years since this process began. So you can imagine what stage the colonization is in today."

He remains thoughtful for a moment and takes a sip of the Chinese liqueur. Ann looks at him blankly, more attentive to the motion of his swallowing than to the significance of his words. She hears muffled footsteps in the hall and he must hear them too, for he waits until they die out before going on. A door slams.

"You're probably going to say to me, If it were true, people would know about it. That's precisely it. In the first generation the conquerors knew that they had come from the outside. But from the second one on, they thought they were earthlings and now, despite the fact that—I don't know, it's hard to calculate—let's say ninety-nine percent of the earth's population is originally from the outside, nobody can tell the difference. No, I should say only a few can; from generation to generation, they pass the secret on to the people who occupy key positions in politics, finance, and the sciences, or to those who are likely to occupy them. They're the ones who know and decide everything. Aside from them, there is a perfect osmosis between the colonizers and the colonized."

"Do you mean to say," Ann articulates with difficulty, "that I am a Martian? That is . . . someone else?"

"No, and it's precisely for that reason that you're here."

Without changing her position, Ann gropes for the little bottle of liqueur set down near the bed. He allows her to take a swig.

"Listen," he says.

"Stop saying listen all the time! I am listening."

Ann didn't even stutter to get the sentence out. She feels absurdly proud of herself. The young man gives her a crooked half smile.

"You're already feeling better. In any case, you're less afraid of me. No," he continued, "you're not . . . like them. Neither am I. And besides, you know that as well as I do."

He takes her by the arm and forces her to get up, brings her over to the mirror of the dressing table, and stands beside her. Slowly he takes off his dark glasses, then carefully removes Ann's. He gazes at their reflection.

"Our autochthonous quality is inscribed in our eyes. The blue of yours is a very pretty one. But that said, you're crazy not to wear contact lenses; anybody could tear off these glasses. I'm used to it, being part of the underground, but you . . . It's a wonder that you've never had any problems."

"Problems?" Ann asks.

"Well, yes. Perhaps you never noticed that you had blue eyes?"

"But a lot of people have blue eyes," Ann stammers.

The young man gives her a blank look.

"A lot of people?"

"Well, that's right."

He reflects for a moment. "I'm beginning to think that you're truly crazy. Listen, you show me someone in the street whose eyes aren't black, and I'll buy you a bottle of champagne; that is, if we ever get out of this hornet's nest alive."

Ann falters. It's absurd. Of course she's right, a lot of people have brown, green, blue, yellow, and also black eyes—that's obvious. But he is looking at her as if she had just told him he was wearing a polka-dot tie instead of an open shirt. It is clear to him that everyone has black eyes, except for a few members of the underground who hide their whole life behind tinted glasses and contact lenses, constantly running the risk of being exposed. If Ann and he went out into the street, and if she were to show him people with blue or green eyes, he would no doubt deny it and swear that they were black. He's a madman. There's not much you can do with a madman, you can't prove anything to him, and now she is in his clutches.

Besides, he is disregarding her interruption, and without taking his eyes off their reflection in the mirror, he continues, "There are very few of us now in Europe. Or rather, we don't know how many of us there are. We know that our race will soon die out, that we are perhaps the last generation, and we're trying to secretly regroup to carry on the rites of the ancients. Captain Walton, whom you know, was in charge of one of these networks, to which I myself belong. I suppose you never noticed, but the series for which you write your little books was a liaison report. He made corrections in your manuscripts—oh, very few—just to convey a message. All over the world, our people decoded them and received instructions. Little by little, after getting to know you better, the captain realized that in spite of your dark glasses, you were one of us, a girl with light-colored eyes, just like old times. That's why he wanted the manuscript, where the truth is written, to be passed on to you."

Ann would like to tell him that she hardly ever wears dark glasses, and anyway, she had never worn them in Walton's presence, but she knows that it's useless. He won't believe her; he brushes aside anything that might threaten his delirious reasoning. She decides against it and asks him instead, "But he's the one who wrote it, isn't he?"

"He didn't write it; he recopied it. You must realize that we can neither print nor distribute a text like that; it would be too dangerous. Some of us copy it so that it can circulate clandestinely. Through various channels we slip in contraband excerpts, like we did in your novels, for example. As I recall, in *Love Is a Bird in Flight*, there's a tiny fragment."

"But then who actually wrote it?"

"John William Polidori, the first apostle of our cause. Look, here's a portrait of him."

He points to the dressing-table mirror with their reflections in it. Then, pressing his hands against the surface, he swings it around to reveal a very ugly picture in the style of religious painting, of a young man with curly hair, gazing off in the distance, with one hand on his chest and another placed on a stack of bound books.

"Our meetings always take place with his venerated image before us," says Ann's abductor with devotion. "You have to understand," he adds in a more natural tone of voice. "Frankenstein, whose name, incidentally, was not Frankenstein, never wrote those memoirs. On the other hand, the encounter that is described between the Byron clique and the scientist surrounded by his living dead did indeed happen. Polidori, who was there, grasped with incredible intuition the truth hidden behind the story told by Elizabeth, the story that Mary Shelley vulgarized in her famous novel. You mustn't forget, as we learn from the manuscript, that Mary had been operated on by Frankenstein, so she was part of the first group of invaders for whom she zealously worked by writing the official version, obviously false, of events that were quickly covered up by destroying the archives and assassinating the witnesses. So that, in fact, no one even knows the real name of the one who was called Frankenstein at the inn, since both Mary and Polidori used the pseudonym. But Polidori was in a way the only human witness who was conscious of the invasion. Mary's apocryphal version was such a success that it prevented him from letting the truth be known, and therefore from helping mankind arrest the spread of the evil when perhaps there was still time. His writings were refused publication, he fell into disrepute and was silenced; for the new masters of the earth had already taken charge of all communications, the publishers and the newspapers. Polidori saw and understood what was going on, a powerless bystander to this invisible conquest, and out of desperation he committed suicide. But before that, he wrote about what he knew, fictitiously attributing it to Frankenstein. Fortunately, the manuscript escaped the police of the new masters. For over a hundred and sixty years it's been secretly circulating. Without Polidori, perhaps we would still be in the dark, we would all be men among men, not knowing, in spite of our light-colored eyes, that those who claimed to be our fellowmen are outsiders, and for the most part, don't even know it themselves. We owe him everything," Julian concludes emphatically, "our lucidity and our suffering. And our condition as social outcasts, which is the sign of our own humanity. His name will survive, and one day will triumph!"

He bows to the hideous picture. There is a silence, then the sound of a toilet flushing somewhere in the hotel.

"And what do I have to do with all of this?" asks Ann, who had gone back to sit on the bed during Julian's long speech.

"You?"

He gives her a baffled look and pours himself another drink. A blood vessel has burst in his right eye.

"In your case, the captain recognized you. He was a genius when it came to that. You know, I really think that out of all of us, he was the heir to Polidori's teachings."

"Why 'he was'?" Ann asks.

"I wish I still had hope, but I doubt . . . In any case, he contacted you, he recopied the manuscript for you, so that you'd know the truth and with full knowledge of the facts, you'd be able to choose. So that you could join us, if you so desire. Fight alongside us, for survival. Unfortunately, now you no longer have the choice. You're either with us, or you're dead. I'm very sorry."

"But why?"

"Why?"

Julian begins to pace the triangular room, making a show of his violent despair. His jeans cling tightly to his plump buttocks.

"Why?" he repeats. "Because our network has been destroyed, that's why. Because they've been suspicious of our captain for months and one of their agents has infiltrated his group. Your friend Brigitte with the contact lenses."

Of course, Brigitte doesn't wear them, but Ann once again decides to keep quiet.

"The captain suspected that something was up, and he spent three days here, in this room, to meditate. When he called me the day before yesterday, to put you in my charge so that I could watch over you, he already knew. I remember

177

he said to me, 'You won't be seeing me much longer.' The next day he disappeared. We haven't seen him since; they must have arrested him. And today Brigitte stole the manuscript in your flat. They knew of its existence, but until now, they had never been able to get their hands on it. Well, it's too late now."

He sits back down, picks up his glass, and dramatically crushes it with his bare hand. Then he murmurs, as if to himself, "The rush for the spoils approaches."

He remains like this for a moment, with his head in his hands. Then, looking up, he gazes at Ann with a somewhat calmer expression, bitter but determined.

"You must excuse me," he says. "I'm very upset. I'm going to leave. Now you've got to get some sleep."

He stands up and takes a step toward the door. Panicked, Ann grabs his arm as he passes in front of her. "I want to go home."

He clenches his fists. "You stupid little idiot! Don't you understand? They're probably already there, in your flat. Brigitte turned you in. Get this into your head: you're with us now."

"But," Ann cries, mad with rage—she has nothing more to lose—"what are the risks if they were to find me?"

He opens the door and says in a hollow voice, "Worse than death."

Then, from the outside, he turns the key in the lock.

CHAPTER XXVII

The next few hours are atrocious. The only thing Ann understands is that she's fallen into the hands of a madman. Incapable of reasoning, she clings to the hope that Tom, having gotten a stranger on the phone, might become concerned and set out to look for her. But the slim chance of this happening worries her. She reproaches herself for having affected such a casual air toward the end of their conversation, when she'd told him that she would probably go out, though he could always try calling her later. There is a good chance that Tom, if he was indeed the person who phoned, had assumed the man who answered was one of her lovers and had decided not to come, out of discretion. At this very moment he might be drifting off to sleep, somewhat irritated by her capricious behavior, or at best, disappointed to have missed out on a chance to see her. He couldn't possibly suspect the truth. If she wasn't there, he'd think that she had good reason not to be. Of course, "something might have happened," as the saying goes. She could have been kidnapped by a dangerous madman, for instance. Tom might even envision this remote possibility—Ann is desperately hoping that he will—and say to himself, "It *is* kind of strange." The worst part is that the odds are against her. When someone is not home, there is at most one chance in a thousand that he or she has been kidnapped. Any sensible person would theoretically eliminate this likelihood; if not, life would be impossible. People would constantly imagine their loved ones run over by cars, hacked into pieces, or trapped behind walls. But by the same token any sensible person ought to be constantly aware of this improbable chance. For Ann, the improbability—more than anything else—is horrifying, worse than being hunted down, locked up, or crying out for help when she's certain that no one can hear her.

Frightened, Ann calls out Tom's name, wishing she could glide into his thoughts, set off an alarm that would keep ringing, draw him nearer. But she knows full well that he can't hear her, that he can't come to her rescue, because he's thinking of all of those good reasons that further deter him from the truth. After repeating them to herself over and over, vainly attempting to find a flaw, she finally falls asleep.

When she awakes, she realizes that her watch has stopped. Light filters through the thin crack between the metal shutters and the window frame. It must be a nice day. Ann's mouth is dry and the back of her head throbs. Her clothes stick to her skin, emanating a sour odor.

She gets up, checks to see if the door is still locked, and while examining the window, notes that the latch and the cord to the blinds are both missing. She wonders if they had taken this precaution while she was asleep, or if it had been that way before. She drinks some water out of the sink faucet but her throat is still dry.

She drums her fingers on the door, almost timidly, as if she only wanted to relieve herself of an obligation. No one appears. She sits back down on the bed and ponders the situation. It's unlikely that anyone is looking for her. No one will begin to worry before three or four days, at best. She suddenly remembers Julian's preposterous speech the night before: his story about a Martian invasion, an underground network, and a clandestine population with light-colored eyes—the typical ravings of a madman. Once an absurd premise is established, everything is interpreted in terms of that premise—more simple, in this case, since according to the assumption, the plot is invisible and blends into normal, everyday life. It's also typical, she thinks, of the delirious reasoning of those who speak of a pure race—the true population of the Earth—and the outsiders who secretly manipulate everything. She had often heard such enlightened individuals talking nonsense in pubs, squares, or on Speakers' Corner. At the time they had struck her as picturesque. They maintained precisely this kind of discourse, explaining that the planet's confusion was due to conspiracies by the Jesuits, the Freemasons, and Qaddafi's fanatic disciples. It was the same paranoia, the same underlying racism, but Julian's reasoning was based on a more elaborate system, enhanced by sacred texts, occult traditions, and an entire interpretation of history. Who knows? Perhaps if she had listened to some of those single-minded maniacs to the end, they would have backed up their denial of reality with equally coherent explanations. The only difference is that one of them is now holding her prisoner, subjecting her to his raving, and involving her in his delirium. Besides, Julian is definitely not alone. He must belong to some kind of sect, which for days, perhaps months, has been trying to attract and convert her, by fair or foul play. Yes, a neo-Nazi sect obsessed with the purity of the race, drawing their invincible and twisted arguments from an apocryphal text written a century and a half ago by a suicidal doctor and, no doubt, assassin; a crime syndicate presided over by Captain Walton.

Captain Walton. That courtly little man, that endearing, aging bachelor with his romantic den of shady business, his menagerie of young snobbish women, his T-shirts laundered in Melbourne . . . it didn't seem possible.

Yet, one reads similar stories every day. The Yorkshire Ripper's wife thought it impossible that her husband, the most gentle of men, the ideal father and exemplary neighbor, was at the same time a bloodthirsty monster. Perhaps the people whose brothers, friends, and children joined Charlie Manson's family thought them perfectly normal on the outside. Former models, friendly marginal types dressed in fringed, bell-bottom jeans, multicolored shirts, and Indian scarves— people who had parties, smoked grass, and exchanged restaurant addresses. . . . Captain Walton now strikes her as a kind of Manson from London; civilized, eloquent, easy to get along with, but in reality an evil guru, ruling over this tribe of chic young women who come to tea every Friday in his office full of Chinese curios in Mecklemburgh Gardens. They are all fascinated by him, devoted body and soul to the cause that he must have revealed, little by little, persuading them that they were the chosen ones. All of them completely mad.

And what about Brigitte? Brigitte, her best friend for so many years, whom she sees almost daily, only interested in sex, coke, keeping her body in shape, and gossip about her friends? Brigitte, the healthiest and most stable girl she knows, with all that those virtues imply, including a slight narrow-mindedness. What is her role in this?

Julian accuses Brigitte of being a double agent, working for the Martians to destroy the network that she has infiltrated. Unless Ann is to believe the Martian story, she must find some equivalent in Julian's delirious ranting that corresponds to reality. So, is Brigitte a member of the police who has worked her way into the criminal organization headed by Walton? But then why would she have gotten Ann mixed up in it, without saying anything? So that she could serve as bait? It doesn't make sense, but nothing makes sense. Or then again, there's always the possibility that she had a sudden change of heart. Brigitte might have belonged to a sect and, in a flash of lucidity, decided to double-cross them. Now, that would be more logical; the pieces of the puzzle are falling into place. Brigitte had begun to work for Walton several months after her accident. It's conceivable that he took advantage of her confused state to convert her, luring her with a cause to give her life meaning, that kind of nonsense. Then Brigitte might have served as a conspirator in the hunt, without thinking she was doing anything wrong, with all due affection for Ann, because she thought her worthy of joining the ranks. She, too, knew how to seize the perfect opportunity when Ann had just broken up with Jim and was looking for work six months ago. . . . So Brigitte had introduced Ann to her guru, and the time it had taken for Ann to write two absurd books had served as her probation period; she'd been observed and finally chosen. Yes, that makes sense, even if after two years of this militant lunacy, carefully hidden from them all, Brigitte's sudden rebellion is not that easily explained.

Now another idea, even more appalling than the others, begins to take form in Ann's mind. All the girls from Mecklemburgh Gardens, including Brigitte, have been subjected to the same ordeal: the stolen alarm clock, the calls from the wake-up service, the story about the manuscript that begins like a parlor game, a treasure hunt, and turns into a nightmare of confinement. Like Ann, they rebelled, resisted, and tried to escape the madness. But they had still ended up joining the sect. Their struggles had been in vain; they had all been driven crazy. And now the same fate awaits Ann. When she is let out of the hotel, if she ever is let out, she'll be convinced that extraterrestrials have invaded the earth, that she is one of the last genuine earthlings; that everyone but her has black eyes, that one must fight in the underground to preserve one's identity, protected by colored contact lenses, and participate in the activities of the network. And the worst part will be that she'll enjoy it, she'll be delighted to do so. She'll meet up with the other girls, Laura Fitzlowins or Sabrina Holygeorge-Nights, who will smile at her and tell her about the months in which Ann's initiation had been prepared without her knowing, like a party. They will be glad that she is now one of them. And Ann will be just as glad; she'll lure other young women and men into this nightmare, which will seem like a salvation, an obvious choice, the only way to live. She will be insane. And if she isn't, they'll kill her. They kill the unyielding ones. Julian had plainly said so: either you're with us or you're dead.

She would soon be dead.

Or insane.

Ann closes her eyes for a while, hoping to reopen them in her own home, to wake up and be out of anyone's reach. But once she has finished fantasizing, she is still in the triangular room. The horrible portrait of Polidori faces her. She walks over to the dressing table and presses against the painting so that the mirror swings back into place. She'd rather see herself than him, although she's afraid to witness the progress of her madness, should it already be visible on her face. Soon she'll be catching herself with an expression of vacant serenity, like the cretins in the Hindu sects who parade down the street shaking tambourines and bells, chanting their hymns to Krishna. But there must be a secret spring that she doesn't know how to trigger: the portrait refuses to budge. She tries desperately, scratching the painting with her nails. When Julian enters, he catches her crouched on top of the dressing table, pushing with all her might on the stormy sky behind the prophet's dramatic pose.

"I brought you some tea," he says, setting the tray on the floor near the bed. "Get down from there."

She obeys. He is dressed just as the night before, except he's now wearing a worn fatigue jacket that clashes ridiculously with his grotesque jeans.

"I want to get out of here."

"Not right now. It would be too dangerous, for you and for us. The minute you get outside, you would go to the police and turn us in, and they would operate on you."

"Then you're keeping me locked up?"

"We're protecting you."

"At least let me take a shower. Change my clothes."

"That can be arranged. The shower is at the end of the hall; you can take one later. As for the clothes, I'll go buy some, if you give me your measurements."

"Oh, because you aren't taking any risks when you go out?"

As he slips his Ray-Bans back on, he gives her another one of his weary, heroic smiles. Ironic and ready for anything, like some B-movie.

"I'm used to taking risks."

An hour later he comes back with an armful of packages. He takes out a T-shirt and some underwear, as well as a very short, sheer dress, which he lays out on the bed. Ann has to admit that his taste isn't too bad.

He escorts her to the bathroom, removes the key, stands in front of the door while she showers, then takes her back to her room. They pass no one in the dim hallway. Before leaving, Julian puts a toothbrush and a bottle of gingival lotion from Hong Kong on the sink shelf and tells Ann to knock on the door if she needs anything.

Once she has slipped on her dress and brushed her teeth, Ann feels more lucid. Her headache is gone and she notes with satisfaction that she's still far from the brink of madness. Calmly she analyzes the situation. On the one hand, someone will eventually get worried about her. Tom, for instance, unless he decides to sulk, to get even for having been stood up, but that isn't like him. Or else, friends or perhaps even the concierge of the building, will call her up and get no answer. But that may take some time.

On the other hand, it seems obvious that the sect is in desperate straits. In concrete terms, Julian's speech about the imminent rush for the spoils, the omnipresent enemy who is preparing to wipe out the last division of real earthlings, can only mean one thing: the police are on their heels; they had probably arrested Walton on the basis of Brigitte's denunciation. Whether she had betrayed the sect from the beginning or had made a recent turnabout is of little importance—she would somehow get Ann out of this mess. She must know where this Chinese hotel is; soon a squadron of cops in combat uniform would be descending upon them.

However, it is a lot less reassuring that the scattered sect is apparently allowing Julian to be the sole master of his fate, a lost soldier left on his own. So that when the police arrive, he might decide to make a last stand, pull one of those "you'll never catch me alive" numbers in which Ann will play the role of the hostage. Since he acts like an urban guerrilla in a TV sitcom, she fears that it's entirely possible.

As luck would have it, he returns in the late afternoon with a tray of bacon, eggs, biscuits, and tea. He sits back down on the black vinyl stool, assuming his air of the fatigued warrior determined to stick it out until the very end, and announces that things are apparently settling down. They definitely have Captain Walton in captivity, but the network is in the process of reorganizing itself. Ann asks if this improvement in the situation means that Julian will be able to free her soon, but he replies that for the time being it is still impossible, and walks out of the room. He leaves her a package of fig cookies and a bottle of water.

Ann has a horrendous night. Julian's words have dashed her hopes; moreover, the admirable, optimistic arguments that she'd constructed during the day do not hold up in the dark. She keeps turning the light on and off, incapable of choosing between her fear of the dark and her fear of the room itself. The yellow light of the ceiling lamp shines on the peeling, flowered wallpaper, on the sharp corner that arrests the eye as if drawing it into an abyss, and in particular, on the portrait of Polidori, which she stares at for hours with fascinated repulsion. Later in the night she becomes so frightened that she rushes to the door and starts to pound on it, shouting. Julian appears almost immediately, his fatigue jacket draped around his shoulders. Ann grabs the bottle of water, fortunately made of glass, and in a rage, vainly tries to knock him over the head. It hadn't even occurred to her to stand behind the door and take him by surprise—besides, the door opens onto the hallway, which makes the ambush even more awkward. Julian overpowers her, and without getting angry, simply asks her what she wants. Stammering, her face clouded with tears, Ann begs him in a shrill voice to get rid of the portrait. He does what she asks and leaves without further comment.

The rest of the night is even worse. Ann imagines the portrait on the other side of the mirror, upside down, with Polidori staring at her from below. She is sure that dozens of people have gone crazy in this room from his stare. Exhausted, she drifts into a fitful sleep and has nightmares.

The next day she no longer has any sense of time. She could have been there for an hour, or twelve years, she can't tell the difference: she's there and she'll always be there. While she was asleep someone lowered the blinds; the crack of light has disappeared, if it had ever been there at all. She keeps the overhead light on all the time now, and consequently loses track of the alternation between day and night. Her sole means of marking time is through Julian's visits with his tray, and her trips to the bathroom, under his surveillance. Ann goes there to shower and defecate as well, since the room is equipped only with a sink, over which, if need be, she can straddle her legs to pee. The sink is directly across from the dressing table, and Ann looks at the spot behind the mirror where the upside-down eyes of Polidori must be, right in line with her genitals, at which he probably casts his covetous glances. Nothing surprising about that, she thinks, if they were taking out their vengeance on the hotel guests by carefully booby-trapping the rooms. This idea makes her laugh hysterically for a good hour—or perhaps it is only five minutes. All of a sudden, her laughter turns into panicked hiccups. She is going mad; the sect's tactics are working.

She lies on the floor for a long time, curled up in the sharp corner of the room, so sharp that lying there, squeezed between the moldings, she feels trapped. It is as if she were in a vise, the walls slowly closing in, and soon the room will be nothing more than a straight line and she will have disappeared inside it, like a car sent to the junkyard, then wrapped in steel jaws so powerful that the old heap is reduced to next to nothing. The room will no longer exist, just a line, and in this line will be Ann. She peers at the walls and is alarmed to see them moving, at the same time she recalls, word for word, Julian's speech. And what if it were true? It wouldn't be any more horrible than her present situation. She surmises that if only she truly believed him for an instant with all her heart, the walls would spread apart, the angle would get wider and wider until it turned into a straight line—but one behind her, so she would be on the outside.

So what if it were true?

She had always felt different, foreign, false. Now, that was a fact.

No!

She hears herself crying out. No, she mustn't start to think like that. That's exactly what they want. They handpick people like her because it's easy to persuade them, to tell them, "Look at your life, and everything you have experienced up until now. You must be aware of it—besides, haven't you always felt that you were different? You know that you aren't quite the same as everyone else. Well, there is a reason and now you know why. That's also why you should join us; we're just like you, we stick together, and would never do one another any harm."

No.

She has probably been crying out often, without realizing it. She hears footsteps rushing down the hallway; Julian is coming, he's on guard, right nearby. He picks her up, carries her to the bed, sponges her forehead with a damp washcloth, and murmurs soothing words.

Later she recalls a book that she had read during her adolescence, *The Three Musketeers*, a French historical novel; in particular, the episode where the wicked Englishwoman, Milady de Winter (with whom she totally identifies) is held prisoner by an incorruptible Puritan called Felton—or Fenton. Milady, who is beautiful, manages to escape by seducing this Felton character. Ann figures this might work with Julian. He's also a fanatic, the kind of narrow-minded man who could be turned inside-out like a glove. First she'd have to pretend to believe him, enter into his game.

When he brings the meal tray, she tries to strike up a conversation, hiding her nervousness. She inquires if there is any news from the network.

"Nothing new," he replies. "They haven't found us yet; that's all that can be said."

"Are there a lot . . . of our people in the hotel?"

Julian looks at her with surprise. She realizes that the "our people" hadn't gone over so well, and bites her lips. Premature. Milady had acted more subtly. However, he doesn't pick up on it, and simply answers the question.

"They all are. They're Chinese. One really can't be certain, but it's likely that the invasion spread more slowly outside of Europe: in Asia, Africa, and South America. At the beginning of the century they colonized in massive numbers, but it was more difficult than here. Naturally, there they all have black eyes. All over the the world, there are still entire tribes of humans. They're the ones we're counting on for the great uprising. But it takes a long time to recognize them and make them aware of it. And of course, the others work faster than we do. Much faster."

He pauses for a moment, lost in his thoughts. Ann wonders if she hasn't been a bit hasty in comparing his delirium to some form of neo-Nazism. After these last words the messianic sect has begun to take on shades of a pro–Third World point of view. Soon he'll be presenting Colonel Qaddafi as the Middle Eastern equivalent of Captain Walton. So the little multicolored flags on the planisphere in the captain's office must stand for the reservations still inhabited by humans, scattered all over the globe; by using the book series as a screen and earnestly marking off these areas, the hidden teachings of Polidori are being transmitted to the four corners of the earth.

Ann walks over to Julian and places her hand on his arm. "I believe you," she says with conviction.

He gently disengages himself and stands facing her for a moment, scrutinizing her face as if he could read her mind. She thinks she has scored a point, but then, as gently as ever, in a tone suggesting that nothing matters anymore, he says, "Don't bother."

He heads toward the door and closes it behind him.

She's blown her chance.

CHAPTER XXVIII

Time passes. Ann isn't afraid anymore; she's beyond that now, merely discouraged. Collapsed on the bed, in the menacing corner of the room, she looks at her hands, arms, and legs, pinches her body, and tells herself that her life is over; little by little, she will grow old listening to the noises just

outside, and stay here forever, die in this hotel room in the
London suburbs. There will be an investigation, and then it
will be dropped. Nearly two hundred people each year are
reported missing in England—she had read it in a magazine.

It is over.

Julian doesn't come to see her anymore, either because he
knows the story about Felton and prefers not to expose himself
to temptation, or because he is disgusted by Ann's childish
and blasphemous pretending, or perhaps he has business
elsewhere. It hardly matters.

Instead, the fat Chinese woman whom Ann had seen the
first day in the lobby brings the tray and escorts her to the
shower. During this activity Ann feels too weak to attempt a
violent escape. It seems as though she goes to the shower
more and more often, or else time has been going by more
quickly in her comatose, half-awake state. At this rate it will
soon be over.

It is over.

CHAPTER XXIX

The rust-stained shower is full of long black hair and dead
insects, clogging the drain. While Ann washes herself with
soap, muttering like an old woman, she notices some kind
of window, or perhaps a dumbwaiter on the shower stall wall
above her: a removable square wooden trapdoor measuring
about forty centimeters on each side. She starts to play with
the small latch.

A black hole gapes before her.

She reaches out and feels something metallic running down
the wall inside.

Steps.

An air shaft, she thinks. It must go all the way down the building.

Ann can barely swallow; she tries hard not to tremble. The water is still running, a whirlpool of dead cockroaches swirling at her feet. She leans over again and looks up the shaft. There isn't any light indicating an exit on the roof—she had better go down.

She cannot remember ever having seen the entrance to the air shaft before, and her frazzled mind has almost come to believe that it exists only in the present; if she lets this chance go by, it will have disappeared by the time she comes back. And furthermore, something could happen to prevent her from ever getting back to the bathroom again. No. It is now or never.

Fortunately, she has gotten into the habit of taking long showers. The Chinese woman won't become impatient, at least for several minutes. But Ann doesn't remember how long she has been there, mindlessly rubbing herself with soap. She will have to act quickly.

The sound of the water pelting the shower floor will cover her. She unhooks a large towel and tosses it around her shoulders, like an athlete after the game. Propping herself on the wooden shelf used for soap and shampoo, she bends over, then throws her leg over the side, into the dark passageway. She feels the comforting touch of the metal rung beneath her foot, and swings herself inside. Before going down, she childishly attempts to close the trapdoor again, as if this would protect her during her escape. But in the process, she pulls it so hard that it bangs against the doorframe, making what sounds to her like a deafening noise. On the verge of tears, Ann fiercely bites her lip. Then she hastily descends, step by step. Her room, and therefore the shower, are on the third floor. Groping in the darkness, she soon feels another doorframe—behind it, the sound of running water, indicating that there must be someone taking a shower on the second floor as well. She continues her descent, fearing that at any moment the duct will be flooded with a ray of light, only to reveal the Chinese woman leaning over the side, watching her escape and already calling for help. Another dumbwaiter: that means she has reached the first floor.

One more.

Then another.

Ann is shaking. And what if she were doomed to an eternal descent? One door after another, one shower after another, one floor after another, an infinite number of stories, when she knows very well that there are only three. And what if she were truly crazy?

She touches a firm surface with one foot.

She's made it.

Her arms outstretched, she realizes that the duct has gotten larger, and that she has indeed reached the basement. She gropes her way along a hot cement wall. She's drenched with sweat. Finally the wall angles off and a step rises out of nowhere from the floor. She bumps into it and cruelly stubs her toes. Barely able to stifle her cry of pain, she hops on one foot, then continues. The cement corridor becomes increasingly brighter, and a halo of light indicates the next bend. She freezes, suddenly on the lookout. It is terribly hot now that she has left the duct. The incessant humming of machines produces minute vibrations all around her. She must be approaching the boiler or an electric generator.

She takes a cautious glance in the direction of the light and her intuition is confirmed: huge machines, not terribly modern, whirring under the feeble glare of a naked bulb, which hangs from the low ceiling. A steady drip of water makes an irritating sound as it plunks into a puddle, perhaps in a pail, or a tin can used for this purpose.

There isn't a soul around.

Ann crosses through the room full of machines, then pauses a moment, protected by a blind angle. She wipes her face and breasts with a corner of the towel, still draped around her shoulders. Then, hugging the wall, passing behind the most imposing machine of them all (a washing machine—through the window, she can see clothes twisting with infuriating slowness), she looks up to find a small crescent-shaped basement window. There are bars behind the frosted glass, and beyond it, darkness. Ann has no idea of the time, but realizes it must be night. She hears a car passing, then the voices of a man and a woman, which get louder and soon fade out, along with the sound of footsteps. High heels.

In the darkness in front of her is a flight of steps. She climbs them.

A door.

She hesitates, then with infinite precaution—the kind that triggers catastrophes, she thinks—turns the lock, which offers no resistance. She pulls the door toward her; it opens. She is intoxicated by the air outside, the air of a summer night, thick with the odor of rotting garbage.

She finds herself below street level, in the narrow passageway that surrounds the building like a castle moat, over which span the stairs to the lobby. To her right and left are symmetrical flights of stairs that lead to the sidewalk level, roughly six feet above her.

This is the final step; afterward she'll be in the street and then all she has to do is get away from the hotel as quickly as possible. Obviously, dressed in nothing but a bath towel, she wouldn't go by unnoticed. Most important would be to find a taxi right away, or a policeman to whom she could explain her predicament.

Suddenly there is a voice from above.

Julian.

He must be standing on the steps to the lobby.

"Stay on the lookout in the street, behind the building," he says breathlessly. "I'm going down to take a look in the basement."

Ann wants to scream; she gnaws at the dried blood on her lip. They are hunting her down. She'll never make it. From beneath the railing that runs along the sidewalk, she can already see two legs, like a compass, in a pair of tight-fitting creased jeans. Julian is coming toward her hiding place; in a few seconds he will find her.

She looks around wildly and spots a carton of empty bottles in a pile of garbage. Her fingers tighten around a cracked plastic neck.

Julian is right in front of her, on the last step of the left stairway.

"Now, now, that's a good girl," he says.

He starts to move toward her.

Ann takes a step backward, searching with her heel for the first step of the stairway behind her on the right. The moment Julian rushes to grab her around the waist, she kicks the pyramid of trash bags, which slowly spill open, momentarily blocking the path of her pursuer. She races up the stairs and pushes open the gate. A taxi has just pulled up in front of the hotel, and the passenger, one leg out the door, is about to exit. Diving in, she pushes him back onto the seat, and screams at the driver to get going. He obeys, and the car pulls away just as Julian has his hand on the door. He presses his face—contorted with rage—against the window for a split second, and then he's nothing more than a gesticulating figure on the sidewalk, veiled by the exhaust fumes of the taxi.

Ann shivers, gasping for breath, her hair in her eyes. She is stark naked, having lost the towel during her escape, and the vinyl seat sticks to her thighs. Someone places an arm around her shoulders and a voice murmurs in her ear, "There, there . . . it's over now." She jerks her head around toward the passenger in the taxi.

It's Allan.

CHAPTER XXX

"What time is it?" she asks.

"Almost four o'clock," a nearby voice replies.

"What day is it?"

"Thursday."

She rolls over in bed and pulls the sheet over her head. Four o'clock in the morning or the afternoon? She drifts back to sleep.

She wakes up in her room. Slowly she gazes at the space surrounding her, checking the place of each object: the typewriter on the table, the bedspread she'd pushed aside, trailing on the carpet, the old leather armchair, the messy pile of records near the stereo, the plastic cube of photos on her night table, near the alarm clock, which now says three o'clock. It is dark. The window is half open, and a gust of warm air enters the room. She is thirsty, and would like to get a glass of water from the kitchen. Then she notices that she has neglected one small detail in her inventory. There is someone sitting in the armchair—Allan—who is watching her with a half smile. The moment she sets foot on the floor, he stands up and tells her to stay in bed. Disappearing into the kitchen, he returns with a glass of water, which she drinks greedily, her head thrown back. She knows it isn't poisoned.

"Don't move a muscle," he says. "You still have a fever."

Ann puts the glass on the night table, near the cube of

photographs, sits up, propped on the pillows, and rubs her eyes. Something has happened, but she doesn't remember what it is. Her right foot throbs with pain. Allan is still looking at her with his friendly half smile. She realizes that she trusts him.

A while later she tries to get up again.

"My head is spinning," she moans.

When she finally wakens, rays of light stream through the large bay window.

"It's going to be a nice day," Allan observes. "It's Friday."

He brings her breakfast on a tray. Coffee, at last. Ann hasn't had any for several days, only tea. And there's a big glass of orange juice, and toast, which he smears with butter and rhubarb jam. Then he runs her bath, where she relaxes for at least an hour. She can hear him putting on some music, a record by Bryan Ferry, and she hums one of the songs, "Tokyo Joe." Then she remembers that the record is scratched near the middle, and dreads the moment when the same line repeats itself, along with an unpleasant grating sound. For that very reason, she never plays this record while she's taking a bath. It's a shame: it would be the perfect way to start a summer morning.

The record skips only once. Allan immediately lifts the arm of the stereo and places it on the next groove. She sighs with relief thinking that he is someone she can count on. Being able to anticipate a snag in the smooth progress of a song like "Tokyo Joe"—that's a good sign.

She returns to the living room, now flooded with morning light, without bothering to put her robe back on. She's not embarrassed to walk around naked in front of Allan. She wonders if they have already made love, but there's a huge blank in her recent memory and she concludes that they haven't, but suspects that it's bound to happen soon.

"Do you feel better now?" Allan inquires.

Ann hesitates to ask him what he knows. She asks herself the same question, but has no answer.

"Don't you think we should notify the police?"

"No," Allan says calmly. "It's a hassle and a waste of time. Are you coming with me to Brighton?"

"Sure, if you'd like me to."

CHAPTER XXXI

By early afternoon, they set out in Allan's car, an Aronde, a model rarely seen during the past fifteen years, even in France. Finding it parked outside her building sparks hazy but unpleasant memories; Ann shrinks back in a moment of hesitation, then opens the door and bravely slides onto the seat next to Allan. The car stalls twice before the engine starts. She finds something very conventional about his disheveled, awkward charm, yet it doesn't bother her a bit— quite the contrary.

They talk a lot during the ride, as though they had known each other for a long time. On the way, Allan explains in great detail the rules of the murder party. While listening to him, Ann is also thinking. Fragments of her incredible adventure start to come back to her and she begins reconstructing the developments of the past few days. She idly repeats to herself that perhaps the police should be notified. But in the light of the day and in this car, as they drive leisurely through the peaceful countryside of green meadows with white fences, her recollection of the nightmare is becoming increasingly clear. Soon she will remember the chronology, yet it also seems more and more unreal.

Ann knows she hasn't been dreaming or taken any drugs.

She is convinced that she had been locked up and had escaped, having been lured into a plot in which the man driving
by her side may perhaps be involved, even if he's been playing
the admirable role of the last minute saviour. But she's not
afraid of him—it's over. She feels relaxed, rested, serene.
She tosses her head back, stretching her neck, leaning against
the seat. With all of the windows open, she is constantly
smoothing back her hair, which blows wildly in the wind.
Allan calmly changes gears, casually talking about fictitious
crimes. Everything is back to normal.

They arrive in Brighton in time for tea. The imposing white
façade of the hotel stretches across the oceanfront, about a
hundred yards from the pier, where a crowd of adolescents
are huddled around the slot machine and video games. Families in their vacation gear—shorts, sandals, shrimp nets—
stroll down the boardwalk along the beach, stopping in front
of the stands that sell ice cream. Balls are thrown into the
warm air, the shapes and silhouettes pulsating slightly, partly
due to the gas fumes. A few people walk around with enormous
cassette players blaring. As they pull into the hotel parking
lot, isolated from the boardwalk by a thick hedge, Allan
agrees that Brigitte had been right: Brighton is truly impossible during August. The gravel crunches under their feet as
they head toward the impressive row of columns decked with
lamps that are undoubtedly lit at night. Ann suddenly remembers Brigitte; she'll call her later.

"Have you seen her, in the past few days?"

"No," Allan answers. "We've only spoken on the phone.
She's been working nonstop so that she can finish her book
by Monday."

They are given a key at the front desk, and an envelope
as well. Ann makes no comment on the obvious fact that they
will be sharing a room. In the elevator, he hands her the
envelope. She opens it. Inside is a piece of hotel stationery

with a brief message typed on it, saying that from now on no one is to think about—much less mention—the words murder party. The dinner that night, like every other year, will be a reunion of Prince College alumni and the Victoria School alumnae.

Once they are in their room, which faces the sea, Allan takes Ann in his arms. They undress and soon they are making love. Allan won't take off his glasses until the moment of orgasm. He laughingly explains afterward, for Ann's benefit, that they give him more control in case of extreme excitement, and this happens to be one of those cases. Ann laughs along with him, puts his glasses back on, and he immediately gets another erection.

CHAPTER XXXII

Dressing for dinner, Ann puts on a very sheer but elegant suit, and Allan, a tie that is too wide and a blazer with a Prince College insignia embroidered on the breast pocket. In the hall, a woman who resembles Margaret Thatcher comes toward them looking very agitated. She cuts short the introduction Allan tries to make (so that Ann is unable to catch her name), and says that they've run into a little problem: Doris's daughter has had an attack of appendicitis and needs an emergency operation, and as a result Doris won't be able to play her part—she has just called to let them know. Allan thinks for a moment, then tells her that it's not all that serious. His friend Ann can replace her—she simply has to be told what to do. Margaret Thatcher gives Ann an appraising glance, as if she were sizing her up. She must have arrived at a satisfactory conclusion, for she asks Ann if she truly wouldn't mind filling in. Ann assures her that she wouldn't

mind at all, and Margaret—her name is indeed Margaret—
clasps Ann's hands with gratitude. Interrupting this effusive
gesture, Allan steers Ann into a corner of the enormous hall
where there are plushy armchairs grouped around low tables,
forming a series of small, comfortable sitting rooms.

"It's very simple," he says. "I'm Jeremy Ballister, professor
of literature at Prince College. Doris was supposed to play
the part of my wife, and you'll replace her. She's a housewife,
so you won't have to know any of my former students. You
can just assume a simpering air and ask them if they have
fond memories of my classes, silly things like that. The main
thing is that during dinner—naturally we'll be at the same
table—everyone should notice that things aren't going well
between us, that our marriage is on the rocks. Every so often
you should put me in my place, and then look offended when
I say something back. It's a cinch."

"Then I'm the one who kills you?"

"No, it won't be you. This is just to put everyone on the
wrong track; they won't follow it for long, for that matter. It's
too easy and they're too smart for that, as you'll soon find
out."

"And when you die, what am I supposed to do? First of
all, how do you die?"

"With dignity. The big show is being saved for the second
murder, tomorrow. I'll be poisoned with curare. Drinking a
glass of mint liqueur, I'll suddenly collapse, squeezing my
glass so hard that it'll shatter in my hand."

"You're going to cut yourself," Ann warns.

"I've had practice. At that point, you scream, panic, and
later, when my death is announced, you play the part of the
tearful widow. But in an excessive, hysterical manner, so
that everyone doubts your sincerity. That's about it. In due
respect for your suffering, the guy who plays the cop won't
interrogate you tonight."

* * *

They reach the spacious dining room (hunting engravings on the wall, a fireplace big enough to roast a herd) where the guests are assembled by tables of six. Ann examines the assortment of people, more heterogeneous than she had imagined. She had pictured an army of old ladies resembling Agatha Christie; although there are a few who look that way, many of them are young, clearly middle-class couples. They take their seats in front of the plates with their place cards, and Ann is slightly uneasy when she notices that Mrs. Ballister, whose role she is playing at the last minute, goes by the first name of Bernadette, like the heroine of *The Fickle Beauty*.

Even before dinner is served, Allan, who has discreetly glanced at the other place cards, begins to call everyone by name and makes inquiries as to what they've been doing since the good old days in college. Given the age difference, it seems highly unlikely that an elderly couple from Texas, who have flown in from Houston specifically for the occasion, would have wasted their time under the professorial tutelage of Jeremy-Allan. But the couple in question coolly enter into the game, and the husband explains to his surprised neighbor that Abigail and he had taken a sabbatical five years ago to spend their old age in the typical atmosphere of an English college as auditing students. Abigail nods to confirm this realistic touch and Allan, reassured, sets out to establish the same scholastic complicity with the other pair of former students; a guy in his thirties with a fierce mustache and a falsetto voice named Edward, whom he immediately calls Ted, and his petite red-haired wife, Josephine, with a determined expression on her face, who immediately becomes Jo. Ann realizes that at each table an accomplice like Allan must be in charge of making contact with the guests, to make sure that the taboo words murder party are never uttered. After a few minutes the conversation has reached a lively pace. They trade memories about their studies, dormitories, innocent punishments, and practical jokes played on the rector. Ann notes with surprise that the Texans prove to be the most inventive, overflowing with anecdotes, and never taken aback. And in listening to them recount—one picking up where the other leaves off—how the husband, Bill, who is over sixty, would climb over the wall to rendezvous with Abigail at the Victoria School, Ann wonders if they aren't by chance part of the group of accomplices, like Allan and her. No, four at the same table, that still would be too many.

Unless the entire murder party were a farce they were performing merely for her benefit, using it against her, in which all the guests were actors, and she the only one who didn't know her part, unaware . . . To banish the thought, and remembering Allan's instructions, she decides to ham it up, and docilely slips into the role that he has assigned her. During every one of Allan's tirades she rolls her eyes to the ceiling and drums her fingers on the tablecloth. When he is overly pleased with himself for having singled out Ted—the man with the mustache—as the dunce who traditionally inaugurated his classes by burning pieces of rubber behind the radiator and creating a foul stench, Ann gives such an exasperated sigh that Bill, surprised, gallantly asks her what the matter is. She dryly assures him that everything is quite all right, thank you. Allan ostentatiously ignores her, constantly turning toward Jo, the little redhead, who is delighted to have been chosen by the leader of the game. When he knocks over his glass, Ann bitterly complains about his clumsiness, asking the guests to bear witness that he is always making a mess of everything, and she's the one who has to launder his clothes, which he soils once he's barely had them on. Now it's Allan's turn to roll his eyes. This sudden display of marital discord based on trivial pretexts ruins the agreeable atmosphere of the dinner. The guests conceal their embarrassment by trying to outdo one another with forced gaiety. Ann realizes that they are wondering whether this marital scene is for real, or simply a good performance, essential to the story, in which the Ballisters would be expected to quarrel. They must realize that there are actors in the gathering, that Allan and Ann are probably a part of this group, and in all likelihood they are congratulating themselves on having been randomly seated at a table of such strategic importance. Perhaps they are already waiting for someone among them to die.

The desserts and after-dinner drinks are finally served. Laughing at an amusing story that Bill is telling him, Allan pours a glass of mint liqueur and brings it to his lips. Ann grips the edge of the tablecloth. Allan makes a slight grimace, the corners of his mouth sag, then tighten, his eyes open wide, and meanwhile Ann thinks that someone truly might have poisoned the liqueur. As planned, he crushes the glass in his hands, then, leaning back and straining his neck, he tries to breathe. The chair falls to the floor, he keels over backward, and Ann screams, cutting short the jovial uproar in the dining room. A second later Bill is on his feet; everyone is rushing over to their table; cameras are clicking; flashes are going off—the murder party has begun.

CHAPTER XXXIII

It's just before midnight when Ann gets back to her room. Allan is lying on the bed naked, waiting for her.

Ann lights a cigarette and gives him a report. As the ambulance left with the supposed body on a stretcher, screeching around the corner with the sirens screaming, Allan returned to his room by a back stairway. Meanwhile, a heavy-set man who had introduced himself as Superintendent Breathwaite began to interrogate all of the guests present at the moment of the tragedy. Aside from the few who had snapped pictures, anxious to have souvenirs of the weekend, everything had taken place in a fairly realistic manner. The superintendent had dutifully collected the shattered glass with a handkerchief, and had forbidden anyone to leave the dining room, patting Ann's shoulder. Prostrate with grief, she had remained with her head in her hands, occasionally letting out a heartrending wail. Then, as the waiters still had to clear the tables, the crowd retreated to the bar, where the super-intendent went around to each group, asked questions, and took notes on his pad. Ann had heard Ted and Jo insinuate that the Ballisters did not get along—while hypocritically explaining that they bore no prejudice against the unfortunate widow. The news traveled around the bar. Little by little, Ann picked out the most zealous of the sleuths: first, Ted and Jo, but also an old maid, the type of person Ann thought would be attracted to this entertainment; finally, a pair of plump and pimply high school girls, twins, whose parents had given them this exciting weekend for their birthday. In light of the suspicion already hanging over her head, Ann appreciated Bill and Abigail's presence by her side through-out the evening—their comforting words, cups of tea, and tissues, into which she could hardly bring herself to shed any tears. They even escorted her, if not all the way to her room, at least up to the elevator. In the hall, the three of them stopped in front of a large billboard where the first clues revealed by the investigation had been thumbtacked: scho-lastic reports that were not particularly flattering to certain students, signed Jeremy Ballister, director of English lan-guage; a class photo, where the same Ballister (Allan in his

casual university attire, tweed jacket and cordoroy slacks)
was posing, surrounded by his students; and two or three
other pieces of evidence, all related to the college.

"Well done," Allan concludes at the end of her report.
"You did a wonderful job. It's good practice."

He pulls Ann onto the bed and they make love again. It's
even better than it was that afternoon, now that they're getting
to know one another. Ann is surprised by how quickly this
intimacy is developing. Once the lights are off, Allan continues to caress her for a long time, then finally drifts off to
sleep.

Despite, or perhaps because of the evening's excitement,
Ann is unable to fall asleep right away. She gets up and looks
out the window for a while at the oceanfront. The starless
sky forecasts cloudy weather for tomorrow. The wind blows
a wad of newspaper, which bounces along the boardwalk. A
trio of late-night strollers pass by her window. One of them
skips around the two others and even begins to sing an aria
from an Italian opera, loud enough so Ann can still hear it
after the night owls have vanished from sight. Almost directly
below the corner window, she notices a terrace that gives out
onto the sea and an even thicker hedge than the one in the
parking lot, which must block out the exhausting commotion
of the boardwalk during the day. Hoping that fifty people in
the hotel won't have the same idea, she vows to go down there
the following day to sunbathe, even if there isn't any sun.
The furnishings on the terrace (a table, a garden chair, and
two chaise longues) suggest an exclusive retreat rather than
a communally shared space. Ann decides that it must be a
private terrace, reserved for the owner or the manager of the
hotel, whom Allan probably knows and who would let her
use it.

She gets back into bed. Allan is asleep, lying diagonally
on his stomach, his arms folded. The moonlight, emerging

from behind a cloud, shines on his slender back, casting a lacy shadow on his protruding vertebrae. Seated on the bed, with her back against the wall, hugging her knees, Ann watches Allan sleep, and it strikes her that she is falling in love with him. She tries to reason with herself: it's easy to be in love with a man lying in a position of such careless abandon, his back illuminated by the moon, arousing a pleasant feeling that something is going to happen, tomorrow. But the one thing for certain is that she feels safe with him. His presence drives off the specters; or rather, tames them. She unclasps her knees, lies down next to Allan, almost on top of him, closes her eyes, and falls asleep.

CHAPTER XXXIV

They wake up at the same time. It is too late for breakfast to be served in the rooms. Allan tells Ann to hurry if she doesn't want to miss the morning events. There will be interrogations, suspicions, fresh clues, but no crime before five o'clock, he explains. As he lathers her with soap in the shower he gives her instructions: the superintendent and most likely a crowd of amateur detectives will question her about a play performed by the theater troupe at Prince College two years ago. Bernadette and Jeremy Ballister had both acted in it. During the rehearsals the couple had gotten friendly with a former student named Gordon Castleton, a strange character who would be arriving at the hotel this afternoon. Rumor has it that he and Bernadette had had an affair. If anyone is to bring this up, she must vehemently deny it, too vehemently to be believed. Besides, her entire role is based on calculated exaggeration designed to arouse suspicion.

Descending the stairs, Ann adopts the same expression

she had mastered the night before, the tearful but suspect widow. She somehow endures the interrogation by Superintendent Breathwaite, surrounded by a group of the most assiduous detectives. At the end this heavyset man, playing the role of the policeman with debonair malice, gives her a wink on the sly. He must know that she's replacing Doris at the last minute, and is discreetly complimenting her on her self-assurance. In spite of his professional admiration, Ann begins to tire of the imposed decorum, the stifled sobs at regular intervals. The ever faithful Bill and Abigail continue to treat her with tender consideration.

During breakfast everyone tries to look glum and grief-stricken, but several can barely conceal the extreme state of excitement into which the investigation has plunged them. The high school girls, in particular, make a mad scramble to be at the same table as the number one suspect, whom they carefully observe. The old maid, sitting nearby, casts them a fond glance for their amateurish naïveté: in the eyes of a hardened detective, Bernadette is obviously cleared by the strong presumptions hanging over her.

Then the interrogations resume, still led by Breathwaite, who takes his role to heart. As planned, Ann denies any extramarital involvement and swears that Gordon is only a good friend. Around five o'clock she manages to slip away, and after a brief visit to Allan, leaves the hotel to buy the cigarettes and Cadbury Fruit and Nuts chocolate bars he requested. As she walks through the lobby, heading toward the revolving door, a few keep an eye on her. Although the laid-back superintendent hadn't specified any restrictions of this nature during the investigation, everyone follows certain imperatives on their own that prevent them from wandering too far from the ongoing drama, for fear of missing some new development. Ann strolls down the boardwalk for a while, which is deserted because of a light drizzle. She deposits a few coins in the slot machines located under a glass roof along the pier and around which the entire summer population of Brighton has apparently taken shelter, and walks into a to-bacco shop that also sells newspapers. Then she recognizes the two acned twins, busy examining a revolving stand of books. Drawing nearer, she notes several works from Captain Walton's collection, including *Love Is a Bird in Flight.* She considers recommending this purchase to the high school girls, who more or less fit the cynical image she has formed of her readers, but nods at them instead and goes over to the cashier to ask for the cigarettes and chocolate. While paying for them, she hears an uncommonly deep masculine voice, one of the twins, and she shudders. Either she has misun-derstood, or the girl had, in fact, just asked the shopkeeper if he carried, by any chance, *Frankenstein.*

"The monster story?" he inquires. "No, I doubt it. Every-thing is on the stand."

Handing Ann the change, he smiles conspiratorially. "They read strange things at their age," he comments. "It must be the programs on TV, putting those ideas into their heads."

Ann forgets to pick up her change and races over to the door, where the two adolescents are walking out, setting off a bell that definitely hadn't been in operation when she first came in.

"What was that you asked for?"

The one who had spoken earlier comes to a stop and stares at Ann, shifting her weight from one foot to the other. Her sister starts to imitate her—they look like a pair of music-hall dancers in a bumbling parody.

"Umm . . . *Frankenstein*, by Mary . . . Shelley," says the first, unfolding the piece of crumpled paper where she must have jotted down the name of the author.

"Does that mean anything to you?" the second one throws in slyly, as though she had some kind of secret.

"But . . . why?" Ann stammers, realizing that her confusion only accentuates the triumphant, evil smile that symmetrically breaks out on the moon-faced girls.

"So it really doesn't mean anything to you?" the second one insists.

And she nudges her sister with her elbow. Then both of them burst out laughing and take to their heels.

Ann can feel the drops of rain. It's starting up again. She stands there paralyzed for a moment, clutching her package. It starts to rain harder. All around her, people are running to take shelter under the vending stands, grabbing their towels and rubber rafts in a panic. They're crazy, Ann thinks distractedly, to have gone back to the beach simply because it cleared up for ten minutes. She returns to the tobacco shop, under the awning that protects a thin strip of sidewalk. The surrounding asphalt is now dripping wet. Others join her under her temporary shelter, determined to wait until the downpour is over.

In spite of their predictions the rain is not letting up. Ann prefers to make a run for it to get back to the hotel. Soaked to the skin, she disappears into the revolving door and shakes herself off in the lobby as the two girls, sitting on a love seat with a tray of tea and Danish pastries, look on with foolish smirks. She decides to ignore them, and tries to keep her dress from sticking to her skin by gathering it between her thumb and index finger. She walks over to the billboard near the elevator, where the clues are exhibited. A new document has been posted: a mimeographed double page, the program of the production at Prince College in June 1982, of *Frankenstein, or the Demon of Switzerland*, a play in four acts by Richard Brinsley Peake, adapted from the novel by Mary Shelley, with the following cast:

210

Frankenstein	JEREMY BALLISTER
Elizabeth	BERNADETTE BALLISTER
The Creature	GORDON CASTLETON
Justine	HELEN WINTERFIELD
William	THADDEUS WINTERFIELD, JR.
Captain Robert Walton	MARCEL NUMERAERE

The elevator doors open, letting out a dozen extremely upset people, including Bill and Abigail. They advance toward Ann and Superintendent Breathwaite, who gives her another wink of complicity as he passes in front of her.

"It's awful," says Bill. "There has just been a second murder."

"Yes," Abigail confirms. "They've just found Thaddeus strangled in the winter garden."

Ann doesn't know who Thaddeus is, but with the sudden turn of events, she figures she never will, given the lack of time. All these details must remain obscure: young Thaddeus (how did she know he was young?), the production of *Frankenstein* in which she and Allan are supposed to have performed under their pseudonyms, and the return of Captain Walton on the billboard. . . . Everything is happening so quickly, that she's caught up in the movement; it's hard for her to think, as it would be hard for a man to breathe when his head is repeatedly being plunged into a bathtub. She knows only that something is going to unfold, at once. Indeed, as if she had willed it to happen, the tumult behind her increases, then suddenly it's drowned out by the booming voice of the superintendent. "Ah, there you are, Mr. Gordon Castleton!"

Ann turns around, bewildered. Peering through the crowd, she sees Julian, around whom a circle has formed in the lobby. This time he is wearing an elegant off-white summer suit, and has just set down his travel bag. Satisfied with his

theatrical entrance, he takes a step forward, feigns astonishment, and answers clearly, articulating every word, "Yes,
here I am, indeed. But why all the commotion?"

"I have a few questions to ask you, Mr. Castleton," says
the superintendent in an ominously good-natured tone.

The audience buzzes with curiosity. Riveted to the floor,
Ann stares at him. Her chin quivers, and behind her back
she wrings her hands, crumpling the paper bag of cigarettes
and chocolate. Abigail looks at her anxiously: Ann seems to
be truly beside herself. Julian eyes the audience, his nostrils
flaring, with a mocking, arrogant air. Suddenly his shifting
glance falls onto Ann and remains there. He smiles. The
magnetism he exerts is so great that everyone notices he has
stopped his inspection. Following the direction of his green
eyes, they all turn toward Ann.

Now everybody looks at her, as if she's been put under a
spotlight. She takes a step backward, her eyes on the floor,
and lets go of the paper bag. A stir follows, a confused
shuffling. Fifty pairs of shoes move forward, tightening the
circle surrounding her. Out of the corner of her eye she can
make out the red legs of one of the twins, pushing her way
into the front row in a rush for the spoils.

She looks up and searches out the portly Breathwaite, as
if he really were a policeman whom she could ask for help.
The superintendent merely gives her a little nod of approval,
as if to say that she should continue, that she is doing a fine
job playing her part.

The role of the victim.

The elevator, behind her.

No one can stop her.

She turns around and dashes into the open cubicle. She
randomly presses a button, recalling that the metal doors are
slow in closing. They have all the time they need to follow
her inside.

But they don't budge. They encircle the elevator, as if surprised by the violence of her reaction. Way in the back, near the reception desk, Breathwaite frowns. Does he realize that something is wrong, that this episode hadn't been on the agenda? And what about her, Ann? Was she delirious, responding to a simple game with a fit of hysteria?

Bill, the old Texan, takes a step forward. "Bernadette . . ."

She inches back to the rear of the elevator; the doors still haven't closed. She must have pushed the OPEN button instead. She presses the one marked 2 as hard as she can.

"Bernadette, my dear . . ." Bill repeats.

The metal doors vibrate and finally slide closed, and like a shrinking movie screen, the scene in the hall is slowly blocked from sight. The elevator feels as though it has dropped down a little to prepare its ascent, then lurches upward. Ann doesn't understand anything anymore, and fights back her tears. Ever since her stay in the Chinese hotel and Allan's rescue, everything has unfolded like one of those horror films in which, after a terrifying scene, developed at length, comes a grand finale with fireworks. The heroine, suffering from shock, believes she is safe, and everyone heaves a sigh of relief. But the audience knows full well, as any heroine should, that if the words "The End" do not immediately follow, if the camera complacently lingers on the fact that everything is back to normal, the music now upbeat, there has to be a reason. The last image will reveal the monster still alive, indestructible; that he has, for instance, taken refuge in the pipes of the bathtub, where the heroine lounges with her eyes closed, trying to relax after so many abominations. And then suddenly he'll spring on her, snickering contemptuously for the very last time, while the audience remains riveted to their seats. That is what awaits her, this last image; inevitably it will happen. From the beginning the nightmarish figure has been coming back, each time more and more convincingly, nearer and nearer, only to withdraw at the last minute, varying his horrid exit only so he can continue his torture, secure his hold over her. Ann would like to remain in the elevator to evade him. She could always press another button as soon as the doors start to open. She would be safe here, out of reach.

That is where she has always wanted to be. Out of reach.

But it won't work. If they really want to get hold of her, the members of the Polidori sect, assembled in the hotel for this special meeting, would find a way to intercept the elevator. She mustn't, absolutely must not, let herself get cornered. Getting out on the second floor, where her room is located, she inspects the deserted, spacious hallway.

She removes one of her shoes and sticks it between the elevator doors, which are closing. A little time gained here, but very little.

She walks down the hallway, leans over the stairway, and sees no one. Strange, she was expecting a mob rushing up the stairs, four steps at a time, their clawing hands outstretched to seize her.

Where now? To her room? That would be throwing herself into the lion's den—Allan is unquestionably part of this. But she can't ask anyone in the hotel for help. Naturally, she can't go to the clients of the murder party either, nor to the other guests. They've already seen it all—the stretchers, the swarms of people in the hallway, the painted cadavers. . . . They would smile, raise their eyebrows. In this hotel, anyone can murder whomever they please with impunity, and they'll gain precious time over the police. She could be dying in a hallway, a knife driven into her stomach—the chambermaids would glance at her distractedly as they went by, a bit annoyed by this waste of tomato sauce and this childish entertainment of the rich, which leaves them only with a carpet to clean.

She keeps her other shoe on, shivering in her soaked dress, and hobbles toward her room.

"The lion's den," she murmurs.

The lion's den.

A game.

"A game," she repeats. "It's only a game. The main thing is to prove I can play along. I've had practice now."

She knocks on the door.

The soft patter of footsteps. Allan must be barefoot. He is, in fact, naked when he opens the door. This guy spends his life in the nude, she thinks.

"Wow, you got drenched," he observes, stepping aside to let her in. "Good timing; the laundry service just brought back your dress."

Ann has never given a dress to the hotel laundry. Of course. Laid out on the bed in a plastic bag, she recognizes the one that Julian had bought her at the Chinese hotel.

Only a game.

She mustn't scream.

The sound of Allan's voice behind her. "You should change. You'll catch cold."

She remains standing, frozen in place. He draws nearer and slides his hands under her wet dress to help her slip it over her head. He unhooks her bra and presses his palms against her breasts. Ann offers no resistance. There is nothing more to be done, she isn't even clenching her teeth. Okay, the last image has already come to pass, but the game continues. Allan kneels down to take off her panties and her one shoe. She obediently shifts from one leg to the other to facilitate the operation. Now she waits with curiosity. Noting that Allan has an erection, she thinks this should reassure her. Theoretically, that can't be faked. But it doesn't matter anymore.

She raises her arms, like a resigned victim about to be sacrificed, so that he can slip on the dress from the Chinese hotel.

While he puts on his clothes, stumbling as he shoves his feet into his already shabby-looking loafers, he drags her toward the window and points to the small terrace she had noticed the night before. It is almost dark. There isn't a soul on the boardwalk, where the rain beats down; she feels even more isolated, protected by only a thin roof. In spite of the eaves, she can still see the chaise longues, and a table on which a candelabrum has been placed. The five candles cast shadows of the trees, blowing against the railing, onto the tiled floor. Two white, electrifying forms catch her eye: the trousered legs of a man, who stretches them out on the chaise longue, then crosses them. From where she is standing Ann can't see any more than that, but she concludes that this man is Julian. Soon she will have to go down to the terrace. She is very calm.

"Villa Diodati," Allan announces, like a groom presenting his ancestral mansion to his bride. "The planet's destiny is in your hands," he adds.

At that moment there is a knock on the door of the adjoining room.

"Ah," says Allan. "It's the captain. Now we can finally begin."

He slides the latch to open the door. It is Captain Walton, of course, dressed in lightweight canvas trousers and, for lack of a T-shirt, a short-sleeved shirt exposing his slender, adolescent arms. His childlike smile suggests a kind of benevolent excitement.

Allan takes her gently by the shoulders and leads her over the threshold of the door, into the next room. The captain walks ahead of them in silence. Ann can feel the carpet beneath her bare feet, fiber by fiber. She takes slow, light steps.

The captain goes up to a large closet in the back of the room, with double doors. Instead of pulling them open, he pushes the doors toward the inside, and Ann realizes that it's not a closet at all, but a secret stairway. She has already figured out that it must lead to the small terrace—through the thickness of the wall, or God knows how else.

As gently as ever—but then, she offers no resistance— the two men push her into the closet. She finds herself standing on a rectangular platform above the narrow stairs; the first few steps are illuminated by the light of the room, behind a row of empty hangers.

Their gestures are in perfect harmony; one would think that it was part of a play. They start to close the two doors of the closet; leaning toward her with the same kindly but excited expression. The crack of light framing their faces begins to narrow, like the scene from the elevator doors earlier on. They both watch her. And then she is alone.

CHAPTER XXXV

During the last days of the summer of 1815, with the sudden eruption, east of the island of Java, of a volcano located inland and thought to be extinct, red-hot lava poured all the way down to the coasts, taking with it the houses and a large percentage of the tribes. The violence and length of the cataclysm made some believe that the unleashed fire would overrun and burn the three other elements. It petrified the earth surrounding the source of heat along the entire width of the island; it covered the waves with an incandescent blanket along the coastline, burning even the air to a cinder. For several weeks the sky was nothing more than a thick opaque cloud of a texture that seemed denser than that of the atmosphere: a rough blackish material, full of snags and rips, that the angry gods had stretched over the island, concealing the sun, the moon, and the stars from the survivors, to the point where they had begun to doubt the alternation of day and night behind this curtain. But it was an ephemeral conquest, as nearly all conquests are. Little by little, the land that had been vanquished by the fire recovered its natural independence. First, conforming to the laws momentarily violated by nature, the waters eventually extinguished the flames. Soon nothing else remained from the firestorm that had raged along the coast but blocks of solidified lava, strewn like pebbles by the sea; rocks and reefs whose incredibly compact mass imprisoned entire boats with the petrified bodies of the crews, caught in their brief agony just as they were trying to escape from shore, from the raging earth, not knowing that there was no longer a shore, earth, nor open sea, only a red-hot blanket of fear enveloping their lives, destined to become a stretch of immutable desolation. Many of these rocks later became meeting grounds for a cult, where to appease the spirits, human were sacrificed, leaving the victims, their throats slit, to the petrified statues that had been victims of the gods. With the effects of wind and rain the sacrificed were rapidly transformed into skeletons, then into dust, whereas the mineralized humans were subject to a gradual erosion. It took more than a century for these ghastly realistic shapes to become blunted; their resemblance to the sacrificed was attributed to one of nature's whims. Cults persisted even longer at sea than on land, undoubtedly because the victory of fire over water—albeit for a short time—is more striking to the imagination than its victory over the earth. Yet entire villages and their inhabitants, caught by surprise in the midst of their daily activities, remained fixed in the carapace of the cooled lava, which now covers the whole eastern section of the island. In a few years new villages, new cultures, and identical lives had superimposed themselves onto this crust of villages, cultures, and bygone lives, and doubtless other crusts as well. For in the past, tradition has taken similar catastrophes into account, and even the earliest inhabitants always knew that they were treading, rushing about, taking their naps, reaping their harvests, and making love and war on the surface of land that owes its fat, its fertile soil to innumerable layers of fiery destruction.

But here lies the strangest fact of all: one might have thought that the conquest of the sky would be the most precarious, that it would only take several days for the moving, ductile air to scatter, consume, or annihilate the monstrous cloud of ashes that had taken it by storm. And indeed, volcanic rocks and black rains fell to the earth; various other signs were observed, proving that the purge was following its cycle. But when the sky swallowed up the cataclysm, it triggered an even subtler mechanism, a circuit more vast than the natives had ever dreamed. When the oppressive lid above them had lifted, when the stars were visible once more, when it was clear that neither their location nor their movements had been altered, the battle was considered won, since the cloud hadn't been carried off to other lands. Which is nevertheless precisely what did occur. During the entire winter— our winter—the winds transported the volcanic slag from the eruption, and the dust and ash that had spread into the atmosphere then drifted in an extremely orderly manner, with a casualty rate as low as that of the migrating birds, who several months earlier had flown in almost the opposite direction. As a result, in the spring of 1816 an enormous black cloud hung over Europe, filtering the rays of the sun, inducing such a marked fall in temperature that the year was later recorded as the coldest of the century in the Northern Hemisphere. The meteorologists, sniffling and wrapping their mufflers tighter, did not take long to determine the cause of this phenomenon—particularly because the spectacular Javanese eruption had created a great fuss in their milieu, and the displacement of its residue in the atmosphere during the winter had them far more concerned than any political events, to which only the laymen paid much attention.

So, for the Javanese villager, the summer of 1815 was the season of the wrath of the gods. His European equivalent only noticed the fall of the empire; the smell of burning villages and gunsmoke did not give him the chance to follow the celestial itinerary of the volcanic ash, being ignorant of its very existence. And when this smoke and these ashes hung over his head, he barely paid attention to the meteorologists' explanations, but figured—without even realizing it, without any conscious reflection—that this general darkening of the sky and the dirty, acrid air he was breathing were from a nearby blaze, one that had just been put out and in whose hearth they were busy holding meetings, restoring monarchies, furbishing new hopes, or claiming that history had reached its end. No one, in 1816, was surprised when darkness followed the bloody fireworks, that the sun, defeated at Waterloo, had disappeared, and no one, or almost no one knew that this darkness, this long eclipse had been imported, the result of another sort of fireworks on the other side of the world, where the wrath of man had no hand in the matter.

Like Ann in her closet, Mary knows nothing of the Javanese cataclysm and merely tells herself that it isn't worth coming to the mountains, only to find, after wiping one's face with a handkerchief, that it is stained with grayish streaks and shiny black particles. The shepherds and the mountaineers resemble chimney sweeps. Besides, in general she is less and less sure that this summer holiday was such a good idea.

It's particularly at night that she starts to have these doubts, when she is alone (or with Claire, which is worse) and the storm breaks. Yet she loves these storms, and recalls the delightful terror she experienced, pulling the blanket over her head, when she was a little girl—which is not terribly long ago: she is still so young.

Now, half-sprawled in a chaise longue that she'd dragged over to the doorway, this slim blond girl dressed in a man's bathrobe (though somewhat garish for a man: it's a present from Albé) alternately glances with her magnificent gray eyes at the downpour—the big drops of melted tar beating down on the charcoal surface of Lake Geneva, drawing a curtain across the mountain chain that one normally sees from the veranda—and at a disorderly stack of papers on the portable writing desk in front of her, resting on the arms of the lounge chair.

She can barely make out the lake or the orchard behind the railing of the small terrace where she sits, which gently descends toward the pebble beach and the floating dock. There's no point in her remaining on the lookout for Percy's return, she thinks; he would suddenly turn up at her side before she had the chance to see or hear him approach. She might as well concentrate on her letter to Emily; it's important.

In the meantime she vainly tries to drive off the images that have come between her eyes and the pages she now holds in her hands, like an orator preparing to read a speech truffled with Greek and Latin quotes; only yesterday Albé had teasingly accused her of being pedantic. All of these images link Percy's person (Percy is a person, she says to herself, and even though there's nothing terribly new about this information, the alliteration troubles her. Perhaps she should begin her letter to Emily like that, try and explain, tell her at the very outset of the game, to avoid any misunderstanding, that Percy is a person; repeat it twice, three times, as many times as necessary to persuade her—indeed, it's not all that obvious) yes, these images associate Percy's person with the aquatic element.

He doesn't know how to swim; he's more like an elf than a water sprite. And still, he loves the water. Ever since Albé and he rented the boat, they've gone out on the lake almost every afternoon, braving the storms. In the past few weeks the rain generally begins fairly late. During the day the sky darkens with clouds, which get thicker and thicker, and the storm breaks in the late afternoon. Every evening the two navigators return soaked to the skin, enchanted by the risks they have taken, singing refrains with incomprehensible words at the top of their lungs, which Albé claims are Albanian songs. Albania, where he had traveled in the past, and where the pasha of Janina complimented him on his hands and ears—the most delicate he'd ever seen—often comes up in his conversation. He praises the climate, the gentle ways and liberal morals of its inhabitants (to shock Claire, he boasts of having seduced children who hadn't even reached puberty), he flaunts the rank of colonel given to him by the Albanian army, and describes his grand uniform. It's precisely for this reason that Percy and Mary nicknamed him Albé, L.B., also standing for his initials.

A water sprite incapable of swimming, she repeats to herself. And she? She knows how to swim; she had learned quite young. It had been one of her father's many educational principles that Percy now teases her about, having once made such a fuss over them—but in his own way, with none of Albé's cynicism. If one thinks about Percy's person, it is even strange to try and comprehend his total absence of spitefulness. It is as though he lacked one of his senses: he knows no more how to be malicious than how to swim, and couldn't master the necessary technique, even if his life depended on it. He can be evil, all the same.

So Mary knows how to swim, but isn't terribly fond of the water. She's afraid of it, more for Percy than for herself. Every day at the same time—at precisely this hour—she imagines him drowning, getting thrown overboard, carried off by a wave and passively allowing himself to sink without a struggle. These fears amuse Percy. Come to think of it, she wonders whether this isn't in fact a form of spitefulness— the only one accessible to him—jesting about it that way. He even enjoys frightening her. Percy, who can't bear to hurt people, loves to scare them. He knows that she's afraid of the water, and whenever he teases her, will ask if she had also been afraid in Dover.

It's always Dover, always that memory. It had happened two years ago, only a few days after he had stolen her away from the home of old Godwin. It was the first time they had left England together (and already, Claire was along with them). Days of riding in the coach, bags that barely closed, flea-ridden country inns, days of wild happiness. In Dover, they had waited for the boat to Calais. It was summer—an English summer—which tonight, all of a sudden, is something she misses. The beach was only a narrow strip of pebbles. They gained access to it by climbing over a freshly painted white fence that had stained Mary's dress. She took it off and rinsed it in the sea to get rid of the two large white stripes; then at the request of Percy, who was grinning like a child, she got completely undressed and went in for a swim. Now, stretched on the chaise longue, her writing desk open before her, she distinctly remembers the exquisite, cold sensation of entering the water. The feeling of the stones beneath her feet, their sharp edges, how she had shivered when she had gone in up to the waist, and what her genitalia had looked like. Her patchy blond fleece inflated like a sponge, as if it were no longer a part of her. Then she had moved in as far as her breasts and armpits. Her loose hair floated around her shoulders; she hadn't cared about getting it wet. Once in the water, she glanced back at Percy, who had also undressed, and was plowing through the little waves to join her. Since he was taller than she, he could still touch bottom where she was swimming, and they made love. He had been carrying her, standing with his feet planted as firmly as possible in the sand that was slipping between his toes and under his heels, and that had slid out from under him so quickly that they were suddenly in the open sea, without realizing it. It was only once she opened her eyes after the orgasm that she was able to gauge the distance they had covered, and then realized that Percy could no longer touch bottom, that his sole anchor was not the ground, but inside of her. And now that he had emptied himself—a hot stream had erupted in her belly and the whitish threads, fine and sticky like gossamer, had merged with the foam all around them—now that Percy was about to withdraw his member from her, nothing else was holding him up. He would sink and drown. Apparently he still hadn't realized it himself, or else he hadn't been disturbed by the prospect. She feared that she wasn't strong enough to bring him back to shore, and above all, that he would panic, like anyone who doesn't know how to swim, vainly splashing about, hanging on to her and hindering her movement. In a case like that, she had been told that the only solution was to knock the struggling swimmer unconscious, or plunge his head underwater. It is easier to haul in an unconscious body than a floundering monster whose uncoordinated gestures interfere with the rescue. For a moment she had pictured herself hitting Percy with all her might, while he was still unaware of the danger, smiling dreamily with half-closed eyes. She had imagined the look he would give her, and the crazy idea that might pass through his head before he swallowed a mouthful of water. Mary, with whom

he had just made love, wanted to kill him; she had always
wanted to kill him; she had followed him and pretended to
love him merely to arrive at this point, so that she could
murder him with impunity at the moment he least expected
it—assuming that a moment could ever exist in which he
might have expected it more. Horrified that a thought such
as this, dictated by an obvious misinterpretation, could possibly arise in Percy's mind, even fleetingly, she had suddenly
felt drained of all her strength. She closed her eyes. A violent
pain throbbed at her temples; she had felt a dizziness behind
her forehead and over her brow, burning into her brain; her
ears pulsated with blood. Then she heard a long scream, a
strange, sustained note coming out of her mouth. And at the
same time—since she could hear it—she reentered the world
of sound, obliterated a moment earlier. Behind the sound of
her scream was the distinct and gentle lapping of waves on
the pebbles, and the waves breaking against her bare flanks,
the moving pebbles digging into her back. The cries of sea
gulls. She had opened her eyes onto the circle of sun, as
close to her as the eye of another person. Then she had closed
them, reopened them—she was on the beach. Percy, leaning
over her, was massaging her shoulders and looking at her as
if he didn't know what to do, as if astonished by the situation
and reduced to this useless and awkward gesture. She had
fainted in the water, in his arms, he told her later. Out of
pleasure, he thought, and she hadn't corrected him. Besides,
perhaps he was right, perhaps it had all gone through her
mind at the moment of orgasm.

"But how did you bring me back to the beach?"

"I carried you. It wasn't easy. You were shaking so and
clinging to my shoulders. I could barely keep my head above
water."

"So you swam?"

"I don't know. Yes, I suppose I did."

Had he really swum? For a moment it was no longer Percy, but someone else, a stranger, holding her. At any rate, he had never swum again. He doesn't know how, he never has. But whenever Mary gets worried about him, he brings up Dover, changing the story slightly each time. Should she tell Emily about Dover? Mary wonders. But how?

She heaves a discouraged sigh, and then, as if this sigh needed a motive, something to justify it, she returns to the letter she has just begun.

My dear,

As I have a million things to tell you, and don't know how to begin my letter, I shall apologize for not having written sooner—it's been almost two years. I could make pages of excuses, but that would only keep me from getting on with my story. Besides, I have had this plan in mind for several days now. Tonight, as every night, I settle down in front of the darling little desk that Percy brought back from the village so that I can work comfortably on the terrace (but you hardly know who Percy is, or to which terrace I am referring), take out a piece of blank paper, and hesitate. Will this page be the first of a letter that I owe you or the first of the second chapter of my novel? I can already picture you shaking your head: little Mary, writing a novel! Don't worry, it isn't very far along, but I think about it constantly. I know the characters, the plot, I have drawn up the outline—all I have to do now is to work on it.

As for the letter, well, that's another story. In all truthfulness, if I were able to write you the letter that you deserve, the novel would almost be finished by that time. My dear, you must think that all the traveling and the poetry have gone to my head, and you certainly wouldn't be mistaken there. Tonight, in any case, I have made a heroic decision: I am putting the novel aside, and now I am already on the second page of my letter to you.

We have been here for almost a month, in a villa called Montalègre. It's on the shore of Lake Geneva, and you can't imagine the exquisite sight stretching before my eyes, to the point where I'm tempted to put down my letter and watch the sun sink into the sky and disappear . . .

Mary finishes rereading the first page. She makes a face and tears it up. Then she picks up the second one.

. . . behind the golden hills. Since I have given in to that temptation for three days in a row, I swore to myself today that I would stand firm, and that even when it becomes too dark to write, I shall ask for a candle. It does attract mosquitoes, but out of love for you, I am prepared to be covered with little red spots that make Percy cry out as if it were his own skin being mercilessly bitten, and on which he would then be forced to apply vinegar. Every evening he takes care of me as seriously as if he were saying Mass, and for nothing in the world would he allow our physician, Doctor Polidori (I say "our physician," but he isn't really ours, even if he would like to be mine), to carry out this dedicated task. When he kisses me, he grimaces, his mouth full of vinegar. And he kisses me a great deal.

How difficult it is for me, my dear, to picture you in London, in a corner by the fireside, perhaps, or at the window, busy reading this letter, which is taking forever to get going! I am certain that you are getting impatient; you are crumpling the thick wad of paper, searching through the pages to see what extraordinary news I have to tell and that I have put off revealing. You skip over all the pages that follow, where I continue to talk about mosquitoes, the view from our terrace, the marvelous weather we are having, and all that nonsense.

*Very well, then. No, you shall not have to skip over them,
because there won't be anything to skip. Now I shall truly
begin, I give you fair warning.*

The second page ends there, and Mary tears it up as well.
Then she gazes at the little pieces of paper scattered around
the chaise longue. A gust of wind slowly pushes a few pieces
to the edge of the terrace, and they disappear into the invisible
orchard, swamped in blackish rain. One can hardly see a
thing, even on the terrace, and even if Mary had wanted to,
she couldn't have gone back to her writing without candlelight. It is almost night. Percy and Albé should have been
back by now. Perhaps they have gone directly to Diodati, she
thinks bitterly, without bothering to come and fetch her. A
bolt of lightning splits the sky in two, followed by a rumble
of thunder in the mountains, the rustling of leaves in the
wind. Silence. Then the sound of a child crying from inside
the house. William must have woken up. He's hungry. The
pattering of footsteps in the hall behind her. Claire will take
care of it, which is fine with her. What does it matter if she
thinks that Mary is a bad mother, or if she lets it be known
with that mournful, dignified air of hers? Mary doesn't feel
like seeing her son right now, nor does she feel like seeing
Claire. In fact, she doesn't feel like doing much of anything.

Earlier on in the afternoon, when she had gone to sit on
the terrace after Percy had left, she really wanted to write to
Emily. And now that the enterprise appears to be doomed to
another failure, it seems even more imperative than when she
had written those first banal words; if they rang false, it was
more out of habit than conviction. Yet she owes nothing to
this friend from childhood. And if she really wanted to carry
on a regular correspondence, it would be more logical to send
it to her father, for instance, or to one of her sisters. Mary
hadn't written to them for almost a year; she wouldn't know

how to go about it now. If Emily is the only one to enjoy this privilege (at this rate, she'll never get a letter), and if from Mary's point of view, she represents the ideal correspondent, it isn't owing to any particular affinity for this somewhat ordinary girl—it is more for everything that now divides them and permits Mary to measure the distance she has covered since her flight.

Emily is a year older than Mary. When they were children, Mary had been struck by her self-assurance and offhand manner. She was the kind of exhilarating family companion who never stopped playing practical jokes, who would burst out laughing, and talk back to adults with such gay insolence that no one knew how to control her. In comparison, Mary had seemed shy, almost retiring. At age fifteen she had honestly thought that Emily was destined to a romantic fate, while she herself would marry some nice but slightly dull young man. Besides which, Emily had always encouraged their belief in this assignation of roles. However, it was Mary and not Emily who had eloped one spring evening with a young poet, more handsome than all the heroes in the novels they had read; she was the one who, without getting married, was leading a nomadic life of makeshift homes, traveling through Europe, spending her evenings in the company of the celebrated and scandalous Lord Byron—to whom Emily, two years ago, had referred as a kind of seductive scoundrel, proud that a friend of her mother's had met him while at the home of Lady Caroline Lamb, then his mistress. Since she had left, Mary had had time to realize that Emily's insolence and eccentricities were the kind of thing that families tolerated and even appreciated, because they know that it will never go beyond a certain point; that it's the guarantee of a peaceful life, graced with a touch of imagination that satisfies everyone and worries no one. In those few days Mary and Emily hadn't actually traded roles; it was just that Mary's departure had shattered the reassuring image that had given these roles their meaning. Emily had remained the life of the party, and Mary had said good-bye to that life and to parties, and without losing her serious, meditative, and sometimes ferocious temperament, had forever abandoned the world in which Emily had been left behind. Emily embodies that world gone by, and now that the difference in character of the two girls has been rendered meaningless by time, Mary feels that by writing to Emily, she is addressing herself to a former Mary, painting a portrait, or trying to, of what she has become, but still doesn't comprehend.

To make herself understood by this former Mary, whose part is conveniently played by Emily, she will have to start at the beginning and tell her everything that has happened. And it's hard to tell everything. Of course, she can enumerate certain events, retrace the different stages of their travels, mention their crossing to France, their arrival in Switzerland, talk about Claire, tell her that William was born—Emily doesn't even know that she has a child. But she would also have to talk about Percy (Percy is a person, and then what? He doesn't know how to swim, but what about Dover?), and the nights they had spent under the stars or in abandoned castles in Cévennes, reciting poems and telling each other stories; Percy's outings in the boat when night falls and how worried she gets; how much she loves Percy and how frightened he makes her, how horribly frightened. She would also have to talk about Lord Byron, of the opulence that surrounds him and the almost evil way that this opulence, this aura, affects everyone around him, Percy and herself included. In short, she would have to put down on paper the thoughts, sensations, and feelings of two years of her life, everything that made it so that in the past few years, Mary Godwin has been Mary Godwin and not Emily Meadows. This abundance of detail renders the letter as difficult, for the same reasons, as the famous novel she claims to be writing. There, for once she had spoken the truth: if she were able to draft the letter, set down all that she wished to explain, it would no longer be worth slaving away on the novel. All things considered, however, it must be easier to relate the life of an imaginary person than it is to tell one's own story. The other day, when she had begun writing the first lines, "I am by birth a Genevese," she felt invested with a power that deserted her as soon as she tried to set down, in a necessarily jumbled order, her memories of the past two years. The hero of a novel, she thinks, deserves a simplified, exotic biography, one that can be summed up in a series of striking events. She doesn't need to talk about the warmth of the sun on his skin one summer afternoon, or the precise taste of his beloved's lips, or what happened at Dover. It's true that this novel is something to take her mind off more disturbing things, and this wager represents an easy way out of her dilemma. Still, it's not that easy, and as usual, she has lied on this score: she'll never send the letter, she isn't even certain anymore that Emily exists, and yet she's lying to her. Naturally, she doesn't know a thing about either the plot or the general outline! Like the letter, the novel grinds to a halt whenever she must come to the heart of the matter (in other words, find out precisely what the matter *is*), stop being evasive, stop blackening pages (a good fifteen already) with tiny falsehoods, whether it's a question of dainty inlaid writing desks or radiant sunshine or the youth of this hero who is "by birth a Genevese," about whom she knows only (since yesterday) that his name is Victor Frankenstein and that he resembles (depending on her mood) Percy, Albé, even Polidori—all the men around her.

So far, the only thing she has come up with is a clever way to stretch out the introduction, to preserve the intoxication of that first day, when she discovered the freedom of breathing

231

life into a paper hero. After all, a hero (even an imaginary
one) who announces that he is "by birth a Genevese" is
obliged to make this announcement somewhere; he isn't writing in a void, but at a precise place and moment in his life.
And so, to play for time, Mary concentrates on this place and
this moment. She hopes to create a dramatic effect by having
her hero tell his story (but what story?) on his deathbed,
under tragic circumstances. Percy, who has a keen interest
in geography, has recently described to her some engravings
he saw, pictures of the frozen North, where the ocean teems
with gigantic icebergs like those seen by whaling men. So
fascinated is she by this image that she'd thought at first about
making Frankenstein a whaler, then about setting the beginning of his story—the moment when he decides to write his
memoirs—on board a whaling vessel whose captain has rescued him. Now at last she'd had no difficulty writing a pro-
logue to her novel, which she presented as the work of this
captain, whom she named Walton, Robert Walton. This Walton relates how he found Frankenstein, adrift on an ice floe,
dying of exhaustion, and how he inherited his manuscript,
or rather—this is a better idea—how Frankenstein dictated
it to him during his last days. To avoid having to face the
manuscript in question, she could endow Walton with
the same biographical scruples that motivate Frankenstein;
the captain could begin with a detailed narrative of his own
life ("I was born in Liverpool") before explaining how the
hero dictated his memoirs to him and why he decided to
publish them. She'd been brought up short, however, by the
prospect of having to invent for Walton a destiny extraordinary
enough to justify such a digression (in which case she was
simply changing the name of her hero, and she preferred
Frankenstein), or to write an infinite series of preliminary
chapters, each one being its author's explanation of how he'd
met the author of the following chapter—without ever getting

to the story itself. She had finally decided simply to give her captain a sister, to whom he writes regularly (which relieves him of the obligation to relate his entire life's story each time, as Mary would like to do with all those Emilys she has invented for herself ever since she was old enough to hold a pen), and she had resisted the temptation of having the sister write an introduction, and then having one of the sister's neighbors write another, and having the neighbor's father confessor write yet another. Walton is the last crutch she will allow herself. She must have faith in Captain Walton, or else abandon the whole thing. At the moment Mary is quite close to giving up; she cannot understand why she's at a standstill, why it's so hard for her to invent a story. Perhaps because Percy is constantly encouraging her to write, and she's afraid of disappointing him, just as she's afraid of revealing her true thoughts to him in their joint diary.

Strictly speaking, Mary is not much given to keeping a private diary. She prefers to write letters: to herself, to correspondents who are wholly imaginary or as abstract as Emily. Still, ever since she began living with Shelley, they've each kept a record of their thoughts in the same notebook, thoughts that are mostly about their life together. At first she found this practice delightful. Both of them strove to be honest, precise, scrupulous, and they believed this daily effort made each of them transparent in the other's eyes. Whenever one —or both—of them would feel a certain strain, whenever some misunderstanding, a gesture or an awkward silence, would threaten to put the slightest distance between them, they knew they could clear it up by reading each other's version of things that very evening, and they had such confidence in their sincerity, as well as in their powers of expression, that they felt these shared confessions banished every obstacle. Shelley dreams of a society in which politics will be conducted by these means, through notebooks in which every citizen might, with perfect freedom, set down his wishes or air his grievances. Extraordinarily enough, their confidence in each other was well founded, at first, for at that time nothing serious had ever come between them. In the first flush of love, in that life of shared exaltation, they could believe themselves to be a single being without fear of any contradiction—save in minute differences of opinion on this or that subject, which they hastened to commit to paper, marveling all the while at how speedily these differences were resolved. From time to time Mary leafs through their notebooks from the year before, in which her elegant and orderly writing alternates with Shelley's more exuberant and capricious hand. Never, she thinks, had she been so happy, nor would she ever be again. Their arguments, which never lasted long, were usually over Claire, her half sister, whom she had believed at first to be in love with Shelley. As it turned out, however, Claire had set her sights on Lord Byron. Taking advantage of his distress over his divorce and the confusion surrounding his imminent departure for the Continent, she had forced herself upon him. Bluntly put, she had offered herself; the poet had not refused her advances, but had quickly grown tired of this unhappy, jealous woman. Mary and Percy had had to console the abandoned Claire, then advise her on her plans of reconquest, which they viewed with indulgent skepticism. All the same, they had invited her along with them on their travels, hoping she would forget this necessarily short-lived liaison. Claire's presence is burdensome to Mary, but Shelley, always the gentleman, will not hear of sending her back to England.

And so, smuggled in by Claire, Byron had invaded their diary like an enemy spy, in Mary's opinion. Percy had mentioned his name once or twice in earlier entries, but these had been enthusiastic literary observations, and there had

been no way of knowing that in three months' time they would
encounter the notorious poet himself, purely by chance.

Mary remembers their first meeting perfectly. It was at the
end of May, before they had rented Montalègre, when they
were staying at the Hotel d'Angleterre in Sécheron, a large
town near Geneva. Each morning they would go for a walk
in the countryside, and sometimes they would take a rowboat
out on the lake; then the sky would become overcast—with
the arrival of volcanic ash from Java—and they would return
to the hotel. Shelley had just begun work on a new poem,
which always made him quite cheerful. Mary was reading
Gibbon, taking care of little William, and faithfully filling up
the diary that bore witness to their happiness. She was also
building a collection of dried plants for botanical study. As
for Claire, she preferred to stay by herself, and often sulked
in her room. One day, as they returned hand in hand from
their walk, Percy and Mary found the hotel in as much of an
uproar as if hordes of barbarians had pitched camp there.
The couple stood openmouthed on the threshold, loath to
make their way through a maze of trunks so gigantic they
reminded the Shelleys of those instruments of torture called
iron maidens, which they had seen in Lyon. Some of them
were already open, as though their owner had intended not
only to occupy all the rooms in the hotel with his retinue,
but to take over the lobby as well. Luxurious fabrics, silks,
velvets spilled out upon the carpet, while a turbaned black
man unpacked an assortment of silver articles—plates,
dishes, drinking cups—which he placed carefully on the
steps leading to the Shelleys' room, pausing occasionally to
buff a piece on his sleeve. When two loud grunts behind
them informed Percy and Mary that they were in the way,
they stepped aside, each pressing back against one of the
columns flanking the door, through which passed two men

carrying an enormous rectangular frame draped with a black cloth. The porters took a few steps, then turned to face the front door, and with a well-timed movement, let the black cloth slip off like the curtain in a theater, thus revealing the object to be a mirror with a delicately engraved frame. Unfortunately, there was no time to admire it. Turned toward the door, the unveiled mirror at first reflected Percy and Mary, who were still standing at the entrance like sentinels, petrified with astonishment; then, in the background, they saw the hotel garden drenched in sunshine (the weather was still pleasant in the mornings then); finally, at the precise moment when the two young people were exchanging looks with each other's reflections instead of face to face, a man dressed in black appeared. Initially no more to them than a face and torso as he climbed to the top of the steps, he rapidly acquired legs and planted himself resolutely in front of the mirror, in which he studied his reflection with an expression of exasperated self-satisfaction. Only then did he notice the figures of Percy and Mary reflected on either side of him. Walking over to the doorway, he turned to Mary, bowed, and kissed her hand without saying a single word. Then he turned to Shelley and was obliged to lean backward as he looked up at him, for he was much the shorter of the two. Turning back to the mirror, he observed its progress toward the staircase as it pivoted ninety degrees, thus picking up a goodly portion of the lobby, notably the large reception desk, behind which stood Monsieur Verrières, the proprietor, who had not been able to see anything except the backs of the two porters throughout this entire silent scene. The new arrival stepped over to the desk, and it was then Mary noticed that he limped. Leaning his elbow on the polished wooden surface, he stared at the flabbergasted Monsieur Verrières as though he wished to hypnotize him, and said softly, "My name is Noel Byron." (He used his second Christian name so that his carriage, which was a perfect copy of Napoleon's, could be emblazoned with the same initials as well. When Mary learned this later on, she boldly nicknamed him, not Albé, but Nota Bene.) He then turned to watch the antics of a magnificent greyhound that had just entered the lobby. It was not the fact that his guest had looked away precisely when he felt obliged to make some sort of reply that upset Monsieur Verrières, but his inability to make any reply at all in English, since he spoke not a word of the language and knew nothing whatever about modern poetry and racy society gossip. He told the visitor meekly that other English tourists staying in his hotel would perhaps be willing to act as interpreters, and looked imploringly at Shelley, whose lower jaw had dropped precipitously when the stranger had given his name. Stepping forward, Shelley introduced himself and Mary, and then launched into a long, rambling speech of welcome in praise of the poet. They quickly became good friends.

Upon hearing his name, Mary had thought at first of all the rumors linked to Byron, and then of Claire. A few minutes later, after she and Percy had gone back outside—in hopes the fresh air would restore their composure and return a semblance of order to a world turned upside down by that display of luxury and scandal—she had stammered her misgivings to Percy as they walked along the street, pointing out to him how dangerous the company of such a man could be. Her husband had reacted almost angrily, saying that if the greatest poet of their time was held in contempt, then it was the fault of the times, not the poet, and that Mary would disappoint him greatly by swelling the ranks of the rabble who were always quick to disparage genius. To calm him down, and tease him a little bit as well, Mary pretended to become angry herself: he, Shelley, was the greatest poet of their time, and Byron was but a poor second, because since she, Mary, had chosen to live with a poet, she would never

admit that he was anything less than the best. Shelley, misunderstanding her jest (but she hadn't really been joking),
heatedly defended Byron's poetry and began reciting whole
passages of it. A minute later, as they strolled along the edge
of the lake while Shelley recited *Childe Harold*, he placed
his arm around her shoulders and drew her to him, kissed
her, and called her his love. All that day, however, he spoke
only of Byron, admiring his lavish generosity and sumptuous
retinue (which would be considerably reduced, as it happened, within the next few weeks). In their joint diary Mary
noted ironically that it was amusing to hear Percy pleading
the cause of luxury, extolling the virtues of an ostentatious
display he seemed to consider the only proper setting for the
poet's glory; this from Percy who, born to riches, had turned
his back on them to elope first with a café proprietor's daughter, then with the daughter of a penniless philosopher whose
debts he paid by going into debt himself—Percy, for whom
happiness consisted in living on fruits and books in a lowly
hut with the woman he loved. An affectionate argument ensued. From that moment on, Byron had become the hero of
their diary.

A few days later, through the Chevalier Pictet (a friend of
Madame de Staël's, whom the poet had visited at Coppet),
Byron rented the elegant Villa Diodati, where Milton had
once stayed, while the Shelleys went to live in the more
modest Villa Montalègre.

The two villas are within five minutes' walk of each other.
Claire is forever trudging along the path through the orchards,
full of hope each time she goes to Diodati, and despair each
time she returns to Montalègre. Byron is perfectly willing to
sleep with her on occasion, but definitely does not intend to
saddle himself with this possessive woman, whom he considers to be a fool and about whom he often complains to
Shelley. In any case, he explains boorishly, he already has

enough trouble with Polidori, whose sullenness is quite exasperating: the poet has been reduced to taking care of his own physician.

In spite of the Claire problem, which in general takes the form of nocturnal excursions and much ill temper (tired of being rebuffed by her lover, she eventually shuts herself up in Montalègre and lavishes all her affection on little William), the two households are drawn closer together with every passing day. Shelley and Byron have rented a boat together to go sailing on the lake, and they make plans for long excursions up into the mountains. They admire each other enormously, a friendship that openly displeases Polidori and the neglected Claire. In Mary's case, things are more complicated. Byron is friendly to her, even charming, but she has only to leaf through the joint diary to see how the poet's intrusion has subtly disturbed the couple's harmony, already threatened by the invasive presence of Claire, the birth of William, and simple habit.

Every day Shelley sings the praises of his new friend, notes down his remarks, quotes his verse. Mary, on the other hand, hardly ever speaks of Albé, but she must admit she is obsessed by him as well. She admits this to herself and would like to confide in the far-off Emily, just to make things clearer, but for some strange reason she's reluctant to admit it to Percy, reluctant to speak of Albé the way her husband does so freely. Thus she is cheating, and finds herself committing the only sin that truly frightens her: defying Shelley, keeping secrets from him. Since the beginning of June she has been writing another diary, in different guises, but always in secret: whether she's starting a letter to Emily that will never be finished, much less mailed, or recording her feelings in a private notebook kept in constantly changing hiding places —a trick she once used to foil her father's curiosity—she feels guilty of deceit, of treachery.

It's not that she lies in their joint diary. On the contrary: duplicity has driven her to observe the most exacting standards. She shares with Percy every single misgiving caused by his relationship with Albé. When she feels abandoned by her lover during meandering late-night conversations on the terrace of Diodati, excluded from an exchange in which the two poets exclaim at the harmony between their dissimilarities even more than at their shared interests and opinions, she reports this faithfully, even confessing that it pains her. On the next page Percy scolds her tenderly, criticizes her foolishness, assures her—and she knows he's telling the truth —that he loves her more than anything else in the world. Come, now, she's not going to start being jealous, making scenes! She's not Claire or Polidori . . . and the insulting comparison exasperates her. She writes this down, replying point by point, but without giving in, without swallowing her resentment. She is sincere, truly, and the joint diary continues to fulfill its official function. Percy is now careful never to leave her out of a conversation (Mary is often irritated by the clumsiness of his efforts) and he presses her to join in the outings on the lake, but she refuses.

What is it, then, that she entrusts to this private diary, which she would hide from Percy at all costs? She'd rather die than let him see it! In the first place, she has been engaged in an exercise of mental gymnastics for the last two weeks, since from now on it's understood by Emily and herself that this second diary, this secret compartment, is even more sincere—more intimate, quite honestly not meant for anyone else's eyes—while the first one, the joint diary, must nonetheless remain as sincere as possible. Although she's putting herself in what would seem to be an untenable position, she's still playing the game, trying to reveal as much as she can in the first version (which Percy will read), knowing all the time that she may set down a second version in which she must strip away yet another mask—her own skin, if she has already been truthful in the first account. And she has been, with only one exception. She's willing to humiliate herself by stooping to the level of Claire or Polidori when she reveals her wounded feelings to Percy, but she doesn't want to wound him, and she senses that she risks hurting him now if she lays bare her heart. Not even to avenge her suffering could she bring herself to tell him of the strange fascination Byron holds for her, a fascination that has nothing to do with love. No matter how deeply she looks inside herself, she cannot discover the slightest trace of carnal desire for that man, who is fighting a losing battle against corpulence despite his ascetic habits, and whose flesh inspires in her a kind of repulsion. The idea that he has been or is Claire's lover is also repellent to her. Yet daily contact with him has given her the vague impression that everything she has lived until now, everything she would like to share with Emily or weave into the plot of her novel, the freshest and most intense emotions of her love for Shelley, all this is mere child's play, the naïve exaltation of newly independent adolescents, when compared with real life, that grown-up and adventurous world in which Byron moves with such splendor. His theatrical entrance, his Napoleonic carriage, the aura of prestige surrounding him that seems to ennoble every one of his gestures—these things somewhat overshadow, however unreasonably, the formerly unique (and therefore incomparable) charm of a walk in the country with the bucolic Percy, his botanical observations, his childishly serious enthusiasm for the French revolutionaries or the famous subjects of Plutarch's *Lives*. In just such a way had her father's difficulties and ideals lost their importance two years before, when she was drawn into Shelley's dazzling orbit. And seeing once again how the exclusiveness of her feelings for her husband is giving way to a life in which there is room for comparison, in which Byron is the embodiment of all that is seductively new and exotic, she fears that one day Shelley will come to mean as little to her as her father now does. Of course, she is not like Claire, who loves only famous men, but she is afraid to compare Byron's enormous celebrity with Shelley's obscurity, afraid that she will lose confidence in her husband's genius, which she nurtures and cajoles (it's true that she could never love the world's second-best poet). She's even forced to admit that Byron's professed admiration for his fellow poet has helped greatly to keep that confidence alive. Can she tell Percy this? Can she beg him to leave, to take her away with him, start over again the way they were before, without Albé, without Claire, without William, just the two of them? He wouldn't understand. And she reflects that it's precisely because he wouldn't understand, because he's never had the slightest misgiving, because Albé's glory means nothing to him, that perhaps nothing is lost after all, that she can go on loving him. Reaching under the writing desk, she pulls out the secret notebook, opens it, and writes in a firm hand, "I love him."

A second time.

She would like to shout it out loud.

CHAPTER XXXVI

Her pen freezes in midair. She has just heard a creaking noise from one of the wooden steps leading down to the orchard from the porch. This noise alone is enough to tell her that the new arrival is not Percy. No one ever hears him entering or leaving a room. No one (and this thought makes her love him more than ever) moves as quietly as he does. He is elsewhere and then here. Absent and suddenly present, without any transition, as if he didn't have to cross the space that separates his lips from Mary's. Each time she is astonished to find herself in his arms.

For Polidori, whose face is illuminated by the flickering flame of his candle as he approaches, the same space seems twice as long, twice as treacherous. For that matter, everything about Polidori seems treacherous, as though all the forces of the earth, even the inanimate ones, were constantly plotting behind his back, and if he himself seems treacherous, which is incontestable, it is not so much a result of his true nature, apparently, as an attitude he has been forced to adopt by a hostile universe. Unless his true nature—if he has one—is just that: to provoke the hostility of the universe. When Percy enters a room, one notices it right away, but this is due to him and not the circumstances of his arrival, which appear to vanish immediately in the magic of his presence, whereas one notices Polidori's furtive entrance instead of Polidori himself. One day when Byron was in a surly mood, he expressed surprise at how Polidori, despite his insignificance, was still able to inspire antipathy—which, he added, was a sentiment reserved for superior beings like himself, for example, who took pride in provoking it in almost every breast. "But when you strive for this effect," Polidori had replied, "you must work hard at it, with your poses and attitudes. With me, it comes naturally. That's one more thing in which I am your superior."

Polidori's superiority over Byron has been a subject of pleasantries ever since the day the little doctor voiced his astonishment at the way the Swiss customs officials treated the two of them as equals, addressing them both as "Milord" and bowing with the same dignified respect to George Noel Gordon, Lord Byron, and John William Polidori. This attentiveness (which was actually rather shortsighted, since everything in their demeanor proclaims the difference in their stations) so impressed the young man that for a moment he had believed it well founded, especially since at that time he still considered himself a brother in poetry to his illustrious patient. "After all, what can you do that I cannot?" he had asked the sorely tried Byron, who then replied, "Since you force me to tell you, at least three things: I can swim up the river we are now crossing by carriage, shoot out the flame of a candle at fifty paces with a single pistol shot, and write a poem that will sell fourteen thousand copies in one day." It was Polidori himself who told Mary that anecdote. His conversation consists essentially of self-deprecating remarks disguised as pathetic buffoonery, alternating with sudden, brief bursts of arrogance, which lead to new fits of self-abasement, abetted by Byron, who although indulgent in the beginning (that's one thing she has discovered, this disconcerting good nature), is now obviously unable to bear his companion. Polidori speaks boastfully, for example, of the three tragedies he is currently writing, which will bring him literary glory that he fondly hopes will change his personality, about which he complains sometimes the way Byron complains about his clubfoot. Then, after reflection, Polidori realizes that it is precisely the irremediable mediocrity of his personality that presents an insurmountable obstacle to success. "Instead of stringing rhymes together," Byron advises him, "you should write some great work of medicine, which I would then put into verse, and we could sell fourteen thousand copies of it in one day, you'll see." Polidori is obsessed by this fame, these fourteen thousand copies, in fact more so than by the writing that must precede such a large edition. And he is astonished, even irritated, to see that Shelley, a poet who has published so little and is largely unknown to the general public, seems completely unaffected by this obscurity, which in no way lessens his self-esteem or least of all Byron's high regard for him. The first time Polidori told the story about the Swiss customs officials, Shelley laughed merrily and ob-

served that he didn't know how to swim either, or shoot a
pistol, or sell his poems. As Mary looks at Polidori, who
silently returns her gaze, she thinks back to that incident,
remembering how she was wondering a little while ago about
Percy's cruelty (or whatever it was in him that would take the
place of this necessary ingredient in human nature), and she
suddenly realizes that his reply, which might seem both modest and considerate toward the unhappy physician, was actually, and unintentionally, deeply humiliating. For while
Shelley admires Byron, he does not consider himself to be
the other man's—or any man's—inferior. And by saying that
he, Shelley, did not fulfill any of those criteria of superiority
either, he was implying that these criteria were false: a conclusion drawn from his own case and not from Polidori's, thus
leaving it understood that the latter was his and Byron's
inferior after all, even if this opinion, which happened to be
correct, followed in this instance from an error in logic. At
the time, of course, Mary hadn't thought all this out. When
she looks attentively at Polidori, however, and since one need
only look at him to see how much he suffers, she realizes
after the fact that he must have immediately performed the
tortuous intellectual operation required to show that Shelley's
apparently friendly reply was in reality offensive. She thinks
of him and of what he might be feeling, instead of considering
him as a piece of furniture—as she usually does—or as a
ghost, as the image of an inferior order, a position she sometimes suspects she might fill in relation to Shelley (which is
an idea she tries to reject with all her strength). This is the
secret motive for her reluctance to associate with the young
man, her distrust of any similarities she might discover between them (or between Claire and her), and now she is uneasy
at having been able to follow his train of thought so well.

She hates herself when she sees this unhappy young man
standing before her chaise longue; he is constantly insulted,

whether deliberately or not, but it comes to the same thing, somewhat like—she'll remember this all her life—one of her aunts, a very kind, very sweet, very ugly old lady, really quite hideous, in front of whom her brother, Mary's father, had loudly announced one day while carving the roast mutton at the family dinner table that he had just seen someone very ugly in the street, a truly ugly person. And, since it was his habit to formulate general principles from the most innocuous particulars, he had explained with a kind of indignation that such ugliness could only be the stigma of a profoundly corrupt soul, that this person's face carried the mark of Satan, and that one had only to see it to be warned. Without intending any malice, he had then interrupted his tirade to observe to his sister, "Of course, I'm not talking about you, Sarah Jane." Sarah Jane had blushed and found the courage to smile, but even little Mary, not yet ten years old, had suddenly felt how much her aunt was suffering from the violence of an insult made without any desire to wound (because old Godwin was not a bad man either, no more than Shelley was). From that day on she understood that the righteous cause even more harm than the wicked. Percy, for example. Or herself, sweet, innocent Mary, hurting the feelings of someone like Polidori, who is constantly analyzing and picking apart everything people say, looking for material to feed his pain. To exercise his intelligence. Because it must be admitted (it has never seemed so clear to her) that Polidori is intelligent, even quite intelligent. She immediately feels curious about him, compassionate toward him, and congratulates herself hypocritically. Compassion distances one nicely from the person in question.

"Oh, Polly," she says to the silent young man leaning on the balustrade, smiling crookedly. "I was just thinking of you. I was just thinking how very intelligent you are."

As she speaks she wonders whether it's better to call Polidori by his name, his given name, or the nickname they all use, which seems to have been invented by Albé: Polly-Dolly. The nickname is humiliating, of course, and he is hurt by it, as he is by everything else. To abandon it suddenly, however, would confer too much seriousness on words that are already serious enough. And besides, by addressing him in the usual manner, with the demeaning nickname he hears every day, she credits his intelligence with the ability to decipher her implied recognition of the fact that this intelligence consists precisely in his extraordinary ability to detect the slightest offense lurking in any word. And so, thinks Mary, her words function not only as an unexpected compliment but also as a test of their own accuracy: if he understands what type of intelligence is deemed capable of appreciating the combination of a hateful nickname and flattering praise, then it will mean she was not mistaken. But no sooner have the words left her lips than she hopes she has made a mistake, wishes she could go backward, wishes she had not been thinking just now the way Polidori constantly does, always reading a deeper meaning into the most innocent remarks. She wishes she hadn't seemed—if he understood everything—as though she were sounding him out, making up to him. She must be sympathetic, but not understanding, above all. She must never again let herself be drawn into his words, into his terrible way of giving meaning to words.

His only reply is a short laugh, the laugh of a young hyena who carries a cane to make himself look older, according to Albé. Luckily, his guard is up: he must suspect a trap. He merely turns toward the southern end of the porch, from which one can see the Villa Diodati, and points out to her a distant light glimmering and moving in the darkness. It has stopped raining, but they can still hear the rumble of thunder.

"Have they returned?" she asks.

"Fifteen minutes ago. Shelley sent me to fetch you. Miss Clairmont will take care of your son."

Mary rises and goes inside to change her clothes. When she knocks on Claire's door to tell her she's going out, the other woman answers crossly, and Mary leaves it at that. William must be asleep; if he wakes up at some point, Claire will take care of him. She can at least be useful that way, thinks Mary spitefully, and this wicked thought hides an even worse one, which she admitted to Emily yesterday before tearing up her letter yet again: she wishes she weren't a mother, wishes William were dead. She wishes above all that she could stop thinking. As she mechanically goes about her preparations in the bedroom, she suddenly remembers that she has left her writing desk and secret diary on the chaise longue. Hurrying back to the porch, she sees Polidori leaning over her papers with an air of interest, just as she had feared. She gathers them up quickly, nevertheless relieved to see that he has touched nothing and could not have been able to read anything. Hugging the writing desk tightly to her chest, she goes back into the house and wonders yet again where to hide her notebook. She must be wary not just of Percy, but also of Claire, who would be only too pleased to learn of her half sister's unhappiness. And the villa is so bare. . . . This time she slips the diary between the folds of a dress on the bottom of a pile of clothes at the back of the wardrobe.

Polidori is waiting for her on the porch.

"You, too—working hard, I see," he remarks.

Mary doesn't reply. Polidori leads the way with his candle as they set out, for the road through the sodden orchards is rough and hilly. As they walk along, she feels more and more angry with herself over her friendly impulse, which she would like to purge of even the smallest trace of compassion. It's still too much to feel sympathy. Pity—that's all. Polidori's intelligence busies itself only with the stuff of humiliation, with dismantling its mechanisms. One has to draw the line. As soon as anyone shows the slightest interest in him, he becomes conceited and unbearable. By speaking to him just now, Mary imprudently encouraged him to establish between the two of them the complicity of helots in league against their tyrants. Of course, his "you, too" seems primarily intended to exclude the two poets, who spend their time out on the sailboat telling each other silly stories instead of writing poetry. On a second level, his words establish a parallel between Polidori's almost servile position in Byron's household and Mary's relation to Shelley (whereas if he's dead set on finding a kindred soul, Claire would ask nothing better). Finally, on a third level, they foster confidence between the friend of one poet and the wife of another, both dreaming of becoming famous through their writing but not daring to work openly toward this end for fear of being ridiculed, secretly showing each other their manuscripts, offering each other advice, casually disparaging those of their friends whom fortune and glory have favored.

To prevent this from being true, she must stop understanding the way Polidori thinks.

What's more, he limps. Nothing could be more ridiculous. It's as though he wished to imitate Byron in his faults, since he doesn't possess a single one of his virtues. Furious, Mary doesn't even reproach herself for this unkind thought, when the unfortunate man had sprained his ankle the week before while attempting to behave gallantly toward her. Byron and his physician had been watching from the veranda at Diodati as she approached, slipping on the muddy path. "What are you waiting for, Polly?" Byron had asked. "Why don't you go help our friend?" To show off, Polidori had jumped down from the veranda, a distance of about six feet, instead of using the stairs, and he'd hurt himself badly. A chronic hypochondriac, he had been using a cane ever since and was afraid he would never be able to walk normally again.

Mary is angry with herself, with him. Angry over his limping, over understanding him, over his unformulated offers of alliance, over his forcing her to think about how far along she is with her novel. It's been more than ten days now since the four of them, inspired by the reading of a German anthology of fantastic tales, decided to produce their own collection of terrifying stories. On the evening when Albé proposed the wager, Percy, always easily fired—whether for a parlor game or the cause of Irish freedom—spoke at length about the plot of his story, which was intended to evoke the fabled Persian Assassins, that fanatical sect whose leader, the Old Man of the Mountain, fed the flames of their violence and determination by sometimes having them transported, while they were in a hashish-induced trance, to a marvelous oasis, where in the space of one night their luxurious surroundings, the delicacy and profusion of the banquet dishes, the lascivious beauty of the women (and boys, added Albé) gave them a foretaste of the paradise promised to all those who excelled in battle for the Prophet's glory. With the approach of dawn, they were again drugged and returned to their sordid cells, so that they believed they had been dreaming, but this dream they had all shared and the memories they whispered to one another helped sustain their lives as soldier-monks deprived of all pleasures, save that of killing. Shelley had decided to tell the story of one of those nights, and everyone had applauded his idea, which he had later abandoned, just as Byron had abandoned an even more nebulous project. Prose suits neither of them: they begin by writing in verse, and then translate. Mary ought to have withdrawn from the contest as well at that point instead of engaging in an absurd competition—for lack of other rivals, since there's no question that Claire would ever participate—with Polidori, who is acting mysterious and dropping hints about vampires. She had been imprudent enough, however, to announce on the very first evening that she would not be satisfied with a story—she intended to write a novel. Ever since then it has been like a conspiracy, since they ask her about her novel every single day. While the collapse of the other projects is passed over in silence, as though unworthy of comment, and Polidori's story is of interest only to him, Mary's novel has become a familiar topic of conversation. One would think she were pregnant again, that everyone was waiting eagerly for the first little kicks of the child inside her womb—it's awful. She'd like to drop this project, go back in time to the moment when she first boasted of it, to erase it from everyone's memory and free herself of this enormous, shapeless, sticky burden, this empty form that harbors all her worries and resentments without ever amounting to anything. "I am by birth a Genevese. . . ." Since then, Captain Walton and his sister have intervened, without this delegation of power serving any purpose beyond that of gaining a little time. If only this damned imaginary captain could really write in her place, invent the story of *Frankenstein!* Some days Mary dreams of sending a packet of white paper (how many sheets? About three hundred and fifty—that's a good length; her father will be impressed) under cover to the British Admiralty, addressed to Captain Robert Walton, who would send the pages back to her filled with writing. Does a real Captain Walton exist somewhere? Quite possibly; it's a common name.

She sighs.

They have arrived.

CHAPTER XXXVII

Unlike the rectangular porch at Montalègre, a worm-eaten wooden structure covered only by a lattice, the veranda at Diodati is of stone, with a roof supported by columns in the antique style and a balustrade with thick shafts mossy from the dampness. Byron, who much favors this part of the villa, has furnished it after the fashion of the winter garden at his home on Piccadilly Terrace. Ordinarily, the wax-encrusted candlesticks standing on a long marble table shed enough light for an entire ballroom, but this evening only one candle is burning, or else the wind has snuffed out the others. That single flame, however, does not waver; perhaps the two poets wished to create a fitting atmosphere for the macabre conversations in which they have been deeply absorbed, according to Polidori, since their return from the lake. The little doctor seems troubled by their preoccupation.

Shelley is sitting astride the railing with his back against one of the columns; he waves to them as they approach. Seen from a distance, with his tousled hair, his flowing shirt, and gray knee breeches, wearing neither stockings nor cravat, he looks like a scarecrow; as one draws closer, his beauty becomes astonishing.

Mary reflects that she loves him. She is apprehensive. He is alone on the veranda. She joins him, perching sidesaddle on the edge of the balustrade. They embrace. Ill at ease, Polidori begins to light the other candles with his own, but Byron extinguishes them immediately when he returns from the pantry carrying a bottle of wine, thus confirming Mary's intuition.

"No, Polly, no. Tonight, let us allow the shadows to invade this veranda . . . and our hearts."

Shelley smiles. The two of them seem to Mary like conspirators, as though they've been preparing some sort of elaborate deception that will prove to be at her own and Polidori's expense.

"How did your day go, Percy?" Shelley asks Mary.

"Quite well, Mary," she replies.

She has obediently supplied the answer he expected, but

this beginning increases her misgivings. Until just a few weeks ago, exchanging their respective roles was a familiar private ritual, a naïve but strangely effective illustration of the dream they fondly cherished, a dream in which their souls were joined as one. Lately, though, they've been merely going through the motions, because misunderstandings have made short work of perfect communion, and they've grown tired of this game. They used to play at it like virtuosi, just as they had excelled in keeping their joint diary, spending hours talking together, each on the other's behalf, each imagining and expressing the other's thoughts and hearing his or her own thoughts on the other's lips or, more often, thoughts the other had invented and which were no less revealing. But they don't do this anymore. They don't even mention it, for fear of having to wonder out loud why it has become so difficult for them. And now, without a word of warning, Percy is starting up again, running the risk of putting on a clumsy performance before a strange audience, like an aging acrobat bullying his partner into attempting the daredevil stunt that was once the triumphant climax of their act. She knows they will fail, will fall into the net, but she cannot show her reluctance openly. She must put up a good front. Why? For whom? Has Percy guessed what is troubling her, read her secret diary? Does he want to find her again, or allay her suspicions while luring her into some intricate game that he and Byron have probably spent all day concocting?

"Were you careful out on the lake this afternoon?" continues Percy. "I'm sure you behaved rashly again, and Albé encouraged your recklessness, as usual. . . ."

Mary thinks for a moment, wondering if she would have said that; it's a harmless remark, but not unlikely, especially the hint of reproach (a habit she would like to break) that Percy would certainly have noticed.

"For my part," she replies with a smile, "I'm sure you

were worried, as usual, imagining me drowned or even worse. You ought to remember Dover, however." (Percy makes a face: on target, but an easy shot.) "I'll wager you spent the afternoon walking up and down on the veranda, watching for our return. Did you do any work, at least?"

It is a wager: if Percy answers yes, she'll be willing to play the game with him. If he does this, if he tells her that she worked without interruption, making progress on her novel, then it will be as if she had really done so. She would so like to have worked, and it's up to Percy, to him alone, right now, to make this come true, to change the past, all the past— not only what she did this afternoon, but all these wretched weeks whose significance can be entirely transformed by his reply. If she has been working, if he has her say that she was able to work, then chaos will return to order, all will be as it was before, as if William, Byron, Claire did not exist, and it will be her novel that exists instead. Her life depends on it; she will find her subject this evening, with Percy's help, or never. She is in his hands. He must surely have divined the note of supplication in her question—or else he has known about this for a long time, has understood everything, planned to tell her so tonight, she'd like to kiss him!—because he answers, "Yes" without a moment's hesitation.

"I hardly thought of you at all, my love," he adds. "I was too wrapped up in our dear Frankenstein."

"Frankenstein?"

Startled, Mary can't quite understand. Percy was coming to her rescue, turning back into an angel, and now he's sneering at her again, frightening her. How could he know the name of her hero when she hasn't told him what it is? She has been very secretive about her work. He must have been spying on her, stealthily reading the first pages, from Captain Walton's narrative. And perhaps her private diary as well. . . .

"Yes, Frankenstein," he repeats calmly. "The hero of my novel is called Frankenstein. It has a nice ring to it, don't you think?"

She wishes the others weren't there, listening. She'd like to take Percy's face in her hands, draw it close to hers, and break off the game by asking him for the truth. Has he been reading behind her back? If so, what? Does he want to save her, bring her back to him—even at the cost of prying into her secrets—or finish her off?

"Frankenstein . . ." says Albé dreamily behind them. He repeats the name, rolling it around in his mouth as though he were savoring a choice wine. "You're right," he concludes. "It does have a nice sound."

Trying to distract her again.

"And what happens to this Frankenstein?" asks Mary.

She studies Percy's face as he puts a finger to his lips and smiles. She recognizes that smile, into which she pours everything she wants from him: love, support, an intimacy she'd thought lost and that suddenly reappears in the upturned corners of his mouth. It's truly Percy, as he used to be, coming to get her and put an end to her fears. Even if he had read her secret diary, it wouldn't be important now; he was free to read it, for wasn't she really writing it for him?

"Hush," he says. "I'll tell you when we're alone together."

Saved. She grows bolder.

"You've spoken with Captain Walton? Has he told you everything?"

"Hush," he repeats, still smiling.

He has understood, of course. He'll tell her tonight. She'll learn what *Frankenstein* is all about. It's strange, and she has only just noticed this, but since the beginning she has been convinced that this subject could not spring from her imagination as the result of a happy combination of ideas and daydreams, because it actually exists somewhere, so she must find it rather than invent it. She seeks it as one looks for buried treasure; she finds herself thinking of Captain Walton as a kind of pirate who possesses a map showing the hiding place, the shipwrecked galleon, and she thinks of Percy as a guide who could help her find this Walton, help her bargain with him in some disreputable, smoke-filled tavern down by the docks. He doesn't know how to swim, but he always gets along well with sailors.

"Who is Captain Walton?" pipes the shrill voice of Polidori.

"You, perhaps—who can say?" answers Mary playfully.

She knows she'll find out this evening, and that Percy will help her, but anyone could be useful, even Polidori. The aspect of the world has changed. The ponderous force that was dragging her down is now drawing her up toward the surface. Soon she will emerge, delirious with joy.

"Well played, my dear," says Byron suddenly from the depths of his armchair; he has been following the conversation and has apparently understood everything. (Would Shelley have spoken to him? At this thought, the world grows dark again.)

"Well played, but I should warn you: don't put too much faith in Polly's imagination, nor Shelley's. He's absolutely worthless at prose, like myself, I might add. If you're counting on him to write your novel, he'll set you off on some foolish vampire story like those we were telling one another on the boat a little while ago."

Shelley frowns in irritation at Byron, who, unaware of the exchange of roles demanded by the game, has addressed his comments on the match—which is not yet over—directly to Mary instead of to her partner. Pleased at Percy's reaction, she reaches for his hand on the garden side of the balustrade, where the others cannot see, and squeezes it tightly. Now she, too, wants to continue the game, to shut herself up inside it with him, leaving Byron to stamp impatiently outside the door. Percy turns his hand over, pressing his palm against hers. They are together, united, and nothing can happen to them.

"Really?" he exclaims, still speaking for her. "You're mistaken. That might be quite useful to me because my *Frankenstein*, as it happens, is going to be a vampire story. Tell me more."

No, thinks Mary, this won't do at all. She lightly pinches his palm, as one might touch spurs to a horse, but she has no bridle to lead him gently back in the right direction. This is not the time to go off the track. Tonight she must find the subject of *Frankenstein*, not beat aimlessly about the bush. The treasure map they must wrest from Captain Walton is obviously not a guide to the land of vampires. She doesn't know what Frankenstein will be, but she knows very well what it won't be. In any case, Polidori has already taken vampires for himself, and she's not going to fight with him about it.

As if on cue, Polidori intervenes to protect his claim. Sitting near the table, across from Albé, he pronounces each word sharply and distinctly. "Then we shall be competing against each other."

Since he never looks anyone straight in the eye, Mary doesn't know if he is speaking to her or to Shelley, and so cannot tell if he is observing their rule or is unaware of it, like Byron. Shelley settles the question by replying before her. "And why should that be? Would you pick the same theme as mine?"

The question irritates Mary; she would certainly never have asked it. Everyone knows the answer, knows that Polidori has begun a vampire story and is afraid someone will take his idea. She'd like to stop the game for a minute, speaking in her own name to set things straight, but no—she remains in character.

"Come, Mary," she says to Shelley, "you know very well that Polly reserved vampires for himself at the outset of our wager. Why trespass on his territory?"

"To make him angry, of course!" Byron laughs. "Of what use would he be, our dear Doctor Polly-Dolly, if we couldn't put him up on his high horse whenever the conversation starts to flag? Come on, Polly, defend your claim, erect barricades around it, protect it against these bandits who are getting ready to set up camp there, following my unfortunate example!"

Leaning back in his armchair, delighted at having regained control of the evening, he looks at each of his three companions in turn, his gaze lingering on Polidori, who attempts to smile with an air of amused superiority.

"For you are doubtless aware," continues Byron, "that the real author of my verse is Polly. That is why I keep him with me constantly. Whole poems issue from his fertile brain at every moment. I stay at his side, noting down his slightest remark, and like the bad boy I am, I usurp his reputation. And that is also why our friend is often irritable, preoccupied, with a gloomy expression and bitter mouth. That is why Childe Harold is not a charming companion like myself. Polly has given him his melancholy temperament, which is completely justified when you consider how this innocent victim has been so cruelly despoiled. Isn't that so, Polly?"

The little doctor is still smiling, but his hands are trembling, and he grips his glass of wine so tightly that his knuckles have gone white. Byron stares in fascination at the glass, as though weighing the odds that it will finally shatter. Noticing his interest, Polidori sets his glass down on the table.

"It's quite true," he replies in a tone that strives to be offhand and gives Mary a distinct desire to be elsewhere. "It's so true, Milord, that the vampire story upon which I am working will present an unvarnished picture of my plight. I shall depict myself therein under the touching guise of the victim, and you as the vampire who survives by stealing the blood and souls of mortals. I shall recount your entire life, taking care that the public will recognize you, and the secret motive behind your exploits, your scandals, and your legend shall finally be brought to light. Lord Byron is a vampire. Isn't that a wonderful subject?"

Byron has listened to him in silence; the sarcastic look on his face is tinged with surprise. It's not unusual for Polidori to launch into long tirades, but ordinarily he loses the thread and dries up in the middle of a sentence, aware of having made a fool of himself. This time he has outwitted his assailant by borrowing his own weapons. Byron has recognized himself in the cadence and inflections of the other's speech and is disconcerted by this surprising reversal.

"A marvelous subject, Polly, really marvelous," he says softly.

Pouring himself a glass of Bordeaux, he looks over at the Shelleys, who are as astonished as he is by Polidori's prompt riposte to his attack. Huddled in his chair, the doctor seems crouched to spring, ready to ward off any new assault.

"I'm eager to read your story," continues Byron. "And I will truly take great pleasure in signing it."

"Would you dare?" asks Shelley, and Mary cannot tell if he has forgotten their game or is making her fly to Polidori's rescue.

"Of course. In fact, this narrative will show to its best advantage only under my name. The poetic effect of a confession, above all a disguised one, is always greater than that of a denunciation."

"Watch out," says Polidori threateningly, intoxicated by his recent victory. "Our friend," he observes, nodding toward Mary, "might well denounce you in her *Frankenstein* as well."

"Would you do that?" asks Byron, feigning the amazement of one who finds himself betrayed by his closest ally.

"You are the one who has encouraged her to do so," insists Polidori. "In stealing from me, she denounces you. That makes two witnesses instead of one. You are lost."

"How infernal your logic is this evening." Byron sighs.

"You must all set your minds at ease," announces Mary, to revive the game and return to the topic she wants to explore (it's tonight or never, she's sure of it). "Don't worry, Mary will let you settle your accounts among yourselves. She has no intention of making Frankenstein into a vampire."

"What, then?" asks Percy in a disappointed voice.

She turns and stares at him with wild eyes. It isn't possible. Another about-face, another betrayal, as though he had been turning her in circles ever since the beginning of the evening, twirling her around by the shoulders, then suddenly letting her go so that she loses her balance and stumbles; taking her by the hand, he sets her turning once more, releases her again, and she falls, falling lower each time. He has regained her confidence, persuaded her to play along with his game, promised to find Captain Walton and the treasure map for her, and now he's slipping away again, abandoning her, leaving her all alone. Putting on that act, pretending they understand each other only to maneuver her into a position in which she's helpless. When she falls, he is the one who has pushed her. Now she knows that he means to hurt her. To make her admit that she has no ideas, no imagination, that she's even more of a fool than Polidori. At least he has a subject—all one had to do was listen to the way he talked back to Byron, like an ordinarily timid animal that becomes brave and aggressive to defend its young. Only she, Mary, has nothing. Except a feeling of dread.

What, then?

Byron and Polidori have stopped squabbling. They're well

aware that something much more interesting is happening on the balustrade. They smell blood, and close in.

Percy is watching her closely. Like the others, he's waiting for her to give herself away.

What, then?

"Well, it's your story, after all," she shouts harshly, dividing her rancor equally between Percy and herself (she hates him; she hates herself). "It's up to you to find a decent subject. What do you do all day, out on the porch? I always see you there when I come home, hastily gathering up your papers so that I won't be able to read them. If it's your novel, tell us what it's about, tell us what Captain Walton has to say. And if it isn't your novel, what is it? Don't say it's our diary; you hardly write a thing in it anymore. Don't say you're writing to Emily, who never answers you; we all know she doesn't exist. What are you doing, then? What are you doing?"

She's screaming. Shelley grabs her shoulders, frightened and aghast. She breaks violently free. A new mask: poor, poor Percy, completely mystified by this fit of rage she directs against herself while pretending to express his own thoughts. He would never say such things; look at how kind and sweet his face is. He would never conduct such an inquisition, for his interest in Mary's work is affectionate, fraternal, never indiscreet. He would like—look at his awkward gestures, so full of love—he would like to embrace her, to soothe her, to put an end to this game he was wrong to begin, it's true, but he had no idea she was in such a nervous state, so fragile. It's not his fault if she pushes away his hands, his face drawing near, not his fault if his panicky contrition infuriates her, makes her want to scratch, bite, be cruel. She won't let herself be calmed down this time; he has pushed her too far. He wanted to make her fall. Well, she's clinging tightly. It's she who will drag him down into the depths, but not before she has told him to his face, in front of the others, that she knows exactly what he is: an insulting and carping spy, intent on doing her harm. She grows drunk on the sound of her own voice—hissing, hateful—and the pleasure of doing and saying irrevocable things.

"I know perfectly well what you're up to," she continues, grabbing him by the shoulders in her turn, holding him firmly, as though she were going to slam him against the column. "You're quite incapable of writing the least little book; you want someone to whisper the whole thing to you on the sly. You've been looking in vain for a story these past ten days now, you're relying on captains who don't exist, you're not writing to Emily, you're no longer writing in the diary. You're jealous, that's all, and embittered. And you're stewing in your own juice, you wish I were dead, that William were dead, that someone would strangle him, you hate him. That, yes, you write that down, you make it into a private diary, full of your wretched secrets; you don't show me that one, you hide it, in a different place each day. But what you don't know is that every day I look for it, I find it, I uncover your childish tricks each day, I read your nasty little girl's nonsense. I revel in it, I laugh at it. What a pity I don't have it on me, I could have read you some passages from it—you'd be amused, Albé, your name often crops up there. . . ."

She sobs as she speaks, as she screams; she can no longer see the others through her tears, just the vague form of Percy bending over her, afraid to touch her. If only she could faint, to escape the appalled silence that will reign when she has grown quiet; she will soon stop speaking, she hasn't enough strength to go on, to faint—she will have to face them. She babbles incoherently to push back this silence, this moment when everyone will stare at her in astonishment without daring to say a word. She doesn't want to think about what will happen when she has ceased speaking. They'll have to stand up, take their leave quickly; she and Percy will walk along the road in silence, and then? If she doesn't commit suicide tonight, perhaps no one will ever mention it again, and things will go on as they were, a little worse. An unpleasant incident . . . they happen sometimes. Mary, sweet Mary, had a fit of hysterics, said terrible things, behaved like Polidori on one of his worst days, but Percy showed the patience of an angel, and we had to cut the evening short. "Women are positively unbearable," Albé will announce repeatedly, and that will be the end of it. If the irreparable isn't crowned by a catastrophe, that's what will happen, and *that* is even worse. Now the damage is done, the outrage committed, and she no longer has the strength to go on, she's going to fall silent. Tears are coursing down her cheeks; she feels their bitterness at the corners of her mouth, a gust of wind rustles through the trees, a branch strikes Percy's face but he doesn't push it away, she has stopped speaking. There, now, the silence is here.

She has uttered her last words.

What, then?

What will happen now?

It's for Percy to decide, for him to rise to his feet: brief excuses, embarrassment, hasty departure. But he doesn't move. They're no longer touching each other, sitting face to face on the balustrade, each one leaning back against a column, like two prizefighters, Jackson and Angelo, panting in the corners of the ring. It's not possible, however, that they should stay that way, here, that the evening should continue peacefully after that outburst, a digression simply to be ignored.

That is precisely what happens, isn't it, every time Polidori makes a scene? They let the storm go by, they smile, they take up again where they left off. But she isn't Polidori, or Claire. They can't treat her like a child who breaks her toys in a rage and obtains only a scrap of halfhearted attention with this havoc. Not her. She must die.

She can still hear the sound of her voice, the horrible things she said, mingled with her shuddering breathing, which is growing calmer. She has closed her eyes. She must never open them again. If she manages not to open them—or her mouth—ever again, that will be fine.

She has no idea how much time passes at this point. Not a sound around her; everyone must be keeping perfectly still.

Finally a voice, Polidori's, saying what shouldn't be said, obviously. (But what should have been said? Nothing. Eternal silence. Leave it at that.)

"What, then?"

And so, it starts up again: Byron taking advantage of the opening to carry on, a mountebank whose words tumble out, capering around to stifle the silence.

"Well, since vampires are just between Polly and me from now on, an area in which we would no more welcome the intrusion of a third party than you would relish our making ourselves at home in your bedroom, my dear lovebirds, there still remain hundreds of delightful subjects that only await an encounter with your fertile imaginations."

Without opening her eyes, she hears him move. The neck of a wine bottle clinks against the lip of a glass; the wine gurgles out. An armchair pushed back, its feet dragging across the stone floor. A limping step—he must have gotten up. Back and forth. Will he ring for the servants, ask them to bring some supper? Will they sit down at the table? She'll have to join them, or else stay where she is, on the balustrade. Mary's sulking, never mind her, she'll get over it. True, they haven't eaten yet. Byron limits himself to a few biscuits in the evening, for he takes an obsessive interest in his physical condition: constantly weighing himself, looking in the mirror to make sure he's not getting fat, that he's still a svelte athlete, trim and supple, but it's a losing battle. In spite of his ascetic regime, the hours of swimming, the dumbbell exercises, he grows portly, his jowls are fleshier; it seems he weighed more than two hundred pounds at the age of eighteen. On the other hand, he insists that his guests be well fed; the servants will certainly appear, and if the meal is served on the veranda, they'll be present, wondering why Mary is staying in the corner with her eyes closed. It's even strange that none of them has showed up yet this evening. It's as though the four of them were alone in Diodati. No, Albé isn't ringing the servants' bell. His steps draw nearer; he's now quite close to them. He must be handing Percy a glass of wine; yes, she hears her husband thank him with a word. She imagines them around her, waiting for her eyes to flicker open—Percy still motionless, a worried look on his face, ashamed of having gone too far, and Albé standing there, bottle and glasses in hand, luxuriously but carelessly dressed. She remembers his clothing: the double-breasted tartan jacket, hanging loosely over the shirt, open at the neck; the braided cap of purple velvet; the nankeen trousers flaring at the bottom to hide his foot. What is he waiting for? For her to grope around after the wineglass he must be holding out to her? No, he sets it down on the balustrade, within her reach, and moves away. No one has taken advantage of the conversational gambit he provided, but no matter, he'll do all the talking.

"Listen to this," he says. "Three days ago I was dining with Madame de Staël, at Coppet. You didn't want to accompany me, Polly, as you recall, and everyone missed you. Your visit left such a fine impression that for my part, I felt as though I were simply being tolerated in the hope that one day I would bring back my delightful friend."

New pause. No reaction. Mary wishes all this would stop, that the lamp heating up in her head would go out.

"I was seated to the right of a very elderly lady," continues Albé, "an Italian princess whom everyone addressed as the Principessa di Massimo, who kept telling me stories about relics belonging to her family, such as the heart of King Louis the Seventeenth of France, the slippers of Louis the Fourteenth—I suppose that the family in question was originally French. Since I have been well brought up, despite what anyone may say, I pretended to be deeply interested in these anecdotes. The princess promptly invited me to come see with my own eyes all this royal debris, which is preserved in the Palazzo Massimo, in Pisa. She even promised, in a confidential tone, to take me down into the palace crypts and show me the chapel of Saint John of Ambéda. I then put on my most pious expression and asked if Saint John of Ambéda was a di Massimo—it's the kind of family, like mine, that has everything in it, even saints. The princess seemed quite shocked by this question, which betrayed my ignorance. 'Oh, no,' she replied, 'no indeed. But he resurrected a di Massimo.' "

Silence.

"Amusing," Polidori finally remarks with a sneer.

"Isn't it? As it happens, I even wondered if she might herself be the one brought back from the grave. When a person tells you a story without specifying who the hero is, you can bet that it's about him. I've often found that to be true."

Mary grits her teeth. Each word in this labored badinage rings false, reinforcing the uneasiness he's trying to dispel. And Percy puts in his two cents' worth. His voice is unnaturally high.

"No offense, dear Albé, but I find the vampire story Polly has fashioned from your life much more entertaining."

"Ah, but not everyone has our friend Polly's genius! I do the best I can. I admit that tales of wandering Jews, pacts with the demon, or elixirs of immortality are banal and that it's difficult to measure up in this domain to the likes of Monk Lewis. However, leaving aside Monk Lewis and Saint John of Ambéda, you know that the resurrection of the flesh is not just a dogma proclaimed by the Roman Catholic Church and the Old Man of the Mountain to keep the rabble waiting patiently, or an attraction reserved for those who visit the Principessa di Massimo, but an actual scientific reality."

"What do you mean?" asks Percy.

They've forgotten Mary, who has ceased to exist.

"Once again we must turn to Polly," says Byron, "since he is my source of information on this topic. Polly, be a good fellow, tell us the story that so impressed me the other day. I suppose you have no intention of turning it into a novel to reveal my crimes, and so can have no objection to relating it before an audience."

Silence. Polidori must be hesitating. He hates to be called on to perform like this. When people make fun of him, he suffers, but he feels at home; he can even strike back, as he did a little while ago. If someone tries to let him shine, however, he becomes wary, not knowing from which direction the blow may come.

"Go on, Polly."

"It seems unbelievable," he says at last, "but it happened this winter in Glasgow. A man named Matthew Clydesdale, condemned to death, had just been hanged. As soon as the sentence was carried out, his body was taken to an amphitheater in the university, where Jeffrey, a professor of anatomy, and Ure, a chemist, subjected it to a series of shocks from a galvanic battery. The cadaver sat up, opened its eyes. . . ."

Mary half opens her own. Without being observed, she can see through the veil of her eyelashes. Polly is seated, motionless save for the slow movement of his lips. He is looking in her direction.

"The audience screamed in terror. Clydesdale was a tall, husky man. He waved his arms, took a step, and seized the neck of Professor Jeffrey in one hand. He would have strangled him if Professor Ure hadn't severed his jugular vein with a lancet, whereupon the man died a second time."

Polidori falls silent. He continues to stare at Mary, as though the story were intended especially for her. She has never noticed before that he has yellow eyes, and closes her own again to escape their gaze. Either the others are as frightened as she is, or else she cannot hear them anymore. Blood is pounding in her ears; she feels a hand, Percy's, laid on her shoulder. She wishes he would stop touching her; she wishes to be alone, far away. On the inside of her eyelids, as on the screen of a shadow theater, pass confused images. Polidori's silhouette is imprinted on her retinas. A black shape, a pale face, yellow eyes. Those around her are still silent. Percy's hand grips her more firmly. Is he afraid, or has he guessed that she is afraid? Does he want to reassure her? To draw closer to her? She is feverish.

Finally a voice. Percy's, right next to her, but deformed, almost metallic. "Were you present at this experiment?"

She does not hear Polidori, although he must have answered. Unless he merely nodded.

"But"—Albé, this time—"I thought you studied in Edinburgh."

Polidori. Hollow voice. "Professor Ure was my teacher in Edinburgh. I accompanied him to Glasgow and assisted him during the experiment."

Mary squeezes her eyelids shut to keep them from opening, to keep from seeing Polidori. She hears Byron laugh and claim that Polly says whatever passes through his head, that he hadn't told him that last part the other day. Polidori doesn't answer, but he's there, behind her eyelids, with his yellow eyes. His image grows larger, like that of a fish approaching behind the glass wall of an aquarium.

She can't take any more and opens her eyes, wide, without

changing her position, so that she sees in front of her the chair where Polidori had been sitting, empty. She shivers; he's going to appear suddenly at her side, to cut her throat with a lancet.

But no, he is standing there, to her left. Mary trembles. Albé is holding forth, but his voice seems to come from far off; she glimpses his mouth jawing away on the edge of her field of vision. At a great distance.

"I didn't realize that we had among us an authentic resurrectionist. This certainly brings up the tone of our gathering. What do you say to that, my friends? Polly, our Polly, is practically the equal of God."

"The equal of Prometheus," whispers Percy.

She turns toward him and as she does so, manages to free her shoulder, leaving Percy's hand suspended in the air. Then, as though he didn't know what to do with it, he runs his fingers through his curls, brushing them back. His face stands out against a mass of foliage. In the background, a pitch-dark sky. Suddenly he stretches his long legs, swings the one hanging down on the garden side of the balustrade over to the veranda, and stands up. He strides up and down, but makes no noise on the worn flagstones. As he approaches or moves away from the single candle, his shadow on the wall changes size and shape. All of a sudden, it becomes gigantic. Without leaving his seat, Byron leans his head back to follow Shelley with his eyes. Polidori remains standing, as straight as a poker in his black clothes. He no longer has his cane. Mary avoids looking at him; she senses that his yellow eyes are staring at her. All this was planned, it all fits together: the speeches about vampires, the servants given the night off, this absurd banter, Polidori's horrible story, this theatrical setting. . . . They've set it all up on her account. A short while ago Polidori came to get her on the porch at Montalègre as one summons an actress from her dressing room to join her colleagues already assembled onstage, where they are reciting a text she has never heard before, acting out a drama in which she must somehow take part, play her role. Everything was planned beforehand. If Percy didn't take her home after that scene she made, it's because there is some pressing reason why she must stay, and she is the only one who doesn't know what is expected of her, whether she's supposed to protest, to demand that they stop all this or at least explain to her what is going on, reveal what the rules are.

"Mrs. Shelley."

She doesn't want to answer, to turn her head. She recognizes Polidori's voice easily. Who else in this present company would call her Mrs. Shelley?

"Mrs. Shelley. . . ."

He comes over to her, the metal tips on his shoes clicking against the stones; she doesn't want to look at him, looks at the others instead. Shelley has stopped pacing to stare at them. Byron too—both of them watch Polidori take a step sideways to plant himself in front of her.

"Mrs. Shelley," he says, "if you like, this story is yours. There you have it: *Frankenstein.*"

The others' voices, a great way off.

"The modern Prometheus!" (Shelley, as though he were announcing the title of a poem.)

"A pretty present," remarks Byron. "I'm going to become jealous, Polly. You scream bloody murder whenever I gather up the slightest crumb from your poetic feast, and now you're offering Mary this sumptuous bounty. Make good use of it, Mary; a gift from Doctor Polidori is such a rare thing."

Before her, his yellow eyes are riveted on hers. She is afraid, doesn't dare understand. Whispers, so that the others can't hear, "Captain Walton?"

Behind them Albé raises his glass as though to propose a toast. No one follows his example. A gust of wind nips at the candle flame; the tree branches toss and sway out in the garden. Byron throws the dregs in his wineglass on the floor. Silence. Polidori turns on his heel and disappears inside the villa, returning a minute later with a bottle that he sets about opening as though nothing has happened. No one has moved during his absence: not Mary, still sitting on the balustrade; not Byron, leaning his elbows on the table; not Shelley, standing a few paces behind him, his face drawn, his arms hanging at his sides. The only sound is the rustle of leaves, which swells in Mary's ears like the murmur of an ocean as one draws near.

The cork pops. Polidori fills the glasses. Byron sulkily places the flat of his hand over his glass to show that he does not want any more. Everyone is quiet. The wind rises briefly, then dies down. A large insect begins to fly heavily around the candle, then falls to the table, where it folds back its wings and crawls slowly along. With the same gesture he used to refuse more wine, but faster, Byron crushes the insect.

Silence.

Mary breathes. She feels her chest rise and fall regularly. Her mind is completely blank, and she breathes as though she had forgotten to do so for a long while. Air rushes into her nostrils, her mouth, down into her lungs; she forces it out. The odor of damp earth; a sudden calm. She would like to unfasten her bodice, touch her breasts.

At that moment she catches Byron watching her, lying in wait for the gesture she has not yet made. He breaks the silence, reciting a few lines of verse:

> "Beneath the lamp the lady bowed
> And slowly rolled her eyes around;
> Then drawing in her breath aloud
> Like one that shuddered, she unbound
> The cincture from beneath her breast;

Her silken robe, and inner vest
Dropt to her feet, and in full view
Behold! her bosom and half her side—
Hideous, deformed and pale of hue—
O shield her! shield sweet Christabel!"

Mary recognizes the poem by Coleridge sent to them last week by Murray, but she has no time to wonder what inspiration, what sudden perception of her own desires has led Byron to declaim the most macabre lines from the work. She sees him as though through the doorways of a long series of rooms: he is seated, gazing intently at her as he recites, and Percy is standing behind him with contorted features, his eyes staring at her as well and growing ever larger, while his hands float up toward his face; the fingers touch his cheeks, pulling at them as though to flatten out a mask. If Byron could see him, he would interrupt his recital in horror. If Mary could beg him to stop—but no, she can't. Percy would catch her signaling him to be quiet.

When Byron does fall silent, she understands something awful is about to happen. Percy's expression, that mixture of hatred, terror, helplessness. . . . She knows it, has seen hints of it when he makes faces at her, playing at frightening her. But right now, it's the real thing, it's truly the other side of the loving smile. She has never seen anything like it on a human face. And Byron doesn't notice a thing, excluded from the disaster he has brought about, for now he is reduced to ashes by the looks exchanged over his head between Percy and Mary, who is distraught, on the verge of screaming.

All of a sudden it is Percy who shrieks. A long, inhuman howl. Byron leaps up, overturning his chair. Polidori remains motionless. Mary is petrified. All three of them watch as Shelley, still screaming, covering his face with his hands, careens into the wall like a blind man. Staggering back, he collapses again, picks himself up—he's foaming at the mouth. On all fours, crawling along the wall, howling as though he were never going to stop, and still staring at Mary. Not at her eyes, at her breasts, as Byron did a minute ago while evoking the witch's bosom. Now he is practically writhing, and hits his head, screaming all the while.

Byron and Polidori approach him warily, awkwardly. They close in on him with all the caution of animal tamers trying to subdue a maddened wild beast. Whether or not he fully understands the reasons behind this fit, Polidori is the first to discover its immediate cause when he realizes what Shelley is staring at, and taking the terrified Mary by the arm, he turns her around, leading her to the other end of the veranda, out of Shelley's sight. Then he returns to the madman, whom Byron slaps repeatedly and grabs by the ears, shaking his head. The shriek collapses into hiccups; the poor man's hands wave about frantically. Stepping behind him, Polidori grips him around the waist and hauls him to his feet. He cannot stand up without this support; his knees half bent, he looks like a broken jumping jack. Byron fills a glass with water, then throws it in his face. Taking the glass from him, Polidori wets a napkin to moisten Shelley's forehead, holding him upright while he murmurs words Mary cannot hear, leading him like a sleepwalker into a little drawing room just off the veranda. The two men help him lie down on a divan. Byron suggests a few drops of laudanum, and goes off to get the drug. Polidori remains alone with the sick man in the drawing room, which is faintly lit by the candle out on the veranda.

Mary stays outside, trembling all over. This fit of terror came over Percy while he was looking at her; she is the cause of it. Did he want to reply to her hysterics, go her one better, take his revenge? Is it all an act? He likes to scare people, always has. Suddenly pretending to be mad so that Mary, and doubtless Harriet before her, and before Harriet his sisters, all devoted to their older brother, would think they were no longer in the presence of Percy—their brother or lover—but of another, a monster, a wild animal that has taken his place. He likes that. Byron as well likes to play the vampire, the gloomy hero, but he could never frighten anyone as Percy does. His face lacks mobility, and the studied expressions he affects have caused the muscles to lose (if they ever had it) that elastic quality Percy exercises and exploits, which allows him to look old, or stupid, or furious in the twinkling of an eye. He hasn't indulged in this kind of foolishness for some months now, but it has also been a while since he has trotted out the game of changing places: it's as though he wished to draw her into those abandoned territories tonight, proving to himself that he is still the master there.

She drains her glass of wine in one gulp and goes over to the balustrade, where she leans her elbows on the railing. In the distance, reflected lights gleam on the surface of the lake. That beacon over there, that's the fortified gate behind which scowls the town of Sécheron. Its steep streets often run with water coursing down from the mountains. The night sky is black, so black. It must be terribly late. Her head spinning, Mary buries her face in her hands, then turns away and walks toward the drawing room.

She looks inside, through the half-open door. They have lit the candles, and Byron, who has his back to her, is holding the candelabrum aloft in a picturesque pose. Actually, the spectacle framed by the aperture resembles one of those genre paintings, a nocturnal scene illustrating some dramatic passage from a novel. She remembers an engraving that appeared in an edition of her father's famous work, *Caleb Williams*, a picture that terrified her when she was a child. Byron and his candelabrum occupy the foreground. The light falls on the far end of the divan where Percy lies, unconscious or simply resting quietly—she can't tell which. Polidori is at his side, almost crouched down, and his eyes meet hers. He immediately glances furtively at Shelley and, satisfied that his patient is not watching him, turns again toward Mary, placing his finger on his lips. How many times has someone made that gesture this evening? She takes a step back, and Percy's face slips out of sight. She thinks she hears his voice. It occurs to her once more that all three of them are plotting together, that Percy has warned them about the mad fit he was preparing to stage, but again, why? What is going on tonight?

Polidori gets to his feet, walks in front of Byron and out of the room. He rejoins Mary, takes her by the arm, and leads her over to a blind angle of the veranda, where they will not be seen by the others.

"It's nothing," he says in a low voice. "A hallucination. He should rest for a moment."

"But what did he say? I heard him speak."

"Do you want to know?"

The dedicated physician has vanished. It's Polidori the embittered, the jester in yellow and black, who stands before her now, his face livid, his lips twisted into a lopsided smile.

"He said that you weren't Mary, his wife, that you weren't Mary, the mother of his son William, that you were someone else, an enemy, and that your nipples were eyes staring at him, eyes that meant to do him harm. That's what he said."

"You're lying," whispers Mary.

"Ask Milord."

Byron has left his candelabrum at Shelley's side and is standing in the doorway; he walks over to the two young people.

"Ask Milord," repeats Polidori, chuckling. "Do you think I have enough poetry in me to make up such visions?"

"Be quiet, Polly," interrupts Byron.

He pushes Polidori away abruptly with one hand, slips the

other through Mary's arm, and draws her away from the little doctor, who sits down in the armchair and pours himself a glass of wine, still smiling triumphantly.

Whispering suits Byron. It limits the range of his affectations, and what his voice loses in strength it gains in persuasiveness. He has his arm around Mary's shoulder, trying to reassure her, but she remains wary. She knows they are in league against her, all three of them.

"It's over now. Percy is lying down for a moment, and you need some rest, too. We've talked too much about ghosts. It has upset us all terribly."

Gently, effortlessly, he walks her to the little outside staircase leading from the veranda to a mezzanine fitted up as a sitting room, and helps her climb the steps. In the semi-darkness, she recognizes the room where she has occasionally awaited the others' return, when they were out sailing on the lake. She collapses obediently onto the sofa. The screen behind her is decorated with paintings of Jackson and Angelo, two prizefighters whom Albé professes to admire.

"Wait here," he says. "I'll get you some light."

He leaves. The tiny room is stifling, so Mary reopens the French windows that give onto the narrow landing, which forms a balcony over the veranda. Through the clouds the full moon sheds a pearly radiance. The candles flicker on the staircase as Albé returns with a candelabrum, which he places on an end table, near the sofa. Throughout the entire evening, she reflects, he is the one who has been bringing and withdrawing light. Everything is out of the ordinary: the absence of servants, that stinginess with the candles, as though someone were afraid we would be seen from outside, from the villas that rise in tiers on the other side of the lake. It's unusual for Albé to be concerned about the attention of strangers, even curious ones. One day, while she was studying the opposite shore with the telescope she had given to Percy for his twenty-fourth birthday, she noticed the flashing of another eyeglass pointed at her. The people who lived over there were spying on them, probably imagining that the Englishman's villa was the site of riotous orgies. Albé had laughed when she told him this, but tonight he is making them all follow his example and behave as though they were thieves, or secret guests. When he moves to leave her again, he seems like a conspirator. She calls him back.

"Albé, please tell me what Shelley said to you!"

"But it was nothing, my dear, nothing at all. It's just his nerves. Rest, now."

He goes back downstairs.

If he had told her the same thing that Polidori said, the ghastly story of those black eyes on her nipples, Mary would be certain they had all invented it together, to scare her. Byron's discretion argues against that interpretation. So it must be true, then: Percy really did say that, and Byron is keeping this from her so as not to frighten her. Percy did have a vision of Mary as an enemy. As more than what she was earlier this evening, a woman deeply hurt. He saw someone else. A monster.

Black eyes on her nipples. Black? Did Polidori say black, or is she adding that detail at this very moment? She will never know. If she asks him, right now or tomorrow, he will certainly deny it and look at her as if she were crazy. So far no one has said anything further about her tantrum, the scene she made in front of Percy; it's as though it never happened.

She wishes that her heart would stop pounding, that she could recover her composure. Stretched out at full length on the sofa, she leans her head back, listening to her own breathing. She unfastens her bodice, sits up, and caresses her breasts with her hands, cold flesh against cold flesh, stroking the erect, leathery nipples.

At this moment, he's resting on a divan a few yards beneath

where she is sitting. Judging from what she can remember of how the house is laid out, this little room is directly over the large drawing room. Is he asleep now? Has he fainted, or is he smiling to himself, delighted at the trick he has played?

She wonders whether she could stand to be held in his arms now, to forget all this, even to laugh about it with him—or whether she would still feel afraid.

To go downstairs, walk over to him, run her fingers through his hair, unbeknown. She doesn't dare. If she were to risk going down there, who would be lying on the divan? Whose face would she see?

She tries to picture his face. In vain. A little while ago she'd already had that same impression.

A little while ago: he was sitting on the balustrade of white stone that surrounds the veranda, leaning back against one of the columns. He had turned his head away, as though the conversation did not interest him (it was when Albé and Polly were bickering about vampires; the game of changing places had been temporarily abandoned). Straining to see his vanished profile, she stared at the brown hair curling over his ear and down upon the snowy white shirt, wide open at the throat. Mary had felt her heart beat suddenly faster, racing from an emotion that seemed more like a vague feeling of anguish than an effusion of love (and yet, at that moment, she had trusted him; he had just announced that he had seen Captain Walton). Percy is a person, she thought to herself over and over again, but all she knew of that person was a patch of light material, shining in the stormy night, and above that bright patch, the outline of his curly hair, the sketch of a face that her memory was already unable to complete.

A long face, an aquiline nose, the prominent nose of the Shelleys that she had already recognized, jutting from an unhealthy fleshiness the artist hadn't even tried to disguise, on the day she saw a portrait of his father, Sir Timothy. She had never met him, had seen only this portrait for a mere few minutes, yet she remembered it precisely and had even felt, a little while ago, that the only thing that could help her recall Percy's face was this memory, this briefly glimpsed portrait of the old squire whose flabby face, which she had been taught to hate, was as clear in her mind's eye as if it had actually been shown to her just now. You couldn't really say that Percy looked like him, but since she no longer knew what Percy looked like, she was forced to fall back on this pitiful model, to assemble around the Shelley nose—the only trustworthy guide, since even Percy admitted that inheritance—a series of features she could describe, but not visualize. She could hollow out the cheeks, cover the forehead with a tangle of hair, choose a more delicate curve for the mouth, make the lower lip less pendulous, sharpen the chin, but these corrections served no purpose: Percy's face had vanished. She would have liked—she would like—to possess a portrait of him at that very moment. One remembers an image more clearly than the reality, a book more clearly than one's own life (and if she ever does write *Frankenstein* one day, she will be able to recall this night, and everything about it that escapes her now). When Percy was sitting on the balustrade, she had wanted him to turn around, face her, and remain still. Above all, to remain still. To abandon that game of changing places, which she had already known would lead to disaster. His features are too mobile. He plays with them too much, growing excited, frowning, wrinkling his nose, making his eyes flash, moving beyond her reach, frightening her. She had stared at his profile with a deliberate intensity, hoping that the weight of her gaze would make him turn around, which sometimes happens, and hold him captive. But he had not moved. She had felt like shouting, pleading

279

with him, had been at the same time afraid that he would give in to her cries, to her pleas . . . and that it would no longer be him.

It was at that moment he had turned around to say, "What, then?"

Did that happen, really?

They are far, so far away from each other.

It's nothing, Albé said. All this talk about ghosts has upset us.

And a little while ago, on the veranda (was it a little while ago or is she falling asleep, becoming feverish?), she was staring at him, she is staring at him once more, and despite her concentration, her longing to win him back, to find him again—oh, let him turn around, let it be him!—she is the one who is distracted, by the same means. Watching him, she feels, she knows that she herself is being watched, and not by him, of course. Even before she turns her head, she knows that her observer is Polidori.

Polidori. He must still be downstairs, sitting in the armchair on the veranda, masquerading as Captain Walton. And what if it were true? What if Captain Walton were an imposter? (Instead of an imposter passing himself off as Captain Walton? She's beginning to get lost.) Those yellow eyes, that pallid face, the clothes of a young minister soured by hatred. . . . What if Captain Walton turned out to be all that?

She had closed her eyes to escape from the yellow light. And now she sees him quite distinctly: the gaunt, rumpled student, the doctor exhausted by illness, lying down on his bed; he had left the laboratory late at night, very late, has lain down fully clothed, taking a brief rest from his monstrous labors. Beset by nightmares, he mumbles something, that he is by birth a Genevese: that's all he knows. Murmuring, he plunges down into the fever of sleep, as into a burrow, digging deeper, ever deeper, to flee from the surface, yet he knows that it is always dangerously close, that he can never go far enough or deep enough: it's only just behind a door, the door to the laboratory. Does one push it, or pull it open? She knows, as he does, that the detail is important, but why? The faint click of the latch—there it is—warns him in his dream that he can dig away, burying himself under the covers soiled by his black stockings, the filthy boots he didn't even bother to remove after hours of tramping around in the muddy cemetery—it's all useless: an enormous hand draws back the curtain protecting the bed, tears off the covers, and the horror is there, standing at his bedside in the yellow light, the horror he set on the path to his own destruction, the creature who will threaten him, kill those he loves and would like to see dead, strangle little William, who is crying in his cradle (and Claire doesn't hear him, where is she? Where has Claire gone, no one ever sees her anymore—what if she were dead as well, in her bedroom?). And of course the face of this horror—finally fixed, finally arrested in its flight, no more averted profile, no more grimaces, no more portraits of Sir Timothy—this face belongs to Percy.

CHAPTER XXXVIII

Did she scream or not?

Is she hot or cold? Impossible to tell that, either. She's shaking, in any case, and all this evening she hasn't stopped shaking, or being afraid. It comes in waves; she thought each time would be the last, the final horror brought forth tonight, her whole life concentrated in this one night, and it would begin again, one terrible thing after another: insulting herself through Percy's mouth, Percy moving away from her, then coming close again but as a different person, for now he's an enemy who sees malevolent black eyes on her breasts, and Polidori is laughing spitefully, speaking out with unbelievable boldness (is it really him?), and he has killed Captain Walton, taken the place of the man from whom she must find out where the treasure is, the true story of Frankenstein, and Byron keeps snuffing out the candles. . . . All this has a meaning, it leads somewhere, but she's not there yet. The laces of her bodice are undone; she lowers her head, resting her chin on her naked bosom glistening with beads of perspiration. It has begun to rain, she hears large drops battering the roof, tearing at the trees.

Did she scream?

Probably not. Her cry would have attracted attention, interrupted the conversation, because there are people talking outside. Someone would have come. Or rather, no, perhaps they want her to think that she didn't cry out, perhaps also they know very well why she is screaming, so it's not worth bothering about, since there's nothing anyone can do, and besides she's got good reason to scream.

People are talking outside, on the veranda. Loud enough for her to hear. She recognizes the voices, which are unusually clear and drift upward on the warm air, gliding through the French windows. They're talking for her benefit, raising their voices for her, speaking distinctly so that she doesn't miss a single syllable. She can scream all she likes. They don't want to hear it, it's not part of her role. What they want is for her to listen. It's even as though they started speaking at the precise moment when she was sufficiently awake to overhear them. (And suppose she did scream, forewarning them?)

"It's all very well to resuscitate bodies," says Byron. (His voice has that studied, casual tone used by actors speaking for the audience—not for their fellow players—and who listen to themselves speak.) "But I must admit that neither our Lord, nor Saint John of Ambéda, nor any *Lives of the Saints* can give me that thrill of fear we seek. As related by you, my dear Polly, and despite the fact that I don't believe your claim to have actually been there, the experiment in Glasgow might possibly be seen in a somewhat frightening light. But a resurrection is never more than just that. You've got a man condemned to death, you wind up with the condemned man coming back to life—it's a bit skimpy, don't you think?"

"Then whom would you like to revive?" asks Polidori.

"But I don't want to revive anyone, that's just it. Living is difficult enough the first time around; no one should be forced to go through it all over again. I find your ghosts' persistence quite tiresome. No, rather than return to a lifeless body the same soul that has just escaped therefrom, I should find it much more intriguing to replace it with another."

"And where would you find it?"

"Anywhere. I'm sure that this world, or the others, can offer many wandering souls who would like nothing better than to become flesh."

Shelley, now. He has left his divan to join them. "It would be a strange consequence of the plurality of inhabited worlds. That those who live on the moon, for example, should be plotting invasions and take advantage of our experiments to breathe their lives into our dead."

"Wonderful!" exclaims Byron. "Imagine that diffuse, secret conquest, our world gradually invaded by Selenites who disguise their arrival by taking care to behave exactly as we do."

"Soon," observes Shelley, "they would be masters of the earth. We native inhabitants would cease to exist. They would have replaced us and be following the course of our history without us."

"Do you think there would be any difference?"

"And what if this invasion had already taken place?" continues Shelley, ignoring Polidori's question. "How would we know it? What if there had been dozens of them in the past, what if this earth we believe to be ours no more belonged to us than does this villa, which houses a series of tenants doubtless as different from one another as Selenites are from Martians, and Martians from Saturnians?"

"That could have happened," remarks Polidori (how this entire conversation seems scripted in advance. . . .), "only if the art of resurrection had already existed for a long time, when in fact the first experiment occurred last winter—"

"You were there, we know," interrupts Byron. "But you have the arrogance of all men of science, Polly. You take for brand-new whatever you have only just learned. How do you know such methods haven't existed since antiquity?"

"The invaders would need only to have removed all traces of their arrival each time," says Shelley, "in an effort to keep from being invaded in turn. When you move into a house that has been burgled, you make sure to change the lock."

"Above all," insists Byron, "how do you know that your experiment—your resurrection, if you really must call it that—is the only means of access to these empty carcasses we call our bodies and which may be taken over by all the inhabitants of the cosmos, one after the other?"

"What would you say about poetry?" asks Shelley.

"Ah," sneers Byron, "don't discuss poetry with Polly, that's his domain, just like vampires, and we are but dwarfs compared with this giant. We dwarfs, however, can see details that may escape his lofty gaze."

"A poem," declares Shelley solemnly, "is a door through which may rush pell-mell all the forces of the world."

"And those outside it, too," adds Byron. "And what do you make of dreams, my good Polly? Aren't they an invitation to visit us, do they not draw souls from the ether as this candle attracts insects?" (The dull thud of a hand striking the table.) "Who the devil do you think comes to haunt us during our sleep?"

"To replace us," says Shelley.

Why are they talking about these things? Why do they want her to hear this?

"I have studied dreams," protests Polidori. "I know that the circumstances of our lives appear transformed in them, altered by the subtle working of our minds. The stranger in a dream is but our own image, which we ourselves have carefully disguised. I am ignorant of poetic matters, perhaps, but I am well versed enough in the sciences to tell you that dreams are like those Spanish inns where you eat nothing save what you have brought with you."

"He seems quite sure of himself," jokes Byron.

"But then what have you to say about premonitory dreams?" asks Shelley. "History certainly furnishes us with enough examples, beginning with Caesar's. Do they not show that this inn is not as ill supplied as the Spanish variety and that one may sometimes find dishes there that one could not have furnished oneself without being able to see into the future?"

"True enough," says Byron, "But be careful, Shelley. You would then have to ask yourself, Who is the innkeeper who has supplied these dishes on our behalf? And this is a dangerous question for you, since it might lead you to contradict your previous avowals of atheism."

"Why?" replies Shelley. "I hate the God the Christian religion has invented for itself, but I believe in demons, in the spirits that surround us, in the plurality of worlds. We are not alone on this earth, or in our souls. It is these demons or gods who keep the inn where we spend our nights, and it is also they who dictate to us our poems, our stories, and our lives. Call them Selenites, if you like. But rest assured that your galvanism, your Scottish resurrections are not the only methods we have to summon them. We need merely invite them in our conversations for them to appear, insinuating themselves in our words and even in our stead."

"To frighten Mrs. Shelley, as did the demon who possessed you just now," says Polidori.

"I was frightened as well," replies Shelley in a low voice.

Silence. A gust of wind. The candle flames dance in the sitting room; Jackson and Angelo come to life on their folding screen, as though sparring together. Mary sits up on the sofa, then crosses the room to the French windows. She senses that the strange current that has carried this entire evening along in its wake will begin to flow again. The perspiration has dried on her skin; leaving her bodice unlaced and her breasts bared, she passes silently out onto the balcony. All her fear has vanished; she now feels only the excitement of an actress at the moment of going onstage. She doesn't know what play it is, and it's only when she steps into the wings that she can hear the scene in progress, hear the other actors establishing their characters, outlining the situation in that labored, didactic tone one often notices at the very beginning of a play; they have to warm up, work their way toward the moment when the plot takes shape and she makes her entrance. They're waiting for her. She mustn't miss her cue, the line that will soon tell her she's on—it's up to her.

She leans over the balcony. The others haven't seen her yet. Do they know she's there? She can tell they are expecting her. From her vantage point she can observe everyone's position on the veranda. Byron has not left his armchair, nor Polidori his seat on the other side of the marble table, on which burns the sole candle, still casting its faint light upon the scene. Byron cannot see Percy, who is standing behind him, leaning on the back of his chair. Both of them are looking toward the staircase; their gaze moves slowly upward, as though picking out one step after another, finally reaching the balcony where Mary is watching them. At last they notice her. Polidori, realizing that something is happening, turns around to find out what they are looking at. Mary stands there, her breasts bare in the moonlight. She is no longer afraid.

Silence.

Byron's voice. He stretches his arm out in a dramatic gesture, pointing at Mary.

"Look at our friend, who is about to join us. How do we know that it is still Mary herself?"

At that moment a bolt of lightning streaks through the murky sky. Only Mary can see the mountains light up, the lake shudder like a sheet of molten metal. They are all silent, waiting for the thunder that, when it finally erupts, coincides with the instant when Mary, holding herself absolutely erect, sets foot upon the first step. As the rumbling dies away, a second flash sheds its electricity over the lake, the countryside, the orchards in which every branch stands out as precisely as if etched. Mary's face is completely expressionless. She wills this, enjoys it, and even the climactic pleasure of love is nothing compared with this: she imagines the face with its delicate, almost angular features, the fragile bones, the skin so pale as to seem bloodless, the naked breasts and shoulders, the mauve stain of her dress, her arms dangling at her sides—she sees herself clearly, this apparition heralded by a second clap of thunder and which so impresses the three spectators that even Byron's voice seems unsteady, unusually high-pitched, when he tosses off a mediocre witticism.

"One more knock, and the curtain will go up!"

The third bolt of lightning is slow in coming, however, and silence descends once more on the veranda, snuffing out the dying candle. Is it the wind, which had spared it up until this moment; is it the depletion of the wax, now melted, absorbing the flame in one swallow; or is it Byron himself who has blown it out, to put the finishing touch on the stage setting?

A crash, the sound of a window breaking. No, someone must have knocked over the bottle of wine, which had been sitting on the floor.

In the darkness, Mary takes one step down, then another. She tries to picture the shape of the map formed on the flagstones by the spreading pool of wine. She swallows; this extreme awareness steadies her nerves, and each detail helps her to concentrate. She is no longer Mary Godwin, no longer even one of those imaginary correspondents from the series that infinitely multiplies Mary Godwin in time and space, she is no longer anything, anywhere, she is someone else, a young woman who has just left a dark room, backstage, a closet, and is going downstairs in the dark, to a white veranda.

One more step, in the darkness. She goes downstairs.

Soon—the last bolt of lightning.

CHAPTER XXXIX

There it is.

It reveals and immobilizes the three men waiting for her on the white veranda, engraves their outlines in the brilliance of high noon.

Blackness once again; the rumble of thunder.

From the last step, she feels for the flagstones with her foot, moving out into the darkness. She can sense them around her, holding their breath. A patch of white, straight ahead: the shirt of the tall young man with curly hair, who is standing near the balustrade. When she reaches him, she holds out her hands, touching his face. With her fingertips she traces the bone structure, the arch of the eyebrows, the bridge of the nose, the hollow of the cheeks. She lifts her mouth to his, thinking that it's happening at last, they're unknowingly exchanging kisses. Although she hasn't said anything, he has understood, and as he moves his lips lightly across her cheek, brushing them against her ear, he murmurs, "Unbeknown to whom?"

All of a sudden, a light; not the harsh glare of lightning, which illuminates shadows and turns brightness inky black, but the reassuring amber glow of a candle. Another one. The stocky man near the table has just lit all the candles in the big candelabrum—except the one that went out moments before and cannot be revived.

Although she can see him now, she continues her blind exploration. Her fingers linger on his bare neck, the throat where the Adam's apple rises and falls as he swallows, for his mouth is dry. The young man looks at her, smiles at her. She smiles back at him.

"Here you are at last," he says. "We were waiting for you."

She wants to tell him she doesn't like that "we," she doesn't know those others, she has finally found him, and only he matters; she says nothing. The young man gently takes hold of her wrists, but does not interfere with her searching fingers. He slides his own down her bare forearms, across her naked breasts, caressing them. He is still smiling.

Behind them, the heavyset man begins to speak, to her.

"Well, you've arrived safely. You weren't afraid. That's good."

It's true, she isn't afraid. She has been afraid all her life and now it's over; she has arrived.

"Where am I?" she asks.

The young man holding her wrists remains silent. She hears the other man speak in a musical, stagy voice.

"At the lakeshore. Look."

He brings the candelabrum over to them, and by stretching

out his arm, tries to illuminate the landscape with the four meager flames, a halo that gleams precisely where it is carried without ever dispelling the darkness. In the foreground loom the twisted branches of fruit trees.

"There is no lake at Brighton," she says.

"Hush," whispers the tall young man.

"There is one in Geneva," answers the man with the candles. "We're in the Villa Diodati, where Milton once lived. Come over here, Captain." Captain Walton steps into the circle of light. He is a small man, with a wrinkled, Chinese-looking face.

"Tonight, call me Polidori," he chides him. (In his voice, the calm majesty of a royal personage enjoying his incognito, when he is satisfied that everyone has guessed his secret.)

"We thought you weren't coming, up until the last minute."

She turns away, looks at the young man holding her wrists. "Who are you?"

She waits for his answer, certain that he will tell the truth. He smiles again, glancing at the captain either to seek his approval or to make sure he cannot hear them.

"At the moment," he murmurs, "Percy Bysshe Shelley."

"Seventeen ninety-two to eighteen twenty-two," adds the wrinkled little man, as though he were a prompter in a theater. He is standing quite close to them and has heard everything. She turns around, upset.

"Eighteen twenty-two?"

The man calling himself Shelley—for the moment—looks reproachfully at the captain (no, Polidori), who carries on regardless.

"Almost six more years. Don't worry, you can do many things in six years, even be happy."

She knows that; she read it. But she no longer remembers exactly how the story ends.

"With a drowning," says Shelley softly.

"Of course," adds Polidori. "These things happen. I can tell you about it, if you're interested."

Without waiting for a reply, he continues as calmly as though he were reading out loud to himself.

"You will be living in Casa Magni, an isolated villa between Lerici and Sant'Arenzo, on the Gulf of La Spezia, in Italy. It will be summertime; the weather, hot and humid. For several weeks the peasants will have been waiting anxiously for the rains, which will be late, unlike this summer. Each day processions of priests and monks will wind along the rocky road behind the villa, imploring the heavens for rain. Finally, on the eighth of July, their prayers will be answered by a violent downpour. Also on July eighth, Shelley and a friend whom you don't know yet will leave Livorno, where they will have had some business to attend to, and set out for La Spezia aboard their new boat, the *Don Juan*, named in honor of our friend." Completing the introductions, he nods toward the stocky man, who bows. "This name will displease you, as it would displease you today. The fog will roll in as they set sail, and the wind will die away to nothing. They will disappear. No one will see them alive again. You will be dreadfully worried. On the fifteenth some fishermen will find two badly decomposed bodies, covered with seaweed and swollen from long immersion in water, on a beach near Viareggio. Shelley's body will be identified from the book of poems by Keats someone will find in his pocket. You will weep."

She has a lump in her throat already.

"Because of administrative complications," continues the little man, "the funeral will not take place until a month later, on a beach at Viareggio, where the black sand is strewn with wreckage, and a forest of pine trees lines the shore. One can see the island of Elba on the horizon, and white buildings all along the coast. The weather will be lovely; many people

291

will attend the ceremony. You will not be there, but Lord Byron will. Around noon, the remains of the drowned men will be placed on a funeral pyre. Lord Byron will take Shelley's skull, claiming that he intends to clean it, have it polished, and use it as a goblet—which he will never do. The resinous wood of the pyre will blaze up quickly; Byron will feed the flames with wine and salt. The heat and stench will be appalling. By four o'clock the bodies will have been completely consumed, and what remains of the pyre will be pushed into the sea with logs. Then Byron, stripping off his clothes, will plunge into the water to swim out to his boat, the *Bolivar*, riding at anchor in the bay. He will feel old and unwell, however; his body will let him down. He will vomit, and his spew, floating on the water, will form a revolting ring around him. He will make his way back to the beach as best he can. Two years later he will die. That is one of the story's endings."

"It can't come soon enough," sighs the stocky man, who has seated himself in the armchair.

The young woman looks angrily at the little man, who appears to be quite satisfied with his prophecy.

"What about you? Won't you ever die?"

"I'll be the first," he replies. "In four years. While you are all in Italy, I will commit suicide, back in London. These things happen, it's only natural: too many nightmares, too much hatred, too much opium. . . . That's one of the beginnings of the story."

"And me?" she asks, to complete the obituaries.

"You will live to a ripe old age, Mary," answers Polidori. "You'll outlive us all by some years. Now, that ending isn't interesting: old age, sadness. . . . Not worth talking about. But soon you will write *Frankenstein*. You will make a great book out of the story I gave you tonight, and your name will never be forgotten. You will also hurt me very much."

She is sorry, deeply moved. At the same time she is delighted to hear about *Frankenstein.*

"Will you always be angry at me?"

"Always, until the end. But I'll always be angry at everyone—at Milord because of *The Vampire*, at Shelley, at you, at myself most of all. I'm only half angry at you, though. You've robbed and humiliated me like the others, but you haven't written the right story. Or you won't write it, whichever you prefer."

"Which is the right one, then?" she asks anxiously. "The one about your death? The one in the Chinese hotel? Black-eyed Martians taking over the bodies of earthlings with light eyes?"

"In 1816 we call these creatures Selenites," Byron reminds her. "Watch out. These anachronisms give you away."

"What's one anachronism more or less?" says Polidori. "We've committed enough of them. In any case, no—the right story is not the one about the Selenites. Well, it is a good story, but it isn't *the* story. Only one branch among others, a limb on which we ventured out, as it were, just to see. The real story would be the entire tree, all the stories four talkative souls could tell one another or imagine on this June night in 1816, on the veranda of Diodati. The invitation is theirs; we are the visitors."

"Or the other way around," muses Shelley. "Who knows who started it?"

"That depends. Do you think our hosts can imagine London as we know it: the Chinese hotel, the murder party? Do you think they can imagine our names?"

"They can always invent some," remarks Byron. "For example, Ann, Allan, Julian, Captain Walton. . . ."

"You're cheating, Milord," observes Polidori in mock reproach.

"Not really. We already know Captain Walton, at least.

293

Mary has been calling on him for help in writing her novel for several days now."

She would like to tell Albé that there is no reason for him to know this, that he's cheating even there, but never mind, she lets it drop. There are other things she would like to understand. She turns back to Polidori.

"Is your name really Robert Walton?" she asks.

He smiles. "Yes. And I'm even a captain, in the Royal Navy. Perhaps that's it—the starting point of the story. Merest chance, and everything falls into place. Since you weren't able to come up with the subject of *Frankenstein*, Mary, you dreamed of assigning this task to Captain Walton. You even wondered, if you recall, whether there might exist somewhere a captain bearing the same name you had just invented. Perhaps there was one in 1816, I don't know; perhaps he even had a sister."

"That's right, the sister," says Mary. "We'd forgotten her."

"Things are already complicated enough, aren't they? One must know when to stop. The important point is that in 1984, long after we are all dead, a real Captain Walton will come across your book, and this accidental homonymy will inspire the game that has enabled us to reply to our hosts' invitation. To be behind the door at the right moment."

"To push it when they pulled it," adds Shelley, seemingly much impressed by his own words.

"There's one thing," says Byron, "that I haven't quite figured out. I almost asked you the other day, when I left you to go fetch Ann and shut her up in the hotel."

"Now, I really think you overdid that just a bit," observes Shelley.

"Oh, you know how it is—one gets carried away sometimes. Caught up in the improvisation." He turns back to Polidori. "No, what I don't understand is why you've chosen to play Polidori in all this when you could have been the ringleader, after all. In your place—"

"In my place, you would have chosen the role of Lord Byron?" interrupts Polidori, who is obviously enjoying himself. "But Milord, that is why you play the role so well. I do not have your natural aptitude. I prefer my subordinate position, which leaves me free to direct the story as I please, behind the scenes, and besides . . ." He hesitates. "And besides, it's a question of temperament, similarities of character. Let's leave it at that."

The others are quiet, momentarily ill at ease. For a fleeting instant Mary reflects that sorrow is the only true motive for making up stories, and that there's no point in pressing the captain further, since he would only elude their questions.

"No matter," says Byron. "We're here, and that is all that counts."

"Are we going to stay here?" asks Mary.

"I don't think so," replies Polidori. "Soon it will be daybreak; our hosts will be tired. It's hard for them, to say what we say, to keep everything straight. To pay no attention to that, for instance."

A car drives by, behind the hedge. Mary listens as the sound of the motor grows fainter. She knows that Polidori is right, as usual: they won't be able to hold on to Ann and the others. Her companions are already stumbling; it won't be long before they send the visitors away.

"They're going to send us away," she says sadly.

"Where will we go, then?"

"To Brighton. We'll return to our rooms, to sleep."

"Or to the moon," says Byron.

"But there's nobody left on the moon," objects Shelley. "Now that the Selenites have invaded our world, the moon is right here."

"Only in this episode," murmurs Polidori. "In this episode."

"Even so. At this very moment we are the Selenites. I find that remarkable."

Shelley turns to look at Mary; he is still holding her wrists. "Your book must prophesy all this. You must start writing tomorrow, and tell the whole story."

"Impossible," snaps Polidori, cutting him off.

"Why?"

"Why?" He seems sad all of a sudden, like the others. "Because tomorrow you will have forgotten it all. Everything our hosts have said, everything we're saying now. . . . I alone will remember. Only I could write the true story of Frankenstein."

"And of tonight," adds Mary.

She would like him to do so, would like this story to exist, even if she never reads it. Or else she'd like Allan to have hidden a tape recorder somewhere on the veranda.

"But you won't write it, Polly—I know you," observes Byron.

"Who can say? Perhaps I won't, perhaps I'll forget everything, like yourselves. But Captain Walton"—he winks at Mary—"won't forget so easily. He'll write it one day, in the empty house, after living through the last days of poor John Polidori—which you will know nothing about. At all events, he'll write down a few scraps of it: the story of the Selenites that you like so much, for example. No one will believe it, no one will read it. It's not important."

"Are you trying to tell us that your host is more intelligent than ours?" jeers Byron.

A smile returns to Polidori's face. A sad, lingering smile. "Haven't you noticed, Milord? He's the captain, after all."

"True," agrees Byron. "You have been more witty than

usual tonight. It's even distressing to consider that for once in your life you will have really sparkled, but that not a trace of this brilliance will remain. A mirage."

"Distressing indeed," agrees Polidori. "But nothing prevents you from making a note of my remarks. As usual."

It is his turn to issue a challenge, to lay a wager. He knows he will win it, and Mary feels like crying when she sees him so sure of himself. She'd rather he remained Captain Walton instead of turning back into that awful Polidori—without whom Captain Walton would not exist, however. She would like to suspend all movement, keep going just as they are, without changing anything, without losing Allan.

"Too late," says Byron. "I'm tired. When news of your death reaches me, Polly, I promise you that I will reflect on all this. My thoughts will be vague, uncertain, muddled by the irritating memories I'll have of you, your easily wounded feelings, and your wretched tragedies. But I'll tell myself over and over, to convince myself, that one night in June of 1816, John William Polidori, doctor of medicine, unfortunate poet and killjoy companion, astounded us all by leading a game in which others took our places."

"You'll forget, Milord. The harder you try to remember— let us suppose that you will try—the deeper this memory will lodge itself in your brain. Confess, it would already be impossible for you to say how all this began."

Mary takes up the challenge. "Why not write it down this minute?" she cries. "Do you have a pen, some paper?"

Polidori rises and disappears into the house, returning with a writing desk. The young woman seats herself at the table, takes pen in hand, and tries to think how to begin.

"Tomorrow morning it will all seem like nonsense," predicts Polidori. "You won't understand a word of it."

Oh, she thinks, if only one of them had a tape recorder!

She would never hear the tape, which would exist nevertheless, a hundred and sixty-eight years later (she has already heard this calculation made, but when?).

"Tomorrow morning is already here," announces Shelley. "Look, the sky is growing light."

"In the proper order," says Mary, ignoring his remark. "First of all, we talked about vampires, didn't we?"

She writes on the piece of paper, *"Spoke of vampires with Lord B., P. and S."*

She stops, hesitates. Should she also note down her violent fit, the insults she hurled at Shelley? Deciding against this, she continues. *"The conversation then turned to the living dead and P. told us about an experiment he had witnessed: the galvanic resurrection of a man condemned to death. I know that I have found the idea of* Frankenstein, *and P. graciously makes me a present of it."*

"How kind of you to note that," comments the little man, who is leaning over her shoulder to see what she is writing. "But you'll forget that, too."

She lets this reproach go by. *"Lord B.,"* she continues, *"then recites the verses of 'Christabel' that concern the witch, and Shelley is much affected by them. He cries out while looking at me, as though I were frightening him. Lord B. and P. make him lie down on the divan to rest."*

"You can also write that he imagined you had eyes on your breasts. It was true, you know."

She makes a face. "Black eyes?" she asks.

"So, you still remember that? The sunglasses, the contact lenses? It was a rather timid transposition, I admit. Do you remember the Chinese hotel? Write it down."

Obediently she writes, *"Shelley imagines me with black eyes on my nipples."*

Then she puts down the pen. The Chinese hotel. She has

approached it all wrong. She shouldn't have started out like that; she should have begun by talking about the Chinese hotel, about how Julian tried to make her believe that Martians (Selenites, she corrects herself) had invaded the earth, and that they all had black eyes. Now she'll have to redo the whole thing, and from the beginning—but which beginning? She has to talk about the hotel, the manuscript, Brigitte, Allan, Brighton . . . and even Bernadette, Gérard, the boxer Tim Bishop. Keeping Allan, above all, she must keep him, must write down his name. She writes it. There: she has that, at least.

"Allan."

Stops again.

"I can't get it right." She sighs.

"Naturally," says Polidori. "I wouldn't know how to tell the whole story either. I would have to remember my death, four years from now, the empty house, Teresa. You don't even know who Teresa is, but it doesn't matter. And then the opium, the doors you have to pull toward you if you want to get back up, the captain's cabin, the manuscript written for you, lying on the dressing table, the Chinese hotel again, and this is the point where you come in, the moment when you can take over the story, if you remember it. But you don't."

The other two aren't watching them; they've been abandoned. Now she's angry.

"But where should I start? Where does it begin?"

"Nowhere," sneers Polidori. "It could begin immediately, on this sheet of paper, if you were able to go on. Let it drop."

Don't obey him, above all. She rereads what she has written, adding the words "tape recorder," and continues.

"Lord B., observing the state of my nerves, persuades me to go lie down in the small room above the drawing room. There

I have a nightmare in which a pale medical student, who resembles both P. and S. in turn, breathes life into a monstrous being. I know that this creature is going to persecute him. . . ."

Hesitation.

". . . and will kill William." She presses so hard with the pen that she tears a hole in the paper. *"This will be the story of* Frankenstein."

"You will remember that," prophesies Polidori. "Which is already a great deal, isn't it?"

If it were true, at least. . . . She writes on, already beaten. *"I awake in great agitation. I hear my three companions conversing on the veranda. They are saying that the monster is actually a foreign soul, a Selenite, and that such souls are gradually substituting themselves for our own. It then seems to me that I myself am becoming someone else."*

"There you are," crows Polidori. "It *seems* to you. A little while ago you *were* someone else. It's all over. As soon as one starts to write, it's gone."

Looking up, she sees Shelley and Byron straight ahead of her, leaning their elbows on the balustrade with their backs to her as they watch for the sunrise. The blanket of fog on the surface of the lake is beginning to fray. This is the moment when the layers of clouds accumulated each evening melt away, when the stars finally become visible, only to disappear. They are quite pale, fading fast.

"It will be a beautiful day," declares Shelley.

He says that every morning, and every day the weather is overcast.

It's because of the volcano, she thinks. In Java.

He comes over to her. Drowned in six years.

"We should go home."

Byron stretches. "Tonight has tired me out. We drank hardly anything, though."

Two empty bottles on the veranda, one of them lying on its side. Very little, in fact.

"But we talked too much," says Polidori, and she's surprised to see how eager he is to disperse the shadows of the night, the phantoms stirred up by the four of them, who now go their separate ways, returning to their rooms. In the corridor they pass the hotel maids, who must think they are drunk; the telephone at the reception desk is ringing.

She should try to make herself keep writing, but it's impossible; she knows it would only end in regret and disappointment. She looks down at the paper in disgust. That's not what she ought to have written, not the right story. Picking up the pen again, she idly records a few words that are already losing their meaning: "Captain Walton. Chinese hotel. Brighton." (She knows Brighton; she went there on vacation as a child.) "William. Jim." (She no longer has any idea at all who he is.) "Catania." (Why Catania?) "La Spezia." (She draws her pen through that last name, knowing full well that no amount of ink can blot it out, for she'll remember that one. Only six years, just over six years, alas. . . .)

She gives up, this time for good. Her head is throbbing, her body aching and exhausted. She feels empty. Empty, more than anything else. She'd like to sleep for three days straight, lying next to Percy.

She stands up and goes over to him; he takes her in his arms. There, the sun is rising behind the mountains. Byron squints as if the sunlight, although pale, were bothering him. He breaks off the neck of a bottle of sparkling water on the balustrade, cutting his lips as he drinks from it greedily. Without commenting on her disheveled appearance, which she hasn't even noticed, Percy tenderly refastens her bodice. How could she have walked around like that, with her breasts completely naked?

The custom at Diodati is to dispense with good-byes and

thank-yous. Albé has already disappeared into the house with his bottle after giving them a wry smile, a trickle of blood at the corner of his mouth. She picks up her piece of paper from the table, slips it into her bodice, and gives Polidori a friendly little tap on the shoulder as she leaves. In the light of dawn he seems suddenly old and wrinkled, with the pinched face of a Chinese mandarin.

Chinese hotel.

He smiles automatically. Soon he will die. She knows it, and so does he. Alone until the end, always alone.

Percy is waiting for her at the top of the steps, which they descend together.

CHAPTER XL

The road to Montalègre, which runs through the orchards, is slippery with mud. Raindrops still cling to the leaves and shower down on them as they brush by the trees. They walk slowly, both of them barefoot: they've forgotten their shoes at Diodati but are so anxious to get to bed that instead of going back the short distance to the villa, they prefer to arrive home with muddy feet, and pick up their shoes later on, tomorrow.

Tomorrow the weekend will be over; they'll return to London.

Percy puts his arm around her shoulders, and even though this makes it difficult for them to walk because of the difference in their heights and the unevenness of the road, she hopes he will hold her close until they reach the house. When they arrive, they'll let go of each other only long enough to undress and climb into bed, where they'll entwine their legs, he'll caress her breasts, and that is how they'll fall asleep, with the window open, the sun flooding into the room, gleaming on the wooden paneling, warming their bodies. . . . She feels as though she were already asleep. She walks along with her eyes half closed and a pleasant sensation of heaviness in her legs, hardly feeling the brambles that scratch her as she passes by. When they must step aside to let a peasant and his donkey trudge past, the man's greeting and the tinkling bell on the beast's halter bring her back to her senses: she had been about to fall asleep while still walking, lulled by the procession of pictures behind her eyelids, glowing with light. The web of tiny veins, the pale red curtain of flesh turns objects into shadows of themselves: a branch, a tree, a boulder. As one might recall a dream within another dream, she remembers her nightmare, the yellow light, the monster. She must not forget that, or Captain Walton, or any of this night. She feels the folded piece of paper lying between her breasts, and Shelley's hand upon her shoulder. As they walk his fingers lightly touch her clavicle, tracing the line of the bone. They will remember everything, together. He is close to her, at this moment. Who was it who said he would drown? Probably herself, since not a day goes by that she doesn't think about it, fearing the arrival of some grieving rustic, twisting his cap between callused hands, tongue-tied at the prospect of telling her the tragic news. She shakes her head, looks up at him. He smiles absentmindedly, then, noticing her eyes fixed intently on him, leans closer to her.

The wooden stairs creak beneath their feet. Bathed in sunshine, the little veranda of Montalègre seems more decrepit, and the balustrade looks shabbier. Luckily, Claire must still be asleep, after spending the night waiting up for them. She would hate to confront her right now, parading the sorrowful face of an abandoned woman. While they were gone, Claire put away the chaise longue, and perhaps searched for the notebook. It doesn't matter. This morning the notebook no longer serves any purpose. If they weren't so tired, she would willingly show it to Percy, and together they would laugh at her childishness. She has already told him about it tonight, hasn't she?

They haven't made any noise, haven't awakened Claire or William. Now they're in the bedroom, where the walls smell of resin and sunlight filters through the half-closed shutters, as dust motes dance over the loose floorboards. They can hear the stream outside, and insects. Wooden shoes, on the road that runs uphill of the house.

One by one, he unfastens the buttons of her dress, which falls down about her feet. He takes the piece of paper folded over three times and places it on the night table, on his side of the bed. He handles the paper with respect, as though touching a precious object.

Naked, she stretches out on the bed and throws back the covers, which would keep them too warm. It's his turn to undress, which he does with his back to her, looking out the window and through the branches of the apple tree, through luminous gaps opening onto the lake. She waits patiently for him to come lie down next to her; he will come, and it's because he will come soon to lay his weary body next to hers that he lingers at the window while she watches him.

"The sky must be beautiful now, east of Java," he says, and she doesn't ask him why.

They have plenty of time to think back on tonight, together.

Six more years, she thinks quickly.

The tinkle of bells on the road. The singing of birds.

He turns around, comes toward the bed. She opens her arms, and he's at her side, bending his leg over hers. She tans easily, while his skin remains white, and is so delicate that folds of the finest, sheerest material leave red marks on it—like scars—she traces softly with her lips. The half-open window directs a shaft of light along the entire length of their bodies. Perhaps this new day will be truly beautiful, all day long. It looks as though this particular storm has washed the heavens clean. Tomorrow she'll write; she'll really begin working on *Frankenstein*. But right now they're going to sleep, for a long time. Their bodies are already settling into familiar positions, both of them lying on their sides, Percy's stomach against Mary's back. Words are straggling along in her head, open-sesames that no longer open anything, but it will all come back; they'll search together. She closes her eyes, wondering if he has closed his. She ought to be feeling his eyelashes fluttering against the nape of her neck.

No, he's stirring, withdrawing the arm lying under her side, moving away. She moans softly to make him return; she wants him very close to her, right next to her.

The bedsprings make a harsh, grating sound.

A flint is struck once, twice. Why light the candle?

She turns over halfway, blinking, and sees him touch the piece of paper to the glowing red tinder.

"What are you doing?"

She sits up, leaning on her elbow. The paper is burning rapidly.

"Nothing. Go back to sleep."

"But . . . that's what I wrote a little while ago."

She tries to stop him—too late; the flame licks at her fingers. He drops the last corner of the paper, which turns to ashes on the night table.

"A little while ago," he says, "you were asleep."

She stares at him incredulously, distraught. It isn't possible. He hasn't the right to do that, to start frightening her again. Not after tonight. They must remember it, both of them, and each one of those words must exist for them, even if they cannot recall their meaning.

Brighton, the Chinese hotel, Captain Walton. . . .

She repeats them. He must repeat them as well, and return to her.

"You've had a nightmare, my love. You should sleep."

His air of concern and his solicitude upset her. She'd like to spit in his face. He hasn't the right. The others can deny everything as much as they want; she knows they will—but not him. Not him.

He places his hand on her shoulder. She pushes him away, looking at their feet still crusted with mud from the road, the fresh scratches on their calves. They've just come home; he can't deny that.

He realizes where she is looking: more proof that must be destroyed.

"You walked in your sleep tonight, on the road. I followed you. You were saying the same words over and over again, words I didn't understand."

The stranger again, the crafty enemy who can take advantage of everything. It's true that she used to walk in her sleep when she was a child. And if she asks him what paper he has just burned, he'll say it was a few verses he wasn't pleased with, anything at all that might seem reasonably likely. He'll say they left Diodati around ten or eleven o'clock, and the others will confirm this. They conspired together to make this happen and now they will all pretend that it never did, as though she were crazy. But why? Why? Is it on Captain Walton's orders? To erase everything, wall up the door they've opened tonight?

"You're lying. You're lying," she repeats, trying to convince herself.

She's afraid she'll wind up believing them in the end. He smiles at her, bends over her, while she would like to scream, to claw her way with her bare hands through the surface of the smooth, blind wall until she finds the door again.

Behind it, Ann and Allan are sleeping peacefully. They have abandoned her.

"Calm yourself, my love. . . ."

His face, so close to hers. His black eyes stare at her without blinking, candidly, lovingly. She is imprisoned with him forever, on the other side of the wall, and it isn't him.

She holds him in her arms, tightly, to avoid looking at him anymore. Whispers into his ear.

"In six years," she murmurs.

Silence. The sunlight streaming through the shutters has now reached the pillow.

"Sleep. . . ."

She turns toward the wall.

ABOUT THE AUTHOR

Emmanuel Carrère is the author of three other novels, *L'Amie du Jaguar* (1983), *The Mustache* (1986), and *Hors D'Atteinte* (1988). *Gothic Romance* (1984) won two literary prizes, the Prix Passion (1984) and the Prix de la Vocation (1985). Carrère lives with his wife and son in Paris.

ABOUT THE TRANSLATOR

Lanie Goodman currently resides in Nice, where she teaches Comparative Literature at the Université Canadienne en France. She has translated Emmanuel Carrère's *The Mustache* and *The Cannibal Kiss* by Daniel Odier.